The Military Advisors

Adventures of a Jump Space Accountant

Book 6

Andrew Moriarty

Andrew Moriarty

Special thanks to my dedicated team of beta readers – Alex, Bryan,
Catherine B, Christopher G, Dave M#1, Dave W, Dave M#2, Djuro D,
Greg D, Haydn H, Jolayne W, Keith C, Kent P, Michael G, Michael R,
Peter B, Scott, Skip C, Susan G, Tigui R, Vince, and to my editor
Samantha Pico.

CHAPTER ONE

The jump countdown on Jake's board reached thirty before the collision alarm bonged.

"Not again." Nadine tapped her screen. "Jakey, your stupid alarm is going off again. Fix it."

Jake switched on the threat radar screen. Empty. He shared this with the four crew occupying the control room. "We're on course. I don't know why it's triggering. According to the computer, there's nothing there."

Nadine pivoted the far left control chair to face Jake, who was sitting in the back of the control room. "Then why does your computer say it is?"

"Not my computer." Jake stilled the alarm. "It's the ship's jump computer."

"But you are the only one who knows how it works," Yvette, the backup helmsman and primary Free Trader representative two stations to Nadine's right, said. She muttered in Francais to Odette, her deputy.

Jake shut the alarm off. "Emergence in ten, nine, eight—"

"We can read, Jakey. We don't need you to count," Nadine said.

The counter ticked down to zero, and the blue glow of the jump field faded from the exterior cameras.

"Passive sensors say nearspace is clear," Odette said. "Doing radar scans."

Nadine tapped her screen, and a red planet sprung to life on the main screen in front of the consoles. The terminator was visible sweeping across it. The light side was undifferentiated red, the dark side only black.

"No visible indication of anything," Nadine said.

1

"Quantity one, airless, waterless, peopleless planet."

"Nothing on long range radar except the three moons from the charts," Odette said. "No ships or stations."

"This isn't working," Nadine said. She slapped her screen. "There is nothing here. We need to go home. We've come far enough."

"Odette," Jake said, "any beacons broadcasting?"

Odette shook her head. "Nothing, el supremo, we see nothing. This system is dead, like the others."

"Please don't call me that," Jake said. "Call me Jake. Or captain, if anything."

"N'est pas possible," Yvette said. "Free Traders only call the master of the ship captain. You are just the owner."

"We're not Free Traders," Jake said. "We're a Delta crew."

"Not your crew. That is why we wear our own uniforms." Yvette gestured at her clothes.

Her skinsuit was dark blue, like her coveralls, and had Free Trader emblems. Odette wore the same. Nadine wore a custom-fitted skinsuit with a blue jacket over it. Jake covered his own skinsuit with gray Militia coveralls.

"I've told you not to wear those," Jake said.

Yvette winked. "Of course. Then, you will help me take them off later in my cabin?"

Jake blushed. "I meant, wear the Delta uniforms, like I do." Jake pointed at his own clothes—plain skinsuit and plain blue-gray coveralls with a Delta patch on the right breast.

"Perhaps I will compromise and wear just a smile, then," Yvette said. "What will you do then?"

Jake bit his lip. Yvette had done her black hair in a tight braid that exposed her slender neck. Jake had a thing for necks. And her Free Trader uniform was tight enough to leave no doubt she was female.

"What about me?" Odette said. "I can smile, too. And I fixed my hair." Her hair looked like she had fallen out of bed. Her uniform was tighter than Yvette's, making her appear as Yvette's younger, more wanton sister.

"I don't want to see you naked," Jake said. Keep your eyes on their face. Don't look anywhere else.

"That's not my information, Jakey." Nadine folded her arms across her chest. "I heard you're pretty ambitious about that."

"Nadine," Jake said. "We can talk about this later."

"No, we won't, Jakey," Nadine said. "Because, later, I'm going to be busy turning this ship around and heading back to Delta. This exploration has gone on long enough. Time to get back to civilization."

"Dashi said we're to explore until we reconnect to the Empire."

"Did he say keep going through empty system after empty system until we run out of fuel?"

"There's no shortage of fuel in any of these systems," Jake said. "There's been hydrogen everywhere. Even this one. I see a gas giant on that screen. Odette, can we have a course, please?"

Odette typed on her screen. The main screen beeped, and the course appeared. Accounting Error was a larger version of the standard freighters Jake was used to. The bridge had two rows of four consoles. Nadine sat in the primary pilot position, with Yvette and Odette in the row next to her. Jake sat alone in the second row.

"We're going to starve to death," Nadine said. "Four systems so far and no people, no Empire, no habitable planets, nothing."

"We won't starve to death," Jake said. "We've got plenty of trays."

"Red-green-blue trays," Nadine said. "Frankly, Jakey, I'd rather starve."

Yvette and Odette exchanged mutterings in Francais and then they both laughed.

"What's so funny, Trader chickees?" Nadine asked.

"You are. You and your worry about foods," Yvette

said. She looked Nadine up and down. "Perhaps a little less food might be good for you. What is the standard word, porky?"

"Porky?" Nadine flicked her hands, and a knife appeared. "I'll give you porky. My problem is that I'm not eating a balanced diet. Not enough vitamin C. It's messing with my complexion. Jakey, do we have any liver in the food stocks?"

"Liver? No. No liver."

"I need some liver, Jakey. If you don't get me some, I'll have to find it myself." Nadine spun the knife in her hand. "Yvette has a liver. What say I take a closer look at it? Chop it up, make it into cream, and see if it clears up my skin."

"Nadine, liver isn't really a good source of vitamin C, more like Vitamin A—"

"Shut up, Jakey." Nadine spun the knife again. "What do you say, Trader chickee—want to help me solve my dietary problems?"

"I'm happy to help," Yvette said, pulling a pink revolver from her arm holster and pointing it at Nadine. "But I think your problem isn't vitamins. It is minerals. You need some iron. I can give you some, a few grams at a time."

Jake swallowed. "Revolver bullets, frangibles, are actually a form of concrete—"

"Shut up, el supremo," Yvette said. The hammer clicked. "What about it, blondie?"

The hatch clanged open behind them. Nadine and Yvette continued glowering at each other, not moving their eyes.

"Captain Jake," Professor Willowby said, climbing in. He surveyed the tableau. "Am I too late for the gunfight?"

"Not your concern, Willy-me-boy," Nadine said. "Not serious at all. Yvette and I were just having a friendly chat. Nothing to see here."

"Looks pretty serious," Willowby said. He was fat,

bald, and old but had magnificent facial hair—a bushy beard and mustache. "But not my responsibility. Dashi made me chief engineer, not captain or pilot or navigator for that matter. But are the weapons necessary?"

"Please leave us alone, Professor. We are conducting medical research," Yvette said. "We will see if she can dodge a bullet."

"I've seen her practice with those knives. She might be able to," Willowby said. "But speaking in my professional capacity, the console behind her probably won't, and I'd like to reduce damage to our irreplaceable pre-abandonment equipment where possible—or even where not possible because of that 'irreplaceable' part."

"I can shoot her without hitting the console," Yvette said.

"Doubt it," Willowby said.

"Knives don't hurt equipment," Nadine said.

"Nope," Willowby agreed. "They don't. But you've only got one. What will you do when her fellow merchant officer over there pulls out that revolver that she's so cleverly hidden under her arm?"

Jake stretched sideways for a better view. Odette had her hand in a pocket, a pocket big enough to hold her revolver.

"Ladies—" Jake said.

"Shut up, Jakey," Nadine said.

"Not now, el supremo," Yvette said.

Willowby snickered. "I'm guessing that this system is empty as well, and the ladies want to turn around."

"Not you, too?" Jake draped himself over the back of his chair, so he could face Willowby. "You want to give up?"

"Nope. Dashi appointed me to be an engineer on a voyage of discovery. And I want to keep going till we discover things. But this isn't exactly a democracy, so what are your orders, Captain Jake?"

"Nadine, Yvette," Jake said. "You two have had your

fun. Can we have a serious discussion now?"

The two women still glowered but both lowered their weapons. Jake couldn't tell who went first.

"There's nothing out here," Nadine said. "This is the fourth system we've been in. Nothing. We're going the wrong way."

"We have records that Delta was remote before the abandonment. Not completely cut off but a difficult shortcut between two sectors," Jake said. "That's why we had such a big food and fueling infrastructure on Delta. To fix and reprovision passing ships."

"We're going the wrong way," Nadine said. "We should return to Delta and try a different set of jumps."

"That will just give us the same problem but in a different direction," Yvette said. "But I don't care that much. If this is the wrong way, why not try another?"

"There is no wrong way," Jake said. "We're between two sectors—according to the university. Isn't that right, Professor?"

"Don't drag me into this," Willowby said. "I'm just the engineer. I left all that professor nonsense back at the university."

"Doctorate of electrical engineering and a masters in astrophysics isn't nonsense," Jake said.

"Is to me. Mostly a hobby, to be honest. Never thought I'd use it."

Yvette bit her lip. "You should be the captain, Professor."

Willowby shuddered. "I should not. I am not. And thank the spirits of dead Emperors for that. This way, I get to stick with my books and papers, and you youngsters have to do all the hard work."

"You are the foremost expert on Imperial technologies and trade routes on Delta," Yvette said. "You should be in charge of this expedition."

"Yeah, I've read a lot of books about how things were a hundred years ago, which has nothing to do with how they are now. And in terms of practical things—Chief Engineer? When the kids in engineering come to see me with an engineering question, I just say 'And what do you think you should do, Meadow? The backup compressor? Good, start it up.' I don't even know where they keep the tools."

"Engineering lockers are on the side of the compartment—" Jake said.

"What I mean, Captain Jake, is that I have no practical experience. Ms. Nadine here is one of the most experienced pilots in the system, and Ms. Yvette is a close second. Her compatriot Free Traders have skills in navigation and are reasonable engineers. Me? I can't pilot a ground car. If you make me a navigator, I'll be running us into the sun so I can take a closer look. And if you give me a wrench, I'll break a bone when I drop it on my toe. Nope, I'm happy to be the engineer emeritus here."

"What does emeritus mean?" Odette asked.

"It's from the Latin 'emeritus,' meaning e for 'out' and meritus for 'deservedly so,'" Willowby said. "A good status for washed-up, doddering professors." He cracked his fingers. "Now that you've worked out your boredom and frustration with rage and threats of violence, should we set up for refueling and a jump to the next system?"

"Yes, please, Professor," Jake said. "While we're waiting, I need to check why the jump computers and sensors keep giving the wrong info."

"Will do. Oh, and your two trainees are ready to report for duty," Willowby said.

"Don't they have more tests to take?" Jake asked.

"You mean the hundred and thirty-seven useless delaying prerequisites you assigned them a month ago? They finished them all yesterday. I checked them and certified them as passed. They're done with the academic parts of their training. Time for the work term. They belong to you now."

"We don't have time for training some newbies,

grandad," Nadine said.

"I'm not your grandad, and even if I was, I certainly wouldn't admit having such an ill-mannered progeny as you."

"Ill-mannered?" Nadine rudely gestured with her hands. "I'll give you ill manners."

"The defense rests," Willowby said. "But, regarding trainees, I don't have time myself. It's all you two."

"I'm not training anybody," Nadine said. "I have lots of important things to do with my time. Sleeping. Eating. Knifing."

"Pontificating," Jake muttered.

"What was that, Jake?"

"It's not a priority for us," Jake said. "They can learn somewhere else. From somebody else."

"Dashi impressed upon me," Willowby said, "that we needed to educate people, young people, in the new ways of doing things. Young people with few ties to the existing power structures in Delta. Young people that could learn new skills."

Jake and Nadine shook their heads, so Willowby continued. "You two had to learn from others. It's your turn to give back."

Jake and Nadine shook their heads again.

"Fine," Willowby said. "I'll just have to tell Dashi that you two were too busy to take the time to teach those two, when he not only explicitly said that it was something that needs to be done but picked the two trainees himself and impressed on me how important that training was." Willowby raised his eyebrows. "I guess the two of you can tell him yourself—when you meet him—that you were too busy. Too busy napping, and... whatever."

Jake compressed his lips. Dashi was neat, clean, quiet, and smiled a lot. He was also Jake's boss and possibly the Emperor of the known human universe. He never did anything himself, but anything he set his mind to would happen, and it was hazardous to life and health to be on the wrong side of him.

"I'll come back and see them," Jake said, unbuckling his harness.

"What about our course?" Nadine said.

"Gas giant," Jake said. "Find us some hydrogen."

"There's nothing out here," Nadine said. "Nor in the next system on the list."

"As much as I dislike agreeing with the chubby one here," Yvette said, "in all probability, there is nothing in the next system."

Odette leaned over to Yvette, whispered in Francais, then pointed at her screen.

"Something?" Jake said, swiveling his head.

"Nothing. Sensor glitch," Yvette said. She cleared Odette's screen before Jake could see.

Jake turned back to Willowby but kept the corner of his eye on Yvette. She waited till he moved, then typed a code into Odette's screen. A long code.

"Dashi will be unhappy if we turn back before absolutely necessary," Willowby said. "We should go on."

"We've found plenty of hydrogen and oxygen in every system we've traversed," Jake said. "And we have enough food for two more jumps before we have to turn around."

"Which leaves us zero margin for error," Nadine said. "Even I can read an inventory list. What if we have a problem where we have to fix the jump drive or just take an extra week or two to find fuel in the next system?"

"There are risks, but we promised Dashi we would explore. So, explore, we will," Jake said. "After we get fueled up, what are our options?"

Nadine guffawed, then tapped her board. "There are two systems within jump range from here. Both red dwarfs. One slightly larger than the other. I'm sure our glorious leader can work his jump computer magic and get us a course to either."

"Either way, I'll be in engineering," Willowby said, swinging the rear hatch open.

"Try the bigger one," Jake said, unbuckling his harness to stand.

"El capitaine, we should try the smaller one," Yvette said.

"Why?"

"Just a feeling."

Jake rubbed his forehead. "Do both of you have a feeling?"

"Yes, we should go to the smaller one," Odette said.

"Hey, merchant chickees," Nadine said. "Is this some sort of secret merchant travel thing? Is this the secret merchant burial ground?"

"Just a feeling," Yvette said.

"'Cause if it is, I'm happy to help." Nadine grinned. "Help, you know, with the burial."

Yvette faced Jake. "A feeling. A good feeling."

Jake flicked his eyes to Odette's console. It showed an empty sensor screen. "Why not. After we fuel up, I'll set up a jump to the smaller one." He stood, followed Willowby through the hatch, and closed it behind him.

Willowby pointed at the closed hatch. "That, Captain Jake, that's why you're in charge. Practical things. Like closing hatches. Sensible things that keep us alive. That's why Dashi didn't appoint a doddering old fool like me to anything important."

They were under light thrust, so the ship's stern was down. Jake used his fingertips to propel down the central shaft wall. "You're considered one of the smartest professors at the university in generations. The only reason you're not the rector is that you didn't align with any of the political factions in the university. Nobody benefits from appointing you, so they didn't."

"I'm a nonpolitical type. I just like to do my research. I enjoy the academic world. Always wanted to be a professor. Stay home and mind my own business." He drew a deep breath. "I love the smell of flowers. How do you do it?"

"Humidifier sprays mint water in from a reservoir."

"What happens when we run out of mint water?"

"It's a powder. We mix up more. If you're such an academic, why did you join the Militia when you were young? Nadine recognized you. You were a contemporary of Admiral Edmunds. She said you came to dinner at the house a lot."

"The admiral's late wife was an excellent cook."

"I asked around. You were on track to be fleet engineering officer. Why didn't you stay in the Militia?" Jake asked.

"That was a long time ago," Willowby said. "I get spacesick."

"I don't see any evidence of that here," Jake said, grasping a seam and pulling himself along. "Nor did the owners of several Free Traders that you served on after your Militia service. One of them was Yvette's second cousin. He speaks highly of you. Said you could have been a Free Trader captain if you wanted."

"Never did like the commercial side of things," Willowby said, grasping the seam. "Not my cup of tea."

"Yvette's cousin says you still own shares in several ships. 'Extremely profitable ships' were his exact words."

"You have been checking up on me, Captain Jake," Willowby said. "Sounds like you don't trust me."

"I don't trust anybody. I don't trust anything. I check everything. You know why Dashi put me in charge?"

"It's not your winning personality, that's for sure," Willowby said. "Or your command presence. Those two women near killed each other and no way you could have stopped them."

Jake hung from a grab bar and ran his fingers along the bulkhead. "Everything in this ship is smooth. All the walls are polished like thruster nozzles."

"Better manufacturing techniques. Higher quality construction materials."

"Will we be able to build ships this good?" Jake said.

"If we recontact the Empire."

"Only if we find a real shipyard, not the jumped-up repair places we have on Delta."

"Maybe we'll find one in the next system."

Willowby traced a design on the wall. "And maybe Nadine and Yvette will swear eternal sisterhood and spend their spare time braiding each other's hair."

"Nothing would happen," Jake said. "It's just alpha dog posturing, female version. If they were men, it would pass without comment. They're just arguing about who is the most badass girl on the ship. It's so close between them they'll never sort it out."

"Badass girl or badass person?"

"Girl," Jake said. "I run the ship."

Willowby laughed. "You believe that, Captain Jake? What if one of those ladies said no to one of your orders—really said no?"

"They won't, not when it's important," Jake said.

"You don't strike me as the blindly optimistic type. How do you know that?"

"Because I'm smarter than them, and they know it," Jake said. "I've always got a plan. And they know that, too. We've worked together before. They're fighting over who will be my executive officer."

"Well, aren't you the cocky one then," Willowby said. "I never heard you talk like this before."

"You never asked these questions before," Jake said.

"You've got the girls pegged. What about me?"

"Dashi needed a spy on board to watch me. An obvious spy. That's you. You'll report back to him, back to the admiral, and back to the Free Traders. You're keeping him informed about everyone and keeping everyone informed about him. That's in addition to being... what did he say, 'one of the best minds of our generation'? Something like that. And when we do find the Empire, you'll be invaluable. Maybe."

Willowby placed his fingers on the wall and hung for a

moment. "Well, thank you for that, youngster. Glad to know you think I'm of some use. But what if I'm not...of use, that is?"

"I can ignore you," Jake said. "I'm in charge, after all."

"Some folks believe I might be better in charge than you. Does that bother you?"

"Not at all. I can take care of you if need be."

"Take care of me? What, physically?"

"Sure," Jake said.

Willowby laughed. "You? Take care of me. I might be an old dog, but I know some new tricks." He snapped his fingers, and a revolver appeared in his hand. "Think you can beat that?"

"Nope," Jake said. He propelled himself through the door. "But I don't have to. I've got people." He blocked the door. "I don't buy your doddering professor act. You're on this ship because powerful people wanted you here. You're no threat to me now, but if you ever cause me any problems, I'll have you removed."

"You don't have the guts," Willowby said. "Or the skills. Everybody knows you can't shoot to save your life."

"I can't." Jake unblocked the door. "But Nadine can. So can Yvette. They'll be happy to shoot you up if I give permission." Jake smiled over his shoulder. "Not only that, but they'll thank me for the opportunity."

CHAPTER TWO

"Fill the glass all the way to the rim," Nadine said, pouring vodka to the brim of the shot glass.

Gabriella, the dark-haired woman across from her, took the proffered bottle and filled her own glass. "How full is it? Stupid glass." The vodka overflowed. "Emperor's ears."

"Don't worry, you'll get it," Nadine said. "It's these metal ship glasses. Hard to measure with. Dirtside, we'll get proper glass ones, and they're easier. Now the beer."

Gabriella did a better job with the beer mug, hardly slopping any. She needed two hands to lift it for inspection. "Is this right, madame pilot?"

"Call me Nadine. Gabriella, what do you go by, Gaby?"

"My mom calls me Gaby. It's okay."

"You need a ship name. I'll call you Brie. What do you think, Brie? Are we ready?"

Brie examined the lounge table. Four shot glasses of vodka and four larger mugs of Belter beer sat between them. "I think so."

"Right, first the vodka." Nadine tilted her head back and shot the vodka in one gulp. "Then the beer." She drank it down and slurped the last drops. "There we go. Got it?"

"I think so," Brie said.

"Now you try. For now, with hands. Later on, I'll show you how to do it while you're handcuffed."

Brie took the shot glass. She breathed in, then out, then tossed the shot into her mouth. She gasped and dropped the glass, then cupped her hand over her mouth as she

14

choked half of the vodka out onto the table. Her eyes watered, and she wheezed.

"Good, good." Nadine shoved the beer across to her. "Now the beer."

Brie grasped the beer in both hands and sipped from one.

"No sipping. Drink. Drink," Nadine said.

Brie tilted the beer more and gulped it down. It sloshed onto her shirt, but she continued gulping. After twenty seconds, she dropped the glass on the table and heaved. "Huuuuuuh."

Nadine picked up the beer glass and drained the remainder. "Not perfect but a good start."

"Emperor's ears, that tastes horrible," Brie said.

"Brie, what did I tell you about your swearing?" Nadine said.

"Sorry, Ms. Pilot—I mean Nadine." Brie took a breath. "The Empress's hairy vagina, that tastes horrible."

"Much better. If you're going to curse, do it properly," Nadine said. "Again." The two repeated the process with the second round. This time, Brie spilled less and drank more.

"Nadine," Jake said, climbing into the lounge with a younger man in tow behind him. "What are you doing?"

"Teaching my trainee," Nadine said. "Like you told me to."

"By filling her full of vodka? What's she learning with that?"

"How to be a pilot."

"What's drinking vodka have to do with being a pilot?"

"This is why you're so lousy at the controls," Nadine said. "You don't understand piloting."

"What's going on?" Yvette said, arriving from the forward control room.

"Nadine is getting her trainee drunk and stupid," Jake said.

"She's an expert at being at least half of that," Yvette

said. "Is that vodka?"

"And Belter beer," Jake said.

"It's disgusting," Brie said. "This Belter beer."

"No kidding," Yvette said. "But be careful, Capitaine El Supremo here is a Belter."

"You're a Belter, Capitaine El Supremo," Brie asked.

"Yes, I am a Belter—wait, did you call me Capitaine El Supremo?"

Nadine extended a hand to Yvette. "High five." Yvette slapped her hand.

Brie swayed. "Did I do something wrong?"

"Absolutely not," Nadine said. "In fact, you passed your first lesson. Star pupil."

"Oh, good." Brie burped. "Capitaine El Supremo."

Jake grimaced. "Yes?"

"I don't feel so good." She swayed again. "I think I'm going to—" Brie leaned over and barfed on the floor.

The vomit cascaded, splattering Jake's ship slippers. Jake jumped back but not fast enough. Brie got down on all fours and heaved again, then dropped to the deck and gasped. Small dribbles of vomit ran down her chin.

"That's your idea of teaching her to be a pilot? Having her lie on the floor in her own vomit?"

"Yup," Nadine said. "That describes pretty much every pilot I know. What you think, merchie?"

"I agree." Yvette nodded. "We all end up there sooner or later. Best to get it over with."

Brie dry heaved and mewled like a wounded cat.

"I make that exact sound after I puke," Yvette said.

"Me too," Nadine said.

"Huh," Yvette said. She scrutinized Nadine, then turned to Jake. "Well, as much as I enjoy assisting in a youngster's education, the computer is telling us we're going to be coming out of jump early—unexpected gravity well, and I wanted you in the control room to make some decisions, Capitaine El Supremo."

"We'll all come up." Jake spoke to the young man

behind him. "This will be a good part of your training, Kivi. As soon as we arrive, you can set up a list of all the potential refueling sites in the system and what fuel we'll need to reach them, along with a listing of probable time to refuel and calculate the necessary adjustments. Good practice for you."

"And since you don't need a pilot till that's done, I'll stay here and get drunk." Nadine poured a shot and held it out to Jake's trainee, Kivi.

Kivi, a serious-looking young man with dark hair, shook his head. Jake turned and climbed the bridge. Kivi followed, but a moment later, he dashed back, grabbed the drink out of Nadine's hand, downed it, gasped, wiped his chin with his hand, and raced after Jake.

"Kid's got potential," Nadine said to Yvette.

Yvette nodded and extended her hand. Nadine poured another shot and handed it to her. Yvette drank it down with no change in expression and had placed it back on the table when the collision alarm bonged.

The crew raced to the control room. Nadine, Brie, and Odette sat in the first row. Yvette took the console behind Odette, and Jake and Kivi filled in the second. The jump countdown was on everyone's screens, but they were all preparing for an unscheduled return.

"Helm is up," Nadine said. "Brie, mirror my board and watch what I do." The pale-faced girl strapped in next to Nadine and nodded.

"I have backup," Yvette said. "And backup sensors."

"Scan's ready," Odette said.

Jake tapped the intercom. "Engineering?"

"We're ready down here," Willowby said. "Did you miss a planet again when you set up our jump course?"

"I did not miss a planet," Jake said.

"Easy things to miss, planets, in the general scheme of things," Willowby said. "Small compared to stars. Much smaller."

"I did not miss a planet," Jake repeated. "The radar is

triggering on an unexplained mass. We're coming out just beyond the jump limit. There shouldn't be anything there—the planet and moons are inside of it."

"Then why all the bonging and banging and going to stations?" Willowby said.

"Probably a malfunction," Jake said. "Stand by."

"Standing by to stand by," Willowby said.

Jake mashed the intercom offline. "Arrogant twit."

"What should I do, sir?" Kivi asked.

"Think," Jake said. "What's the worst that could happen when we exit the jump?"

"We hit something," Kivi said. "A planet, like the professor said."

"That's not the worst," Nadine said. "We hit a planet—bang, we're gone. Not even enough time to yell at Jakey there and blame him for his lousy navigation. No, the lousiest thing would be we hit a piece of space debris, something sharp that smashes through the hull, cuts into the control room, and slices your suit open, spilling your guts out and leaving you screaming in pain as you watch your insides boil away into space. Or even worse, we come out close to a planet but don't hit it. Just far enough in the atmosphere that we can't rocket out, and we have to watch the cooling and shielding systems fail as we burn up in the atmo, so we'll have plenty of time to feel ourselves cooking from the outside in. Except for your lungs, of course. They burn up first."

"Wow," Brie said. "You have a great imagination."

Nadine grimaced. "Not entirely imagination. Let's say…personal experience."

Brie paled. "That's going to happen to us?"

Nadine stared her down, then giggled. "Gotcha. No, that's not going to happen. Had you going for a while, didn't I?"

"You did. Do those other things happen?"

"Things like them do," Nadine said. "And I do know some people who burned up or got shot or sliced up. But it doesn't happen often."

"Why is the alarm going off, then?" Brie asked.

"Like Jakey said, most likely a malfunction," Nadine said. "It's detecting something that isn't there. Give our gallant captain his due. He's very particular. He wouldn't drop us somewhere with debris."

"We're outside of the Hill sphere of the planet," Jake said. "We're dropping so far out that we're beyond anything in a stable orbit. The planet will be below us. Anything that is this far out will eventually break orbit and fly off into interstellar space."

"What's setting the alarm off, then, sir?" Kivi asked.

"We'll know in twenty seconds," Jake said.

The system counted to zero, then the displays changed to indicate the jump field was down.

"It will take the sensors a few seconds to scan locally," Jake said. "Then the alarm will stop."

"Sensors are all fuzzy," Odette said. "Have to wait till they clear."

The alarm didn't stop. A second alarm joined it. The ship rocked as something hit.

"Not a malfunction," Nadine said. She grabbed the controls and rolled the ship counterclockwise a quarter turn while pitching up. Relative to their vector, she stood the ship on its tail and turned sideways.

BANG. The ship shuddered and slowed, throwing the crew sideways into their restraints as it slowed.

"Hang on, I'm climbing out of the ecliptic." Nadine fired the main engines, and they were pushed back into their seats. "What's out there?"

"Debris field," Yvette said. "Heaviest at the equator of that planet."

"A moon?" Jake asked.

TING. The ship twisted. Another hit.

"Only if it was made out of metal," Yvette said, "and was in an equatorial orbit."

"We're too far out for an equatorial orbit to be stable,"

Jake said.

"Who says it needs to be stable?" Odette said. "Metal. All I see is metal. It's below us now."

"How much?" Nadine said.

Jake examined his screen. "Not a lot. Could have been a big station. Or a ship, or a group of ships. They broke up, though. It's a wide debris field, I'm trying to chart it now."

"What makes a debris field this far out?"

"Ships coming out of jump and breaking up," Jake said. "Lots of ships. Nadine, that debris is in a fairly narrow band. See if you can slow us relative to the planet while we figure this out. Try for a polar orbit. A high polar orbit."

A cautious half hour later, they were drifting along while everybody worked whatever sensor they could find.

"Emperor's toenails," Jake said. "That's a lot of debris. Looks like it was a series of ships that were destroyed as they came out of jump."

"How many ships?" Yvette asked.

"Can't say. It depends on how big they are. If they were all our size, hundreds."

"Or if they were bigger, like Imperial warships, dozens," Odette said.

"But how is it out here, this far out?" Nadine said. "This far out, we should be safe."

"They're not in stable orbits. A lot of them will drift away over the next few years. We're just running into the debris of an old battle."

"How old?"

"Don't know," Jake said.

"I found a station," Odette said. "Strange orbit but definitely a station. Lots of debris near there, too."

"What's it broadcasting?"

"Nothing. No radio. No infrared, either. Just dark."

"There's nothing on the planet," Jake said. "Let's go look at this station."

"Are we sure it's a station?"

"Looks like one. But whatever it is, something destroyed most of this system, and we need to find out what and why."

CHAPTER THREE

"Radio check, one-two-three-four," Jake said, climbing out of the air lock. His air supply hissed in his ears.

"Bite me. One-two-three-four," Nadine answered. "Emperor's sake, Jakey, we've tested these radios a hundred times. Stop being such a wuss."

"It's good technique," Jake said. "Safety is important. I'm hopping now." He braced his feet and pushed hard. He flew away from Accounting Error.

A single-ring orbital station loomed ahead of him. It was dark, deserted, and pieces were missing.

"What is this word wuss?" Odette asked over the radio.

Yvette climbed out behind Jake. "It is another word for fearful or scared."

"Why do the rest of us have to stay behind while you two inspect this deserted station?"

"The rest of you have to stay behind," Jake said, "because I'm the only one who ever lived for a long time on a station like this. I know the most about their construction, their dangers, and I'm the only one who had friends die in blowouts or electrical malfunctions when I was a kid. I'm the only one who knows what we're getting into here, and I'm the best zero G person here."

"Belters, very prickly people," Yvette said.

"I'll say," Nadine said. "Annoyingly prickly. And lousy shots."

"Nadine," Jake said, "if I need some broken piece of electrical equipment shot, I promise I'll have you come over. In the meantime, I have a solution to your question about the spin problem."

"What about the spin?" Nadine said. She'd had problems maneuvering the ship as it closed the station. "What's wrong with your ship? What did you do to it?"

"I'm sure there is nothing wrong with the ship," Yvette said. "Nothing that a competent pilot couldn't have fixed."

"Maybe I'll try to figure it out right now," Nadine said. "Why don't you go stick your head in the thrusters while I fire them off. See if you notice any problems."

"Yvette," Jake said. "Roll one hundred eighty onto your back and look at Accounting Error as you drift."

"Men," Yvette said. "So traditional and boring. 'Roll over,' they say, on your back—oh. That does explain the maneuvering problem."

"What do you see?" Nadine asked. "What's going on?"

"There is a spaceship embedded in number five container," Yvette said.

"A what?"

"A spaceship."

"It's not a spaceship, it's a pinnace," Jake said. "Or parts of it."

"What in the Empress's name is a pinnace?" Nadine asked.

"It's what's stuck in number five container," Yvette said.

"It's a small boat, used to shuttle crew between warships. Engines, but no life support."

"How did it get there?" Nadine asked.

"We must have hit it," Jake said. "That was the thud when we came into the system. It just stuck, didn't smash for some reason."

"Well, get rid of it," Nadine said. "It's messing up our maneuvering."

"Later," Jake said. "I see some other damage. Some of the sensors. I'll check later. For now, let's check this station out." He rolled gently to face the approaching station. "I'm going to lock on next to that air lock. Try to open that door."

Yvette pointed. "Or we can just climb through that big hole next to it."

"We don't know what's inside that hole."

"We don't know what's in the air lock, either, but we're going to climb in there."

"Humor me. I'm the captain," Jake said.

"For now," Yvette said.

Jake and Yvette landed hard on the station shell, rolled to dump velocity, then clamped on with magnetic boots. Jake tried the air lock door but couldn't budge the locking wheel. They tromped over to the ten-meter-wide roundish hole spinward and examined it. The outer skin was bent inward, so they climbed down and peered inside.

"Seems safe enough," Yvette said.

"Watch out for sharp edges," Jake said. "Broken beams, that sort of thing."

"They all seem squished. Whatever did this melted everything as it went by."

Jake ran a gloved hand over a nearby beam. The edge was smooth, like the metal had liquefied, sagged, then froze back. "Something not only punched a hole into the station but also melted everything metal it touched."

They maneuvered from melted beam to melted beam until they could climb into an inner corridor and walk the ring.

"Can't see you on the cameras anymore, Jakey," Nadine said. "Your radio's fading, too."

Jake unclipped a radio booster from his belt and attached it to the wall. "I left a repeater, and I'm sending my suit camera out as well. We're walking spinward. Yvette and I. No lights. No gravity. No atmosphere, either." He punched his suit lights on. "I can see fine with my suit lights—no dust. Metal floors. Numbers and such on the walls. But no loose items."

"No evidence of fire or explosion," Yvette said. "Just that giant hole punched through."

"We can see a lot more of those holes, now that we

know what to look for," Odette said. "Infrared shows no heat. This happened a long time ago."

"Why no fire?" Nadine said. "Or no explosions?"

"Must have been no air when it was destroyed—nothing to explode out," Yvette said.

"Like it was abandoned and then destroyed," Jake said. "Are all the holes round?"

"Mostly," Yvette said.

"Professor, are you watching this?" Jake asked.

"I'm here, Captain Jake," Willowby said over the radio. "We've got it up on the screen here in engineering. My youngsters think these were kinetic weapons, and I agree."

"Kinetic weapons?" Nadine asked. "Like you use in a mass driver?"

"But bigger and faster," Willowby said. "Like you'd find on a warship. That's why the round holes with the melted slag on the edge. Somebody fired hunks of metal into this station. Fired fast. They went through so fast the friction melted everything it touched."

"But no secondary explosions," Jake said. "Strange."

"Any bodies?" the professor asked.

"No," Jake said. "Should there be?"

"Where were the people, then?"

Jake and Yvette continued walking the outer part of the station's ring. The doors were unlocked, so they peeked into the empty rooms. Some had furniture bolted to the floor or wall. Mattresses and chairs remained, and, sometimes, they found cups and plates but no clothes, no pictures on the wall, and no portable electronics, just dead screens and displays.

Jake stopped after the fifth room they inspected and asked Yvette, "Where's the reactor?"

"It will be at the core, like all stations."

"Not this core," Jake said. "I don't remember seeing it. Nadine, can you see a reactor?"

"We can't see the core from this angle, Jake. Do you want me to move the ship?"

"Yes, please. Look for the core spindle."

Nadine and Odette talked as they maneuvered the ship. "No spindle," Nadine said after a minute. "Just the spokes coming together and the usual round shaft broken off above and below. It looks smaller than it should be."

"That's because this station was much bigger than we're used to," Jake said. "We're used to single or double or triple-ring stations. We just assumed that this was a single-ring station. Stand by. Yvette, come with me."

Jake walked them back through the dark corridors and shone his light on the wall where a spoke corridor intersected. Like all stations, when working, this one had used centrifugal force to mimic gravity. When the station spun and the outer rim was 'down,' which meant when you were traveling through the spokes, you climbed up and down stairs, then walked around the rings. Stations had a standard nomenclature—rings, where letters listed from A, spokes numbered from 0, and segments extended spinward from each spoke. Jake shone his light on the wall and saw a sign. Q3. Ring Q, spoke 3.

"Crap," Jake said. "We're missing at least sixteen other rings."

***

Back in the ship's control room, they watched the station fragment shrink as they sailed away.

"We got rid of the parts of the pinnace stuck in number five container," Yvette said. "The container was damaged, but we didn't have time to survey the contents."

"What do you mean got rid of?" Jake asked.

"Levered them out and shoved them at the station."

"This wasn't a station," Jake said. "It's a part of a station. A very small part of a very big station."

"A destroyed station," Yvette said. "This is all that's left."

"Who destroyed it?" Odette asked.

"And why did they wreck it?" Nadine said. "Perfectly good stations are hard to come by. If this is just a fragment, imagine how many people could have lived in it. Was this an Imperial fleet base or something?"

"Not according to our records," Jake said. "But they're pretty incomplete and old. The university had some things from back then, but most people didn't keep track of that type of thing."

"People keep track of those things," Nadine said.

"No, they don't," Jake said. "It's amazing what things you know that you don't realize you know that aren't written down anywhere. You've lived on Delta your whole life. How many stations are in orbit?"

Nadine opened her mouth, then closed it. "I don't know."

"And think of a station you've been to. Do you have a plan or a record of where things are on it or how big it is?"

"They give me that info when I get there," Nadine said. "There're maps in the computer."

"Maps on computers," Jake said. "You get one when you arrive, and you dump it when you leave because you don't need it anymore."

"Somebody must have a map," Nadine said.

"Why?" Jake said. "I grew up on a station. I never saw a map. We all knew where everything was, and when ships visited, we walked them where they needed to go. The caf, offices, stuff like that. There weren't any plans."

"We don't know what this station was?" Nadine said.

"We don't. It's not in any of our records," Jake said.

"Nor any of ours," Odette said.

"Your records?" Jake said. "You have your own records?"

"She means we didn't read anything about it in the database here, either," Yvette said. "The data you showed us, that's what we mean. But if this was a big station, where's the rest of it?"

"Maybe that's what we hit on the way in?" Nadine said.

"Could be part of it," Jake agreed. "That could be true." Jake turned but kept a view of Yvette and Odette.

Yvette raised her eyebrows at Odette. Odette shook her head.

Nadine missed the byplay. "But if it was destroyed, where are the bodies or the random junk you find during a blowout. There's none of that there," she said. "This is the neatest destroyed station I've ever seen."

"Seen many?" Yvette asked. "Destroyed stations?"

"Destroyed a couple by crashing into them. Want me to show you how I did it? Let's take your head—that can be the ship, and this bulkhead is the station. Now, if we slam your head into the bulkhead like so—"

Kivi had been quiet this whole time, listening to the others. "Maybe they left, then blew it up. You know, evacuated and then destroyed it."

"Destroyed a station this big?" Jake said. "Why?"

"It would explain why there's no random junk," Nadine said. "They packed up everything good, then ran away."

"Shut down the reactor, turned off the power. Emptied the air, then blew it up," Odette said.

"But why?" Jake asked. "Why destroy a perfectly good station."

"They were scared," Brie said.

"Scared? Scared of what?"

"Something," Brie said. "Something was coming, and they ran away from it because it scared them, and they didn't want to give it any idea where they went or any ability to follow them. And it kept whoever was chasing them from using this station."

"But the Empire was huge," Kivi said. "And powerful. What's scary enough to make them run away?"

"Your trainee has it right," Willowby said, sitting next to Jake in the lounge. "I put the problem to the students, and me and the youngsters came up with a theory." He tapped his console, and a schematic came up on the main display.

"You know that they're not really students?" Yvette said. "They are merchant officers."

"And Militia officers," Nadine said.

"They're not that young either," Jake said.

"Stuff and nonsense," Willowby said. "Anyone younger than fifty is a youngster to me, and if they're working for me, well, they're students. I'm teaching them things, after, all. Who's to say otherwise?"

"Never mind," Jake said. "What are we looking at?"

"Imperial accommodations block. For a base or a station. This is where the workers would stay. The shipyards were a different design, and so were the fueling stations. This is what they would put into a system where they needed lots of people to live. Quarters, warehouses, logistics hubs. Entertainment sections—restaurants, bars, gyms, those sorts of things. Let's say they put a refueling station into a system or a repair station. Those were standard designs as well, and they had accommodations attached, but this was for the other services people needed. Transients, that sort of thing."

He pulled up a picture of the ring next to the blueprint on the screen. Their station fragment matched a ring on the bottom half.

"They were all about standardization and modules," Willowby said. "The Empire would build a repair depot—a small station with its own accommodation and logistics units. Then they'd build a fueling station—with tankers to skim the gas giants or mining ships to haul in ice. Or both. That had basic accommodations, too. Then a mining station to pull in metals, fabricate metal plates if nothing else. Then a light manufacturing station. Pretty soon, they'd have five or six of these in the same place—couple, maybe three thousand people between them. If there was no suitable planet nearby, they'd build one of these accommodations blocks, give people on the station somewhere to go for short leaves and to handle overflow from each station."

"This accommodation block was always a part of a bigger complex?" Jake asked.

"Always."

"Where's everything else, then?" Jake asked.

"Some of it is sticking out of number five container," Nadine said. "The Empire must have blown it all up."

"And did a good job of it, too," Willowby said. "This ring is all that's left intact."

"So, the Empire destroyed, preemptively, their biggest station in this sector and retreated," Jake said. "Just to make it harder for anybody to follow them?"

"Seems like," Willowby agreed.

"Do you need more time to study any of this?" Jake said.

"Got what we need. Not much more to find out."

"Onward."

"Jakey, you said we had enough food for a few more jumps," Nadine said.

"Yes, I did."

"That was a few jumps ago. How much now?"

Jake grimaced. "We've got enough for one more jump, then we'll have to turn around."

"So, onward to the next system?" Nadine said. "Then we turn around?"

"We do have some indications that there was a colony there. A small one, according to the records."

"No Imperial base? Like the one here?"

"We didn't know this one was here," Jake said. "But no, not supposed to be a base."

"Well, let's get this over with," Nadine said. "We'll go investigate your colony. If there's nothing there, we turn back?"

"We turn back," Jake agreed. "If there's nothing there, we've gone as far as we can, and we'll have to let Dashi know we failed." Jake looked at the cup of basic in front of him. "I'm not looking forward to telling Dashi that."

"Don't think of it as failing, Jakey, think of it as..."

"Failing?"

"Well, yes, that's exactly what it is," Nadine said.

"Don't lose hope, el supremo," Yvette said. "We might find a colony after all."

"Or," Odette said. "We might find the reason that this station was destroyed. Or who destroyed it. They might be waiting there. Waiting for us."

CHAPTER FOUR

"I almost miss the alarm," Nadine said, waiting for the jump counter to hit zero. "Did you ever figure out what the problem was, Jakey?"

"Self-tests went okay," Jake said. "It's more sensitive than I knew. It picks up even small anomalies, far away from our emergence."

"What's an anomaly to a jump sensor?"

"Any sort of mass that isn't listed in the database."

"And our databases are nearly a hundred years old, which means that they'll always be wrong. Hello, constant bonging."

"Not always," Jake said. "I've got Kivi converting the scans to orbital data and updating the databases with every system we've visited so far."

Nadine smirked at Kivi. "Go to space, learn to type. Useful skills you're learning, Kivikins."

"Kivikins?" Kivi asked.

"Everybody needs a nickname—that's yours now," Nadine said.

"I don't like it," he said. "Can I be something else?"

"You don't like it? Even better. And you don't get to choose your own nickname, but the worse you hate it, the more other people will use it. Enjoy your database, Kivikins."

"What's Gabriella's nickname, then?" Kivi asked.

"Brie. Nadine calls me Brie," Gabriella said.

"You get Brie, and I get Kivikins?"

"Best you learn now that life isn't fair," Nadine said. "Brie, get ready to take her once we come out of jump."

"You're having Brie do the piloting?" Jake asked. "Now?"

"If not now, when?" Nadine asked. "You have to learn sometime. Besides, according to your beloved jump computer, this is as simple an emergence as we're liable to have for a while. Why, even you could pilot us out of this, Jakey."

"Let's not be hasty," Yvette said. "El supremo wasn't hired for his piloting skills."

"Thank the Empress for that," Nadine said.

"And it's not my 'beloved' jump computer," Jake said.

"Really?" Nadine said. "I thought that was the only action you were getting at all these days."

"I-I—" Jake shut his mouth.

A light flashed on Brie's board. "Emergence in ten."

"Take us in, sister," Nadine said, leaning back and putting her hands behind her head.

Inky black regular space replaced the blue jump glow on the monitors. Brie tapped a minor course change on her board. Nadine watched but didn't move her arms.

"Nothing on passive," Odette said. "Radar is running."

"No beacons," Yvette said. "And ours is broadcasting."

"No alarms," Brie said. "Nothing in front of us."

"What have we got for planets?" Nadine asked.

"Rocky, rocky, and rocky," Yvette said. She tapped her screen. "But not exactly right where the navigation database said they'd be."

"They are out of orbit? What moves a planet?" Nadine said.

"Nothing. Perhaps we're out of orbit." Odette frowned at her screen.

"There's supposed to be one habitable planet," Jake said. "With population. Let me put it on the screen." He tapped his console, and a picture appeared on the main display.

A picture of empty space.

"Did you lose a planet again, Jake?" Nadine asked.

"I've been told that's easy to do, them being so small and all."

"Computer says it should be right there," Jake said. He tapped through his screens. "I'll find it."

"I'll believe that when I see it," Nadine said.

Odette swiped through several displays. "Here it is. Looks nice. Blue. I'll share the coordinates."

The crew busied themselves with checking out Odette's position report. Jake put his plotted system information on one screen and the scanner output on another. They didn't match. He kept an eye on Odette's screen as Yvette walked up to talk to her. As Odette continued switching screens, Yvette typed in a long code.

"Sir, I have lights," Kivi said.

"On the planet?" Jake said.

"I pointed the infrared telescope at it, like you said. I can see light patterns on the dark side."

"Well done, Kivikins," Nadine said. "You found them."

"Why haven't they contacted us?" Jake asked. "At least called us?" He looked at his screen. "Our beacon is on," he said.

"Could be nobody is watching for beacons?" Nadine shrugged. "Let's go closer and look."

"Or just give them a call," Jake said. He typed a message on his screen. "Here, I'm broadcasting on the Imperial emergency channel. Let's see what they say." Jake hit send, and they sat back to wait.

Nothing happened for two minutes, then a voice channel came online.

"Vessel calling. Identify yourself," a voice said.

"He's talking standard," Odette said.

"Better standard than you speak, merchie," Nadine said.

"Why don't you—"

"She's right, mon ami," Yvette said. "The accent is perfect. Very perfect, like those old vids with the actors from the core."

"Must be the Empire," Jake said. "Planet, this is Accounting Error from"—Jake paused—"from a lost colony. We seek the Empire."

The round trip delay was five seconds. "You're from a colony?"

"Yes."

"You seek the Empire?"

"Yes."

The voice laughed. "The Empire? Which one?"

***

Accounting Error pulled into a polar orbit around the planet, identified as Magyar, per the radio voice. He refused to answer questions, saying he had to "speak to the baron" but told them they would be welcomed at the main and only city on the planet.

"I see it in the telescope," Odette said. "Between those two landlocked seas." She popped the image up on the main consoles.

A large continent stretched across the equator from the northern to southern hemisphere. Icecaps covered the far north, mountains to the south, grasslands down to the equatorial sea, and more grasslands below till they petered out in low hills in the far south. Two large seas occupied the eastern and western centers of the continent, separated by a giant peninsula sticking up in the middle like a thumb.

"Do those two pieces of land meet?" Jake asked.

Odette magnified the image. The continent stretched across the middle, separated by ocean into two halves. For several dozen miles, the north and south shores were no more than five or ten miles apart. In the middle of the northern side was a crooked inlet with a city built beside it.

"That's the big city, according to them," Odette said.

"Doesn't look that big," Jake said.

Odette highlighted a building next to the water. "That is a fusion plant there, and that looks like an Imperial colony complex beside it."

"No mass driver, though," Jake said.

"Gravity is lower than Delta," Yvette said, reading her screen. "Low enough we can land and take off with that lifting thing—if we don't load too much."

"Well, let's go see them," Jake said. "First, we load up the boat."

"The boat? What boat?" Yvette said.

"The landing boat, the ship's boat. That's what I'm calling it."

"You mean the lifting thing."

"I mean the landing boat."

Yvette rolled her eyes. "Fine. Who goes down?"

"Me and Nadine."

"And me," Yvette said. "In case Ms. Nadine has a problem and you need someone else to fly it back."

"What sort of problem will I get into?" Nadine asked. "I'm pretty good at solving problems."

"Maybe stabbed by a jealous wife?"

"That could happen," Jake said. "But I'd also like to have a second pilot who can lift, if we need to stay behind. Come along and help me load up."

Jake had twenty-four sample cases he needed to put on board the landing boat. The landing boat clamped on the dorsal side of the jump ship, accessed through the dorsal air lock. Since they were under thrust, the cases had to be lifted out of the pressurized cargo bay, carried up the ladder through ship and boat locks, then dragged back to the boat's cargo bay to be latched down.

Nadine and Yvette helped begrudgingly, and Jake told the two trainees they could come as well, provided they helped load.

Brie hauled a sample case over the coaming of the interior boat air lock and dragged it to the tie down straps. "What's in this one, Jake? Lead?"

"You should probably call me Captain Jake or something like that," Jake said.

"Nadine calls you Jakey or el supremo or el capitaine."

"El Capitaine is Francais for captain. And you're using Nadine as a role model?"

"Why not? She's the one training me, she's a great pilot, and she tells amazing stories. Did you know she shot an ex-boyfriend in the chest three times?"

"I do know that," Jake said. "And it hurt a lot."

"How do you know how much it hurt?" Brie asked.

"I'm the ex-boyfriend."

"Huh," Brie said. She cocked her head and inspected him. "You probably deserved it."

"Two of them," Jake muttered. "That's all I need."

Nadine appeared. "What's in this case, Jakey? Lead?"

"Your apprentice just asked that," Jake said. "And no. That's case number eleven. That one has copper and zinc. Lead is in number seventeen."

"You have copper, lead, and zinc?"

"And iron, aluminum, nickel, scandium, tungsten, vanadium, chromium, and manganese. Pretty much the whole periodic table. I did some reading before we left. Metals will be our best bet for trading things anywhere we meet."

"There's metal everywhere, Jakey," Nadine said. "Every system has aluminum and iron and... all those other things you said. The nickledanium and stuff."

"True. But not every system has orbital zero G smelters that can boil it to the purity level we can reach. Everybody has copper, but our copper is ninety-nine point nine nine nine percent pure. That's hard to do on a planet. We can command high prices. And this case"—Jake hefted the case in his hand—"has rare earths. Samarium, europium, neodymium, and others. Samples. With those cases we've got samples of everything for them to test and check out. Then we can land container loads or partial container loads anyways."

"Well, you're the trading guy, that's for sure. Pay close attention there, Kivikins. Don't know how he does it, but whenever you trade with Jake Stewart, you end up thinking you won. Till you find out later that however much you made on the transaction he made a hundred times more."

"You're just jealous," Jake said. "Yvette and I will be back in the passenger compartment."

"Jealous? Of that skill, yeah," Nadine said. "It's uncanny."

"Uncanny? Maybe he's possessed by a demon," Brie said.

"That could be," Nadine said, walking to the control room. "How do we get rid of this demon."

"We need a pentagram," Brie said, "a live goat, a knife, and a lot of blood."

"Tell me more," Nadine said, buckling in. "As soon as you're ready back there, Jake."

Jake delayed them for fifteen minutes while he set up an automatic sensor sweep to record more data on the system. He also spent a few minutes looking at Odette's logs and launching another more complex program he had to go to the jump computer to start. Then he had a long chat with Willowby and gave him some ship operating codes.

The deorbit was uneventful, except for Nadine and Brie discussing how they would have to carve Jake up to remove the trading demon possessing him. Scooping Jake's intestines out figured prominently in Brie's solution.

"And then we cut them into four pieces and burn each piece in a special container called a scone. With some incense," Brie said, mirroring Nadine's screen. "Till there is nothing left but ashes. And then we take all the ashes and bury them at a crossroads at the dark of the moon."

"A crossroads?" Nadine said. She sat at the controls of the "ship's boat," as they called it. "Why a crossroads?"

"I'm not sure," Brie said. "I can ask my mother. She's a witch."

"You mean spells and stuff?" Nadine asked.

"Yes. And cutting out intestines."

Nadine looked out the front windows, then down at the control screens. "Dirtside in five. Ramjet will shut down shortly. We're landing right in the middle of that big city, in the harbor near the fusion plant. There's a clear path between those big sailing ships on the right and that bunch of barges on the left. Clear path across the harbor, with markers of some sort. Must be the landing channel. Should be close enough to shore that they can tow us in." She tapped her screen. "Did she ever do that, cut anybody into pieces?"

"She threatened some of my old boyfriends with it."

"But never did it."

"Well, one went away and never came back..."

"Jake," Nadine hollered back to the passenger compartment. "I absolutely love this girl. I'm so glad you recruited her."

"Nadine," Jake yelled from his seat back in the passenger compartment. "Please stop thinking up elaborate ways to kill me and concentrate on landing us in that harbor."

"Spoilsport," Nadine said. "Here I am, trying to help you out by getting rid of your inner demons."

"I have no inner demons," Jake said. "I have outer demons, and one of them is flying this landing boat right now. Please concentrate."

"I've landed unpowered gliders, ships, shuttles, this stupid lifting body around mountains, rivers, lakes, with people shooting at us or trying to ram me. You think I can't land in this wide-open harbor in clear weather? What could possibly go wrong?" Nadine turned to Brie. "Who does he think he is? I mean, with me doing all this piloting—"

"Boats. Sailboats!" Brie pointed to the view port.

A fleet of sailing boats zoomed in from her right side. Each was six meters long, wooden, with a single mast and a single sail. At least thirty appeared from behind the sides of the larger sailing ships to her right, then streamed directly into her path.

"Brace, brace, brace," Nadine yelled.

The landing boat clipped the top of the first sailboat and knocked it over. They clipped the top of the mast off the second and third ones. More carnage ensued after that, but they didn't see it because the third boat's sail billowed up and wrapped across the forward view ports and cameras. They hit more masts bang-bang-bang-bang, then were free. Brie threw up a stern camera. Thirty or more boats were spinning in circles, locking rigging, or lying tipped over in the water. Knocked-over crewmembers swam for their boats.

The landing boat hit the water with a splash, glided to a stop, then rocked in the waves. Jake climbed into the control room as the covering sail slid off the bow of the landing boat. Rescue boats sailed or steamed in all directions on the cameras. People lined the quay in front and were yelling and shaking their fists. A siren wailed in the distance.

"Nice landing, rocketsocks," Jake said.

"Bite me," Nadine said.

Brie giggled. They both glared at her. She wilted. "Any landing you walk away from is good, right? Besides"—she waved her hands—"that was fun, right?"

After Nadine's carnage, the locals were initially too involved in rescuing their sailors to come over to the landing boat. But after twenty minutes, a barge chugged over. Jake had climbed out of the upper air lock and stood on the surface of the floating ship's boat. He'd learned that from previous trips and had stripped extra weight and fuel so they would float. They were low, but they wouldn't sink. The landing boat had tie-downs for tug lines at the bow and stern. Nadine had unlocked the covering plates, and Jake attached the throw lines.

After four lines were attached, the barge maneuvered

until it was close enough that a crewman could jump over. He looked at Jake's knots, shook his head, and retied them.

"That's the worse bowline I've ever seen," the squat bearded sailor said to Jake.

"Not a lot of call for rope knots in space," Jake said.

"You ruined the baron's cup final."

"Pardon?"

"Baron's cup. The race." The sailor pointed at the mélange of sinking sailboats behind them. "I had a lot of money on that race. Bluey was ahead. He was going to make it. I had fifty credits on him."

"I'm sorry. They got in our way as we landed."

"In your way. They got in your way? Pfffft."

"We were landing. From space."

"What sort of idiot lands in the middle of a regatta?"

"Regatta?"

"What do you think those red markers were for?" The sailor nodded to several floating red buoys in the harbor. "That was the racecourse. Supposed to stay clear. Everybody knows that."

"We don't. We don't have racecourses in space."

"Nor bowlines neither, apparently," the sailor said, retying another of Jake's knots. "Expect your spaceships to blow away in a strong wind."

"We don't have—"

"Winds, I know. No winds in space. You don't have much." A sailor from the barge hailed them. "What you want?"

The other sailor called back, "Come back. We're to take them into the royal wharf and tie them up. The baron wants to see them."

"Now you're in for it," the sailor said, yanking the final rope tight. "Baron will be upset you ruined his race. Takes his races very seriously. Wouldn't want to be in your shoes, boyo." The sailor stepped back, then made a running leap from the side of the landing boat to his barge. Once there, he and the other man went into a wheelhouse at the front. Black smoke puffed out of a boiler behind the wheelhouse, and the barge dragged them toward the shore.

"But we came from space," Jake said. He looked back to the sinking boats. "Space."

CHAPTER FIVE

"Anything on the radio?" Jake asked. They were all crammed into the control room as they waited to be towed in.

"Nothing," Nadine said. "That guy from before hasn't come back since he said he gave us those landing instructions. A baron—that's an Imperial rank, right?"

"Yes, one of the lowest ones."

"Have we found the Empire?" Brie asked.

"We've found something," Jake said. "Not sure what."

"Sir," Kivi said, pointing out the view port, "that barge is burning coal."

"You make him call you sir?" Nadine said. "Jakey, have you got delusions of grandeur?"

"He does it himself. That does look like coal." Jake focused on an external camera and magnified it. "That's a boiler..."

"You don't have to call him 'sir,'" Nadine said. "Just Jake or Jakey or Stewart or something like that."

"But he's the captain. He's in charge."

"Less in charge than you imagine."

"It wouldn't be right. It's not... proper to call him anything but sir," Kivi said.

"Not proper?" Nadine groaned. "Another one. You're not his cousin or something? Younger brother?"

"I'm an only child," Kivi said.

"But still formal. Boring. It must rub off from Jake," Nadine said. "Welcome to the great Empire of the universe. Wooden sailing ships. Coal-burning barges. No mass driver. And, apparently, only one radar and spacecom on the planet. Well done, Stewart, well done."

Jake brought up another vessel on the screen. "This one isn't burning coal." He sharpened the image's focus. "That's an anti-grav vehicle, maybe. Or perhaps a hovercraft."

"That's a radar on top," Yvette said from the passenger compartment. "Some of the older Free Traders have that model."

"Annnnnnnd that's a laser," Nadine said. "Pointing at somebody. Us?"

"It's right behind us," Jake said. "And that fellow on the bow has a Gauss rifle."

"Haven't seen one of those since I sold them..."

"Sold them? You sold guns?" Brie said.

Nadine winked. "Whattya need, kid? I can find it."

"You are the best teacher ever. Way better than those old goats at the university," Brie said.

"Please don't use her as a role model," Jake said. "You'll get us all killed."

"At least we won't die of boredom," Nadine said, "like when we follow your advice, Stewart. Or starve to death in the dark."

"Nobody is starving," Jake said. "Speaking of, is that a cow walking down the street there?"

"Big cattle, bigger than we have on Delta," Kivi said. "And that's a horse."

"Big cattle, big steaks," Nadine said. "Outstanding. I am so sick of eating trays. Delta is awash with trays."

"About that," Jake said. "Best we not identify exactly where we're from. Saying 'Delta' is okay—they won't know what that means, but no mention of Sigma Draconis. Just say we're from this sector."

"And why say that, Jakey? The Empire knows Delta. The colony wasn't a secret, at least if those histories I read are correct."

Jake raised his eyebrows. "You read histories? Which ones?"

"Some old thing that I read somewhere," Nadine said. "Not important." She tabbed through her screens. "Look—horse. Cows. Is that a ground car?"

"Nadine read all the books on the reading list that you distributed before the mission started," Brie said. "We talked about all of them during the training. It was an excellent selection of reference books."

Jake rounded on Nadine. She kept her face pointed at the camera and focused on the ground car. Her neck was turning red.

"Nadine, are you blushing?"

"Am not," Nadine said. She glared at Brie. "Traitor. Told you not to say that."

Jake nodded again. "Well, good to know that somebody takes my suggestions seriously. But we have to be careful."

"I thought the Empire would be our friends," Kivi said. "Lost colony and all."

Jake tapped a few screens and brought pictures into focus on them. "Look here. Wooden sailing ships, coal-burning boilers but also anti-grav with radar. Cattle, horses but ground cars and Gauss rifles. This is not what we expected."

One horse stopped, shook itself, then shat a huge pile of dung into the middle of the street. People stepped around it without breaking stride.

"I don't think this is the Empire we're looking for," Jake said.

The barge crew backed them into the dock, with the bow pointing out to the harbor for easy departure. Sailors swarmed over the hull of the landing boat and tied it firmly to the side of the quay, then wheeled over a portable gangplank, complete with stairs and extensible fitting to handle different heights, widths, and tides. It also had hydrogen and water lines. Jake collected his main sample box and led his crew onto the gangplank. After punching a few test buttons, he plugged the Empire-standard fueling hoses into their intake port. He had Yvette start the internal pumps to suck hydrogen and water into the boat. The dock crew didn't complain, but they didn't help, either.

Yvette stayed on board to monitor the refueling, man the radio, and launch the boat if necessary. Jake spent a few minutes in the control room, pointing out some control settings to her, before returning to stand beside Nadine.

Nadine inhaled. "Horse's dung, coal, and rotting seaweed. You take me to the best places, Jake."

"It's not that bad. I can smell oranges, too. I'll bet they have orange juice here."

"I see you didn't ask if you could refuel."

"It's only water."

"And hydrogen."

"They probably don't have any use for the hydrogen. Only good for starships. Same with distilled water."

"Good thing because, given the piles of horse doo-doo out here, I'm not drinking the regular water." Nadine stamped her foot on the gangplank. "They must get regular shuttle traffic here if they have all this."

"Maybe," Jake said. "It's Old Empire for sure—not sure what this alloy is, but it only took two of them to wheel this big thing over. But look there." Jake pointed down.

Nadine clomped down the steps at the end. "Wooden steps. So?"

"It's a repair. A repair with wood. Why wood?"

"Why not?"

"Maybe they can't do metalworking anymore," Jake said.

"Think you're wrong there, Jakey. Look at what Mr. Ironworks over there is carrying. And he's not the only one."

Jake and his group thumped down the last of the stairs to a concrete seawall. Jake gestured to Kivi and Gabriella to wait, and he and Nadine walked three steps and stopped. Approaching them were a group of uniformed soldiers or perhaps police or customs. Another uniformed group held back a crowd at the far end of the seawall. The soldiers were bareheaded, wore red tunics, blue pants, and sandals. They had broad leather belts, complete with brown hilts of swords in scabbards. All four were shorter than Jake and uniformly dark-haired and dark-eyed. All had beards.

"Jake," Nadine said, "your lengthy faults outweigh your tiny list of skills, but one thing that I can depend on is that, if it involves something boring like numbers or math, you are disgustingly precise."

"Thanks for the compliment, but why do I feel suspicious all of a sudden?"

"Not supposed to be a compliment. When we scanned for the planets, they weren't where you said they should be. Did you make a mistake in your calculations?"

"If I did," Jake said, "I did it three times, three different ways, because I always triple-check those things."

"You don't make those types of mistakes once, never mind three times." Nadine grinned. "You do make complete categories of mistakes other times. Shooting. Running. Unsuitable women."

"Depends on your definition of unsuitable."

"Is the computer bust?"

"Keep your voice down. Don't let the kids know." Jake glanced back at Kivi and Brie. "It is. I back-checked. We've been coming into the wrong coordinates every jump. It just hasn't been obvious till we hit something."

"What's wrong?"

"The database reset. When they wiped the files, when the crew—my father—came to Delta with the jump ship, they erased the records so that it couldn't be proven that they were rebels. And—"

"And what?"

"And they didn't know what they were doing, so

instead of just erasing their course, they erased every course in the computer. Everywhere the ship had ever been. Every change since the ship was built. Every update to the database, errors in the survey, errors in the software, things that had been fixed, trade routes that changed, notices of new construction, errors. The lot."

"Should have checked the version numbers, Jakey," Nadine said.

"I did," Jake said. "They doctored them to display a later version number, same as the latest version on Delta. It's only when I pulled the source code I saw a difference."

"Can we still jump?"

"We can jump. But we're jumping with defective software using two hundred-year-old databases."

"What, we'll hit a star?"

"Stars, I can avoid. Planets, probably. But smaller things, nope. Moons, nope. And those systems with lots of debris. We don't dare go back there till we get this sorted out. Otherwise, next time, we might hit the remains of a destroyed station's public bathroom at twenty percent of light speed."

"So, we're stuck here until we figure this out?"

"I need the updates. Both for the software and for the databases."

"Where can you get them?"

"Any Imperial colony has them in their colonial database, probably. I know Delta does. I just never needed them."

"Do they have them here?"

"Maybe. They should."

"Could we just ask for a copy?"

"Can you imagine what that would cost?"

Nadine shook her head. "Oh boy."

"Don't tell the others," Jake said. "We'll talk later. Here come the locals." The approaching group halted within arm's distance. "Greetings," Jake said. "I am Jake Stewart, this is my crew, and we're—"

"You ruined the baron's cup," the first guard said.

"Pardon?"

"The baron's cup, the sailing race. You ruined it."

"I... sorry. We didn't know."

"How can you not know about the baron's cup?"

"We came from space. From the Empire."

"From the Empire? The Empire should know about the baron's cup. Right, boys?" He looked at his companions, who nodded grimly. "Everybody in the Empire knows about the baron's cup."

"Well, that's what we've been told," another guard said. "Stands to reason, how many sailors we produce and all. But"—the other guard looked at Jake—"we haven't talked to the Empire in a long time. Maybe they forgot. Have you Imperials forgotten us here?"

"Here?" Jake said.

"Magyar," the man said. "Here. Where you're standing."

"Well."

"You do know where you're standing, right?"

"I do, but..."

Another group—this time on horses—paraded through the end of the dock. The horses high stepped down the dock until they stopped in front of Jake and the others. The leader was dressed similarly to the guards in front of them in matching colors but with shimmering fabrics and elaborate facings on his collar. He wore armor. Brown straps of metal crisscrossed his chest, shoulders, and hung down like a skirt at his waist.

"All hail the honorable Marchello, grandson to our glorious baron. Long may he reign," a soldier called.

"Long may he reign," the soldiers chorused, dropped to their knees, then went into a full face-plant in front of the crew, facing a short figure on the next horse.

The young man drew up ahead of them. He wore the same outfit as the soldiers, just more expensive-looking. The others wore dark brown, his was a bright, shiny silver, and the fabrics of his shirt and trousers seemed more expensive. Physically, he could have been the brother of a soldier.

"Who are you strangers, that you do not do obeisance to me?"

"Pardon?" Jake said.

The horseman looked at them and at the landing boat. "You are Imperials?"

"Sort of. Yes," Jake said. "We're part of the Empire."

"And you do not know of me? I am Marchello, grandson to the baron."

"The baron," Jake nodded. "I see, the baron. Um, which baron would that be."

"What? You have not heard of the baron?"

"No," Nadine said. "Should we have?"

The young man noticed Nadine, her skinsuit, and her looks. He hopped off his horse. The soldier behind him dismounted and took his reins.

"Where are my manners? Beautiful lady, welcome to Magyar. I am the honorable Marchello, and I am enchanted to make your acquaintance." He bent over, drew her hand to his lips, and kissed it.

Nadine grinned. "See how it's done, Jake? Kivi, are you taking notes?"

"Alas," Marchello said, straightening up. "I was consumed with surprise at seeing Imperials for the first time in many years. My apologies for not greeting you more properly." He looked at Jake. "You will want to see my grandfather, the baron."

"Your grandfather? The baron. Yes, yes, of course. Let's go see the baron," Jake said.

"We will provide you with horses," Marchello said, then snapped his fingers. Five of the other troopers behind him dismounted and led their horses forward.

"Um, is it far? None of us can ride horses."

"Imperial nobles that don't ride horses?" Marchello frowned.

"They're hard to carry on spaceships," Nadine said. She rolled her eyes at Jake. "We don't use them that often these days. Perhaps you can walk with us and talk."

"If that is your wish"—Marchello bowed—"then, of course that is what we shall do." He gestured down the dock. "This way, if you please."

The group collected around him and strolled down the quay.

"What of the Empire? How goes the war?"

"The war?" Jake asked.

"It goes well," Nadine said. "Very well. We are everywhere victorious."

"I thought so," Marchello said. "We've had no news for many years, but nothing can defeat the Empire."

"Nothing at all," Nadine agreed. "I didn't get your... grandfather? The baron's name."

"Arturo. The Baron Arturo. But surely you know this, beautiful lady?"

Nadine beamed at him. "And why do you say that, handsome man?"

Marchello beamed back. "Because he is the Imperial governor of this sector. Appointed by the Emperor himself."

CHAPTER SIX

Nadine flirted with Marchello while they marched up the road, chatting of nothing, but touching his arm frequently. Jake and the others walked behind. They left the dock and the waterfront promenade and entered the city proper.

Market stalls lined both sides of the crowded street. Marchello's guard's shouldered their way through the crowd. The crowd objected—loudly—and pushed back until they got a closer look at the guards' uniforms. When they saw Marchello, they bowed deeply or dropped to one knee.

Conversations hummed as they went by. Jake overheard "The Imperials are back" and "I lost a bundle on that race." He couldn't tell which they viewed as more important.

Horse dung stank in the sun. Flies buzzed. One in five windows had mesh screens, the rest open to the bugs and weather. Shopkeepers and shoppers gibbered at each other.

Jake stopped at one stall lined with bolts of fabric before he asked the stall keeper, "Do you speak standard?"

"Of course, Imperial sir," the man said. His accent was faultless—he could have been a news announcer on an Old Empire vid. "How may we help you?"

Jake pointed at shimmering fabric on the counter. "What type of cloth is that?"

"That is tree silk, Imperial sir." The keeper unwrapped the bolt. "Feel the quality."

Jake rubbed his fingers on it. "Old Earth silk?"

"A local plant. It is as good as Earth silk—better, in fact."

"You grow it here?"

"It comes from the vines of the Bakkan plant. It's similar to Earth silk but based on cellulose. It takes dyes better than Earth silk."

"It's beautiful," Jake said. "So soft."

"What do you offer for it, then, Imperial sir? Name a price."

"We have just arrived from orbit," Jake said. "We're going to greet the baron. Shopping can wait."

"From orbit—so, the rumors are true." The man looked worried and glanced forward, where Marchello pointed to a building, explaining something to Nadine. "Then, you should proceed, Imperial sir. The baron's advisers do not take kindly to those who are late."

"Thanks," Jake said. "Besides, we don't have any money right now. We'll have to trade for it. What do you use for money here?"

"We take gold, of course, and silver," the man said. "And copper and aluminum, of course."

"Copper and aluminum? What would you trade for aluminum?" Jake asked. "Or tungsten and other metals?"

The man flicked his eyes at Marchello, laughing at one of Nadine's jokes, then back to Jake. "You have these metals? In quantity?"

Jake nodded. "We come from the stars, after all."

"Feel the quality, kind sir," the man sang out, pulled more fabric, and stepped to drape it on Jake's shoulders. "Smooth, soft, keeps you warm under the Bakkan cloth," he called out, bringing his head to Jake's ear. He whispered as he wrapped it around him. "My name is Kasem. I can help you trade your metals. When you are at the palace, do not take their prices. I will pay five, ten times what they offer. If it is too much for me, I have friends. Come here to my shop at the close of business any day, and I will deal with you. It will be to your benefit."

"Jakey, stop being lazy. Let's go," Nadine yelled.

"Sorry, Nadine," Jake yelled back. Jake unwound the fabric and gave it to Kasem. "I will see you later."

Kasem nodded and clutched his bolt of fabric.

The party continued up the busy street. Jake walked beside Kivi. "What do you see?"

"They are short of metals." Kivi pointed at a shop on their left. "Household goods. Wooden bowls, wooden plates, wooden cups, wooden furniture. Some stone things—jugs, maybe. But look at the cutlery."

"It's locked up," Jake said. The store was open to browsing, but the display of metal knives, forks, and spoons was in a locked case. "No metals. But lots of fabrics."

Kivi nodded to a vendor on the left. "What's Bakkan cloth? And Bakkan silk?"

"They have a plant called a Bakkan. Bakkan silk feels like real Earth silk. Soft, shiny. Bakkan cloth looks pretty rough. But they have regular Earth fabrics as well."

A sign advertised denim, cotton, Bakkan cloth, and Bakkan silk. The silk was double the price of the cotton.

"Make way, make way," a voice called.

The entire party, even Marchello, squeezed to the side. A truck drove up from the harbor, almost touching the crowds surging between the stalls on either side. The body was a standard construction, but a steam engine replaced the normal electric motor. The back of the truck was piled high with shiny black rocks.

Jake choked on the dust as it went by. "That's coal. Coal-powered truck, and it's hauling coal for somewhere. They've reverted to a coal-based economy."

"But look there—" Kivi pointed at a store sign. "Electrical and mechanical repairs. They have electronics in the shop windows."

"They have pictures of electronics in the shop windows," Jake said. "Not real electronics, and they don't have windows, just shutters that they have open. See any glass? I don't."

"I see personal electronics," Kivi said, pointing to a stall keeper. "Or what could be. That man has a comm unit."

"Not like ours, though," Jake said. "Bigger, different color."

The road steepened as they climbed. Stores lined each side. All with open shutters, none with glass windows.

"No glass, not many metals," Jake said. "But fabric. Cows. Agricultural stuff." He skipped ahead for a moment and touched a guard on the shoulder. When the man turned, Jake pointed at a building and asked a question. The man replied, and Jake grasped the man's hand and forearm in a double-hand grip and shook it.

Jake returned to walk by Kivi. "That armor is metal, but it doesn't feel like iron. Maybe bronze."

The sky darkened, the buildings on either side of the road tall enough to block the sun. The road flattened out and smoothed underfoot.

Jake kicked the ground. "We're on concrete now. No more flagstones."

Kivi dragged his hand on a wall. "And these buildings are concrete, too."

The group exited the laneway, walked under an awning stretched between two sets of restaurants with outdoor seating, then halted in an open square. Three- and four-story concrete buildings topped with solar panels lined three sides. A six-story edifice fronted the far end, surrounded by lower buildings in the same style.

Marchello swept his hands up. "Behold, my grandfather's palace."

"Wow," Gabriella said. "That's just—"

"Just one of the most beautiful buildings I've ever seen," Nadine said. She stepped back and closed Gabriella's mouth with her fingers. "Most beautiful. Marchello, sweetie, why don't you get back up on your horse and go tell the palace we're here and we'd like to attend that levy thing you mentioned. We'll follow on foot, give you time to let them know we're coming."

Marchello frowned. "But I cannot abandon you, pretty lady."

"Your duty calls, and besides, you look so handsome up there on that horse." Nadine beamed at him.

"If you wish, I will inform my grandfather's chancellor of your arrival." He snapped his fingers, and one of his men brought his horse. Then he vaulted onto the saddle.

He didn't quite pull it off. His groin impacted the pommel at the front with a meaty thud. He gasped, then swayed and needed both hands to hold himself in the saddle.

Jake and every male watching winced. "Ouch."

"Farewell," Marchello squeaked. "I shall see you at court shortly." He bounced off, gasping.

"Stellar horseman, your new conquest, Nadine," Jake said.

"Stewart," Nadine whispered. "We need some privacy to talk." Nadine turned to the six mounted troops remaining. "Lead us to the palace, kind sir."

The soldier walked his horse in front of them. Nadine stepped back next to Jake and gestured to Kivi and Gabriella to follow closely.

"Those troops, are they escorting us because we're welcome guests?" Jake said.

"More like we're under arrest to control who we talk to," Nadine said.

"I've already been warned not to trade with the people at the palace," Jake said. "By strangers. The man on the street isn't totally enamored with this baron fellow."

"That's no palace," Gabriella said. "That's a standard Imperial colonial administrative center. The Empire built them by the hundreds."

"Keep that quiet," Nadine said.

"What's happening?" Kivi asked.

"Something dangerous and scary," Gabriella said.

Nadine blinked. "What makes you think that, Brie?"

"You're being polite to Jake, and you've asked for his help. You never do that unless there is some sort of disaster."

"I don't?" Nadine said.

"No, you only take his advice when you've tried everything else. You hate it when he turns out to be right."

"I like her." Jake smiled. "Intuitive girl. Shows great potential."

"Shut up, Stewart. There's no Empire here. They're cut off, too."

"I agree. No recent trade, metal shortage, and they're de-industrializing. Coal. Agriculture. No factories. It's worse than Delta. And something's not right with all this military activity. Look, more soldiers. Different soldiers, different uniforms." Jake pointed at a group marching across the square. They wore green-blue outfits, not the red-blue of their guards.

"According to Marchello, his granddad is a hundred years old. He's been the ruler here since before their abandonment. His father is dead, and he's the heir but not until the grand old man dies."

"He seems a most... attractive man, with excellent manners," Jake said. "I'm sure he'll do well as planetary executive."

"He sounds as dumb as a bag of rocks. He doesn't do subtle at all. I had to practically slap him in the face to get him to answer my questions."

"Perhaps he's being discreet," Jake said.

"Perhaps he's an idiot," Nadine said. "There's a guy called a chancellor. The chancellor runs the planet."

"Who picks the chancellor?"

"There's an advisory council, composed of the leading families. Merchants, landowners, that sort of thing. They elect one of their own as chancellor. Must be a knife fight to win the election. But once you win, you're in charge."

"For now," Jake said. "And I'm not so sure he runs the

whole planet. Why all these swords on people? What are they afraid of?"

"Each other," Kivi said. "Those are household troops. Private armies. That's why the different colors. I've seen at least six. We're seeing the start of a civil war."

"You figured that out by yourself, Kivikins."

"Yes, Ms. Nadine," he said.

"Jake's rubbing off on you," Nadine said. "Marchello talked about 'those outside the city' and 'recent arrivals.' He wasn't complementary."

"Are we in danger?"

"Maybe. Don't know." Nadine quieted as a group of soldiers in red-and-yellow checkered outfits marched by. "Not yet. We need more information." She watched the soldier walk away. "That armor looks a funny color."

"It's bronze," Jake said. "I got a hand on some earlier. Copper and Tin. I got offered big money for some metals earlier. Don't mention what we have to trade, not yet."

They arrived at the door of the palace, aka the Colonial Admin Center. The door guard argued that they should surrender the revolvers they wore on their belts to go into the levy. Jake argued that it was just another weapon and that everyone else had swords on their belts. The doorman said swords and guns weren't the same thing. Nadine said her new best friend, Marchello, had said they could keep their guns. And did the doorman want to check with him or perhaps have her check with him? And perhaps discuss things like why there hadn't been enough public floggings recently? The doorman said guests of the royal family could do as they liked.

"Guests of the royal family," Jake said, pushing through a revolving door. "He's just a baron."

"Good enough for now. Lights still work in here," Nadine said.

"And air conditioning."

Cold air blew out of the ceiling.

"We saw a fusion plant from orbit," Nadine said.

"Not that big. And if they are abandoned like we were, why waste what little power they have on AC instead of factories?"

"Maybe they need it to recharge those Gauss guns?" Nadine said.

Four troops gazed at the flowing crowd from a mezzanine balcony. One had a Gauss rifle, and the others had shock sticks.

The doorman had given directions, but the stream of people entering the building flowed through to a ballroom in the back. Their escort tried to shove them through, but it was crowded enough they were pushed together and mixed with the crowd. Their plain skin suits stood out in the sea of colorful silks in the audience room.

"Imperials?" a man next to Jake asked. "From the Empire?"

"Sort of," Jake said. "We're from a colony in this sector. We're trying to contact the Empire as well."

"Came here on a ship?"

"Yes."

"Have things to trade?"

"Yes."

"Any metals?"

"Who are you again?" Jake said. "We haven't been introduced."

"Don't pay the official rate," the man said. "I can pay ten, twenty times that." A commotion sounded at the back. "We'll talk later." He dropped to one knee and bowed his head.

"All bow before Arturo, duke of the lesser cluster, and Imperial governor of the Draco sector," a voice said.

The entire crowd—except Accounting Error's crew—dropped to one knee, then bowed low, leaving Jake and his companions the only ones standing in the room. A group of well-dressed courtiers entered from the far side, Marchello in the lead, pushing a wheelchair with a gnarled old man in it. He scanned the bowing crowd, and his eyes lit on Jake and company.

"Who are these people?" the man screeched. "They do not bow." He pondered for a moment and gestured to Marchello. "Grandson, shall we cut off their heads?"

CHAPTER SEVEN

"Guards," a red-and-black clothed man behind the baron's wheelchair shouted, "seize them."

Six soldiers wearing red tunics, blue pants, and bronze breastplates drew swords and advanced on the crew. Jake, Nadine, Kivi, and Gabriella shuffled together.

"Jake," Nadine said, dropping her hand to her revolver. "This is where you do something... smart. Get that thinking thing on."

"I am thinking," Jake said.

"Think faster."

Jake put his arms up and turned in a complete circle, then faced the wheelchair. He raised his hands higher. "Is this how you greet the representatives of the Emperor? Threatening to cut off their heads? You are not worthy of your office. Shame, shame on you."

"Wait," Marchello called. The guards halted but didn't retreat. The crowd bowed, but eyes rolled to watch the newcomers.

"I am Jake Stewart, Admiral of the Delta Militia, personal representative of His Imperial Majesty Dashi the First." Jake threaded through the kneeling crowd to the baronial group and halted in front of the wheelchair. "We have not been introduced, but I assume you are Baron Arturo, governor of this sector on behalf of the Emperor. Greetings." Jake lowered his arms and held out his hand.

Arturo stared at the hand for an instant, then extended his own, tiny and shaking. Jake shook, taking care to use only his fingertips and not leave a bruise. "You may call me Admiral Stewart, Baron."

"Admiral Stewart," Marchello said. "You did not say you were an admiral before."

"You didn't ask," Jake said. He waved his crew forward. "Kivi and Gabriella, my assistants. And my personal pilot, Nadine."

"Your personal pilot?" Baron Arturo said. "This pretty woman?"

"She's pretty, yes, but also an adequate pilot," Jake said. "Isn't that right, Nadine?"

Nadine gritted her teeth. "No, not bad at all, Admiral Stewart."

"But her looks are distracting. Perhaps, Baron, that is why your grandson didn't properly introduce me. He was too beguiled by her. I'm sure you were much the same in your youth."

"Ah," Baron Arturo gurgled, "so true. Why, I remember when I was a youngster, not much more than Marchello's age... there was a girl. She was beautiful, had golden hair. We often went riding on our horses. Riding, I had a big bay horse. With yellow tack. Yellow, you recall." He stopped, then narrowed his eyes at Jake. "Who are you again?"

"Jake Stewart, sir, representative of the Emper—"

The man in red and black, who Jake assumed to be the chancellor, said, "Which Emperor did you say again?"

"Emperor Dashi the First," Jake said.

"That's four now," a blue-and-yellow clad man in the back muttered.

"Four what?" Jake said.

"Stewart," Baron Arturo said. "Are you here for the party, the midsummer festival?"

"Sir?" Jake said.

"We have a festival tomorrow," the chancellor said. "The whole city celebrates—well, those that matter—with a formal dinner and ball."

"Looking forward to seeing you at the dinner," Baron Arturo said. "It's great fun. You'll all be there?"

"If we're being invited..." Jake said.

"An excellent idea," the chancellor said. "I agree, Baron. We'll reserve a spot for them."

"See that you do, see that you do. Grandson?"

"Yes, Grandfather?" Marchello said.

No response.

Baron Arturo nodded, his chin resting against his chest. "He's fallen asleep," Jake said.

"He does that," Marchello said. "I'll just take him back to his room. You finish up here, Donat."

"As you wish, your lordship." Donat leaned into a small bow.

"These administrative things bore me," Marchello said. "Once you're done here, perhaps the lovely Ms. Nadine can join me for dinner."

Nadine grinned. "I'd love to, that is, if Admiral Stewart doesn't need an adequate pilot for some reason. He might need me. To do something adequately."

Kivi and Gabriella sucked in a breath.

Jake winced. "We will probably have to go back to the ship, assuming our discussions are fruitful."

"You must stay here and enjoy our hospitality," Donat said.

"Well, we have to—"

"No, I insist," Donat said. He waved to the guards, and they crowded behind Jake's party.

"Perhaps just overnight," Jake said. He typed a code into his comm, then put it in his coverall pocket.

"Till tomorrow, then," Marchello said.

The crowd was silent as he left.

Once he disappeared through the door at the back of the room, the kneeling crowd stood, and the hum of conversation roared.

Jake addressed Donat. "He's the heir to the throne?"

"Marchello? Our very own baron's very own grandson," Donat said.

"How old is the baron?"

"One hundred and seven glorious years. Long may he reign."

"The baron, he runs things here?"

"With the assistance of his council of advisors."

Jake surveyed the people in front of him. "Would I be looking at the council of advisers?"

"You would."

"What do the colors mean?" Jake pointed at the different-colored shirts and neck clothes of the assembled group.

"Family things. Boring stuff. Who's related to who. You wouldn't care. Why are you asking so many questions?"

"Actually, I don't care about that sort of stuff," Jake said. "But I was sent to explore and to trade. And ask questions. Are you in contact with the Empire?"

"What was the name of your Emperor again?"

"Dashi. Dashi the First."

"Never heard of him."

"No reason you should. He only proclaimed himself Emperor just more than a year ago."

"You were cut off from the Empire?"

"More than eighty years. You?"

"No new news in fifty. Before that, we had news of three different Emperors. What have you got to trade?"

"Now you're asking lots of questions," Jake said.

"If you're just a cut-off colony like us, you won't be much help. We have our own problems."

Jake gestured to Kivi, who was carrying the sample case. He snapped it open, rooted inside, and produced four metal blanks before handing them to people in front of him. He divided them between people with different-colored clothes. "Copper. Tin. Cobalt. Tungsten."

Donat hefted the iron, then glanced into the case filled with other cubes. "We can use metal. How pure is it?"

"Five nines," Jake said. "Ninety-nine point nine nine nine percent."

"I don't believe you for a second. Nobody can get that type of purity. Not anymore."

"Not anymore here, I'm sure. But we were a mining colony. Those four are a gift, one for each of these folks here. Test them if you want."

All four slipped the ingots into pockets or handed them to aides.

Donat started to object but changed his mind. "You have more on your landing boat? That shuttle."

"Nope," Jake said. "But up on the ship, we do. Lots."

"Can't get to the ship without your shuttle," Donat said. "You sure it's in good repair? We could take a look at it for you before you go."

"You're not getting on our shuttle. Or our ship. And don't think about launching some sort of attack on our ship with a shuttle of your own. Shuttles don't maneuver well in a gravity well, and missiles and lasers find them easy targets when they're climbing." A boom rattled the windows. "Plus, our other pilot just slipped her lines and blasted up to orbit. She'll come and get us when our... discussions work out."

The assembled council members laughed.

Donat grinned at Jake. "You're smarter than you look."

"He'd almost have to be, wouldn't he?" Nadine said. "Tell us about this party tomorrow."

"You're not just a pilot, are you?" Donat asked.

"So, so much more," Nadine said. "How did Marchello's father die?"

"Drowned in a sailing race."

"How sad. Big storm? Big waves?"

"Rammed a lighthouse in clear weather. He was drunk. Hit his head on the boom, passed out, and drowned in the bottom of the boat, in eight inches of water."

"I see." Nadine bit her lip. "Having met Marchello, that sounds believable. What happens to you all when Marchello becomes the baron?"

"He picks his own advisers," Donat said. "Not an

issue, of course, while his grandfather is alive."

"Not at all," Nadine said. "Jake, we should stay for this party."

"We will. If Chancellor Donat could provide us with rooms..."

Donat issued the orders. While he was talking, the conversations doubled in volume, and a voice called from behind them. "Make way for the ambassador."

A man and two women pushed through the crowd and stopped to Jake's left, facing the council. By his looks, his ancestors had come from Asia on Old Earth. He was as tall as Jake and as thin. Like everyone else Jake had met, he wore a sword, but his accent was pure Old Empire. He wore sandals and long cotton pants. Under a plain blue unbuttoned cotton tree silk shirt, he wore an elaborate blue undershirt, embroidered with red-and-gold thread.

"Chancellor Donat"—the man bowed—"I understand that visitors have arrived from the Empire." He turned to Jake. "Welcome, Imperials. I am Quan, the representative of the Planters."

"I'm Jake Stewart."

"I see the Empire has not forgotten us, at last."

"Welllll..." Jake said.

"Don't get your hopes up, Quan," Donat said. "They're from a colony and cut off like we are."

Quan turned to Jake. "Truth?"

"Yes, it's true," Jake said. "We were sent out by our Emperor to explore and trade."

"Your Emperor?"

"Emperor Dashi the First."

"Great, another one." Quan grimaced. "That makes four. Well, welcome to Magyar. Our lovely planet." He extended his hand, and Jake shook it. "What do you have to trade?"

"We have metals," Jake said.

"Metals? Lots of them?"

"Enough," Jake said. He gestured, and Kivi opened up

his case again. Jake handed Quan an ingot. "Here you go. Tin. Five nines pure."

"Five nines?" Quan weighed it in his hand. "Orbital factories?"

"Yes. We have more than just that. I gave some samples of tungsten and cobalt to the council members."

"Which they will instantly sell, no doubt," Quan said. "Dishonorable way to make money. But to be expected from the likes of them."

"We want to trade," Jake said. "Best I let people test my wares. Besides, as they say, money has no smell."

The woman next to Quan said, "The Roman Emperor Vespasian."

She was tall, like Quan. Her outfit was identical to his, but her pants and shirt were tailored to hug her form, and her undershirt was perhaps cut lower than was absolutely necessary. Her shoulders were firm and muscular. A blue-green gemstone flashed as an earring, and she wore a choker chain woven of gold and silver around her neck.

"Jake Stewart," Quan said, "this is Tam, my daughter and aide. And her assistant, Ket."

Ket had blacker hair, blacker eyes, and slightly plainer clothes. Her shirt was cut just as low.

Jake automatically gave Tam an up-and-down look, then blushed. "Yes, Vespasian said that. He's my second-favorite Emperor."

Nadine huffed and rolled her eyes. "Jakey," she muttered.

"Second favorite? Who's your favorite, then?" Tam asked.

"Hadrian."

"Hadrian?" Tam crossed her arms. "How conventional. I find him overrated, just finishing what his father did. Antonius Pius is a much better choice. Don't you agree?"

Jake's eyes widened. "You know who Antonius Pius is?"

"Doesn't everybody?" Tam said.

Jake sputtered an incoherent response.

Nadine looked into Jake's eyes, then switched to look at Tam. "Geeks flirting. How cute."

Tam turned to her father. "If they are here to trade, we should invite them to our embassy for dinner. We can exchange news and discuss trade options."

Donat broke in. "The trading is already taken care of. We will discuss it with them later. And it's not an embassy. It's Magyar jurisdiction."

"The Emperor says otherwise," Quan said.

"Eighty-year-old warrants—" Donat said.

"Are still as valid as the day they were issued, or are you disobeying Imperial rescripts now? Perhaps we should discuss them. In particular, ones that appoint certain Barons as sector governors?"

A murmur swept over the crowd. Donat's eyes swept from side to side. "We honor the Emperor."

"Then, honoring him and his appointed representatives by allowing these people to attend a dinner should be no problem." Quan turned to Jake. "Mr. Stewart, you and as many of your party as you would like to bring are invited for dinner at five local time at our embassy. We have a wonderful cook and plenty of food."

"Thanks," Jake said. "Uh, what time is it now? We use a shift schedule on our ships, not a clock. And we're not synced with local time."

"It is just after two now. The main clock on the front of the administration building—"

"The baronial palace," Donat said.

Quan glared at him. "The main clock on the front of this building will help you. Will we see you then?"

"We'll be happy to attend. Shall we—"

Another set of voices came from the back of the hall, and a second group shoved through the crowd.

"And here comes the horse people," Quan said.

Two men pushed their way to the front. Both were at least a head taller than Jake, broad-shouldered, dark-haired, with bushy black mustaches.

"Donat, you rascal, you," the taller one said. "Trying to keep the Imperials to yourself, I see. I suppose that's why they made you chancellor." He turned to Jake's crew. "Two leaders. Check. Two assistants. Check. You in the custom skin suit. You're the merchant, this Jake fellow I heard about, aren't you?"

"Jake Stewart. Representative of the Empire."

"You, you're different," the tall man said, turning to Nadine. "You look like you're trouble. What's your name, trouble?"

Nadine grinned at him. "They call me Nadine. But trouble is fine. Who are you?"

"I'm somebody who can handle trouble. But you can call me Vidor. This is my best friend, Arpad. My father is Poldi, the hetman of the Magyar people."

"What's a hetman?"

"Elected leader of the clan," Vidor said. "Old tradition, but we keep it up here on Magyar because it works for us. I hear that you're not from the Empire, exactly, but a colony close by. Where is it?"

"We call it Delta," Nadine said. "Some jumps away."

"How many jumps?"

"Some."

"Not telling us where it is—smart," Vidor said. "But don't worry, no chance of us getting to you. No ships, none at all. Not since the last battle when the Empire left."

"The Empire left? Took their ships?" Jake asked.

Vidor grinned at him. "They did. Long time ago, but we can tell you all our history over dinner. We frequent a tavern across town. You should come out and be our guests. I know you spacers want fresh food—and they've got lots of that. Beef, pork, fresh fish. Made with local herbs to local recipes. Come to dinner tonight at six. What do you say, Miss Trouble?"

"Sounds great to me," Nadine said. "Steak is my favorite."

"It sounds great to me, too, Mr. Vidor, but we're already committed tonight," Jake said. "We promised to visit Mr. Quan here at his embassy."

"Quan's here?" Vidor looked over Jake's shoulder. "Quan. Didn't see you there, turnip farmer. You're such a small person, easy to miss in a crowd. Tam, you're looking beautiful as always. Like the starlight glinting in the sky when we ride our horses at sunset."

"But unlike you, Vidor, I don't smell as bad as said same horse does. Where's your father? Is he passed-out drunk again?"

"I missed you," Vidor said.

"I could say the same. But then I'd be lying," Tam said.

Vidor grimaced. "Always a pleasure seeing you farmers. Even if you're always hiding behind somebody."

"We weren't shouting and making a spectacle of ourselves, chicken rancher," Quan said.

"Shouting? I'm just a big man with a big voice—genetics, you know. Can't help it."

"We don't blame you, Mr. Vidor," Tam said. "Not your fault at all. But you should probably speak to whoever cross-bred your mother with a horse about this outcome."

The crowd sputtered. Vidor and Arpad put their hands on their swords and so did Quan and Tam. So did the guards and the council and much of the crowd.

"I don't understand your meaning, Ms. Tam," Vidor said. "Care to explain?"

"And there's the genetics at work again," Tam said. "Beautiful animals, horses, but not known for their intelligence."

Vidor bared his teeth and stepped forward but banged into Nadine, who had stepped in front of him. Quan had, likewise, moved, but Jake jumped to block him.

"Ladies. Gentlemen," Jake said, "I'm sure this would be a fascinating subject to discuss, but it doesn't exactly involve us, the visitors, does it? Perhaps you could deal with this later?"

Vidor smiled down at Nadine. "That's true, young lady. Not your thing." He looked over at Quan. "Next time, turnip farmer."

Quan said nothing but stepped back from Jake.

"Perhaps, Chancellor Donat," Jake said, "we could conclude this audience. My crew and I need to digest things."

Donat had been smiling as the two groups faced off. "Of course, Mr. Stewart. We'll have some rooms made ready for you tonight in the palace. We're going to be doing some testing of those samples you brought. After, we should meet and discuss these things. Unfortunately, you won't be able to take these folks up on their offers."

"A brief meeting, perhaps," Jake said. "We're tired from our trip."

"Of course," Donat said.

"Shall we say, in a few hours, at four?"

Donat looked at the council. One or two nodded. "Four it is, for two hours. To discuss trade."

"Excellent," Jake said. "But we do need to eat. Perhaps we could have a short dinner meeting at seven, Ambassador Quan?"

"Wait," Vidor said. "You'll eat with this dirt digger but not with me? Whose side are you on?"

"Our own side."

"Doesn't look like it to me."

Nadine broke in. "Jake, we can all go to the meeting with Chancellor Donat at four. But perhaps you can see the ambassador and his people at six, while I can go visit Mr. Vidor's restaurant." She smiled up at Vidor. "You can tell me about what trouble you handle."

Vidor grinned back. "That sounds like an excellent idea."

"Nadine," Jake said, gesturing, "a word."

Nadine drew back, and she and Jake put their heads together.

"Nadine, you've been mad at me since those Francais

girls kissed me. But that was weeks ago, and nothing happened. Well, except you shooting me. But I'm getting used to that. But I see you licking your lips when you look at Vidor, the over sexed cowboy."

"And you're not drooling on yourself when you look at Ms. Big Boobs On Tiny Girl?"

"She's not tiny. She's as big as you. Besides, she's the daughter of an important official."

"And Vidor's the son of the leader of his clan. Whatever a clan is."

"Tam is the ambassador's daughter."

"How do you know he's really an ambassador?"

"I've never met a girl who knew who Vespasian was."

"And you're not likely to ever again." Nadine frowned. "This got way more complicated. Who do we believe here?"

Jake shook his head. "None of them yet. We need more information. If you go by yourself to this meeting, will you behave?"

"Will you behave?"

Jake looked at Kivi and Gabriella. "Chaperones. The trainees. We take chaperones."

"Kivi's so in awe of you he'll jump off a bridge if you say it's necessary. He won't stop you from doing anything."

"And Gabriella will be the voice of reason when she's with you?"

"Whoops," Nadine said. "This kind of backfired on us, didn't it."

Jake frowned, then smiled. "We swap."

"Swap how?"

"Brie comes with me. Kivi goes with you. Then they report back."

Nadine nodded. "That will work." She waved her fingers at the two trainees, and they came over.

"Ma'am?" Kivi asked.

"What's up?" Brie said.

"Kids," Nadine said, "you two are going to a party!"

CHAPTER EIGHT

Yvette climbed out of the ship's boat after docking. Jake had helped her program the auto-release for the dock lines and fueling system, and retied the lines so they could be auto-released. After his notification, she released the tie-downs and popped the fuel hose loose. The Empire-designed system had stopped pumping as soon as it detected the drop in pressure, and she fired the main engines and sped away from the dock for a textbook take-off. Three orbits later, she docked with Accounting Error.

She locked the outer hatch, then the inner behind her and traipsed up to the bridge.

Willowby caught her as she passed through the lounge. "Any update?"

"Things are great. El supremo and his sidekick are stuck on the surface. They did such a lousy job negotiating they've been arrested by these colonial people. They won't be around to annoy Odette, and I, while we figure out what's going on, will decide what to trade and save this mission."

"That doesn't match the update I just got from Jake. He said he's meeting separately with the three largest political units on the planet, and they're all eager to trade for metal that we have."

"You shouldn't believe everything you hear," Yvette said.

"I don't. That's why I don't believe you. Jake said to stay here in case he needs us."

"We need fuel."

"Not right away. We can wait."

"Is there a gas giant we can go to while we wait?"

"Yes, but it's not hydrogen-dense. We'd have to orbit for two days to refuel—could be longer. Jake might need us before then."

"Then we land the ship on the surface to crack water."

"We're not going anywhere till Captain Jake says so."

"I'm the only pilot. The ship goes where I say."

"Only if the engines are running. Which they won't, for you."

Yvette pulled her tiny pink revolver out. "Don't bother us, old man."

"The engineering boards are locked, with a code only I know. Shoot me, and you'll die here. Probably starve to death."

"Jake keeps telling us we have plenty of food."

"We did until somebody stuck the wreckage of a pinnace into number six container and ruined most of our return journey supply."

"I didn't know that."

"Now you do. We need to stay here and wait for them. And I need to get that wreckage out of that container."

Yvette pocketed her pistol. "For now. We'll wait and see. Until I decide otherwise."

"Until Jake decides otherwise."

Yvette waved him off and continued climbing to the bridge. She passed through the rest of the pressurized cargo hold, then the long section where the jump drive and jump controls and their associated computers and fuel resources were, then the hab sections, and, finally, to the control room. She closed and latched the hatch behind her, then went to sit beside Odette. Since it was just the two, they spoke Francais.

"Jake got himself arrested and captured, and everything is a mess. Oh, and we're going to run out of food and end up eating each other."

"Are you sure it's not some secret plan of his that we don't know about?"

"It could be. He's bizarrely unpredictable."

"Should we leave without him?"

"Not now. We have to wait for him to come back. He's the key to all this."

Odette pointed at the intercom. "I listened in. You made Willowby think we were going to leave Jake behind."

"I did, didn't I? That will let us know where he stands. Do you have engine control?"

"He's shut everything down. But discreetly. The self-tests and status monitors all work. It's only if you actually start a firing sequence that things stop."

"He didn't want you to know he could do that."

"We do now. What did our beacons say?"

Odette tapped through her screens till she found one with a password and typed in a long code. "This is the right system. There have been three ships here in the last five years. One just passed through, but the other two stopped and traded with somebody."

"Who?"

"I have some names, but they don't mean anything to me, and they don't match anything we've heard from the planet. Code names. Bird-one and Bird-two."

"Original."

"But effective."

"Whose codes were they using?"

"Free Trader forty-six. Those were the old ones, and the most recent one was shipmaster's code seven. Should I record a message?"

"No. We're not sure who we are dealing with yet."

"The Traders' council said it was a priority to reestablish links with the Free Trader's Association in the Empire."

"Is there anything in our private database as to who owns those ships that were here?"

"Just basic class info. No ownership details."

"They could be pirates or even impressed into one of these many Emperor's navies."

"Could be."

"One thing's for sure, I don't want to give away the location of Delta to other traders, not till we find out who we're trading with. Any idea when the next ship is due?"

"Yes. The last ship put in an expected return date and some coordinates for meeting them for trading."

"When and where?"

"When is now. We're here in the window."

"That's good luck. Where do we meet them?"

"That's the bad luck. There's a problem with that. Let me show you." Odette put a system map up on the screen and highlighted a certain area. "Right there."

"That could be a problem," Yvette said. "A very big problem. And we can't wait forever. If you heard Willowby, you heard that we're going to run out of food."

"Not really."

"Not really? He said we don't have enough food to get the crew back?"

"Not the whole crew, no," Odette said. She looked at the map. "But if we're short four people, we could make it."

CHAPTER NINE

Tam welcomed Jake and Brie into her house after they knocked on the door. "How was your meeting with the council?"

"Exhausting," Jake said. "They all argued that they were our best trading partner for whatever we had to trade. They just kept repeating that. They didn't offer any details."

Tam smiled. "They would. I'll bet they all offered the same low price to buy things from you."

"I was kind of confused with what they were saying. It was hard for me to make sense of some of the offers because they were offering to trade, but that's what it seemed like. I need to see the goods."

"Father is waiting in the courtyard." She looked over Jake's shoulder. "Guards?"

"'To protect us from harassment,' the chancellor said," Jake replied.

"Who is harassing who, I wonder. They can wait out here. Follow me."

She led them through her house. The walls facing the street were nondescript white plaster. Once inside, it was different. The front door opened up to a polished stone foyer, and they walked to a second set of doors that led into a courtyard. The building was a three-story hollow square. The walls were stone, plastered in different colors, some with painted murals. The murals showed rural scenes. On the ground floor, all the rooms opened onto a covered arcade with windows facing a central courtyard. Stairs ascended to the second and third floors and the roof at each side. There were six rooms on each floor, with windows facing in. Water bubbled out of a fountain in the courtyard.

Tam led them through the foyer and across the courtyard. She was barefoot and had removed the formal clothes she had worn to the levy. She replaced them with a tight crop top and loose pantaloons. The pantaloons swished over her legs and hips. Walking behind her, Jake had problems keeping his gaze at eye level.

Quan greeted Jake and Brie as they arrived. "Welcome to my home."

"This place is amazing. I've never been in a building like this," Jake said.

"Masonry beats the heat, courtyard gives shade, and the fountain cools it even more. The water comes from the city water system—carried down from the hills into giant cisterns. Then they use ultraviolet light to sterilize it and pipe it into the city. It's all gravity fed, almost no maintenance. For power, we have solar panels on the roof and a battery backup. It's Empire tech and very reliable."

"You don't have access to city power? We saw a fusion plant," Jake said.

"A small fusion plant. It covers the Imperial buildings, the so-called baronial palace, some small factories, the electric harbor cranes, things like that."

"The palace is a standard Imperial administrative building," Jake said.

"You noticed that, didn't you?" Quan said. "Yes, this was a colony, didn't even have a governor. Run by a senior administrator. It was always going to be a colony. Gravity was light enough that small shuttles could launch and drop. We could make fuel out of the sea water, so it would be cheap to settle."

"Why is this colony here?" Jake said. "What was its purpose?"

"No idea. Maybe just to keep an eye on a habitable planet. There was only the one city when we got here and just random groups of wild people roaming the frontier."

"When you got here? What do you mean?"

Quan led them over to a table covered with pots and cups. "Please sit down. We'll drink first, then eat."

Jake picked up a cup. "I've read about this. A tea ceremony."

Tam laughed. "You read too much. This is coffee. Just coffee. With cream and sugar. Hope you like coffee."

"I don't know," Jake said. "I'm not sure I've ever had real coffee. Where do you get cream and sugar?"

"Cows for the cream, sugar cane for the sugar."

"How do you process it? The sugar, I mean."

"We have mills. Hydro powered—or coal. Lots of coal here. It's not super-efficient, but all we need is crushing and boiling, and you can do that with simple machinery. We built them after our arrival here."

Jake and Brie sat. Tam poured them cups and added cream and sugar. She and Quan took theirs black. Jake and Brie sipped first, then drank.

Jake licked his lips. "I've never had coffee that tastes like this before."

"Fresh cream makes a difference."

Jake drank from the cup. "You're showing off. This is something you want to trade. But I need to know what you mean by 'when we came here.' Do you know what happened to the Empire? And what does everyone mean by 'four Emperors?'"

Quan sipped his coffee. "I only know what I've been told. We've had no direct news of the Empire for more than fifty years. Our ancestors came here about eighty years ago, escaping a civil war in the main Empire. An Emperor—well, a general—who called himself Emperor Vindex revolted. I don't know why or how, exactly. My father might have, but he's dead, and he didn't talk about that time much. Anyways, this Vindex general revolted, and sent troops to conquer local planets. My family and lots of other families from Hispania, when they heard his army was on the way, they collected what valuables they could find, hired some ships, and fled. There was a lot of local animosity between different groups, people who wanted to stay in the Empire and people who wanted to revolt. It looked to be getting ugly, so they hopped on a ship and fled. Good thing they did, too, according to my dad. Later, there was a big battle there, and we heard Hispania was wrecked. Like here was wrecked."

"Here was wrecked?" Jake said. "Magyar?"

"So they tell us. Our family wasn't here yet. But if you ask the locals, they said that Vindex's troops came through here and fought the Empire. They won, but it wasn't much of a battle. The Empire retreated as Vindex's troops chased them but not before destroying most of the Imperial assets in orbit."

"Then this Vindex became the Emperor?" Jake said.

"Not exactly. We got only confused news for a few years—merchant ships came and went. Then an Imperial flotilla—a destroyer and two frigates with some merchant ships in convoy—came through here. They commandeered anything useful space-wise, ships, shuttles, crews, specialists, spare parts, weapons— anything war related—and left. They were off to fight Vindex. Vindex hadn't won, but he hadn't lost, either."

"Which means the Empire was back."

"Back enough. They claimed sovereignty over the planet, and they appointed us the new sector capital. And appointed a new governor."

"Sector capital? That's great," Jake said. "Who did they appoint... Wait, I can figure that out."

"His gloriousness, the baron. Imperial warrant made him governor of the planet and the sector."

"So, he is the sector governor? For real?"

"A sector of one planet. He never left here."

"Okay." Jake drank his coffee in silence for a moment. "Where do you fit in? Who are you the ambassador of?"

"You are speaking to the official ambassador of the

self-governing Imperial planet, Hispania's government in exile," Quan said. He did a seated bow. "Welcome. I will take up my office as soon as Imperial forces recover the planet of Hispania and reintegrate it into the Empire."

"What forces are those?"

"Space-wise? Nothing. Here on Magyar dirtside, some local Militia."

"I see. May I have more coffee?" Jake said.

"Of course. Dinner should be ready," Tam said. "Let's start with that. No more talking business till after."

They switched to a larger, more formal table adjacent to the courtyard. Overhead, fans blew breezes across the tables and out vents. Dinner arrived in courses. First fruit—oranges, expensive on Delta but, apparently, a common appetizer here. Jake offered to trade for oranges.

"What type of fruits are these?" Jake tried to pick a squishy black sphere up with a spoon.

"Eat them with your hand." Tam demonstrated. "Olives. We use them in a lot of our food. You don't have olives?"

"It's too cold on Delta. We have a few greenhouses that grow special items, but they are so expensive I've never eaten any."

"We have plenty of them here. Try the salad."

Jake demolished the salad. Olives, tomatoes, cucumbers, onions, and a type of cheese he'd never eaten before. "This is the best salad I've ever had."

"Take some hummus."

Jake had never heard of that, either. Tam used some flat bread to scoop up some yellow paste, then fed it to Jake.

"Mmmph. Good." Jake wiped his face.

"Missed a spot." Tam used a piece of bread to wipe hummus from Jake's face, then fed it to him. Jake blinked and licked his lips. "Thank you. That was... nice."

Brie bit her lip to suppress a grin.

"Now, try some wine." Tam poured everyone a glass of

white. "To new friends."

"New friends," Jake agreed.

Brie grinned openly this time and gulped down her wine.

"This is incredible food," Jake said. "If any of it will travel, we can trade for it."

"Olives, perhaps. The others can only be eaten fresh. Maybe the wine?"

"A few cases. You need people to have a taste for it."

They discussed trivialities. Jake learned that Tam's mother was dead—cancer. She learned that he had little to do with his family back on Delta. Tam was her father's deputy and co-owner of their holdings. She had no other siblings. Their farms grew vegetables, grain, soybeans, sugar beets, and dozens of other varieties of produce. Their neighbors had citrus, dates, and more grains. The farmland of Magyar was productive—plenty of natural rainfall in the growing seasons, good soil. Too warm for some crops.

Tam learned all about Dashi, Jose, Nadine, and the ship. They talked about how Jake's father had fled the civil war in the Empire but had not told anybody. Jake alluded to problems back on Delta. Brie shared her own experiences and insisted that Jake and Nadine were "not a couple—not right now" into the conversation, which caused Jake to give her a disapproving glance and Tam's eyes to narrow.

"We're here, we're refugees, we're planters," Quan said. "But we're loyalists. We petitioned the Emperor when we could find one, and we got an answer back—we could run our government from here. The governor was to give us land to farm in the meantime, and we had certain exemptions from local control. We grew our vegetables, did what the governor—that was Baron Arturo—told us. He wasn't a bad fellow when he was younger. He did the best job he could, and he's old and senile now, but he tried. He wasn't trained for the job."

"Is he really a baron?" Brie asked, spooning some custard out of a bowl.

"He was a third cousin of somebody somewhere, and the Emperor made him a baron and appointed him governor. That's all legit. Everybody agrees on that. And I don't like everything he did, but let's face it, somebody has to be in charge, and we're loyal citizens of the Empire. If the Emperor appoints somebody, we'll listen to him if he isn't nuts. And he wasn't."

Jake licked his spoon while Tam poured him a second full bowl of custard. "I'll have to figure out a way to keep milk on a spaceship. How long till it spoils?"

"A week at most," Tam said.

"Have to sterilize it or something. What didn't everybody agree on?"

"Pardon?" Tam said.

"You said 'everybody agreed on that,' which means there are other things that everybody doesn't agree on. What are they?"

"Well." Tam finished her bowl and licked her own spoon. Jake watched closely, and Tam saw him watching, so she took a moment longer with it. "The Emperor anointed Arturo a baron and made him the governor. But he didn't make him a hereditary baron, and he didn't grant him any lands. He's not the overlord of the planet. He doesn't own it. He just ran it as an administrator."

"Meaning it was just for his lifetime," Jake said. "What happens when he dies?"

"When Arturo dies, we don't have a baron, a governor, or any Imperial authority."

"What about Marchello?"

"When his grandfather is dead, he won't survive a day, unless he flees into the backwoods. Somebody will kill him. The council is full of factions who want to run the city."

"What then?"

"Then the war starts," Tam said.

CHAPTER TEN

Nadine's feet stuck to the floor of the Cuttlefish Tavern when she and Kivi walked in.

"Kivikins," Nadine said, unsticking her feet from a puddle of something gelatinous. "This is what is called a dive bar. Make a note for future reference."

"Yes, ma'am," Kivi said. "For future reference, how can I tell?"

"Dirty plates and glasses on the tables. Unidentified puddles on the floor. Stains on the wall." She sniffed and wrinkled her nose. "And generally poor hygiene."

"Of the food?"

"No, the patrons." Nadine stepped up to the table nearest the door. A man with greasy hair was drinking alone. "Excuse me, sir. Do they sell breath mints anywhere close by?"

"Down the road, at Darby's Emporium," the man said. "Why do you ask?"

"If you don't know, I'm not going to tell you," Nadine said. "But you should probably do some shopping there soon."

He looked her over. "You're the prettiest girl to talk to me in here."

"Given the way you smell, I'll bet I'm the only girl to ever talk to you in here. Or anywhere. Pretty or not."

"What's that supposed to mean?"

"Maybe you need to do some shopping for those breath mints," Nadine said. "I'm looking for a man called Vidor."

A table crashed over. Vidor stood by the back wall. A

man choked him from behind. Vidor stood up and flipped the man into a table of drinkers, scattering cups and glasses. The shortest drinker stood and punched Vidor in the chest.

"Never mind. I see him. Remember, go visit Darby." Nadine gestured at Kivi and left the man exhaling into his hand and sniffing the result.

"Seems like kind of a rough place," Kivi said.

"No such thing as a rough place, only rough people," Nadine said. She stopped at the bar. "Two mugs of beer."

"What type of beer?"

"The cheapest that comes in the heaviest glass mugs," Nadine said.

The bartender pulled two hefty mugs and shoved them over. "Twelve credits."

"I'm on Vidor's tab," Nadine said.

"Vidor know that?" the bartender asked.

"Let's tell him." She walked to where Vidor was boxing with the short man. A crowd had formed to watch. She waited, slid between two people, waited for an opening, then slammed Vidor's opponent's head with her mug. He dropped to the floor, along with half of her beer..

The crowd turned to her. "Hi, Vidor. We're here. Buy a girl a drink?" She sipped the remaining beer and gagged. "Not this, though. Something better."

Vidor looked at the groaning man. "That wasn't nice. He didn't see you coming."

"Best way to win a fight is for them not to see you coming."

"You should have waited," Vidor said.

"I've been waiting. I'm hungry. You promised dinner for Kivi and I."

Kivi arrived beside her. "Is he okay?"

"He'll be fine," Nadine said. She leaned down and hauled the moaning man to his feet and looked in his eyes. "Probably. A concussion, at least." She shoved him gently to a bystander, who caught him and lowered him to a chair. "Vidor. Dinner? I'm hungry." She drank her beer. "Now would be good."

Nadine, Kivi, Vidor, and Vidor's friend Arpad retired to a table in the back of the tavern. Vidor shouted orders for food and beer to the bartender. Nadine assumed that was the case, but she didn't understand a word of the language he used.

"You all speak perfect standard," Nadine said. "But what was that you were talking?"

"You would call it Hungarian," Vidor said. "Magyar. Like the name of the planet. It was settled by relatives of mine many years ago. Before the abandonment."

"So, you were here before the war—the civil war, I guess they're calling it."

"I wasn't, but my grandfather's people were. My grandfather was born in the core worlds. He was the third wave of colonization. His great-great-great something grandfather founded the colony here, but things were marginal, until the second wave came. They started ranches on the plains to the south. He was fond of history, so they used some ancient cultural designations. He called himself khan and the settlers his horde."

"A horde?"

"It's an ancient term from Old Earth. The Empire didn't care as long as he paid his taxes. It's traditional now. I've been told it was hard living at first. The terraforming package wasn't taking well. Then it reached a critical mass. The field grasses and trees caught on and spread on the plains. My grandfather's family came as the plains were growing. Cattle and horses were reproducing, so we became herdsmen. They had some Imperial technology, so they were able to live in comfort at the ranches. Then the civil war started."

"What happened to your family? Something bad?"

"Nothing major. But we were here, and the Empire went away. Now it's fifty years since we last saw an Imperial ship, a hundred since the one that brought my grandfather from the core with the remainder of the families. We are three times as many of us now as then. We haven't been able to buy any new technology. The teaching computers, comm units, and solar powered generators are in short supply. We've put them with our schools and medical places, but we need more."

"We had a similar problem on Delta, where I'm from," Nadine said. "But we headed off the shortage."

"How?"

"The man Jake worked for arranged for a bunch of people to die. Jake helped. After that, more for the survivors."

"That man, Jake, killed them?" Vidor frowned. "He does not look the type. He doesn't seem... physical."

"He's not. But he's smart. So is his boss. They took control of our planet, and his boss declared himself Emperor. Jake is one of his main lieutenants."

"Interesting," Vidor said. "Then this Jake Stewart is an important man."

"Very important. He's in charge of our group."

"Even more interesting. And the two of you are a couple?"

Nadine grinned. "We were. We're taking a break right now."

"And even more, more interesting. A woman like you will not be long unaccompanied."

"Not long at all. And yourself."

"I am unaccompanied at present. But I am to be married."

Nadine rubbed his arm. "I'm sorry to hear that, big guy. Who's the lucky girl?"

"I don't know."

"How can you not know who you are to be married to?" Nadine asked. "It's kind of something you'd be involved in."

"It does not concern me. My family is in charge."

"Aha. Arranged marriage. With the daughter of

another... whatcha call them, clan chief?"

"No, my parents seek a marriage with one of the families of the city."

"Which one?"

"Whichever one will betray the others." Vidor drained his beer as a waiter brought plates. "The food arrives. Have another beer and try the barbecue, and I will explain."

The meat was delivered on skewers, chunks of beef and pork alternating with vegetables. Some were flavored with garlic, which Nadine had tasted on Delta and some with paprika, which she had not.

"Spicy." She licked her lips and drank her beer. "Tell me more about this betrayal."

"You have traveled in the city, not the entire city, but enough to see much of it. Have you seen any like me?"

"There aren't any like you, big guy," Nadine said.

"No, I mean dressed like me, tall like me, or looking like my people. People of the Ranches."

Nadine furrowed her brow. "Come to think of it, no."

"The council prohibits any ranchers from entering the city, except just a few for trading purposes. My father, me, a few specialists. But just us. The rest are barred."

"Barred? You mean, like, banned."

"Yes. My mother stays at the farm because of this, and my father rarely leaves our city residence except for official functions. The disrespect tires him. This palatial palace"— Vidor extended his arms to encompass the bar—"is one of the few places in town that will serve us."

"It's an open-minded place?" Nadine said.

"They want our money. Many in town are like that. At least here, they are honest about it," Arpad said.

"Why put up with this?" Nadine asked. "Why not just walk right in?"

"There are walls and gates and soldiers," Vidor said. "You haven't seen them yet." He pulled a chunk of beef from a skewer, chewed it, and swallowed. "But the walls are not tall, nor the gates strong, and there are not many soldiers. A group of armed men, well led, could overwhelm all and enter."

"Why would you want to do that?" Nadine said. "Sounds like they're elitist snobs, but are they hurting you?"

"They hoard technology," Vidor said. He gulped his beer. "Most technology, But, truly, they do not have much more than we do. They haven't been able to buy anything for years, either. Do you know what happens when the old baron dies?"

"Tell me," Nadine said.

Vidor explained the same story Jake had heard. The office wasn't hereditary. The Empire's authority would lapse. The grandson was an idiot and wouldn't last.

"My parents are negotiating with some of the council families with suitable daughters. Once the baron dies, we will marry, and with the backing of part of the council I will enter the city with my men. We will proclaim myself the new baron, gain approval of the council."

"Then you'll be in charge of the council."

"No, I will be in charge of the planet. The entire planet." Vidor smiled. "I will be the khan of the whole planet."

CHAPTER ELEVEN

Jake, Nadine, and their escorts had been quartered five buildings away from the administrator's building down a side street. After having returned late from their respective meetings, they met for breakfast on the ground floor the next morning. Every table was packed, and they had to stand till a group of four vacated one by the open window.

"No luxuries for visitors from the Empire," Nadine said, shoving dirty plates aside and sitting.

"We're in the officer's quarters." Jake gestured. "Look at the colors."

"And the ages," Kivi said.

Thirty people filled the breakfast room, and eighty percent of the people in it wore some variation of red and black—red shirts, black pants. Most were men in their twenties, with a sprinkling of women of the same age.

"At least the food is fresh," Kivi said.

"It would be better," Gabriella said, chewing on undercooked gruel, "if it was good as well as fresh."

"As much milk and sugar as you want, though," Kivi said.

"They do well with sugar," Jake said. "Given the red-and-black uniforms, who do we have the pleasure of thanking for his hospitality this morning?"

"Red and black are the chancellor's colors," Kivi said. "His faction. Those two-toned green are a different group but closely allied with the chancellor. Red and blue are Marchello and the baron's private guards."

"The colors represent guilds or merchant alliances or families," Gabriella said. "Mostly related to former

Imperial departments. The families are usually the descendants of who they reported to during the Empire. Customs and administration was the baron, and thus Marchello. The chancellor's group was the finance department—they do banking. The descendants of the secretary of agriculture are now big traders. They're the green and green."

"Red and black was finance, profit and loss."

"Good information," Jake said. "How did you find that out?"

"There's a library across the square from the palace," Kivi said. "I went and asked the librarian."

"A Jake Stewart clone. Wonderful," Nadine said. "Wait till you start saying things about some Roman Emperor or another."

"How did you find out your history lesson, Gabriella?" Jake said.

"Had a drink of rum at the bar and asked some soldiers," Gabriella said.

"A very Nadine way of doing things," Jake said. "A little more practice, and we'll start to question why she's along at all."

"We're already questioning why you're here, Stewart. So far, we have a colony almost as backward as we are, in the midst of an Imperial civil war, at the end of a long and treacherous jump route, with extra strong gut bacteria. And they are sort of kidnapping us. Your record isn't good."

"Or we could say I've triumphed over adversity by bringing us safely through a perilous route, avoiding being destroyed by the remnants of rebel forces, met with divergent political units, enhanced our resistance to changed diets, and discovered exciting new sources of critical resources."

A horse-drawn cart stopped in front of the window. The horse neighed and shat onto the cobblestones. They all recoiled from the smell.

"There's your resources right there, Stewart," Nadine said. "All the horse poop you can carry. In easy form for fast consumption."

"You know," Jake said. "Feces is great fertilizer, If we just brought back a container of it. Wouldn't matter if it froze. We wouldn't even need a container. We could just stick a big ball of it on, and it would freeze."

"I will not fly a ship covered in shit," Nadine said.

"Didn't you call yourself a shit-hot pilot?" Kivi said.

"That would make her a shit cold pilot," Gabriella said.

"Quiet, children, the adults are talking," Nadine said. "Jake, this colony is more primitive than we are. There's nothing here. We need electrical components, solar panels, industrial chemicals. Advanced technology like that."

"And sugar," Jake said.

"On eggs?" Nadine looked down at her breakfast. "Are you drunk? Who puts sugar on eggs?"

"Sugar as a trading commodity," Jake said. "Delta is too cold to grow it. They have fields of the stuff here, miles and miles of it. It might grow wild as part of the terraforming package. We can take the processed sugar, load up containers of it."

"And now we're going to be importing cheap rum," Nadine said.

"It's a feedstock, and we can mix it with the trays we make or the meal bars. It won't take much to produce calorie-dense portable foods that are shelf stable."

Nadine clapped her hands. "See, Brie, that's why we bring Jake along. The man is a trading genius."

"But you just said that he was full of—" Kivi said.

Brie had kicked him again.

Jake scraped his own eggs into his mouth. "Second, cotton, denim, and maybe flax and linen. Again, it's too cold on Delta to grow that. We can take containers of the stuff. I wore dead people's clothes for the first twenty years of my life—we recycled or reused everything on our station. A couple shiploads of fabrics, and we'll be able to expand what we have in the way of clothes. We don't have the machines to mill or weave or anything—not now, but we can make them. We have all the metal we want. And we have power to run them, which they don't. And that tree silk stuff is pretty intriguing. For its weight, it's exceptionally strong and airtight. We could make skinsuits out of it."

The spacers nodded at that. Skin suits were made out of synthetics and were nearly indestructible, but the supply was limited, and a good skin suit was the most expensive thing a spacer owned.

"Okay, food, clothes, fine," Nadine said. "Anything else."

"Coal," Jake said. "We want their coal."

"Why? To burn in the jump ship's furnaces to get us here? Are we going to put Kivi and Brie to shoveling? It may have escaped you, Stewart," Nadine said, "but we have a fusion reactor, as does every ship in Delta orbit, and we've got fusion power, hydro power, and solar power on the moon we call our home. We don't need to burn coal to keep warm."

"Too true," Jake said. "Coal isn't an optimal solution."

"Good," Nadine said.

"Ideally, I'd like oil—petroleum. If they have coal, they have that, too, but they haven't been looking for it because the infrastructure to use coal is simpler. But I'll bet if we go prospecting, we can find some."

"You want us to go out and drill for oil?" Brie asked.

"That would be great," Jake said. "We need to organize that. Maybe that could be your project?"

"If we're not burning coal, why are we burning oil, Jakey? You're drunk on fermented cow milk."

"We're not burning the coal or the oil. They have a ton of uses. All sorts of long-chain carbon molecules. Mostly, we want them to make plastics from. We're short on industrial feedstocks for plastics. We can make them out of petroleum and, in a pinch, coal. This place will be a plastics bonanza for us." Jake drank off a glass of milk. "But I have to figure out the milk issue, too. How do I get that back to Delta?"

Jake finished his glass and put it down. This was a signal to the room—groups of people came over to ask to speak to them or pulled up chairs and talked. They had drawn looks as they sat but no actual conversations. They had been left alone until they finished their meal. The crowd then swarmed them with outlandish questions.

Three young officers in green on green asked about their ship. "You came on a spaceship? A jump ship from the Empire?"

"Not the Empire," Jake said, "But an Imperial colony. We're trying to find out what happened to the Empire. They just left."

"Your cravat doesn't feel like silk," a young woman said to Nadine. "And what are those things on your wrists?"

"These?" Nadine held up her arms. "They're called armbands. The latest fashion."

"An Imperial fashion? Are they popular in the Empire? Is that why you wear them?"

Delta women wore neck collars and armbands because they were easy to put on with a skin suit, a way to jazz it up, without endangering anything. When outside, in the dark, most women folded them up and put them in a pocket.

"The latest fashion," Nadine said. "All the best people wear them. The Emperor himself does."

The women leaned closer to Nadine. "Would you sell them to me?"

"I'll trade," Nadine said. "What will you give me?"

The woman stripped her bracelet off and handed it to Nadine. "Opals. How many of those armbands will you give me for it?"

Nadine weighed the bracelet in her hand. It was heavy. "What's your name, and how do I find you later on? I have some other things you should see."

Gabriella and Kivi got their share of attention. Questions about their clothes, Delta, life on a ship.

After receiving a half-dozen invitations to visit people, Jake said "I'll tell you what. The chancellor has been very hospitable in putting us up. We're to attend a party tonight—the summer festival?" The group nodded at Jake. "Well, before that, we'd like to see the city. I'm particularly interested in seeing more of the harbor, the walls, and the gates, of course—I always enjoy Old Empire architecture—and the commercial quarter. I would be grateful for some guides, and in return, we'll try to answer as many of your questions as we can."

The crowd chorused agreement.

"We could split up so that we can see more," Jake said. "Perhaps, if it's not too much of an imposition, this young lady here"—Jake pointed at an attractive young woman talking to Kivi—"could take one group, and this gentleman here," Jake pointed at a bald officer, "could take another."

Kivi's smile brightened the room.

"Kivi and I will go with you," Jake said, "and Nadine and Gabriella can go with the others."

Kivi's face fell. Brie grinned.

"Something, Kivi?" Jake asked.

"Well, sir, normally, you and Ms. Nadine have things to talk about, and you have the most experience, so I figured you'd take the more important areas, and Brie, and I could just collect some general impressions."

Jake nodded. "Good point. You go with Brie, and Nadine and I will go with—" Jake turned to the bald man.

"Cartier. Jack Cartier." He shook Jake's hand. "Let's go."

Jake whispered to Gabriella, then the two groups separated. Jake and Nadine followed Cartier and two men who were dressed like officers in the chancellor's colors. Four uniformed guards followed at a distance.

Nadine leaned close to Jake. "Who called the guards?"

"They were waiting when we came out. I'm still not sure if we're prisoners or guests."

"That was cruel, making Kivi sweat like that."

"He'll appreciate it all the more for waiting for it," Jake said.

"True. When did you learn that?"

"I learned it off you," Jake said.

"You should practice what you learn," Nadine said.

"How do you know I'm not?" Jake asked. "Practicing on you, I mean."

Nadine was quiet for the rest of the walk. Cartier peppered Jake with questions about space and the empire, which Jake answered in detail. Once they reached the stairs, Jake had his own questions.

"Easiest way is to just walk you along the walls," Cartier said as they climbed up a set of stairs. "City isn't that tall, mostly two stories, and the walls cover the whole Imperial quarter, which was the original settlement." They climbed up to the top, and Cartier pointed out the cardinal directions. "North. The peninsula runs up to the mainland. There, it's flat river bottom—the two rivers run south to the sea, West River and East River, and the land between is fertile. That's where the farmers are. Way north of that is the forest, then the mountains in the farther north. East, the eastern oceans." He turned and pointed south. "City stretches south of here to the water. You can see the harbor in the middle. Great harbor, snug, then the entrance to the straits. South, in the distance, you can see the far shore of the straits, with a settlement there. It's called Far Shore. That leads down to the Magyar plains." He turned ninety degrees. "West, another ocean."

"Called the Western Ocean, no doubt," Nadine said.

"Why would you call it that?"

"It's west. And your names are pretty derivative. West River. East River."

"You don't have rivers on your planet?"

"We do."

"What do you call them, then?" Cartier asked.

"Well, we... Jake?" Nadine looked at Jake. "I've never bothered to learn."

"We number them," Jake said. "We have a monorail that stretches east and west. Places are named after their distance from the main city. Point Thirty-Seven, Point Seventy-Eight. The rivers take the names. If there is a settlement called Point Thirty-Seven, and it has a river, we call it Point Thirty-Seven River."

"What do you call your oceans?"

"We only have one. It's called the World Ocean."

"Well, we call it the Central Ocean," Cartier said. "Least we use words rather than just numbers. You do that with your kids as well? Boy Number One, Boy Number Two?"

"That's an interesting idea," Jake said.

"Sorry I asked," Nadine said. "Does this wall go all the way around town?"

"All the way. Six kilometers long, two meters wide, and four meters high. Pretty big, huh?"

"I've seen bigger," Nadine said.

"She says that a lot," Jake muttered.

"What's that, Stewart? Want to share your wisdom with us?"

"Let's go to the gates," Cartier said. He pointed down. "See the market square? That's where most of the shops are. There's the main road to the harbor—you would have come up that when you landed."

"Different types of stores down there. Is that a blacksmith shop?"

"You bet," Cartier said. "That's Sven's. He makes household items, knives and pots mostly. Not the most elaborate, nothing fancy, but workmanlike."

"And that's a carpenter next to him."

"Now, there, you can spend some money," Cartier said. "Alfonso de Santi. Purveyor of fine furniture."

"What's the difference between fine furniture and regular furniture?" Nadine asked.

"Lots of other woods of different color inlaid into the frame and triple the price. You can get the same chair down by the docks for one-third, one-quarter the cost, but it's simple. No mixed woods, no extra decorations. Just solid workmanship."

"It's all very old-timey," Nadine said. "Blacksmith, carpenter."

"We've always had a mix here. Once the civil war started, we couldn't get imports, so we had to make do with local materials. We have wood, coal, fabric."

"How much metal?" Jake asked.

"Not much. I hear tell you've got a shipload of metal?"

"We have some items to trade," Jake said. "Copper, iron, zinc. Other things."

"That probably makes you the wealthiest person on the planet right now. All that metal. We've got no mining at all. We just use surface deposits. And we don't have any smelters. Processed metal is expensive here."

Jake pointed across the square at a machine visible through a window. "That's not primitive. That's a computer-controlled milling machine."

"Empire tech," Cartier said. "As long as we've got power, we can keep what we have. But it's not much. That milling machine is scheduled out months in advance. The boats and steamship people need it for parts."

"It's a lot to take in," Jake said. "But why have a wall at all. Are there killer animals?"

"Nope. Killer tax dodgers and petty thieves," Cartier said. "We were discovered during the first Empire expansion. The Imperial survey found the planet marginal for habitation, and we were far away from any growing trade routes. They declared it an Imperial preserve, dropped a standard terraforming package, and said to check back in two hundred years."

"Let me guess," Jake said. "Illegal settlers moved in."

"No actual records, but when the first chartered settlers arrived, there were already people here. They homesteaded. They didn't do well. We figure eighty, ninety percent died before the weather stabilized. When the official party arrived, there wasn't so much a colony here as a swarm of near starving poor people. First few years, they'd form raiding groups and storm in and steal just everything. The Empire sent in a few troops, and they built the Imperial quarter behind the walls. First few years, the city was beleaguered. They needed the walls to keep the originals from taking everything. But after about fifty, hundred years, we kind of divided things up. The city people kept to the city, and the originals stayed out. They came in to trade. Of course, then the refugees came in. The farmers, the horse people. A lot more of them than the originals, and they were better organized. The government just gave them blocks of land outside the city and told them to live there. They cut deals with whoever was there already, married in or killed them off or something. Not a city problem."

"What do you mean not a city problem?" Jake asked.

"City is city, and country is country. We city people control who can live here. If you're not from a city family, you can't stay overnight in town, you have to live out there." He swept his hand out. "Which means you're a farmer, or a horser. Or an original. Still some original places out there. Villages, especially far along the Central Sea. People migrated out there years ago. Groups in the mountains. The farmers or the horsers deal with them."

"Why is the city right here, on this bay?" Jake asked.

"Needed water for the fusion plant, and the electricity could run the cranes. Shuttles could land here, and it was easy to defend. The city handled trading, on and off world. It had the only spaceport. The others came in and traded for what they needed. We took their crops, products, what have you. Used to export a lot of cotton and a lot of leather. Not now. No Empire to export it to. Come see the market outside the gates." Cartier walked them along the wall. "There." He pointed.

The gate below was large enough to take two men on horses. Bored guards gossiped with each other. A line of planters stood outside, with carts full of food. The guards checked them in. Some planters had comm units, others printed books. Others waited nearby with their goods. Jake saw a woman and two men dressed in yellow-and-red clothes approach a farmer with a cart of carrots and radishes pulling their own cart. Payment changed hands, and they unloaded the planter's cart into their own and hauled it into the city. The farmer walked over to a city cart displaying leather shoes.

"See?" Cartier said. "Works okay. We get the food we need, they get paid, and they can buy things."

"All the buyers are wearing the same colors," Jake said.

"They belong to the same clan. They handle produce buying. They're the only ones."

"What if you don't want to sell to them?"

"Then, you don't sell."

"Seems like that's a great deal for Cortez and the city, not so great for the planters."

Cartier looked at the farms ringing the city. "Not my problem. They can starve for all I care."

CHAPTER TWELVE

After the day spent touring the town, they collected for the ceremonial dinner. Dinner was, of all things, at a floating restaurant.

"That's a sailboat?" Gabriella asked. "Sailboats are supposed to be graceful and sleek and romantic."

"And they should have sails," Kivi said. "Big white things up on top of the masts. This looks like a box with a smokestack."

"And it has wheels. Does it drive on land?"

"It's a paddle wheeler," Jake said. "A riverboat. They'll burn wood or coal in a boiler. The boiler will heat water into steam. The steam pushes cylinders out that are connected to those paddles. The paddles spin and push it through the water. They don't work well in any sort of waves, so you only get this on small lakes and rivers. Especially rivers."

They joined a crowd lined up at the gangplank. The crowd was a sea of colored outfits—the red shirt and blue pants of the baron's faction, the light-green and dark green of the agriculture-trading family whose name Jake had forgotten, and many others.

"Pretty colorful," Jake said. The group ahead of them wore a yellow-and-orange checkered outfit. "We won't lose them in the dark."

"They fit in better than we do, Stewart," Nadine said, gesturing at their skin suits and plain coveralls. "Everyone can pick us out from a kilometer away."

"Where's your ruffles? And arm and neckbands. You normally dress up on these occasions."

"I traded some to the locals for a fortune in opals," Nadine said.

"A fortune?"

"I learned from the master, Stewart."

"How do you know that they're real?" Jake asked.

"How do you fake opals?"

"You need a laboratory and some heat. Did you test them with acid?"

Nadine's eyes widened, and she tapped the opals on her wrist.

"You're wearing them now?" Jake asked. "Do you want me to check them—"

"Mind your own business," Nadine said, arriving at the door. "Hello, we're the spacers."

"Of course you are," the woman at the gate said. "In those outfits, who else could you be?"

"In these outfits—" Nadine said.

"The space outfits." The crew had discarded all their space-specific clothes – helmets, weighted boots, hard collars, oxygen supply and gloves. Their skit suits were more of a leotard, with some local accessories added on. "But nice opals."

Nadine stuck her tongue out at Jake.

"Mackeson mining, I think. Nice, but last year's."

"Last year's?" Nadine said.

"They mine 'em by the cartload out east," the woman said. "They sort them by color and just release certain colors each year. Last year was blue-green. But this year is black. But you spacers are rich. I'm sure you can buy new ones for your next important event." She consulted a list. "Since you're not nobles, you're seated after the great families in the order of precedence." She grinned at Nadine. "Right next to the ambassadors from the farmers and the horsers." She grinned wider. "You'll have a lot in common. You can exchange fashion tips." The woman led them into the restaurant.

"Sir," Kivi said to Jake, "did we just get insulted?"

"And by an expert, too," Jake said. "Nothing we can complain about, but the message is clear—we're of no account in local politics and society."

"But we're from another planet."

"They don't know how to process that," Jake said. "They don't understand how newcomers will affect them. They think we're not important."

"Because foreigners aren't important?"

"Foreigners are never important. Until we are."

The interior of the riverboat had twenty rows of six tables, each table holding eight people. The baron's tables were near the bow of the boat. The paddle wheel housing intruded into the room two-thirds of the way down, obstructing the view. Down the centerline, vegetables and meat sizzled in oil-filled pans. Jake and his group were conducted to the back of the room, out of sight of the front tables.

"Two of you will be here with the farmers," the hostess said, pointing to empty chairs. Tam and Ket sat at a four-person table at the rear. "And the other two over there." On the far side of the riverboat sat Arpad and Vidor at an equally small table.

"Who sits where, ma'am?" Jake asked.

The hostess laughed. "We don't care which table you sit at, you... folks... work it out yourself. As long as you stay back here."

Jake and Nadine's eyes met, and Jake nodded her across to the Ranchers.

"Brie, you're with me at Vidor's table. Kivi, you go with Jake and clean up when he drools over Miss Skinny But Big Breasts over there." Brie followed Nadine across.

Kivi walked next to Jake as they approached Tam's table. "Sir, were we insulted again?"

"By the hostess or by Nadine?"

"Yes."

Jake laughed as they sat and greeted Tam and Ket.

"Ambassadress... first secretary? I don't know your

title, your official title, that is," Jake said.

"I don't have one. Tonight, I'm just the ambassador's daughter. If I'd had a title they recognized, they'd have to seat me closer to the baron. I'm surprised they didn't put you up front. Are you a nobleman or anything like that?"

"I'm technically an admiral in the Delta Militia. I don't think that counts for anything here."

"It should. But what they're saying, subtly, is that they don't believe you're a real Empire. Otherwise, they would have put you closer to the front."

"Will your father be joining us?" Jake said.

"He has an actual title. With Imperial-signed papers to prove it, so they have to put him up front. Otherwise, they're insulting the Emperor. Their Emperor. And the first families wouldn't stand for that."

"I would have assumed, since we're from another planet, simple curiosity would have put us closer."

"This is the social event of the season," Tam said. "To put the four of you here, they had to kick out a city family. They can't have been that important if they were sitting with the barbarians, so no big deal."

"Barbarians?"

Tam extended her hands and pointed at Ket and herself. "That's us. Meet the barbarian cousins."

"But Nadine and Brie are with the Ranchers—"

"I'll give these city-dwelling snobs that much. They hate us and the Ranchers equally. We're both barbarians to them, as are you now, apparently, if you're not part of the real Empire."

"This three Emperor thing is complicated."

"Four, now that you're here. You have your own."

"We do."

"Well, welcome to the year of the four Emperors, then." Ket raised her glass. "Cheers!"

***

"The pots were originally shields, you see," Vidor said.

Nadine and Gabriella were seated at his table. He insisted that Gabriella sit next to his friend Arpad. Neither she nor Arpad had objected. They sat across the table, conversing in whispers.

"They don't look like shields. They look like big pots," Nadine said. "There's even a name for them. What'ya call them, woks?"

A cook in the central cooking line dashed some oil into his wok, then rolled it to ignite the oil from the fire. The flame flared up four feet.

"Not woks, shields," Vidor said. "My ancestors would slaughter cattle to eat. We used our sharpened swords to slice the meat into strips, then put our shields on the fire and grilled the meat and vegetables on the sizzling metal."

"Your ancestors were cooks?" Nadine asked.

"My ancestors were great warriors of the steppe. I am descended from the great Attila myself."

"The great Attila. Great. Good. Great Attila. Good for him, great for him, the great Attila."

Vidor frowned. "You have no idea who Attila the Hun is, do you?"

"None at all. But if he invented pots for cooking meat in, I'm all in favor of it. I like meat. It smells great."

The cook in the middle rolled his wok again, making the flame flare up.

"I am saddened that you don't know who the great Attila is," Vidor said.

"You didn't invite me to sit here because you wanted to talk about Attila. You either want to try to seduce me, or you want off-world help with some political scheme that you're planning to pull on these stuck-up city people. When do we eat?"

Vidor laughed. "You're very direct."

"I'm very hungry. Which is it?"

"Can't it be both?"

"We can hope," Nadine said.

Arpad, across the table, yelped in pain. Nadine and Vidor stopped talking.

"Sheb pulled myb mistache," Arpad said.

"Men don't wear mustaches on Delta," Gabriella said. "I wanted to see if it was attached."

"She doesn't know about mustaches? So, she tests by pulling them? Does she not know what she was doing?"

"She knows exactly what she's doing," Nadine said. "As do you. Fun later. To business. You don't like these city people at all."

Vidor glared at the crowd. He pointed to a rambunctious group in red outfits with a yellow strip. "I am seated back here, behind a city family that makes mirrors. They hammer them and then polish them, but they don't do the polishing themselves. They send it out to our people or the planters, and we polish for them. In return, they give us small items of worked metal, tools, trinkets." He picked up his knife and tested its edge. "This is good steel, but we cannot make such as this. Not in quantity. We sell them food for a pittance. They buy our freedom with an ax or a saw. This city would starve without us—we raise the cattle and the sheep that they eat, tan the hides that they wear, but we are not even allowed here overnight. My clan has perhaps thirty thousand people—three times that of the city dwellers, at least. But they keep the best technology for themselves. We needed another portable computer, one with a database of veterinarian information. They offered to trade it to us for enough food to feed the city for a year. They eat for free, and we would have nothing for an entire year. I'm not even sure they are using it."

"You hate them?"

"I do. I wish to crush them."

"Why don't you?" Nadine asked. "Sounds like you could."

"My father will not hear of it. They are of the Empire,

and we swore loyalty to the Empire. And I must admit, I feel the same. We are Imperial citizens, not barbarians. Our loyalty to the Empire gave us this land. We should follow Imperial laws."

"No crushing them, then?"

"Not while the baron lives, and not while my father lives."

"That's the only reason you had us seated here, then?" Nadine asked. "Why are you talking to us?"

Vidor called over a server, took four glasses of red wine off his tray, and handed them out to the table. "Why should we not talk? I can ask questions, learn of your world, and plan for the future. We do have good wine here. Drink up and tell me of your planet. And besides"— he grinned at Nadine—"you are most pleasant to look at."

Nadine grinned back. "Buy me wine and tell me I'm pretty. Works every time."

***

"Right about now," Tam said, pointing to Nadine and Vidor, "he's telling her that the pots are corruptions of his ancestors' shields, that they used to cook meat on them."

"Are they?" Jake asked.

"They would be if these were Hungarian pots, like his ancestors were, but they're really woks, which are Mongolian in origin. He's getting two Old Earth despots, Genghis Khan and Attila the Hun mixed up. Genghis Khan was Mongol, and he ruled one of the largest Empires the world has seen. Attila the Hun was a bloodthirsty barbarian."

"He fought the Roman Empire and won often," Jake said. "At least against the Eastern Empire. That takes a fair bit of organization and leadership. He was hardly a regular barbarian chieftain."

Ket grinned at Kivi and whispered. "He got her there.

Finally somebody to call her on these historical things she's always talking about. Half the time, I think she makes them up."

"Captain Stewart knows his history," Kivi whispered back. "And he never makes anything up."

"This will be fun to watch."

"Did you have a question, Kivi?" Jake asked.

"No, sir," Kivi said. "Just excited to learn more about the situation here."

Jake narrowed his eyes but turned back to Tam. "You seem to know a lot about Vidor and his people," Jake said. "But your father doesn't like him much. How did you learn so much?"

"He's an ignorant, arrogant bore," Tam said. She grabbed a fork and stabbed at her plate. "Nearly uneducated, with the mental prowess of a roadkill beef-beast. Nothing about him is worth knowing." She stabbed her fork into the table and snapped the fork in half. She glared at it. "Shoddy city goods." She tossed the broken half of the fork to the floor.

Jake pulled the embedded half of the broken fork from the table and handed it to Tam. "Ex-boyfriend?"

"He was never a friend."

"Bad breakup."

"It's over now. I don't discuss him anymore."

Jake looked at Ket. She nodded. "It was epic. They dated for years. There was talk of marriage. But they had a fight. He said she was boring and wouldn't do anything exciting. She said he was an ignoramus that couldn't buckle his own sword belt, could barely read, and lacked 'mental prowess.' He threw wine on her dress, so she set his beard on fire. They had to dump a bucket of water over Vidor's head to put it out."

Tam waved a waiter over and requested another fork. They sat silently as the party swirled around them.

A plate was propped in front of Jake, and he tapped it with his spoon. "Carrots?"

"Yep."

"Do you follow this rule to not talk business during dinner?"

"Who's to say what is business and what isn't?" Tam said. "Why do you ask?"

"Why are you here at this dinner?" Jake said. "It seems like it's deliberately designed to humiliate you—placed at the worst table, with us. Apparently, the worst table companions you can have or at least the lowest class."

"Low class can be interesting," Tam said. "They often know things others don't. And we're considered the lowest of the low, regardless. These city snobs think we're all equally bad—you, me, the Ranchers over there. But it's important for us to be seen in the city and seen by the first families."

"So that they can remember to put 'humiliate farmers' on their calendars."

"Because we want them to remember something that we have that they don't."

"Which is?"

"Money."

CHAPTER THIRTEEN

Nadine and Gabriella were on their second glass of wine. Vidor and Arpad were at number five or six.

"Then I will take the warriors of my people and ride into the city and crush them." Vidor thumped the table.

"Warriors? I thought you were herders," Nadine said.

"Well, we are. But we are all excellent riders. And we all have swords."

The ship shook as the port wheel thrashed in the water. The riverboat pivoted back, and the bow swung toward the harbor mouth. The port paddle stopped, and the starboard one ticked over. The stern lines were thrown off, and the boat settled on a course for the harbor mouth. Both paddles increased speed, and the city dwindled behind them.

"Having a sword and using it are two different things," Nadine said. "Even I know that."

"My men are brave and bold. We fear nothing. When the time is right, we will carry the fight to them."

"And be bravely and boldly shot to pieces by that Gauss rifle I saw on a palace soldier the other day. It fires thousands of rounds a minute. No way you're getting over a wall with that behind it. To say nothing of a ship mounted laser in the harbor. And, by the way, it was a woman with the Gauss rifle."

"Bravery will conquer all."

"Okay." Nadine drained her glass and signaled a waiter to bring another round for the table. "Let's assume your brave men and women conquer the city. You defeat their guards with ancient weapons, and you somehow hijack or ambush the ones with the modern ones, and you ride in here in triumph. What then?"

"I will be king of the world!"

"Great, Mr. King. You take over the throne, and on the first day, you have a levy and say what?"

"Say what?"

"Exactly."

"I don't understand."

"Let's say you are in charge. How will you feed this city? Handle the people here? Provide for industrial growth. Farming. Industry. What's your monetary policy?"

"Why would I do that?"

"You're the king. You're in charge. You have to feed your subjects. What do you have to do?"

"Well, the planters trade with the city."

"Yeah, but the city people are gone. The leaders, at least. You're in charge now. The planters don't like you, and you don't like them. Why should they still trade with you?"

"If they do not, we will kill them," Vidor said.

"Dead planters grow no grain," Nadine said. "And capturing a city that can't move is one thing—chasing thousands of planters over millions of acres of land is another, horses or no horses. And, while you're chasing, all those men aren't available to handle flocks, slaughter cattle, tan hides. Your whole economy is in disarray."

"What if they fight back?" Gabriella said. "Lots of swords out there."

"Why would they fight? I am khan. I mean, I will be after my father dies. They should obey me."

"What's a khan?" Nadine asked. "And why would we care?"

"It is the name of our hereditary leader," Arpad said. "The leader of our horsemen. Vidor's father is khan now, technically."

Nadine craned her neck. "Will we meet him?"

Vidor squirmed. "Perhaps not tonight. He will be busy

up front with diplomatic niceties. They put him at the table with the farmer's leader, and they do not get along."

"Plus, Vidor is often embarrassed," Arpad said, "when he brings his... companions to his father. His father is most critical."

"We don't have to meet him? Good, I don't want anybody being embarrassed in public by their companions."

"I would not be embarrassed by you, Ms. Nadine." Vidor said.

"Wasn't talking about you," Nadine said. "Brie and I have standards to uphold as well. Wouldn't want people making fun of our choices, would you?"

Vidor and Arpad exchanged glances.

"I don't understand," Vidor said.

Nadine pinched his cheek. "Of course you don't, horse can leader guy."

"It's khan, the leader of our horde of horses," Vidor said. "It is an important title."

"We came here on a spaceship, remember?" Nadine said. "Good for you, but what do we care for a bunch of horses?"

Arpad drank his wine. "This is true. Sometimes we forget how big the galaxy is and how small we are in it. Being khan is not enough. You are correct. We would have to provide good government. You would have to offer more than just rhetoric, Vidor."

The lighthouse at the harbor entrance appeared out the door, and the boat made a slow right turn to the west, starting down the middle of the strait. The water thrashed behind the wheels, but they neither rocked nor rolled. An unsupported glass of wine could sit on the table without sliding off.

Vidor rolled the stem of his glass between his fingers. "I had not considered these items."

"You should if you ever want to be in charge," Nadine said.

Vidor stood. "I will think on this. Let us all go to the deck and see the river cliffs as we wheel by. Arpad, attend me."

He and Arpad exited the dining room, going out to the promenade deck and whispering of policy.

Gabriella lagged behind with Nadine. "Monetary policy?"

"Yeah."

"Do you even know what that means?"

"No idea. But Jake talked about it before, so it must be important." Nadine drained her glass. "Sometimes, I think I should listen to that boy more often."

***

"So, you bribe your way into a better trade arrangement when the baron dies," Jake said to Tam.

"That's the plan," Tam said. "Father's plan. The city has electricity and clean water, but they don't produce much of anything useful. They have some small factories—more like big workshops, but they have to trade for the raw materials. That's where you come in."

"We have supplies of metal," Jake agreed. "But this isn't an economic problem. It's a political problem. You need representation in the government."

"There is no government, just a jumped-up ancient governor who is now a baron. When he's gone, there will be a crisis."

"A crisis is also an opportunity. Why do you have another city person take over? Why not your father or a council or a republic?"

"You say you want a revolution?"

"Well, we all want to change the world," Jake said. "But if you're not happy with the government here, why not wait for a good opportunity to change it?"

"We're farmers, not fighters," Tam said. "And we've

been planning for this. The city's first families might fight it out, but only three groups garner enough support to realistically take over. The chancellor's people, the baron's family, or a coalition of two other of the largest families. The leader of one of them will become the de facto baron, and we've been carefully cultivating all three. They all owe us, one way or another, and we'll escape the worst of the troubles."

"You're very well organized," Jake said. "This would be a good time to seize your own opportunity, so to speak."

"We're farmers, not fighters," Tam repeated. "We plan. We plant. We harvest. We're conservative. We don't take wild chances." She glanced out the window, then stood. "Come out onto the deck. We'll be wheeling past the river cliffs. It's quite a sight."

Magyar had a dozen moons of middling size. Seven were visible in the sky, ducking in and out of the clouds, and the combined light flashed a red glow onto the riverboat. Nadine, Vidor, Gabriella, and Arpad stood by the rail as they floated down the river.

"The current runs with the tide, so we are driving down-current for now. When the tide slows, the boat will use its paddles to move back to the city. Here, the strait narrows at the cliffs. The current is strongest here but doesn't last long. In less than a mile, it widens and slows, with beaches and marshes on both sides." Vidor pointed. "Look there, in the moonlight. You can see some of my clan." On the southern bank, a herd of cattle with six horsemen was visible on top of the cliff, climbing along a hill to a rocky promontory. "They are traveling east before they cross the strait to the city, to a slaughterhouse. They will feed the city people."

"Long way to go for a slaughterhouse."

"It is inconvenient," Vidor said. "And takes a toll on what we can ship. We have no trucks or other transport. Animals can walk. And a slaughterhouse needs power—either coal or electricity. All is available at the city."

"Why no trains?" Nadine asked. "If you have coal and basic metal working, you could have trains. And I know you've got lots of rivers. Why not dams and water mills?"

Vidor took Nadine's arm. "You Imperials are smart. We should hire you as advisers to teach us things."

The light increased, and they could see the deck clearly. "Those moons certainly are bright when they come out from behind the clouds," Nadine said.

Arpad looked at the sky. "But they have not come out. The same five are out as a minute before." He looked back inside the ship. "Vidor, inside!"

Cooking stations lined the middle of the dining room. The wok opposite them had been overfilled with oil, and when the cook ignited it to show off for the crowd, the extra burning oil slopped onto his table, setting it ablaze.

Jake and Tam heard the cries of the crowd and spun around. "Clumsy fool of a cook," Tam said. "When they spray that with water, it will ruin all the food. We'll end up going hungry. And it's a long time back to the city against the current."

"We need to move." Jake stood. "Where are the lifeboats?"

Tam raised her eyes. "Scared of a little fire?"

"Yes. On spaceships, it's what we most fear—we have nowhere to go." He pulled Tam up.

"They'll spray it. Everything will be fine," Tam said.

The fire raged inside, and the startled cook backed away, then tripped over a container of cooking oil sitting on the deck. He yelled as he fell, and the can tipped over spilling more oil that dripped onto the deck before running under the burning counter and pooling. The heat from the burning counter ignited it, and the fire spread. The cook scrambled backward, regained his feet, and raced away.

Most of the dining room crowd was on their feet, shouting at each other. A crew of four raced past Jake and the others and unwound a fire hose onto the deck.

"Is that foam?" Jake asked.

"Out of the way," the crewman said.

Three of them heaved the whole mass of the hose onto the deck and unraveled it. The fourth spun a wall valve.

"Wait," Jake said, "that's an oil fire. You can't put water on an oil fire."

"Out of the way, out-worlder," the crewman said. "Sev, Tern, grab the end." The three crew raced into the dining room, and the fourth continued spinning the wheel.

"No, no," Jake said. "You'll make it worse. Stop, stop."

Water rushed through the hose, inflating it, stopping at a kink. The other crew members inside yelled for more water.

"What's going on?" Tam asked. "Jake, why are you stopping them?"

"Burning oil floats on water. They'll just push the fire along, and it will burn anything else it hits."

Jake raced to the valve wheel and spun it half closed. The crewman yelled and fought him, trying to push it open. "Kivi," Jake yelled. "Tam. Help me. We need to close this."

The two women and Kivi grabbed the man and pulled him back. He yelled and fought, but they piled on and held him. Jake spun the wheel in reverse, cutting the flow down, reducing the water pressure.

He was two-thirds of the way down when the crew inside yanked the hose again, pulling the kink free, and the water surged through. Inside, they held the hose and pointed it at the burning cooking table. The water splashed out and slammed into the burning oil in the pan.

The fire on the burning table died instantly as the water cut off its oxygen. But the burning oil in the pan was blasted off the far side, slopping to the deck and landing on the giant pool of cooking oil soaking into the dry wood. The deck lit with a whomp, and the explosion blew burning tables and chairs in all directions, splashing bulkheads, cooking pots, cans of oil, and people. The cooking oil on the other tables flashed up, and people scattered.

Jake and the crew backed away as thick black smoke blew out the door, followed by a surge of coughing, gasping, and burning people.

CHAPTER FOURTEEN

The smoke and noise of the explosion blasted Nadine and her crew. She grabbed Vidor and Gabriella by the arm. "Out of here. To the back. Away from the fire. Get away." She dragged them for a few feet before they caught up. The smoke poured out of the doorway and leaked out from the windows as they raced to the stern.

Nadine and her party ran back till the promenade ended. The stern of the boat was blocked to them by the lounge that ran from side to side in the back.

"What's going on? Where did the fire come from?" Vidor asked.

"The food tables caught," Arpad said. He coughed, the riverboat still steaming forward, smoke blowing back.

Flames on the forepart of the ship flickered out of the windows, and they confronted each other in the glow.

"Wooden ship, this will burn up quickly," Nadine said.

"They have firefighting equipment," Vidor said. "And plenty of water."

"There—" Gabriella pointed. "There's a hose."

"Get it ready," Nadine said. "Somebody will need it, if not us."

They unraveled the fire hose and heaped it on the deck. Nadine, Arpad, and Vidor grabbed it and pointed it at the fire. The middle of the boat was covered in thick smoke, making them gasp as it was blown back upon them.

People streamed aft through the smokey clouds. They coughed and gasped, and several beat red embers off their clothes.

"I don't see any fireman," Nadine said.

"We will help," Vidor said. "Arpad. Ms. Nadine. Attend me."

Vidor muscled the nozzle up and pointed it at the fire. Arpad and Nadine grabbed behind him.

"Let it rip, Brie," Nadine yelled.

Gabriella gripped the valve wheel and spun it counterclockwise, and the water flowed out. The three temporary firefighters played the stream back and forth, soaking the deck, the bulkheads, and any passengers who came their way.

The increasing water pressure made it harder to handle, and the stream increased in power, knocking over several persons fleeing the fire.

"Cut it back. Back off. Half as much," Nadine yelled as they grasped the surging hose.

Gabriella obeyed, and the water diminished. The hose stopped shaking.

"Forward," Vidor yelled. "To the fire. We must put it out." He advanced into the darkness, dragging Arpad and Nadine with him. Vidor fumbled with the nozzle lever, and the water changed from a single stream to a wide spray, making the hose easier to handle and more effective at covering a larger area.

Nadine stumbled over a crawling body in the dark. The people exiting the dining room were crawling, not running. "Brie!" she yelled.

Gabriella was already there, pulling the choking form backward. Nadine, Vidor, and Arpad advanced with the hose, playing it on anything visible.

The smoke thickened, they all coughed, and the heat rose. A furnace of air blew back at them.

A whistle blew three times, and the paddle wheels stopped spinning. The smoke cleared and rose vertically, but the heat increased.

"I can't see the fire," Vidor coughed. "Where is it? We are just wasting water here."

"We're keeping it from spreading this way," Nadine

yelled. "Just hose down everything, but don't go so far into the smoke you pass out. We need to keep ourselves alive."

The three pushed forward again, coughing. Nadine felt Gabriella behind her, helping hold the hose. The smoke had thinned and was rising straight up, but the heat increased, and flames licked the dining room door. They moved closer and sprayed the door and the wooden frame. There were bodies inside the door and in front of it, but it was too hot to get closer, and the bodies didn't move. They sprayed the water to cool the deck and walls, but as soon as they moved the stream away, the deck smoked and the heat returned.

A bang came from the bow, and sparks leaped upward, visible even through the smoke. More flames rose. The whistle blew again, once, twice, then raised in volume and shrieked nonstop.

"What's going on?" Arpad said.

"Something bad," Nadine said.

The water stream suddenly halved, and heat pressed on them.

"Brie. More water," Nadine said.

The hose sagged, and Gabriella raced back. The hose sagged more, and they retreated aft as the heat built. Then the water returned, and they advanced again. The whistle died off and disappeared.

"That's on full now," Gabriella said, coming up behind her.

Nadine slapped Arpad's shoulder, and they advanced again, spraying the reduced water. They could not get half as close to the dining room as before, as flames poured out of the inside of the boat and the entire deck of the door— all the way to the engulfed paddles.

"We're not winning," Vidor said.

"Got any better ideas?" Nadine said.

"The water is dropping again," Arpad said.

The hose slackened in their hands. Another whistle blew a high-pitched screech that rose to an unbearable volume, then cut off in an instant.

The hose went limp, and the water dwindled to a drip. They stumbled backward, pulling the hose. Coughing crowds blocked the deck and pushed through to clear air. Gabriella shoved through to the hose fitting and spun the valve left then right. "No water pressure."

"Pipes burned away or the pump," Nadine said. "Right, to the back—Emperor's testicles."

The lounge behind them glowed a dull red, and smoke leaked out of the top of the doors. "Fire beat us."

The four clustered together. Forward, the decks and bulkheads were engulfed, and anything past the wheels wasn't visible in the whistling flames. Aft, small fires licked out of the lounge windows, as well as smoke. They were in a clear spot between the conflagration and the haze. Twenty or thirty people were crowded there with them. Many were already climbing the low rail to drop to the water.

Vidor wiped his brow. "We cannot stay here. The heat will get us or the smoke, even if the fire does not."

Nadine surveyed the deck. The few dozen passengers who remained were rapidly dropping off the side. She stepped over to the rail and looked at the water. "Less than twenty feet. We can do it."

"I will go first and catch you," Vidor said. He pointed to the cliffs in the distance. "The southern shore is only a few miles away. If we are careful and husband our strength, we can swim there."

He climbed up on the rail, stood, and dove cleanly into the water. Arpad followed. A blast of air knocked Nadine and Gabriella over. Fire had surged through the door of the lounge only feet away. Nadine regained her feet, climbed onto the rail, and looked back. Gabriella was hovering behind her. "Get up, get up," Nadine yelled. "We need to go."

Gabriella clambered up and sat on the rail next to Nadine, her feet dangling. Vidor and Arpad were treading water below them, both holding their arms up and gesturing. Gabriella yelled at Nadine. Nadine couldn't hear her over the crackling and roaring of the fire. She leaned over and grasped her shoulder. "What—what is it?"

"I can't swim."

Nadine stared at her for a moment, then looked at the fire, then down to Vidor, then back.

"Girl," Nadine said, "must I teach you everything?" Then she hugged Gabriella tightly, set her knees, and shoved them both off the boat. They fell, away from the fire and into the water.

***

Jake kicked a burning piece of chair to the edge of the deck, grasped the end of it, and shoved it overboard through a gap in the railing. Kivi, Ket, and Tam followed, shoving and tossing flaming piles of wood into the water. People surged out of the dining room, knocking them over. They banged onto the deck, rolled to the rail, and climbed up.

"My father is up front," Tam said. "We have to go get him." She started inside but was hit again by the firefighting crew as they ran out, trailing their hose.

"Get back in there, you cowards," Jake yelled. They ignored him and scampered aft. He reached over and pulled a stunned Tam to her feet. "I'll help you. Wrap something over your face, and I'll wet us down. Kivi, help me with the hose."

Kivi and Jake dragged the hose in as fast as they could. It was flipping from side to side as the water surged through.

"Cut the water off for a second," Jake yelled.

Ket ran to the hose and spun the valve shut. Jake and Kivi tugged the hose in hand over hand.

"Crap," Jake said. He had the end of the hose in his

hand. The broken end. The nozzle had burned off, and all he had was a frayed bag. "Give me some water," he yelled. "A quarter turn."

Ket overcorrected, and the hose lashed out of Jake's hand and bounced till she cut the water flow in half. Jake grabbed it and hosed down the four of them, then pulled his shirt up over his mouth and soaked that, too. The others followed, pulling their shirts over their mouth and nose, and Jake noticed that Tam was as shapely as he had imagined.

Even in the middle of a fire, Stewart, really?

People stumbled out of the fire, one or two at a time. Then the exodus stopped. Jake took a final play of water over everybody. He grabbed Tam's arm and motioned to the others behind him. "Hold on to each other. We'll run through to the bow."

Kivi grabbed the back of his skin suit, Tam grabbed him, and they raced into the smoke.

It was pitch black. The smoke blocked all vision, and the heat was fantastic. Jake stumbled along behind Tam, moving with difficulty. The water steamed off his face, hands, and feet.

Six feet in the dark, Jake lost his way. He couldn't see forward or backward. They stumbled, and Ket pitched down and slammed into a wall, then dropped to the deck. Jake piled in on top of her, banging his chest on the unseen chair she had tipped over. Kivi held him tight and tried to haul him back up. Jake dropped to his knees, then down farther. He grabbed Ket's shoulder as she rose and pulled her down again.

The heat was horrible, and Jake's hands burned.

"Back, back now," Jake yelled. He climbed to his knees.

The way ahead was blocked by a wall. There shouldn't be a wall in front of them. It should be open. Jake looked behind him but couldn't see the door, only fire.

Was the fire all around them? Were they trapped?

Kivi had dropped beside him. He couldn't see Tam,

even though he could touch her. Ket tried to get up, but Jake pushed her down again. Where was the door? He looked back and front. Only fire. Smoke blew away, and he saw an open spot in the wall to his right. He grabbed the women's shoulders, then pulled them along as he low crawled to the door. But then Ket surged forward, pulling him along. Kivi grasped his shoulder.

They crawled through the door. The smoke billowed above them, and the heat dropped. Kivi passed Jake, dragging Ket by her collar. Tam yanked him forward, and the four crashed out of the door to the open deck. Smoke billowed above them, and burning sparks landed on them. They stumbled to the railing. Jake grabbed the spinning firehose as they passed and hosed them all down. Tam held the railing and gasped. Ket couldn't stand. Kivi pulled her up and thrust her head over the railing into cleaner air. She was nearly unconscious and gasping.

"That didn't work," Tam said. "I got turned around. We'll try again."

Kivi was shaking Ket and talking to her. She retched over the railing.

Jake played water over the four. "Tam, we can't do it. We should get off this boat now."

"My father's up there," Tam said.

"Ket is in a bad way. Your dad will have to look after himself. She can't do that again. We need to get her off the ship."

"You two take her," Tam said. "I'm going back."

"You got lost and were choking to death," Jake said. "We don't have the right equipment."

"I'm going back in," Tam said.

"All right," Jake said. "Kivi, take Ket back to the stern. There're two big life rafts on the deck above the lounge. Cast them loose into the water and get her out."

"What about you, sir?"

"I'm going with Tam," Jake said.

He played the hose over her, then himself, then her

again, pulled up his shirt, dropped to his knees, and crawled forward. Tam crawled behind him, holding the back of his shirt. They had just entered the darkness under the door when a blow smashed Jake's shoulder into the deck. His back hurt, and he was stuck under a charred beam.

Jake kicked and flailed his arms, but he couldn't get any purchase. He tried rolling to one side or the other, but he was firmly wedged. He pushed his arms under his chest and lifted off the deck, but the beam still sat on his shoulders. He shoved higher and tried to slide back, but got stuck again and dropped to the deck.

No good. I have to move or die.

He shoved again, and the beam rolled onto his neck. He squirmed, and it slid off. He ducked under, and rolled left, knocking a kneeling Tam onto him.

The two rolled out of the smoke and hit the railing.

Jake lay there gasping, Tam lying on top of him.

Tam sat up, crying. "The door is blocked. I saw the roof cave in. We can't get through." A whistle wailed from the bow. "Steam," Tam said. "They're venting the steam so the boilers don't explode. If the steam doesn't vent fast enough, the ship will blow up."

"Back to the raft," Jake said.

Tam grabbed his arm, and they raced back to the lounge. Red flames glowed inside, and smoke seethed out. A crowd of people were up on the roof, wrestling with a large square float—a life raft.

They climbed a ladder next to the door and onto the roof.

Two rafts were tied there, one on top of the other. Each was five meters per side, with grab ropes fixed along the edge and on the top. Just a giant square floating piece of wood designed to be swung out by a crane with a block and tackle.

Smoke obscured the decks as flames billowed from the front of the boat. Jake hadn't noticed when, but the paddle wheels had stopped moving. A group of shadowy figures was fighting to lift the life raft off.

"Listen up," Jake bellowed. "Two on each side, everybody else on the back. Those on the side lift enough to tilt it, those on the back push. Once it starts moving, keep pushing, and it will slide off. Get ready. We go on three."

The shadowy crowd shuffled, and hands moved in the gloom.

"Get ready. One, two, three."

It worked perfectly. The side lifters tilted the float, breaking the friction. Those in the back shoved it forward, and it moved two feet easily and broke free of the other raft. "Again. On three," Jake yelled. "Ready, one, two, three."

The second shove pushed the raft forward, and it kept going. The back crowd pushed faster, and the raft slid out, overbalanced, and dropped into the water below.

"Great job. Now, we take—"

The crowd didn't pause but leaped into the water after the raft. One woman shrieked when she smashed into the wooden raft from twenty feet up.

"The second one," Jake said.

He, Tam, Kivi, and Ket were the only ones left.

"Girls on the side, boys on the back," Jake said. "Get set." The women shuffled to the sides. Jake and Kivi got set on the back. "On three. One, two, three."

The raft didn't budge.

"Too heavy," Kivi said.

"Again," Jake said, then counted out the shove.

The raft didn't move.

"We don't need to lift it," Tam said. "Just shove it."

Behind the raft, on the bulkhead, a fire ax was mounted on the wall. He pulled the ax out of its cradle, turned to the raft, and swung it.

He aimed the swing between the raft and the deck. The ax sliced under the raft and stuck. "Help me lift. All of you." He strained on the ax handle, using it to lever the raft.

The raft didn't move until Kivi and Ket leaned in to help him, then the lever shoved the raft up and forward a few inches.

"Step back," Jake said. He swung the ax and slammed it under the raft again. The other three needed no instructions. They stepped up and helped him lever it up and out. The raft slammed another foot closer to the rail.

"Again," Jake said.

They repeated, and it slid another foot. Smoke billowed up from below, and Kivi coughed. Jake grabbed him, dragged him to the rail, and leaned him out in the air. Tam and Ket dropped beside him.

A whistle shrieked from the bow, blowing on and on.

"That's the emergency pressure release valve," Tam yelled. "We need to get off now before it blows."

"We're not the only ones needing a raft," Jake said. "If this raft stays, it will burn with the ship. Take a few deep breaths, and we'll try once more. If not, over we go. Breathe. Ready? Go."

The four ran back. The smoke was thicker, and Jake missed his first swing. It banged off the deck. He was holding his breath, and the smoke swirled in his vision. He stepped back, set himself, waited for a clear patch, then swung again. The ax jammed under the raft. The four leaned into it, and the raft lifted, then slid another foot.

They heaved, and the raft slid, tipped, and dropped off the ship. Jake threw the ax over the side. They ran to the rail and looked down. The raft had rolled and floated away. The water below was clear.

"Hold hands," Jake said.

The four stood and grasped each other.

"On three," Jake said. "One, two, three."

They leaped, and the dark water rushed up to meet them.

CHAPTER FIFTEEN

Nadine grasped Gabriella tightly as they dropped away from the boat. She smacked into the water, and the impact drove the air from her lungs and compressed her spine. Her legs hurt badly. She sank farther in the water, and the light from the blazing boat dimmed to a red glow. She kicked and thrashed, but the glow dimmed more. The combined weight of her and Gabriella dragged them down but then buoyancy reasserted itself, and they rose.

Nadine tried to kick, but mostly waved her feet. Her legs weren't responding, only her arms. She floundered, and water pounded in her ears. Her vision dimmed, and her feet stopped moving.

The light cut off above her, and two hands grasped her hair and pulled. Another two grabbed Gabriella in front of her, and the light brightened.

She tried kicking her legs, and, this time, they moved a little. The hands above kept yanking her hair, and she kicked harder. Her head broke the surface, then her face, and she swept in a mouthful of air.

"Are you okay? How is Ms. Brie? Is she all right?" Vidor said. He held her shoulder and hair, pulling her away from the burning boat. Vidor pushed Gabriella's arm.

Nadine took a deep lungful of air, then another, then a third. "You ignorant, cow-herding cretin. Who said you could pull my hair? That hurt! Try that again, and I'll stab you in the eye."

The flames crackled and snapped. The hands holding her released, and Nadine kicked her legs, holding her and Gabriella on the surface. Gabriella coughed as she tried to kick. The air shimmered with the smoke, and heat thrown off of the burning ships. The side of the boat boomed as a porthole was blown open by the heat.

"I oughta take your beard and tie it to one of those stupid horses you have and have you dragged across the desert. At Noon. Naked. Facedown."

The boat crackled again in the background.

"I think," Arpad said, "I think that means she is okay."

"Yes," Vidor said. "Even on short acquaintance, I believe that screaming death threats is her default mode."

"It's my happy place," Nadine said. "I go there when I'm stressed. Brie, how are you?"

Gabriella coughed, sputtered, then coughed again. "My legs hurt, but I'm okay."

"Mine too," Nadine said. "We hit hard."

"We must stay together," Vidor said. "It will be easy to get lost in the dark. Take my hand."

"I'll take it all right," Nadine said. "I'll take it and shove it up your—never mind. Brie can't swim."

"But she can float," Arpad said. "And kick. I will get under your shoulder, Ms. Brie. Lie on your back and kick as hard as you can."

"And I'll tow you along, Ms. Nadine."

"If you do that, I'll reinstate my shoving protocol. I'm fine. Help Brie. And where's this shore that you're talking about?"

"Over there." Vidor pointed through the darkness. "Due south."

Nadine swam back to Arpad and Brie. She had rolled over on her back, and he was towing her by her right hand, talking softly to her.

"Brie? What's your status?"

"I can kick, and Arpad is helping."

"We'll be okay. Just keep floating and kicking, and we'll get out of this."

"We need to move along," Vidor said. "We must go quickly. Arpad, swim faster."

"Easy up, Vidi," Nadine said. "Give us a few minutes to get Brie settled here before we move off."

"We cannot stay here," Vidor said.

"And why not? The boat's already on fire and burning to the waterline. What's the worst that could happen to us now?"

"When the boat sinks, the water will reach the steam boiler and condensers," Arpad said. "The cold water will hit the superheated steam and cause an explosion. Red-hot shards of exploding metal and burning wood will explode outward, showering us with debris."

Nadine rolled over. Steam hissed as the boat sank lower. "You heard the man, Arpad. Get towing. Faster. Faster."

***

Jake, Tam, Ket, and Kivi dropped into the water together, holding hands. Tam and Ket yelled "Stride jump" and spread their legs and arms. The women slapped their hands down as soon as they hit the water. Jake's head ducked underwater for only a second, then popped back up.

"Raft dead ahead," Tam said. "Everybody okay to swim there?"

The other three answered yes, and they released hands and splashed away.

Jake reached the life raft and tried to lift out. It floated much higher than expected, so he couldn't reach high enough.

"Like this," Tam said. "Put one foot on the hanging ropes, then step up." She demonstrated by standing and rolling onto the raft.

Jake and the others followed. The four rested for a few seconds, then rolled and looked back at the burning boat.

Fire engulfed it from stem to stern. Bright yellow

flames stretched out of every opening—doors, windows, portholes, skylights. The decks and hull burned, not just the bulkheads. The wheels were stopped, and it floated in a glowing tableau of fire and flame.

The fire crackled loud enough they had to yell.

"The wheels aren't turning, but it's moving away," Jake said.

"The tide will push it along. But the rudder is locked over. It's stuck. See at the back?" Tam said.

The glow of the fire lit the scene, and the curved wake glowed white in the dark.

"Are we the only survivors?" Kivi said.

"Others went into the water," Ket said. "There's another raft. Far back."

"I see people on it, not sure how many."

"Why are there none in the water near us?" Jake said.

"We may have been the last off," Tam said. "The others jumped right away. While the ship was still moving, they will be farther back. Others were trapped inside. My father." Tam sobbed and grabbed her mouth. "He burns."

"No," Jake said. "No, he doesn't. We know all about fire in enclosed rooms on spaceships. It's the toxic gas that gets you. The carbon monoxide. It happens quickly. You cough at first, then you fall asleep and just drift off. It's painless. He won't have known what hit him. He would have fallen asleep in thirty seconds."

"Really?" Tam said.

"Yes," Jake said. "We have records and films. We train for those things."

"Is that true, Mr. Kivi?" Tam said.

Kivi caught Jake's eye. Jake nodded minutely. Kivi coughed. "Yes, ma'am. It happens very quickly. Carbon monoxide is deadly."

That was true, but he was condensing the time by a factor of ten.

Tam continued to snuffle and buried her head into Jake's shoulder.

"What now?" Jake said. "Where are we?"

Ket waved north. "That's the northern shore. It's inhabited. Not densely, but there are farms. My people's farms. If we can get ashore, we can find people who will help us."

"Won't people come to rescue us?"

"With what?" Ket said. "That was the biggest riverboat on Magyar. There are others but none as big, and they will take hours to be made ready to sail. The currents are strong. And how will they find us?"

"Surely somebody had a comm—the baron's guard, at least."

"Look at the waves, and the wind," Ket said. "The wind was blowing with the tide while we were on the boat. That makes for smooth sailing. Flat, smooth waves. The tide will turn shortly. Then the wind and tide will be fighting each other. The waves will get bigger and steeper as the tide and wind fight."

"When they fight, who wins?"

"Everybody on a boat loses. The water will be much rougher than this. Nothing smaller than a big river boat will be able to fight its way down that strait for hours. Even if they wanted to send somebody to rescue the baron, it would be nearly impossible. If they can even find where to look."

"That should be easy," Kivi said. He pointed. "We have a giant burning flare floating along the water there. It must be visible for miles."

The lights brightened. The fire flared and cracked, then the rear of the boat settled deeper into the water. The fires dimmed as the water rushed in. Steam hissed.

KA-BOOM. The back of the boat exploded. A deluge of water, burning wood, and debris rose into the air, then showered down on them. They all ducked onto the raft. Wood pattered into the water. Something clanked next to them.

"Pipe," Kivi said "Whoa, that looks red-hot." He used

134

his shoes to kick the pipe into the water.

Steam hissed as it sank. Jake and the others stood and stamped out burning embers.

The front of the riverboat had split into pieces. Each piece bobbed in the water, then sank. Thousands of pieces of floating, burning wood riddled the ocean. The fires doused as they watched. In two minutes, only six small lights were visible floating in the murk.

"Oh, good," Jake said. "We'll be easy to find now."

***

The light from the explosion reached Nadine first, the noise and shock wave two seconds later. Glowing trails of burning wood rained into the water, then died out.

"Well, that turned out to be a good prediction, Arpad," Nadine said. "Your record is pretty good at this point. What next?"

"We keep swimming. Or, in Ms. Gabriella's case, floating. At this rate, we will be on the southern shore within an hour. Sooner if the current helps."

"And we don't get lost," Gabriella said.

"We cannot get lost, Ms. Gabriella," Arpad said. "That triangle ahead of us? Those three bright stars? That is the southern triangle. Rendor, Gyala, and Ica. It is named after three good friends who traveled our lands. The southern planetary pole is in the middle of them. When we are alone with our herds on the steppe, we use it as our way home. As long as we keep swimming to it, we will be heading south. If we head south, we will strike land. The stars point our way to salvation."

"That's pretty smart, Mr. Arpad," Gabriella said.

"Please, just Arpad."

"Arpad. You can call me Brie."

Nadine snorted. "The stars point our way to salvation? Three good friends? Brie, he's just trying to sound romantic to get into your pants. You're not falling for that, are you?"

"Oh, I know that," Brie said. "No, I'm not falling for it. And we don't need the stars. If I stretch back my head, I can see land ahead. Those cliffs."

Nadine lifted her head higher from the water. "You're right. Not far."

They paddled quietly for a moment. "Arpad?"

"Yes, miss?"

"Just 'cause I see through your plan doesn't mean it might not work. Tell me some more stories."

Nadine laughed as Arpad and Gabriella conversed quietly. "Vidor, you have some stories of your own to tell me? How the horse god insists we strip naked and cover each other with mud to celebrate our fortune."

Vidor paddled for a moment. "We are fortunate, yes, but I feel for the others. There were many on that boat."

"Well, life is for the living. We need to—the Empress's hairy vagina. Your father was on that ship, wasn't he?"

"He attended the baron, as his job required."

"Maybe he got out. Maybe he got up and ran at the first sign of trouble."

"You know as well as I do that the fire moved quickly, and few escaped. We are lucky that we were in the back, near an exit. Our lack of standing secured our lives. No, my father would have been near the head table, surrounded by men and women he despised. He would have sat, eating his meal, even while the table burned under him, rather than shame himself in front of those."

"You're probably right. I'm sorry about your father."

"A man lives as long as he lives and no longer."

"Right, sure," Nadine said. "Is that a religious saying?"

"Something my ancestors said."

"You worship your ancestors, then?"

"No, why did you say that?"

"Well, I mean, you have this whole revere your family, ancestor lore, that sort of thing. I just figured you'd worship them or a horse god or something."

Vidor laughed, then snorted as he inhaled waters.

"We're Christians," Vidor said.

"Christians?" Nadine said. "I've heard of that. You worship the ghost of a dead carpenter, right? And drink lots of wine."

Vidor snorted again. "That is an odd way of saying it but substantially true. We do not drink wine. Or dance. Or sing. We are modest in our clothing and behavior. Quiet. On our feast day, we worship quietly and pray all day. We must have many children and carnal relations before marriage are forbidden."

"Forbidden?" Nadine paddled more. "But I mean, you and your friends, the way you... behave?"

"Behave? Oh, we are reprehensible," Vidor said. "We are poor Christians. But I take solace in being a bad Christian."

"Solace?"

"Yes. We have great room for improvement."

"I see," Nadine said. "Well, good for you. Still, I feel bad about your father. And even the baron. Even the baron. Vidor?"

"Yes, Ms. Nadine?"

"Your father is probably dead, and I'm sorry about that. I don't think many got out of the front of the boat."

"I don't think so, either."

"Since he's dead and his son? And the leaders of the city factions... wouldn't that mean that now you can..."

"Honor my father's memory by instituting a just government of free-born men and women loyal to the Empire, who treat each other with honor and dignity. Yes. I can do that."

"I was going to say seize control with a few hundred of your armed friends, but sure, honor. And dignity. That too. Dignity is always good."

"I will make myself a king, under the Emperor, of course. Ms. Nadine, your questions before dinner impressed me. You know many things, and you think deeply. Will you help us?"

"Me? Think deeply," Nadine said. "Maybe in a relative sense to some people. Not that those people aren't good in their own ways... But no, no, this isn't my fight."

"Are you sure? You could help show me the way. The way to the palace."

"The palace—well, it's not my palace. We're not from here. Not our circus, not our monkeys."

"What is a monkey?"

"I have no idea. My friend Jake Stewart said that once."

"I am sorry. I have been insensitive. Your friend is probably dead as well. I grieve with you."

"Jake? No, Jake won't be dead. No chance."

"You seem certain."

"I am. Jake always has a plan and then a backup plan and then a backup backup plan. If I know Jake, he got off that ship, and he's reclining in a chair, drinking wine fed to him by some half-naked slave girl while he figures out how to spend the obscene profit he made from the ship sinking."

CHAPTER SIXTEEN

"Another bottle, Jake?" Tam said, leaning over to him and putting a hand on his shoulder.

Jake was having problems figuring out where to look. Tam's few clothes that had survived the fire were soaking wet, plastered to her body and now largely see through, leaving no doubt she was a healthy young woman. They had broken out the rations of food and water on the raft and, with no way to steer it, waited to find where the current took them. Midway through the night, they had salvaged random pieces of wood they'd bumped into, including a chest, two chairs, and a case of wine, complete with corkscrew, that floated by. Jake and Tam were on watch, scanning the lightening horizon, sitting in the charred chairs, drinking the wine. The others slept.

"No thanks. But that wine is better than any I've ever tasted before."

"Better, indeed," Tam said. "Ten thousand credits. That's my offer to help us."

"First, I don't know how much your credits are worth," Jake said. "And I can't spend them back on Delta. Which means we need to trade. What type of commodities do you have?"

"Flax. Linen. Cotton. Sugar. Wheat, barley, vegetables. Processed oils. Juices."

"Orange juice? Lime juice? Cottonseed oil?"

"Sure. Give us some time, and we could come up with it."

"We can do a deal," Jake said. "I just need the particulars."

"But you know that's not all we want." Tam took a swig from her bottle. "I want your advice on the political situation."

"Is now the time? I mean, with everything that happened."

"Should I just sit down and cry over my father's death? Drink another few bottles. Is that a better way to spend my time?"

"Of course not."

"He's gone, and he's not coming back. I'll grieve privately. He'd want me to do something. But I need help."

"I'm not a politician."

"You know what I mean. The city people have to choose a new leader, a new baron. We're not used to that. We only have the Empire as a model, and they aren't here now. Having a disinterested person watching over things and giving advice on how to govern a planet would be useful."

"We haven't exactly done a stellar job ourselves," Jake said.

"Yes, but you came to us. We didn't come to you, so you must have done something right." She handed him the nearly empty bottle.

"We've done a lot of things right," Jake said, draining the last of the bottle. "Not all of them apply to you."

"Well, we could make it work. It would be helpful to have you overseeing things."

"Tam, you told me you were just going to bribe you way into more influence."

Tam nodded. "That's what we do. And it's easy. We move incrementally. Every time we help one family or another gains prominence, we've gotten more freedom or better trading options or things like that. Slow and steady wins the race."

"You don't want to rule the city? The whole planet?"

"It's a lot of work and for what? We're largely self-governing now, and there isn't much in the city we need. If we were in charge, we'd have the problem of feeding and clothing and governing all the city people. What would we get? Access to the harbor, better trade deals. We can bribe our way to those right now. The only other thing would be a drafty palace and the Imperial archives and computers."

"Imperial archives? Computers?" Jake said. "What type of archives?"

"Regular planetary ones. The full databases from the Empire survive. That's one of the reasons that the fusion plant was put here. To support the scientific exploration in this sector. There was a—what do you call it? Astrogorp? Department here."

"Astrography? Records of stations and planets and such like."

"That's it."

"Would it have things like navigation charts?"

"Probably," Tam said. "Why? Do you need some?"

Jake thought of their misbehaving computer and their ancient databases. "We have our own charts, but it's always good to have recourse to other copies. For comparison and validation. Not necessary but useful."

"Well, if we ever take control of the baron's palace, also known as the old Imperial administration building, I'll make you a gift of them."

***

Nadine touched ground under the waves and stood, then fell again as the waves smashed her over. She burbled along for a moment, got her feet under her, and staggered closer to the shore. She pedaled her legs and leaned into the water. After ten meters, she crawled on all fours. Then she tried standing again and running forward before clambering out of the water and onto the sand. She continued up past the high tide mark and dropped. Vidor walked out beside her, checked that she was okay, then went to help Arpad and Gabriella out of the surf. The sun had risen, and the beach was still cool. She shivered and clasped her arms around herself. Gabriella stumbled up and sat next to her.

"That wasn't so bad," Gabriella said.

"The fire, nearly burning to death, avoiding breaking our necks jumping, or the nearly killer swim through tidal waters to this barren shore?" Nadine asked.

"I meant the beach. It was easy to climb up," Gabriella said. "Pretty gloomy, aren't you?"

"Sorry," Nadine said. She sniffed.

"He's probably okay," Gabriella said.

"No, he's probably not. I lost my communicator during the jump. Can't call. Can you?"

Gabriella pulled a battered comm unit from her pocket. "I already tried. My communicator doesn't work. Salt water got it. I can't call, either." She rubbed salt water from her eyes. "You told Vidor that Jake gets out of everything."

"He does. He did. I'm not sure this time."

"It's just us?"

"And we're alone in the desert with two near savage herdsman, our friends are dead, and we're miles away from our shuttle."

"On the flip side," Gabriella said, "they're both kind of cute."

"Ah, to be young again."

"What do we do now, Nadine?"

"We need to get back to their capital—the 'city'—and then confirm what happened to the others."

"And then we go back to the ship and fly back to Delta."

"Yeah, about that flying back to Delta," Nadine said. "Since Jake might be dead, you should know. Bad news..." She explained the problems with the jump computer.

"It needs to be reprogrammed?"

"I think more updated and given the latest database."

"And you can do that?"

"Nadine the Programmer, they call me."

"Nadine, you're great fun and a wonderful pilot, but I'm sure nobody in the history of the Empire ever called you a great programmer."

"I'm sure I can fix it."

"You can fix something that Jake Stewart can't?"

"Shut up." Nadine stood. Vidor and Arpad were conferring a distance away. "Let's go see the boys." The two women traipsed over.

Arpad was drawing in the dirt.

"Figuring out a way to get us rescued? Drawing maps of likely ways to build signal fires?"

"Signal fires?" Vidor said. "Why would we do that?"

"Oh, I don't know." Nadine put her hands on her hips. "Because we're lost on a barren, isolated, rocky shore next to a desert, and we're going to die of hunger and thirst before anybody comes looking for us?"

"Lost?"

"Yes."

"Isolated, rocky shore?"

"Look around—do you see anything other than rocks, sand, and this stupid brown stuff?"

"Seaweed."

"Seaweek, water week, who cares? Where are we? How do we get out of here?"

Vidor and Arpad exchanged looks, then Vidor stood. "Ms. Nadine, we are not lost. We are only three day's hike from the city. The road is just over those dunes." He pointed inland. "Perhaps a hundred yards that way. It's a good road here—rock. No mud this time of the year. And it has good fords across all the rivers."

"I see," Nadine said. "What about water?"

"Arpad has been on this very beach before."

Arpad nodded. "Yes, my second cousin's summer grazing is perhaps two miles that way." He pointed east.

"There is a small stream. Not much water, but it will suit for us. We can be there in an hour. We might even find some cattle for food." He smiled. "I played with him right here when I was seven. We made sandcastles."

Nadine kicked the sand. "We're not lost?"

"No, Ms. Nadine."

"Or going to die of thirst?"

"No, Ms. Nadine."

"Right." Nadine looked at the diagram. "So, what are you drawing there?"

"Our plans to seize power. Now that the baron is dead, we will seize the city, and I will make myself king—under the Emperor, of course. Arpad will be my vizier."

"A vizier? Is that good?"

"It's like a chancellor, only better."

"Good for you."

"Will you help us?" Vidor asked.

"As I mentioned before, not my circus, not my don't-know-what-they-are-but-called-monkeys."

"I see."

"Mr. Vidor," Gabriella said, "if you take over the city, you'll be in charge of the old Imperial buildings, too. Like the old Imperial computers and libraries?"

"Of course."

"Do you have star charts and software and the like there? For merchants like us?"

"Why, of course," Vidor said. "My uncle traded with the city family that was in charge of the wharf customs. They had old Imperial computers with many software packages from the days of the Empire. Things for starships. For jump ships. They offered some to him in trade, but he had no use for them."

"Jump ships? There is software for jump ships here?" Nadine said.

"I think so."

Nadine grinned at Gabriella. She grinned back. "Tell us about your plan. To take power?"

"Well, now that the baron is gone, there will be chaos in the capital city. We will take advantage of this. We, the four of us, march in the direction of the city. Within only a few miles, we will find some of my people. We will send messengers, and I will call a thousand of my clan with weapons. They will converge here."

"Here?" Nadine pointed down. "This place?"

"Yes, a thousand brave warriors."

"And what, Mr. Kill 'Em All, will these brave warriors eat while they are standing here?"

***

"Bribery is not enough," Jake said. "You need to take direct action. Before one of these groups gets into power and nullifies all your previous work. Move into town and seize the palace. Or administration building. Whatever it's called. You know what, I'm just going to call it the palace for simplicity. There can't be more than a couple hundred troops there. And they're not even troops, more like armed security guards. You could be there in a day."

Everybody was awake by then, drinking water and eating. The raft contained enough food and water to handle twenty people for a week, plenty for them.

"Who could be there in a day?" Tam said. "Our corps of trained killers?"

"Can we make the shore over there?" Jake pointed at low hills on the horizon.

"Can't avoid it," Tam said. "With this tide shifting, we're going to wash right into that bay. We just sit here, and we'll be ashore in a few hours."

Jake sat back in his chair. "I'm not saying kill people. But if you want to be part of the political process, especially in uncertain times, you need logistics, political leadership, administration, and some sort of police or military. Especially the military. Are those rocks?" Jake pointed at some swells ahead.

"No, that's the start of the swamps. Sandy bottom. Once we get there, we'll be stuck. We'll have to hop off and head to shore."

"Hop off? That doesn't sound good."

"It's not a pleasant walk, but we can do it in a few hours. Jake, you sound like you're advocating a coup. Taking over the government."

"From what you told me, you got dropped here with nothing, made a success of your farms and businesses, organized things. You have your own laws and courts, don't you? Your county thing?"

"Well, yes. Each county has a judge, and we handle legal and commercial matters. If it's just us. It's also where we have the agricultural institute. And, of course, the branch office of our insurance operations."

"You have insurance companies here?"

"It was one of the first things we established. Life, crop, transport, all kinds of insurance."

Jake looked up at the sky. "I love this planet."

Tam hadn't heard him. "In fact, my first job was with one of the insurance companies. I was an auditor for four years. Anything you want to know about insurance, I can tell you."

"What was your job?"

"Long-term planning. I enjoyed it."

Jake looked at her. "You're a Roman-history-loving girl who enjoys long-term planning and working for an insurance company?"

"I guess you could say that," Tam said. "Is that important?"

Jake muttered something that sounded like cruel joke.

"What was that?"

"Never mind. How do you interact with the city people or the Ranchers?"

"If the city is involved or any city people, we have to follow their rules. Which are biased in favor of them. Of course, we can, in theory, appeal to the Emperor's justice, his representative here."

"Which would be the baron?"

"Right, but that never happens."

"Because he doesn't want to deal with you?"

"Because any Planter who did would never be able to deal with his friends or neighbors again. None of the commercial councils would certify her work again. The commercial councils set the standards for crops, weights and measures, handles purely civil matters."

"Let me get this straight," Jake said. "You already self-govern your own area—all of your own lands. You have your judges, your own laws, your own law courts. All certified, legal by the Empire. Do you have your own police?"

"No police."

"We have the sheriffs," Ket said. "They're elected in each county. They enforce the laws and customs of the county. Once they're elected, they set a tax rate, and they hire assistants. They're armed, usually."

"Guns, shotguns?"

"Sometimes."

The raft rocked, and the chairs tipped over. "We just drifted out of the main channel," Ket said. "That was one of the barrier sandbars."

Jake set his chair back upright. "You said they administer a county. What exactly is a county? How big is it? How many people?"

"They vary in size," Tam said, "but the idea is that each farming area has a town, a county seat. And the county is a day's ride in every direction, so anybody who needs services can go to the county seat. When we set up the original land grants, every county seat got some medical and technology. They have a medical clinic, a library, and a school. The county taxpayers pay for the sheriff, a judge, a librarian and their assistants. The trade guilds have collection points there, and we use that to collect crops before dispatching them to trade with the city."

"And each county sends a delegate to the annual council meeting," Ket said. "Once a year, we all meet to agree on any regulations that should be passed and instruct the judges accordingly."

"Sounds like a government to me," Jake said. "And the Empire approved of this?"

"They did. It's in our charter. But they're not here now."

"And you use the sheriffs to enforce public order and deal with miscreants and criminals. Do you have prisons?"

"No. We fine people—either money or work. If it's a serious crime, they're banished. They just ride over the hills and into the wilderness. Outside of the settled areas, it can get wild."

"What if the sheriff and their assistants can't handle things themselves?"

"They call out a posse. They swear in any people they need. We usually ask for volunteers, but we can conscript people if it's important enough."

"Which you do if there is a threat to public order big enough."

"Right," Tam said. "Hang on, here we go."

The water shallowed, and grasses filled the horizon. The waves were breaking on a sandbar twenty feet ahead. The raft slid up and became stuck. Tam and Ket had them hop out to push it forward, and in a few minutes, they were floating up to the muddy grass.

"I'd say that the loss of the entire governing elite of the planet is a crisis," Jake said.

"For sure," Tam said. "But is it our crisis? We could just stay out of it."

"The governor is probably dead. His possible successor is probably dead. Anybody he could have named as his successor is probably dead," Jake said. "Right?"

The two women nodded.

"And you have a warrant from the Empire for self-government, correct?"

"We do."

"How many of those counties do you have? And how big are they?"

"Twenty-four. Average a thousand people. Some bigger, some smaller."

"And each one of those has one of those sheriff people, right?"

"Yep."

"Who can call up a posse in the event of potential civil disorder?"

"Yep. Where are you going with this, Jake?"

"The baron is dead. There will probably be unrest in the city. Why not have each of those sheriffs call up a posse of a dozen people and ride into the city to enforce Imperial laws and take control in the name of the Emperor?"

"In the name of the Emperor?"

"Absolutely." Jake smiled. "Take over the planet in the name of the rightful Emperor—Dashi the First."

CHAPTER SEVENTEEN

"Kivi's comm is right here." Odette pointed at the sensor screen. "Right in the middle of this river or bay or whatever you call it."

"Proper name is a strait," Willowby said. "Connects two pieces of ocean."

Yvette, Odette, and Willowby lounged in the control room. Magyar loomed large on the main screen. A blue dot demarcated a spot in the water.

"Doesn't matter what those dirtside people call it," Odette said. "What matters is that it's also fifty meters below water level."

"He could have dropped it, swam to shore."

"Could have. But did el supremo, chubby girl, and the other child drop theirs?"

"A whole bunch of reasons they might not be responding," Willowby said. "They're busy. Tired. Maybe they're involved in a four-way orgy and don't want to answer comm."

Yvette laughed. "Not Jake. He wouldn't do that."

"Because you think he's an upright individual?"

"Because we tried. Besides, chubby girl would shoot whoever made a move on Mr. Jake. Then shoot Mr. Jake."

Willowby bit his lip. "If that's what you think, why do you keep hitting on Captain Jake?"

"He's attractive. But mostly because it annoys her. A lot," Yvette said.

"We like to annoy her," Odette said.

"One of these days, she's going to shoot first," Willowby said.

"Or we will," Odette said. "The soul of the Empress willing."

"Don't break my ship when you do."

"They are not coming back, Professor."

"They could be involved in something we don't know about yet."

"Possible. Not likely. What is more likely is this." Odette brought up another image on the screen.

It was a thermal view of the paddle wheeler. Red people-sized dots swarmed over the ship. The boilers glowed a brighter red in the middle. Two blue dots shone on the left side near the middle, another two on the right. The recording ran, and a yellow bloom appeared in the middle, then brightened.

Over the next few minutes, the yellow expanded and covered most of the middle of the boat. The red dots swarmed over the side or stopped and merged into the yellow bloom. The blue dots zigzagged back and forth on either side. Two moved right and appeared briefly in the water, dimmed, then winked out. The other two raced to the back of the boat till they were surrounded by the bright yellow, then they departed. One dimmed, then disappeared. The other floated back behind the boat, then sat there.

The yellow bloom brightened and covered the whole ship. A dark green spot appeared on one side of the plume and crept into the side of the yellow. It continued till it reached nearly the center of the frame. Then the whole picture blew out in a cascade of red and yellow. The camera zoomed out, and red-and-yellow fireflies covered the screen and then dimmed. A minute later, only one of two dull red spots remained, a single dim blue one floating away.

"Blue is the comm units, of course," Willowby said. "That one that got away?"

"It sank. We could barely read it."

"The others got into the water? Why didn't their

comms stay on?"

"They're not waterproof," Yvette said.

"It's Old Empire technology. How can they not be waterproof?"

"First, they weren't designed to be waterproof. Especially not for salt water. You can be vacuum proof and not waterproof. Second, they're probably a hundred years old. Definitely a crack or two in them."

"They got off that ship, though," Willowby said.

"But they're not among the survivors picked up, according to the radio reports we heard. It sounded like there wasn't much hope for survivors. The fires spread extremely quickly and then that explosion. Many of the people who went into the water were badly burned, and they died before that hovercraft got there."

"It should have got there more quickly," Willowby said.

"He said the tide was too big—or the current. No, the waves. He said the waves were too big for it to get there quickly."

"What's happening now?"

"He said he had to go into the city to 'consult.' I think the comm facility is not directly in the city—it's up on a hill somewhere. We haven't been able to contact him since."

"This is bad."

"We want to go back the way we came. We found the Empire. We can do some trading. We have scans, notes, comm logs."

"And now we have enough food to get back," Yvette said.

"Just sail back when we've come all this way?" Willowby said.

"Yes."

"What if I say no? Are you going to shoot me?"

"Are you saying no?" Yvette asked.

Odette stopped playing with her screen. Neither woman held a weapon, but they freed their shooting hands.

Willowby bit his lip again. "We need to give him time. There could still be survivors."

"Two days. You said it would take two days to refuel."

"More or less."

"So, we refuel. For two days. Top off our tanks. Count our provisions."

"And then jump out? Leave them here?"

"They might already be dead. But we're not sure. Let's go get fueled up. We can stay in contact with the planet. If they answer."

"Okay." Willowby stood. "Let's go to the gas giant and fuel up."

Yvette and Odette exchanged glances. "Okay? That's it."

"Yes. Okay. We'll get fuel."

"No complaints, no more demands to stay here."

"They might be dead. We need fuel. I'm going to check the engines. Give me an hour, and we can leave." He fumbled the hatch open, then slammed it shut behind him.

Odette changed the display. Dark red groups traveled between concentrations of light in the north and south. "At night, this is quite a sight."

"Yes," Yvette agreed. She rubbed her chin.

"That was too easy, wasn't it?"

"Is there any chance he knows about the other Free Trader ships?"

"I didn't tell him. We didn't tell him."

"I'm suspicious. But we need fuel."

"But he knows something. Somebody told him something."

"Who?"

Yvette tapped the screen and watched the explosion play back again in slow motion. "Are we completely sure that Jake Stewart is dead?"

CHAPTER EIGHTEEN

"Five kilograms," Nadine said, "per person, per day. Two liters of water, and a liter is a kilogram. Two kilograms of food and one kilogram of other stuff, like tools or parts or arrows or what have you. And that's just the men. Horses need water. How much water does a horse drink a day?"

Vidor and Arpad looked at each other. "Well, a lot, but they can use streams—"

"Not a thousand at a time. Not these little streams. They'll clog them up. And what if we need to go somewhere without water?"

Nadine had convinced the two men not to call out the clan to ride to the town till they could figure out the logistics of it. They had to wait until civilization, regardless. Outside of the city, they didn't have comms, just local radio relays.

"And you can slaughter a cow and eat it, but the meat doesn't keep, does it?"

"No, it only lasts two days fresh. We can smoke it."

"How much do you smoke? How long does it take? What tools do you need? How much wood does it take?"

"We usually slaughter one cow a week in my family," Arpad said. "And we eat it for days. Maybe four by the time we sort it out..."

Nadine spent the next four hours helping them plan their campaign.

"If you do get a thousand 'heroes of your clan,' as you call them, somewhere to ride, then you'll need two tons of food, two tons of water, and one ton of miscellaneous items for the fighting men. And fighting women and the horses—you say five liters a day—that's five tons of water just for the horses. And that's every, single, day."

"Ms. Nadine, if I understand your numbers, then five tons a day will not be enough. Most of us, when we are on the range or travelling, we have two or three horses each."

"So, we triple that. You need twenty tons of provisions and water arriving a day, every day, and they have to start out from somewhere, and those people bringing them need to be fed..."

It took the rest of the day to figure that out as they walked down the road.

"We can take the city by storm," Vidor said. "Our men will ride in and capture the palace."

"And what if they don't? There's walls," Nadine said. "And you have to get across the strait. You need to go east first, then cross with boats, or swim it, like you showed me, then head back west. By the time you do that, they'll, for sure, close the gates. Then you'll be picking your nose outside the walls, with no way to get in, getting shot to pieces by those Gauss rifles I saw."

"They only have six," Vidor said. "In the baron's armory."

"That's six more than you have. Those things can shoot five kilometers. What about the other tech I saw in town? A laser on a boat. That shoots ten kilometers. What do you have that can shoot that far?"

"Nothing," Vidor said.

"You have to be prepared to blockade the city if you can't get in or overwhelm them in a big charge. Attack at multiple points at once. Which means you need a lot of troops over there. Which means you need to feed them."

By the next town, Vidor and Arpad knew what to do. Because Nadine told them. They sent out riders to collect food and water at four ranches, each a day's ride from the crossing of the strait. The crossing area was just where the water was narrowest and had no current at slack water.

Once the groups had collected at the staging points, and once they had collected food and what weapons they had, they would move forward in relays. When the tide dropped, they would swim all the horses across at the narrowest point. The supplies could be rafted over. Once on the other side, they would race to the city and try to rush in.

"Working backward," Nadine said. "On the far side, it takes a day to race for the city, a day to cross the strait to get there, and a day to gather from the collection points. You need everybody to be ready at the collection points with whatever food they need to get there and a week's more worth each, food for them and the horses. Make sure there is plenty of food and water for the horses at those staging points."

"We can use the river valleys close by, with plenty of grass. But once we move farther along the coast, it may prove difficult."

"So, three days' worth of water. How will you carry water?"

That started another long technical discussion between the two riders. Nadine and Gabriella walked behind them while they argued.

"I didn't realize you knew anything about horses," Gabriella said.

"Horses? I barely know which end the manure comes out of," Nadine said. "I did spend some summers on a ranch, but I'm not an expert. But this is just logistics. It's like loading a spaceship with fuel and food. So many people for so long eat so often, and that has to be paid for and stored and moved. And somebody has to cook it. Wait till the boys discover that."

"It's still pretty impressive," Gabriella said. "They'll make you their army general if you ask."

"General Nadine. I like that."

"Where did you learn all this? About armies?"

"A wise man once said, 'Amateurs talk strategy,

professionals talk logistics.'"

"Who was that wise man?"

"Jake Stewart." Nadine plodded along. "He's better at this than me. I wish he was here."

***

"We need to get everyone moving," Jake said to Tam. They had spent an hour wading through the swamp until stumbling on the main shore. Fields of grain, orange and lemon trees, and cotton lined the road. The road was built of crushed rock, dry and level. "Get word to your sheriffs and get the posses moving. The sooner we can get them in front of the city gates, the better."

"We need to make sure that we can feed them," Tam said.

"Every one of your towns has a granary and storehouse," Jake said. "Plus warehouses, and you have all these carting companies. Just contract them to deliver the food to that nearest county seat. It's a two-day march from the capital city. Gather everyone there, mount up, and race for the city. The carts can follow behind them."

"We can't just rush into things."

"You need to rush into things. Strike while the iron is hot," Jake said. "Once you are moving, your logistics train can catch up with you. But we need to get this strike force here before the city people figure out what's going on."

"I don't know."

"You can do this," Jake said. "Charge right in while they're disorganized. An organized charge will always prevail over a disorganized opponent. Ancient military maximum."

"Who said that?"

"Septimus Servus."

Tam bit her lip. "I need to talk to Ket." She walked away.

"I never realized that you were this aggressive, sir," Kivi said.

"I'm not. Usually, I'm the one the on suggesting caution. Now I understand why Nadine was exasperated all the time. She was so much better at this than I was. I wish she was here."

"Do you think she and Brie are okay?"

"I'm sure of it," Jake said. "Soon as the fire started, they would have leaped overboard and swam ashore. She knows all about fire. I imagine right now she and her herder friends are roaming around the southern range there in wild abandon. Chasing cattle, having barbeque, lighting campfires, and drinking some sort of local booze, having the time of their lives."

***

"We are going to count them all again," Nadine said. "And, this time, you're going to write it down properly, and if I find any discrepancies in your paperwork, I am going to stab you in the liver, understand?" She glared at the assembled riders.

They had spent the night at Vidor's great-great-uncle's farm—or Arpad's cousin or some such relation. Possibly, they were the same person. With Nadine's help, they had crafted messages to his clan family, instructing them on how to join his horde in their revolution. The first of the provision-carrying groups had arrived at the ranch stable already.

"I have ridden all night to support Vidor, and I don't take orders from some foreign bimbo," a short man in the front said. "You will not speak to me this way. Besides, there's no way you're going to be able to stab me in the liver."

Nadine glared at him, then threw her hands wide and beamed a smile at him. "You know, you're right. What was your name again?"

"Kidar," the man said. "I am Vidor's cousin."

"Third cousin," Arpad said.

"Of course you are." Nadine stepped forward and stroked his arm. "Kidar, sweetie... may I call you Kidar?"

"Yes, of course." His brows furrowed.

"Here's the thing, Kidar, sweetie," Nadine said. "I've been up all night, Vidor and Arpad and Brie and I, planning how to move a thousand people to the gates of the palace. We've been sending messages, getting reports on how many people are gathering, what type of weapons they have, what type of food they're bringing, how many horses, what kind, all sorts of things. I haven't had much sleep. None of us have. We're tired and perhaps a little bit grumpy. You understand, don't you, Kidar, sweetheart?"

"Well, yes, I suppose that makes sense."

"And we're glad that you came and that you brought your sword. Your big sword." Nadine smiled again. "But the thing is, if we get all these people together, and we end up in the middle of the desert with no food, then all of us are going to starve. Or just be killed by the baron's remaining people. I don't want to starve. Do you want to starve?"

"Well, no," Kidar said. "But we won't starve. We have enough food for ourselves."

"For how long?" Nadine said.

"A week? Longer, maybe?"

"And you brought food for others? Some of that preserved cheese you promised?"

"Well, yes, but I don't know how much. We didn't bother to count it. We weren't going far."

"The thing is, Kidar, we have people coming here who have farther to come, so we told them to just ride and not worry about provisions, that we would feed them when they got here."

"They should have brought their own food," Kidar said.

"They were promised food," Nadine said, "by Vidor and I, because you were going to be bringing it. If we don't know how much food you brought, we can't have all of them come here, or some will have to wait till later or wait for more food. Or we starve, or this fight fails. You understand that?"

"Well, yes, I suppose," Kidar said.

Nadine kicked the ground. "Sand. Lots of sand here. And you promised you would bring five hundred pounds of cheese on your pack horses, but we don't know how much you have. Because you don't know how many horses are carrying cheese. Isn't that true?" Nadine raised her eyebrows. "True, right. You don't know how much food you have?"

The group nodded.

"And if you don't know, we don't know, and we need to know to tell Vidor's other cousin how many people to bring—and when. And we need to do that right now." Nadine beamed at the assembled group. "You know what else I don't know?"

Kidar shook his head. "No."

"I don't know where the human liver is located. Not exactly. But I have a plan for that. Would you like to hear it?"

Kidar nodded.

Nadine reached for his arm again. This time, she yanked his hand, pivoted, and slammed his arm up behind his back. Kidar yelped. Nadine propelled him across the room, scattering henchmen from side to side. She slammed him into the wall once, then again. She yanked, tripped him over her foot, and dropped him face-first into the sand. Clouds of dust blew up from the floor. She kept her knee on his back and his arm jammed up between his shoulder blades. She fumbled for her knife.

Kidar struggled to get up, then froze.

Nadine had her knife inches away from his eye. "Here's my plan. I'm going to let you up to go count what types of food you have, how much, and which horses have which type of food. And you're going to write all that down and bring it to me immediately. If I don't get that answer from you in writing in ten minutes, I'm going to hunt you down and stab you a hundred times in different places. One of those places is bound to be your liver. So, in ten minutes, either I know what you've brought, or I know where your liver is. For me, it won't be a wasted day."

She shook his arm and made him yelp. "Any questions?"

"But..." Kidar said.

Nadine slammed his face into the sand and ground his reply out. "None? Good. Remember, provisions or liver. Your choice." She confronted the group of stunned riders. "What? None of you can count? Or write? Go!"

The crowd scattered.

Nadine folded her arms and glared.

Gabriella stepped up to her. "You don't know where the liver is?"

"Dramatic license." Nadine patted her lower right abdomen. "Down here. Vidor, go be nice to them."

"What?" Vidor said. "Be nice to them?"

"Now they hate me and fear me. They need to love you. I'll drive them up to the city gates. You'll need to convince them to ride through with you. Leadership one-oh-one."

"You have insulted them," Vidor said. "They will be upset."

"Yes. But they will also be embarrassed that this happened to them. And scared that they messed up. They know they should have counted. They were just too lazy. When you talk to them, they'll rant at you for a while, then you tell them that you are glad they are here. And don't take this foreign bimbo too seriously, but she is helping. And didn't they say they would bring provisions, and shouldn't they do what they say?"

Vidor bit his lip. "I am not sure—"

"Don't worry," Nadine said. "You'll figure it out. Just be yourself. We need those riders. But we need the food, too. Go now."

Arpad waited till Vidor left. "You weren't upset, were you?"

"Nope."

"This was all an act?"

"They need to love him and fear me. I'll grind 'em into dust all the time, but they'll cheer him and follow him anywhere."

Vidor had caught up with the scampering horsemen. He slapped a few on the back and laughed with them.

"You do this once, you won't have to do it again," Nadine said. "Do it now. Start hard. It's easy to soften up later. It's difficult to get stricter later."

"You know a lot about this," Arpad said. "I am glad you are on our side."

"I'm on my side," Nadine said. "But with the baron dead, this whole ramshackle-governor thing was going to fall down, so I want to be on the winning side. And, of course, we'll be amply rewarded. Trade. A base for our visiting ships. Diplomatic relations. All the rum we can drink. Other things. Those charts would be nice, too, so we can do some exploring in the adjacent sectors."

"You shall have all this," Arpad said. "I will go collect those provisions and numbers. They might avoid you for a while."

"Good, I want that."

Arpad walked away, and Nadine folded her arms again.

"Do you know what you are doing?" Gabriella said.

"I always know what I'm doing," Nadine said.

"That's a lie, but it's the fiftieth one I've heard today, so I'll let it go."

"Any word from the city?"

"Arpad talked to some Ranchers and trading people. They had a telegraph. That's like a wired thing that sends messages. Text messages only. They sent that hovercraft down river as soon as the paddleboat was overdue. But that was twelve hours after it sank. They found three rafts and nineteen swimmers, total, maybe, thirty people?"

"His father?"

"Missing, presumed dead. Same with Marchello, the baron, and most of the important city people."

"Who's in charge in the city?"

"Nobody. There's kind of a free-for-all right now."

"Any fighting?"

"Not yet. You didn't ask about him."

"Ask about who?"

"Jake and Kivi might still be alive."

"Not likely with those odds. Come on, we have a revolution to feed."

"Why are you helping these people?"

"We need the charts. If they win, we get them. Besides, somebody has to run this planet. Why not our friends?"

CHAPTER NINETEEN

"Which Emperor is yours now?" the sheriff asked.

Jake, Tam, Ket, and Kivi had found a house with a radio, and the sheriff had come out from the county seat. His name was Tran and he looked more like Jake's older brother—brown hair and eyes and three-day stubble.

Jake and the others kept drinking copious amounts of water, while Tran sipped on tea.

"The Emperor Dashi the First," Jake said.

"Haven't heard of him," Sheriff Tran said. "But we haven't had news recently. What's his tax policy?"

"Standard Imperial one," Jake said. "No local sales or income taxes but export and import duties. You don't pay anything till you start trading, and then only on goods coming or going off planet."

"Didn't expect you to know that right off."

"Twenty percent duty on off-planet items. Once a colony passes to self-government, which you have, that's the usual rate. Half the money raised has to be spent locally on local projects. The rest goes to the Imperial treasury. That's after expenses, of course. Pays for the upkeep of the fleet, the custom services, some basic satellite services, comm, that sort of thing."

The owner of the house leaned in with a pot, and Tran nodded to more tea. "What about planetary affairs? What's his view on those?"

"Those are local responsibilities," Jake said. "It's in the colony charter. I've read yours—at least the parts relating to the land grants you got. You're really a self-governing colony within a colony."

"Colony within a colony?"

"Self-governing government in exile," Jake said, "to be technical."

"If we're being technical, what about the city?"

"That's direct Imperial control. It was an Imperial precinct under a governor. Well, a deputy colonial administrator. Outside of your jurisdiction."

"There's that word again," Sheriff Tran said. "Jurisdiction. My understanding is that my jurisdiction starts and ends at the county line. At least that's what Q-T used to tell me. Oh, sorry." The sheriff nodded to Tam. "I'm sorry about your father, Ms. Tam. He's not listed among the survivors. He was a good fellow, Q-T was. He helped me get elected, first time, and I thought he always did an excellent job as ambassador."

"Thanks, Sheriff. We still have some hope," Tam said.

Sheriff Tran coughed. "That's good, but, Miss, that hovercraft did a search come morning. The fire must have consumed the boat pretty quickly. Only a handful got out."

"There could be more like us, Sheriff," Jake said, "who go out and swam or sailed ashore."

"A couple. Maybe on the south shore. You folks were one of only two groups that made it in here. And one that had floated into the Central Ocean, but they picked them up and brought them back to the city."

"Sheriff," Jake said. "Who do you work for?"

"Not you, youngster, not you."

"You work for the Emperor."

"I do. Just not your Emperor."

"You work for an Emperor," Jake said, "the legitimate one."

"There is some dispute on who that is."

"Fine," Jake said. "But regardless of who the legitimate Emperor is, your local affairs are your own... affairs, correct?"

"That's true. I work for the county voters."

"Well, the county voters made Tam's father their

ambassador to the Empire because they are Imperial citizens."

"What's that got to do with the price of rice?"

"One of your jobs is to enforce the Imperial peace in areas under your jurisdiction and to assist Imperial authorities when called on. Called on by the ambassador."

"That's true. Any peacebreaking around here gets short shrift. We put 'em to picking rice."

"That's what those people down there…"

"Yeah," the sheriff drained his cup. "The field next to town. They're criminals, such as we have them. Nothing violent, except a few bar fights. Destruction of property. Theft. Unusual to have the theft."

"Why is that?"

"Somebody steals something here, the neighbors never trust them again. They might as well head out to the backwoods—they'll never get another job here. But, this time, that fellow over there," he pointed, " decided to take a month in the fields. He figures people will forgive him."

"Will they?"

"People who won money off him gambling will, those that lost probably not, but that's the law as we do it."

"That's my point," Jake said. "The law as you do it. You have your own authority, whoever the Emperor turns out to be."

"Why you so interested in my authority?"

"You can call up a posse, swear people in. Send them to keep the peace. In the name of the Emperor."

"Which Emperor, and which peace?"

"Whichever one you want—that's up to you. But you told me that the city is in a state of anarchy."

"I talked to a few folks on the radio. It's just city people who are fighting each other. Not our affair."

"But it's the Emperor's affair. And you're supposed to respond to requests for assistance from Imperial officials. What if you got a request to assist in the city from a competent Imperial official? And what if you and your fellow sheriffs collected a posse, people from each county, and went into the city to enforce the peace until the Empire reestablishes control."

Tran pushed his cup away. "I'd need a request from a recognized Emperor," he said.

"Since you decide which one is recognized, I think we can make that happen," Jake said. "And an Imperial official arriving in a spaceship, first one in fifty years, carries a lot of weight."

"So, we get a couple hundred men and women and go in and take over the city. We put you in charge, spaceman?"

"No, you run the city. In the Emperor's name. Until the Emperor or his designate appoints a governor."

"Who would the governor be? You? One of your people?"

"Nope."

"Who, then?"

Jake grinned at Tam. "I have a candidate in mind."

***

"Jake, are you sure we'll have enough food?" Tam asked as they rode through town.

"Nice horse, good horse," Jake said, patting the horse he was on. "Did you have to give me such a fractious giant as this monster?"

"Fractious? Whisker is the gentlest horse we had."

"This is gentle? I'd hate to see the lively ones." Jake pulled the reins from one side to the other. "How do I make him stop?"

"Jake, he just follows the horse in front of him," Tam said. "Whisker will just follow Ket's Buttercup or my Dixzar."

Ket winked over her shoulder.

"Buttercup?" Jake said. "It's shoulders are taller than

167

Ket's head. That's a ginormous horse. Almost as big as mine. Why did you give us such beasts?"

"You've got draft horses. They just plod along. You're in no danger. And it's a nice rest for them from pulling the carts." She gestured back at the line of carts behind her. "Each one of those carts has a thousand pounds of food or weapons. Carrying you is like carrying nothing."

"Your horse is smaller," Jake said. "Can't I have one like that?"

"Dixzar is the best horse in the whole world. She's smart and fast and does everything I ask of her. She's a mighty horse. But, even though she's small and svelte, she can be a handful. Probably too much for you. Hard to handle. She doesn't take direction well, especially from men."

"Just like all women," Jake muttered.

"What was that?"

"Nothing. You were talking about worries?"

"I worry about the food."

"We've got spare horses, spare wheels, and spare carts, and you've got them moving steadily. Given the numbers you've shown me, we'll probably have more food than people to eat it."

"But what if there's some sort of issue and some of the carts don't make it?"

"We've got an allowance for loss," Jake said, "And for unforeseen circumstances."

"We shouldn't have sent the posse out until the food was there."

"Tam, we can't wait. We needed to get moving. If you wait until everything is in place, you'll never get anything done."

"That's not the way I've done things."

"Strike while the anvil is hot."

"You don't even know what an anvil is."

"It's used in a forge by a blacksmith. You probably have some here."

Ket giggled. "Jake, we're a poor colony. Not a stupid colony. There's probably some anvils in a shed somewhere, but we don't do things by hand. We use waterpower or coal power. Look over there."

Next to the road was a river meandering down to the sea. Ahead was a millrace that ran to two waterwheels. Connected to the waterwheels was a brick building with a wide wooden roof. Packed outside were bales of cotton.

"That's a factory," Ket said. "Makes cotton cloth. Combs out the fibers, spins them into yarn, then uses the yarn to wave fabric. All water-powered."

"Don't you need computers or something?"

"The machines are made out of wood. We got designs from the library, and there's lots of wood here. The hard part is harvesting the cotton and maintaining the looms. But we get good production from it."

"You trade that into the city?"

"We use a lot of it ourselves," Ket said. "We sell the fabric to another company, and they make shirts and pants, things like that. Working clothes. The better fabric goes to tailors. They make the custom stuff."

"That's pretty clever," Jake said. "Who owns that?"

"Princess Fabric's mills," Ket said. "It's a common stock company, lots of people own part. I have some. Biggest shareholders are one of the insurance companies and one of the first families."

Jake noted the size and extent of the property. "Dams, waterwheels, factory, and machines. Must be a wealthy family."

"Oh, it is," Ket said. "One of the wealthiest and prominent of the first families. That's why it's called Princess Mills."

"The owner was a princess?" Jake asked.

"An Imperial noble. Not a princess, but that's what the father called his first daughter when she was born. Thus, Princess Mills."

"I wouldn't mind meeting a princess," Jake said.

"Maybe you could arrange an introduction sometime."

"I can do that," Ket said. "Jake, Princess Tam. Princess Tam, Jake."

"You never said you were a princess," Jake said.

Tam blushed. "I'm not. It's just the name of the company."

"We treat her like royalty, though," Ket said.

"Can I have your head cut off, then?" Tam said. "Seriously, Jake, I'm not a princess."

"But she is an industrialist," Ket said. "Now that her dad Quan is dead—or probably, she's the richest woman on the planet. Fabric mills. Farming. Some river boats. Horse herds. And vegetables. The Quan Vegetable Cooperative handles eight percent of our food, and she owns most of it."

"Eight percent doesn't amount to much," Kivi said.

"A small part of a big thing is a big part," Ket said. "And since we all share in the money from the cooperative, lots of people support her. What's good for Tam is good for Magyar, what's good for Magyar is good for Tam."

"Even better," Jake said. "Nothing like a local hero for widespread support. You'll make a great governor. The sooner we get this group of liberators in front of the palace, the sooner we can proclaim you governor, the sooner we can trade, and the sooner I can get what I want," Jake said.

"What do you want?"

"To get off this Empire-damned horse," Jake said.

*****

Jake dropped with a thud when he climbed off his horse that night.

He had to be carried to bed, and the next morning, he could hardly stand. After feeding him breakfast, they propped him onto Whiskers, and he proceeded along the road in company with the others. He sat in misery while the others rode back and forth. Different posses joined during the day, coming in from nearby counties. A western group, a northern, and an eastern group headed over to the peninsula that the capital was on. They were all expected to join up at the last county town before moving on to the capital.

Sheriff Tran stepped up next to him. "You look the most miserable I've ever seen a person be on a horse. Or off a horse."

"I wish I was off a horse."

"Still five more miles. Want to walk?"

"I'm considering it," Jake said. "What's the weapons report?"

"You don't want to talk about food and water like Tam does?"

"I did a count. We have three times as much food as we'll need for a thousand people and water for twice as many." Jake pointed at some barrels going down the road. "And even that's assuming that all the rivers in this part of the world suddenly run dry, and we have to rely on carried supplies. Let's talk about weapons. What type do we have?"

"What you military types would call 'personal weapons,'" Sheriff Tran said.

"I'm not a military type."

"Sure talk like one. What are you, then."

"I'm an accountant. I trained in ship administration."

"Ship administration? That's something you take at school?"

"I studied the history of insurance at the merchant academy, among other things."

"History of insurance? You're like a male version of Tam there."

"Is she really a princess?"

"Closest thing we have. They call you 'admiral'

sometimes. You really an admiral?"

"Closest thing you have."

"You've only got one ship."

"One ship beats no ship."

"Good point."

"Tell me about those personal weapons."

Tran held up a stick. "We have batons."

"We're not breaking up bar fights. We're attacking a fortified city."

"Then, we have a problem. Or you do, Military Advisor. We have nothing to take care of that."

"No guns at all?"

"Shotguns. Revolvers. Plenty of ammunition. We make our own for that. The revolvers, too. Everybody has one, especially out of the city."

"Why so many weapons?"

"Wolves. They came with the terraforming package. Something had to eat wild horses. Bears are too slow. We have some wild cats, but they are too small, and the horses stomp them. We get some brutal winters up in the hills, though, and a wolf pack can take on a herd of horses and win in the winter sometimes. Enough to keep them in balance."

"I've never seen a wolf," Jake said.

"No need for you to," Tran said. "But we've got revolvers and some rifles. If we're fighting out in the open, we're in pretty good shape."

"Nothing long range, though."

"They do have those Gauss rifles."

"Only six, and they can't be everywhere."

"Don't have to be that good," Tran said. "They shoot those little metal pellets pretty far, pretty fast."

"Only a thousand rounds in a Gauss rifle. I looked it up. And they can empty the magazine in twenty seconds."

"Lots of damage can be done in twenty seconds."

"And none at all in second twenty-one," Jake said. "And it can only fire in one direction. And it's hard to hit something when you're nervous."

"You've given this some thought," Tran said. There was a commotion up front, and a rider rode back to them. "Something's going on. Maybe you might have to convert that thought into action."

CHAPTER TWENTY

"What do you mean we have to wait while you dry the horses?" Nadine said. "And what is he doing over there, massaging it?"

"The riders are rubbing oil into them," Vidor said. "Special plant oils that must be kneaded into the horse hide. First, take off the saddle and blanket, then rub the oil in, then let the horse rest for a time, eat and drink, then you can put the saddle back on."

Nadine had forded the strait, with the first group riding behind Vidor. The water was deep, but their horses had swum it easily, leading a string of spare ones behind. Delta had ranches, and Nadine had spent some time on one, learning basic riding skills. Gabriella's cousin owned a ranch, and she had spent summers there. The two women couldn't approach Vidor and Arpad for ability, but they could keep up.

Once clear of the beach, Vidor dismounted and patted his horse.

"First, you make it relax, then you have it slip into something more comfortable and then a meal? What else do you need? Soft music? Dim lights? Brandy?"

"Horses don't drink brandy, Ms. Nadine," Vidor said.

"Why do we have to do this? They're horses. They live outside, right? In the wind. In the rain. They get wet."

"Do you not dry your own horses?" Vidor said.

"On our spaceship? Yes, we have whole herds of horses roaming the corridors of our spaceships. When we jump from system to system, we take them along because everybody wants a horse when they're exploring an airless asteroid in the dark." Nadine waved Gabriella over.

"I forget that you are not from here," Vidor said. "But of course you do not have horses on your ships. Do you have horses on your planet?"

"We live on a moon, not a planet," Nadine said. "And most of us live in orbit or on ships, not all on the moon. And there are no horses on our stations."

"How do you live on a moon? Moons are small."

"Our moon is bigger than your planet, pal." Nadine pointed. "Over there—why are they crushing those plants?"

"The aloe cactus gives us the sap. The sap kills the fungus—"

"What fungus? And why does it have to be killed now?"

"You—oh no. You don't have the fungus."

"We don't have time for fungus," Nadine said. "Now that we're moving on the capital."

Brie arrived. "Yessum, Nadine."

"Get Arpad over here. We need to get those people to stop fondling their horses and get them moving. We're on a schedule here."

"Sure," Brie said. She galloped over to bring Arpad back.

"Wait," Vidor said. "Let me explain."

The news was bad. Along with horses, some Old Earth equine diseases had arrived. This fungus wasn't fatal, but it made the horses so itchy they wouldn't suffer a saddle or a rider. It was present on the ground, and humidity made it grow faster. After getting wet, horses' coats had to be flogged dry or smeared with a fungus-killing sap from the local bushes.

"It does not take long to smear the fungus," Vidor said.

"But we have to unload all the horses, guard their loads, find the bushes, break up the bushes, smear the sap, then wait, reload."

"That is true. But drying the horse takes much longer.

Much, much longer, and it is hard to do properly."

"And how many of those bushes are there? Enough for everybody."

"Plenty of them, just not on this side, the north side. Plenty on the southern side..."

"Where the horses are not going to be after they get wet," Nadine said. She kicked a few rocks. "How many horses can a single bush give sap for?"

"I do not know, but I will find out," Arpad said. "I will go check. We have never had this many of the clan together at the same time."

Nadine watched him go. "Never thought to tell me about horse sap washing?"

"No," Vidor said.

"And why not, Mr. Khan of all the horseman?"

"It's horse sap. Everybody uses it. Horses have to be dried." He shrugged. "Everybody knows that."

It took a complete day of Nadine's threats and Vidor's cajoling before they moved a hundred horsemen off from the river crossing. The remainder were stuck on the southern shore and refused to move out without drying and smearing their mounts.

"In a day, the horse will be afflicted," said one rider. "She'll either buck me off and drag me to my death or just run into the desert and roll in the sand for days. And once the infection gets severe, they go mad nearly, and can't be used for anything. The only real cure is to send them up into the southern mountains—it gets cold enough that the fungus dies. But that takes a season."

They'd found every single bush within miles of the river crossing and crunched it up for sap. The other riders had recrossed the water back to the more heavily forested southern area, then waited in groups. Arpad had found a portable sap-crushing machine. Once workers had crushed and loaded enough sap for a group of twenty, they would move across.

"Great, so it will take two or three more days to get

everyone over here," Nadine said. "We can't wait any longer. We need to get moving. Word will have already reached the city."

"I can't believe that you didn't know about the horse fungus," Vidor said.

"Next time we're on a spaceship, I'm going to put you in an air lock under quarter pressure. We'll see how you feel about skin suits and all that stuff you make fun of then."

"On a starship? Where will you take me? To a life of luxury in the stars?"

"Luxury? Hardly."

"You have computers. Heating. Air conditioning. Showers, of course. Medical robots?"

"And the whole ship smells like feet after a few days. The showers are only a minute on even-numbered days at most. If we're not short on fuel, that is. But we do have medical robots and lots of computers. But they break, too. Or their software does."

The horse in front of Nadine dumped a load of manure on the road with a plop.

"Perhaps," Arpad said, "the smell is not as bad as we are used to."

"Everything isn't better in space," Gabriella said. "Just different. The food you have here is amazing. Even this trail food is better."

"It's just steaks," Arpad said. "Do you not have steaks?"

"Yes, but they are expensive and hard to get. And they spoil on a spaceship. We use trays. They keep forever, and they don't need to be frozen or refrigerated. Just sit there."

"Sounds horrible," Arpad said.

"It is," Gabriella said. "Your food is much better."

"Yet, I have never been farther than two hundred miles from my ranch," Arpad said. "And even then, that's just to the city, the palace. You've been to dozens of worlds and met thousands of strange people. Vidor, the scouts approach."

Vidor and Arpad rode away to meet the returning scouts.

"Hopefully," Gabriella said, "we can get some of this fresh food on the ship when we leave."

"Hopefully, we can leave at all," Nadine said. "If their jump computer software works with ours. I miss Jake. He was a great guy."

"You don't know that he's dead."

"I don't know that the sun will rise in the morning, but that's the way to bet," Nadine said.

"If we can't fix that software, what do we do?"

"You can be Arpad's rancher girlfriend, riding horses and collecting dung for the fire."

"I look great in this outfit, the boots especially." Gabriella stretched her leg out in front of her. "I suppose there are worse things to happen."

"Really? Name them," Nadine said.

"None come to mind right now. Your khan is coming back."

"He's not my khan."

"Right, you didn't buy him, did you?" Gabriella said. "You just rent him for a while."

"He'll be fun," Nadine said. "I just wish he wasn't so..."

"Dumb as a bag of rocks?"

"Quiet. What is it, Vidor?"

Vidor and Arpad had arrived in front of Nadine. "Ms. Nadine, we have a problem."

***

"But you want them to see the weapons," Jake said to Sheriff Tran. "We need everybody to have a sword belt with a sword and a revolver on it."

"Not everybody has a revolver," Tran said.

"Make a group of the best armed troops," Jake said.

He stood beside the road, hanging onto his horse. He could get off by himself, but it was more of a controlled slide than an actual dismount. And he needed to hold on to the horse's mane to keep from falling. "Your top fifty that have revolvers, shotguns, and swords. Put them together in a group. Then a second group, with just revolvers and swords, then the ones with just swords."

"We don't group that way. The different posses come with what they can. Some have swords, some don't. One or two have shotguns, but most don't. Some just have batons."

"We need to group like together," Jake said.

"That would mix up the posse," Tran said.

"Yes," Jake said. And waited. "Yes, we should mix them up."

"We've never done that before."

"No, you haven't. But if you want to get some respect and be part of governing this colony, you need to look like an army. Put the most heavily armed troops in the front."

"Not very efficient. They're not used to working together."

"When we get to the city, we want to look organized, like we know what we're doing. If the city people see two hundred riders in a row, and the first fifty have shotguns, swords, and revolvers, they'll think they all have them. They'll assume that everybody is armed the same, has the same weapons."

"But everybody doesn't," Tran said.

"I won't tell them if you don't. They'll be worried and impressed by the organization."

Tam and Ket rode up, with Kivi behind them. "How are your legs, Jake?" Tam asked.

"Miserable," Jake said. "I hate horses."

"Shssssh," Kivi said. "They'll hear you, and it upsets them."

"They're horses," Jake said. "They can't talk. They don't understand standard."

"There, there," Kivi said, patting his horse's mane. "Don't let the nasty man bother you, Nova. We love you."

"Nova?"

"I named her Nova, like the sun, you know, because—"

"Kivi, I know what a Nova is. Why did you name her? Didn't she have a name?"

"That was her farming name. This is her warrior name," Kivi said.

"Warrior name? With all that's going on, you wanted to..." Jake closed his eyes, his lips moving as he counted to ten. "Outstanding. Great idea." Jake looked at the plodding draft horse he hung onto. "Giving the horses warrior names. The first Imperial Cavalry."

"Should be a legion, right, Admiral Stewart?," Tran said. "Since you're the Emperor's personal representative. Legion Magyar something."

"Legio XXI, Magyar," Tam said. "We've already named it. We're getting it embroidered on the sashes you had us make. The yellow-and-black ones."

"The surcoats. The colors are important," Jake said.

"And the symbols," Ket said. "Polaris. For the Empire."

"We don't have time for embroidery," Jake said. "Just the colors is enough. We need to move along, not wait for some sewing. Anything is fine as long as it's yellow and black."

"We've already ordered them," Tam said. "They'll be here in a day."

"We don't have a day," Jake said. Hooves drummed in the background. "What now?"

Scouts they had sent out had returned. Sheriff Tram, Tam, and Ket went up to confer for a minute, then rode back. Jake waited. It took many long minutes for him to mount, and it was easier if he just waited.

"Roadblock up ahead," Tran said. "That's what all that noise was. Blocking the road into the city. Our outriders turned back. What should we do?"

"Did they shoot?" Jake asked.

"No, but they had weapons. One might have a Gauss rifle. The others have revolvers and suchlike."

"Who are they? How many?"

"Half dozen. City people."

"Which type of city people?"

Tran shrugged. "They all look alike to me."

"All from the chancellor's party, by the colors," Ket said.

"Right," Jake said. "Sheriff, I need you to find twenty of your friends. Friends who can ride the best. Get them together and make sure they all have a sword and revolver on their belt and a shotgun over their shoulder. The shotguns don't have to be loaded. They don't have to know how to use them. They just have to carry them. Tam, Ket, we need yellow-and-black armbands for all of us. The twenty riders, and the five of us. Yellow on the left upper arm, black on the right. Everybody gets them. Then get the riders here. We need to practice something for a few minutes."

Jake patted the cart horse he'd been riding. "Sorry, old girl, you're not quite right for this. I'm going to need a faster, better horse." Jake let go of the horse's mane and stepped back. He wavered on his feet for a moment, then crumpled to the ground. He lay on his back in the dust. "And also, I'm going to need two other riders with me. Help me stay on."

CHAPTER TWENTY-ONE

Nadine, Gabriella, Vidor, Arpad, and a guard of twenty of the better riders rode down the road. Five men and three women blocked the lane in front of them. Another group was visible in the distance. Beyond, the coast road twisted inland along a bay, then disappeared behind a headland. Cliffs compressed the road into a single lane for the entire sweeping curve, with the roadblock in the middle.

"Colorful bunch." Nadine stopped and pointed. "Which groups are those?"

"Pink, periwinkle, and chartreuse," Arpad said. "The first two are distant relatives of the baron and Marchello. The chartreuse is the chancellor's faction."

"Periwinkle? Chartreuse? Those are the colors you use?"

"We didn't get to choose. They all have some connection with old Imperial uniforms."

"Good for you that you didn't get puke-yellow as your house colors."

"One of the families did," Arpad said. "Medical workers way back."

Nadine wrinkled her nose. "So we've got the old ruling class and the new ruling class, but half of them are in that lime-green."

"That's a minor trading group. They run the sawmill in town," Arpad said. "Not a prominent family."

"I'll bet a lot of prominent families have been wiped out," Nadine said. "Sunk in the Central Ocean."

"Too true. The city people's own vanity has destroyed

them."

"Weakened them," Nadine said. "Not destroyed yet."

"They deserve it with those fashion choices," Gabriella said. "Don't know how to use the cowgirl possibilities at all."

"What possibilities?" Nadine asked.

Gabriella said nothing, just rode six feet ahead. She stood in the saddle and bent over to adjust a strap. She and Nadine still wore their skin suits, but they had accessorized them with high-heeled boots, a loose blouse, and a hat. The combination of the tight skin suit, leg-lengthening heels, and a certain... separation of the hips enforced by the saddle caused all the men to pause and stare.

Nadine grinned, then nudged over to Vidor's horse and slapped his arm. "Less ogling, more riding. Let's go see these people."

Vidor jerked and rubbed his arm. "I was not ogling. I was just..."

Nadine high-fived Gabriella as she rode by and led the group to the city people.

The opposing group stood their ground. Nadine and friends rode up and stopped twenty feet away. The different colors were mixed, and half had a black armband on.

"That's far enough, horse people," the lime-green leader said.

"I know you," Vidor said. "You work at the sawmill. You're the one they call Little Bobby."

"My name is Robert. You can call me Robert," Bobby said. "Who are you?"

"I am Vidor, khan of my horde."

"What of your what?"

"Khan. Leader. Of my horde."

"There's twenty of you. That's hardly a horde."

"We have many more behind the point," Vidor gestured back along the road. "We will take a representative to show you. But I didn't want to bring them here. It would be too crowded."

"Don't entirely trust us?"

"As much as you trust us," Nadine said, pointing to a spot of land behind them. "You trust us so much that you have a sniper post at the tip of those rocks out there. Covers the whole bay, from the far point in here and out again."

"You're a spacer," Bobby said. "Heard some of you got out of the fire."

"And here we are," Nadine said. "Going into town. Need to meet my ship. My new friends here are escorting me."

"No, they're not. Turn around and go back," Bobby said.

"We have the right to visit the town at any time," Arpad said. "That was our arrangement. We cannot stay overnight, but we can visit. And we want to visit."

"No visiting right now. By orders of the baron."

"The baron who died in the fire?" Nadine said.

"The new baron," Bobby said. "We had an election."

"Barons aren't elected," Nadine said. "They're appointed or anointed by the Emperor. Has the Emperor made a visit while we're away and appointed a new governor?"

"The baron-elect," Bobby said.

"We should have been part of any election," Arpad said. "If there even was one."

"Only city people were involved."

"Thus these three groups here," Arpad said. "Groups that I know do not get along. But now you are working together. Why?"

"We've got a new baron, and you swore to follow the Imperial governor. The governor says go away."

"Not a real governor," Vidor said. "Not a legitimate one. You are all rebels."

The lime-green soldiers shuffled. "What do you want?"

"What I want," Nadine said, sliding from her horse and

handing the reins to Gabriella, "is to see what happens if I walk over here and put my hand on my revolver." She stepped up to Bobby. "What happens if I do this, Little Bobby?" She pulled her revolver out and held it up.

The sound of a cloth ripping followed puffs of dust and splinters of rocks exploding five meters up the shore, and the rocks pinged and shattered in a twenty-meter line up the cliffs. The entire group of Ranchers struggled to control their horses. Several ran backward. One fell off when his horse bolted. The city group dropped flat at the first shots and lay with their hands over their heads. Pulverized rock smoke billowed and covered the scene. The dust settled, and Nadine's head loomed above them. She was shading her eyes with her hand and peering across the bay.

"There." She pointed to the far side, where something flashed red near the far point. "That sniper post. Looks like a Gauss rifle," she said, holstering her revolver. "Lots of nervous folks here, aren't there? Let me borrow your gloves, Little Bobby."

"My name is Robert, of the family—"

"Yup, sure. Those are leather?" Nadine pointed at his belt.

"I'm not giving you my gloves."

"We won't leave you alone unless you lend me your gloves," Nadine said.

"Leave?"

"Let me borrow your gloves, that is, if they're leather, and we'll all go back along the trail to the corner there. You can stay here. We won't come back this way."

"Ms. Nadine," Vidor said, "perhaps we should discuss—"

"No, Mr. Horse Khan, we should not," Nadine said. "Everybody mount up. Did you see the rate of fire of that thing?"

"Well, it is an excellent weapon," Vidor said. "But surely—"

"Bobby, they can hear us over there, can't they?" Nadine pointed. "Your little sniper nest. I see two carts, some horses, and a lot of rocks. You've got a Gauss rifle in there and somebody listening on the comm, right?"

Bobby nodded.

"Hold out your comm, Bobby," Nadine said. "I want to talk to them."

Bobby gestured at a lime-green clad trooper, who produced an ancient comm from a pocket.

"Holy original Imperial technology," Nadine said, "That's older than that baron dude. Did you find that in a museum?"

"What do you want, spacer?" a woman's voice said from the comm.

"My friends here, they don't understand Imperial weapons. I don't want to die, not by being shot and not by being beaten to death for being a coward, either. I need you to demonstrate again. Give me a high burst. Nice long one, above our heads, ten seconds or so."

Nothing happened for a moment, then the cloth-ripping sound came, and fractures of rock mowed out of the cliff above them and fluttered to the ground. It continued for several seconds, sweeping from one side of the bay to the other.

"Got the whole bay covered from there," Nadine said. "Good siting. Even if we came charging through here at top speed, you'd have us under fire for plenty of time. Plenty enough to cut us down. But rate of fire's not everything. Accuracy and range, that's important, too. You still there, Gauss gun people?"

"We are, spacer."

Nadine shaded her eyes. "Look up yonder. Way up on that far ridge there. I see a tree, yellow-green leaves, right above that white patch of rock. Probably five kilometers away. Chop it down for us."

"Stand by," the shooter said.

They waited almost a minute. Rounds ripped out and

pinged the top of the nearby cliff, then corrected, and the distant tree shuddered and shook. Chunks blew off, and within five seconds, the entire top of the tree toppled off.

"You happy now, spacer?" the voice said.

"Outstanding," Nadine said. "Range, accuracy, rate of fire. A great weapon. Your gloves, Bobby?"

The confused lime-clad Bobby handed Nadine the heavy leather gloves from his belt. Nadine put them on and strode to the cliff, peering at the ground. Halfway there, she leaned over and sifted in the dirt. "Got it. Ow, ow, still hot." She tossed a handful of metal shards from hand to hand, then returned to the far side of the road where the ocean lapped on the sand. She upended her hands, and little splinters fell into the water. It bubbled and steamed. Nadine watched as the gurgling died down before picking the metal needles out.

She returned to the group, juggling the metal slivers. "Vidor, Arpad, catch," Nadine said, tossing them over. "And don't lose them. They're valuable." Arpad and Vidor cursed as they juggled the still-warm needles.

Nadine held one up for everyone to see. "Imperial standard Gauss rifle, fires those metal needles at some stupid velocity. That ripping was mini sonic booms. They can smash rock, as you saw there, and chop through wood no problem, even at four-five-kay distance. Quite a weapon. I had one myself." She grinned at Arpad. "How long will it take you and the boys to ride over to that little fort over there and imagine those little slugs going through your eyeballs while you try it? Nope, we're not going to do that." She turned to the city group. "We're going to go back to the bend there, and we're not going to be coming down this road to the city. We're not all leaving—depends on how things turn out, election-wise—but we'll leave you alone here. For now. I don't want to be shot." She stripped the gloves off and thrust them at Bobby. "These are ruined, sorry. Burn marks, still want them?"

"Keep 'em," Bobby said.

"We're going to go back and talk for a while," Nadine said. "But I'll tell you one thing. We're not going to be bothering you. All you colorful people." Nadine gestured at the group. "I'm a spacer. I don't get the colors. Which families are you?"

The groups introduced themselves with names that meant nothing to her. She nodded politely. "Pleased to meet you. We'll be going. Vidor, Arpad, back the way we came."

Nadine mounted her horse and rode away. The group followed.

Vidor rode up next to Nadine. "Ms. Nadine, I am—"

Nadine held up her hand. "You are not talking till we're past the point where they can't see us because they have sensors and can hear us or perhaps lip-read."

They rode in silence till the rocky cliffs at the point concealed them.

"Ms. Nadine, you have stopped us making a grave error. I would have charged them, and we would all have been killed. But you should not talk to us that way."

"Well, I have a way you can repay me," Nadine said.

"What would you like?"

"I need all of us to get back to the camp, and I need a cheap sword that can be destroyed, a hammer, and a spoon."

"A spoon?"

"Yes, the spoon is the most important."

CHAPTER TWENTY-TWO

"Harder. Hit it as hard as you can," Nadine said.

Shards of slugs fired by the Gauss gun had been clamped into a portable vise. Two burly swordsman tried to hammer them flat, but they wouldn't bend, no matter how hard the two men hammered.

"That's what we needed to know," Nadine said. She bent down and collected a beaten-up sword and a bent spoon, then took a needle and one of the hammers over to where Vidor and Arpad were discussing options with their group leaders.

"Cannot charge them," Vidor said. "With how fast they fire, they will kill us all before we even get close."

"Don't even think of charging them," Nadine said. "Might as well shoot yourselves now."

"So, how do we defeat them?" one of the men asked.

"Easy," Nadine said. "Look at this." She tossed the mangled sword at their feet.

"It is a sword," Arpad said. "Or was a sword. It is what remains of a sword."

"Head of the class, Arpy, head of the class. Now this."

She threw the bent spoon next to the sword.

"A destroyed spoon," Arpad said.

"What a great warrior she is," a sandy-haired man said. "She killed some cutlery."

"Killed cutlery?" Nadine grinned. "Nah, I have people for that. Hey, big guys," she called back to the men who helped her, "what were your names?"

The men yelled something back.

"No idea what they said." Nadine waved at them.

"Arpad, do you know them?"

"Yes."

"Note their names and make sure to thank them later for their help. Now, what do you see here?"

"A pile of mangled metal," the sandy-haired man said. "That you had others break for you."

"What type of metal?"

"Metal metal. What do you mean?"

"I mean"—Nadine tipped a sword over with her booted foot—"that the guys were able to pummel this sword to bits with just hand hammers. 'Cause the sword is made of steel. Not very good steel, either, apparently. And steel is iron and some other stuff. Which is soft. You have iron here? Vidor?"

"Not much," Vidor said. "We smelt some, enough to make swords."

"You all have swords. Swords aren't that expensive, right?"

"Well, my sword is a family heirloom," Vidor said, "and I wouldn't give it away for any price—"

"Not that expensive," Arpad said. "We can make our own swords. But that spoon isn't steel. It's aluminum. And before you ask, Ms. Nadine, I know aluminum is stronger than steel."

"Can you make aluminum, Arpad?"

"We cannot. We have no aluminum smelter. That spoon is Old Empire-made. Access to your aluminum was one of the things that excited our traders. Give me that needle, please." He held out his hand to Nadine. "And the hammer."

Nadine gave him both. Arpad pinched the needle between his fingers and held it upright on a convenient rock. He handed the hammer to the sandy-haired man. "I will hold it up. Strike as hard as you can."

"I'll break your fingers."

"Hit the metal pin squarely. Strike as hard as you can."

"But—"

"Do it now," Arpad said.

The sandy-haired man shrugged and swung the hammer a lackadaisical blow.

Arpad held the needle vertically. It didn't bend. "Again. Harder," Arpad said.

The sandy-haired man swung harder, and the hammer bounced up. He tried again and again. Finally, he set his feet and swung a double-handed blow. The hammer still banged off.

Arpad stood. "What metal is it, Ms. Nadine?"

"Not a hundred percent sure, but probably tungsten. My friend Jake would know."

Arpad grinned and turned to Vidor. "Rejoice, cousin. We have gained a valuable victory."

"By running away from a foe and hammering rocks?" Vidor said.

Arpad shook his head. "We can't refine tungsten on Magyar. If they must have tungsten for reloads, they cannot make more ammunition. They have only what they have with the guns now. And Ms. Nadine, with her taunting, she made them fire many times. Ms. Nadine, you say you had a Gauss gun. How many needles in a magazine?"

"Depends. Five hundred or a thousand. Thousand only with special magazines."

"And they shoot—ten per second?"

"More. Twenty."

Arpad nodded. "They must be almost out of ammunition, then."

"Almost."

Vidor nodded. "We can rush them."

"Hold up, khan of all the horses," Nadine said. "Almost out of ammunition isn't the same as out of ammunition. We could rush them, but a lot of people will still get hurt. I know a better way."

"I'm actually khan of all the horse people, not the horses—"

191

"Details. Arpad, you have those maps? Can I see them?"

Arpad brought the maps, and Nadine and he stepped to the side for a moment. Vidor and Gabriella waited.

"Where did you learn to ride, Ms. Gabriella?" Vidor asked.

"Call me Brie. We have ranches on Delta. I spent summers on one. Nadine as well."

"She is an amazing woman. Smart, feisty, she can ride. She drives your spaceship, does she not?"

"She's the main pilot," Gabriella said. "I'm her understudy."

"You will be a pilot as well. Good for you. My cousin Arpad is quite enamored of you. He speaks of you all the time."

"Does he?" Gabriella looked at Arpad. "I like him well enough. Is he single?"

"He has many admirers. My third cousin over there is one of them." Vidor pointed at a group of female riders standing to one side.

"Your cousin? But Arpad is your cousin, too. She wants to get with her own cousin. Ick."

"Arpad is from my father's side, she is from my mother's. They are related to me, not each other. Different bloodlines."

"Which one is she?"

"The one sharpening the sword and glaring at you."

"Right," Gabriella said. "Very attractive lady. Pretty hair. Big sword."

"She is most upset that you have beguiled Arpad."

"I can take her."

"With a spaceship, perhaps, but she is the regional winner at our rodeo."

"What sort of regional winner? Riding?"

"Swords. She is quick. Does Ms. Nadine like me?"

"What do you think?" Gabriella said.

"She is attracted to me. She wants me to win. I'm not

sure exactly why. Perhaps she just likes the excitement?"

"It's not just the excitement."

"But mostly."

"Did you tell the city that Nadine and I were rescued?"

"Why would I do that?"

"No reason. Just something that the guy at the roadblock said. They are coming back. Let's hear their plan."

Nadine and Arpad came back to the group. "Right, we're going to bypass them. If we rush them, we'll get hurt. But same problem applies to them. They'll get hurt as well. If we leave a group of people here and put them just behind those rocks there"—Nadine pointed at the rocks near the point—"they're shielded from the Gauss rifle. And there is some water here—that stream. They can stay here as long as the food lasts. The limeys will have to come past the corner to shoot at us and then we'll shoot back."

"Limeys?" Vidor said.

"Arpad told me their family name, but I forgot. Doesn't matter, I'll use the color. But we will leave the bulk of our troops here."

"But this group will be stuck here."

"Nope. We're going to go around them, through this dry riverbed that Arpad showed me. We'll send a group through there."

"Ms. Nadine," the sandy-haired man said, "we all cannot go through this path. It is steep, all-mountain ravines for two thousand meters. No water on the trail at all, and we cannot carry enough for all of us to climb. It will be better in the dark, but once the suns are up, the heat will be extreme. We will surely perish if we climb up there."

"I have a plan for that, too, of course," Nadine said. "Listen up."

***

Nadine and Gabriella watched the second sun set. The first group of riders had returned almost two hours ago, a second group an hour after that, and they waited for the last group to come in.

"You sure there's enough light?" Gabriella said.

"Arpad says so, and I trust him."

"You trust him?"

"He wants to impress you, so he's giving me his A game in the hopes that I'll talk him up to you."

"Is it working?"

"So far. Do you like him?"

"Vidor pointed out a cousin who wants to kill me with a sword because she thinks I'm sleeping with him."

"Better sleep with him, then."

"Won't that make it worse?"

"In my experience," Nadine said, "you're going to get blamed for doing it regardless of what happens, so if it's already a problem, might as well have some fun."

"Not very romantic."

"But fun. Exciting."

"True. Vidor is suspicious of you. He knows you want him to win, but he's not sure why."

"He's smarter than he looks."

"That's not hard—what's that noise?"

"Riders."

A group of figures rode up out of the dark. Vidor and Arpad conferred with them, then came up.

"How did it go, Pista?" Vidor asked.

"We did it just like Ms. Nadine showed us on the map, Khan," Pista, the sandy-haired man, said. "We have two caches of water laid out. We left a man with each one, and I've been to both, so I can find them again. The last two riders watered all the way up to the middle one and then took the last pile of water to the three quarter mark. One will stay there, and one will ride back along the trail."

"Very well," Vidor said. "Call the others. We ride. You

will come with us."

"I need a moment to change horses, Khan, and then I will come." Pista rode past the two women and flicked a half salute. "We won't let you down, Ms. Nadine."

"Thank you," Nadine said.

She had selected one hundred riders and loaded them with as much water as they could carry. They rode two hours into the mountains. Half dropped all their water and rode back to the start. The horses could handle four hours in the heat and terrain with no water, and when they returned, they could drink from the stream, retreat along the coast to a major river a few hours down, and wait there.

The second half rode another two hours, dropped half of their water, and drank the rest. Then they rode back to the start as well before drinking some of the water stored at the midpoint. A group of two carried as much as they could and rode further for two hours. Nadine had water supplies cached every two hours. Enough water for a group of forty to ride hard up the mountain and reenter the coast road behind the roadblock—and between it and their water supplies.

Nadine and Gabriella rode up to Vidor, Arpad, and the others. "Everybody ready?"

"All set," Arpad said.

Pista rode up on a different horse. "Blessings to you, Ms. Nadine. What happens now?"

Nadine looked up at the dust streaked cliffs. "We ride."

Twelve hours later, the first sun rose. The group of forty walked their horses down a dry riverbed. The Central Ocean was visible in the far distance.

"At least we're going downhill," Gabriella said. "I didn't enjoy the first part."

"Was it the dust, the snakes, or the thirst?" Nadine said.

"Now that I've seen them, the snakes."

Nadine shaded her eyes. "We're hours behind. We

should have been at the coast by now."

"Slowing down to miss killer snakes does that to you."

"Arpad, why do you have snakes?" Nadine asked. "Did you introduce them?"

"They came with the terraforming package," Arpad said. "They keep the smaller vermin down—and something to do with insect control."

"They're creepy," Gabriella said. "Will that guy be okay?"

"He is in great pain, but he will not die," Arpad said. "Their bite will not kill you. But it hurts more and more for the first day, then releases. If we had left him to ride alone, he would fall off his horse and die of thirst." Vidor had detached two men with water to ride back with a snake-bitten man and collected two of the waiting riders as they passed.

"Better him than me. Where is this other cache of water, then?" Nadine said.

"We should be close," Arpad said.

"We should have been there hours ago," Nadine said. "We don't have much margin for error here." Nadine walked her horse faster and picked her way along the dry, rocky riverbed they were descending.

Vidor led the column, two of the earlier scouts with him. "Any thoughts, great Khan?" Nadine asked.

"All will be well, Ms. Nadine," Vidor said. "We should be at the water point shortly."

Nadine rode up next to him and leaned over to speak. "Everybody is thirsty. The horses, too. Are we lost?"

Vidor spoke softly. "We are not lost. But the last water party was. They may have got lost in the dark and be wandering these hills. We passed the marked water point an hour ago. If they sent a rider back, she did not find us."

"Are we in trouble?"

The group straggled behind them. They had ridden for hours, up and down a two thousand-meter pass, with no food and limited water.

"The horses are not spent, but they will need water soon. The men and women worry me."

"Again, are we in trouble?"

"I think so, yes."

They found the first rider dead ten minutes later.

"He fell," Vidor said. He pointed at the rider's horse. It had bled out in the dark. "Missed his footing. I don't know if they got separated or what happened. But this one has spilled their water. We need the water from the second one. But we cannot see it."

"We can fire a gun," Arpad said. "The other will hear it and come to us."

"And the roadblock people will hear it, too," Nadine said, "and wonder what's going on. And our friends will hear it and think the attack is starting early. They'll charge around that point and right into that Gauss gun's fire."

"We cannot allow that to happen." Vidor stood in his saddle. "Everyone, attend me. We have no more water. We are still some time from our destination. We cannot signal the others."

The group choked out some murmured acknowledgments. The second sun was just cresting the horizon, and talking hurt.

"We will not wait," Vidor said. "A few hours more, my friends. Then we will be on the coast road. Once there, we will collect ourselves, ready our weapons, then charge the city people. Some of us may be hurt. Some may be killed. But they have only the one Imperial weapon. We will surprise them, and they will not react fast. A quick, bold stroke and we will chase these city people back to their lairs. I will do this. Arpad and I." He patted Arpad's shoulder. "I will do this. Who is with me?"

The crowd cheered, and Nadine and Gabriella joined.

"He's crazy," Gabriella said.

"Like a fox," Nadine said. "This could work."

"And if it doesn't?"

"You won't be complaining about the heat anymore."

Andrew Moriarty

CHAPTER TWENTY-THREE

"Again, do it again," Jake yelled. "Once more. Back along the road." He pulled on the reins, attempting to turn his horse, but nothing happened. His horse continued trotting forward, ignoring him.

But this was the third practice attempt, and his two escorting riders knew what to do. They closed beside him and bracketed his horse, then leaned in and muscled her into a turn till he was facing back along the road.

"You are surely the most useless rider I have ever, ever seen, Admiral Jake," the woman on his left said, pushing his horse.

"I'll bet you'd be equally useless, Siblee, on a spaceship," the right-side rider said. "To each his own."

"True, I guess. Back to where we started, Admiral Jake?"

"Yes, thank you," Jake said. "Just one more practice run and we're ready."

The group of twenty riders collected behind Jake's horse and trotted down the road back to their starting point. At the crossroad, they milled around, then turned back the way they came, formed a column of two, ten ranks deep. Tam and Ket followed Sheriff Tran, then Jake and his escorts.

All the riders fiddled with their weapons and harnesses, and when they were ready, each raised a weapon in their right hand. Half brandished a sword, half a revolver.

Except Jake, of course. The first time he tried it, he'd slipped and nearly skewered his horse, so his sword was snapped into its scabbard. Once all the arms were up, Jake yelled, "Get ready! Three, two, one, go."

The lead riders galloped off. Others followed, spaced behind them at one-second intervals. The first two riders approached the next crossroads, but ten meters from it, they split, the right-hand one turning counterclockwise, the left clockwise around the intersection. The two lines behind them split as well. The lead riders slowed, came back together, and turned to face the intersection. In a matter of ten seconds, a circle of riders faced the intersection inward, half pointing swords, half revolvers. A gap was left for Jake and his chaperones to ride up and halt in the middle. They were the last to arrive—the two escorts had to control their own horses, as well as Jake's.

"Well done, all of you," Jake said. "A fine display. We're ready. Let's go show these pretenders what it means to stand against a representative of the real Emperor. Form up."

The group milled around again, then formed up and rode down the road. Woods and orchards blocked their view, but they moved steadily to the crossroads the scouts had viewed.

After ten minutes, they cleared the orchards on either side, and their view opened up. The road wove between fields ahead of them, wagons and people waiting ahead.

Sheriff Tran rode next to Jake. "Pretenders? The real Emperor?"

"Somebody has to run the planet," Jake said. "Why not your people? You seem reasonable and well organized."

"This is a damn fool idea," Sheriff Tran said.

"It will work," Jake said. "They're not expecting an organized force. Once they know what's going on, they'll let us pass or run away."

"They shoot that Gauss thing. They'll slaughter us."

"No, they won't. They've never shot it before. And it's only one weapon, a big weapon, but only one. It can only shoot in one direction, and while they're doing that, we'll be attacking from all the other directions."

"They could gun us down from a distance."

"First, they need somebody who's good at shooting from a distance. All the questions I've asked, nobody has ever seen those guns fired. We don't know if they even work. And second, even if they do work, the 'city people,' as you call them, sure haven't been practicing. And third, do the city people hate you enough to just start firing at random at strangers?"

"People get scared enough, strange things happen."

"They're all alone out here, away from the city. They're more confused than scared. And it's the chancellor's people you said. The dead chancellor. They won't know who they are working for now. Why not us?"

"You willing to bet your life on that?" the sheriff asked.

"I'm right here, next to you," Jake said. "Kivi and I are dressed differently from you. Even if they don't know what a skin suit looks like, they know we're not Magyarian, so we'll be the first to be shot."

"Good point," the sheriff said. "I'll hide behind you. You ready?"

"As I'll ever be."

"Ride," the sheriff yelled.

Legio XXI Magyar, the most heavily armed twenty of them, thundered down the road toward the roadblock. Two men in the chancellor's colors stood next to a cart full of vegetables, probably turnips. They had body armor on, but only copper from the color, and their only weapon was a sword. Four more sat in the shade of a roadside tree. Jake's group approached at a fast but measured pace. As the horses closed, they put hands on their weapons. One unslung a shotgun, and the other slung a Gauss rifle from their shoulder. They didn't point the weapons. Yet.

Jake's group split twenty meters away and formed the rolling circle around the roadblock. The five men and one woman twirled in place, not knowing who to follow. Their heads pivoted back and forth. The shotgun and Gauss rifle men both unlimbered their weapons and held them but didn't point them at anybody in particular.

The circle formed, and Jake's group drew weapons, pointing swords and revolvers into the center. The roadblock crew was a collection of wide eyes and spinning heads.

"What's this? What in the Emperor's name? Who are you?"

Questions rained out.

Jake's escorts slowed his horse, then stopped it between them. He kept his hands in front of him. "Halt," Jake yelled loudly.

"We're already halted, Jake," Tam whispered.

"It's for effect, Tam."

"It sounds dumb, Jake."

"Not now," Jake said, raising his voice. "I am Jake Stewart, Admiral of the Delta Militia, appointed by the Emperor Dashi the First to restore Imperial control of this sector. God save the Emperor!"

"God save the Emperor, and god save his admiral," the planters chorused.

The chancellor's people jumped at the shouted salutation, but several joined in after a pause.

"Who are you?" Jake asked.

"You're that spaceman," the shortest man said.

His uniform was a different color, and he had bars on it like a sergeant. A piece of black fabric circled his right upper arm.

"I am. I'm also the Emperor's personal representative. I asked who are you?"

"We're not supposed to let anybody into the city," the sergeant said.

"I didn't ask why you were here, but thanks for that," Jake said. "But since you mention it, who says you're not to let us in the city?"

"Chancellor does."

"No, he doesn't. He's dead. I saw him die in the fire on the boat. You heard about the fire."

The sergeant nodded.

"The chancellor's dead. The baron's dead. I saw the boat burn. I was there."

"His people sent us here," the sergeant said.

"On what authority? The baron's gone, so is the government. I have orders to recognize legitimate governments. Your government was legitimate, but now you don't have one. I have an Imperial warrant to take over the city till elections for a council has been held."

"The chancellor's cousin sent us out here. Said to secure the road into the city."

"You work for his cousin?"

"No, we work for the chancellor. Well, did work for the chancellor."

"Let me see if I understand this," Jake said. "Some random person with no known authority, who you've never worked for before, told you, the six of you, to go out in the middle of nowhere to guard a road that's never been guarded before, against people you've never had to guard it against before. And meanwhile, the former government of the planet is all dead, and you're going to oppose an Imperial official in performing their duties because somebody's cousin says you should."

"Put it like that," the sergeant said.

"Plus, you're outnumbered," Tran said. "Heavily outnumbered."

"We've got this," the man with the Gauss rifle said, hefting it up.

"One of this," Tram said. "Can't shoot us all."

"I could get some of you."

"You really want to shoot random people you've never met before because some cousin you've never met says so."

"I met him," the sergeant said. "Once." He looked at the others. "Or did I. Was this one the tall kid?"

"No," another chancellor's man said. "This one is the blond one. Works at the bakery."

The silence stretched.

"Sooo..." Jake said, "you're going to get killed for a baker?"

"No," the sergeant shook his head. "Just no." He took his hand off his belt. "What happens now?"

"Any of you in Imperial service?" Jake said. "Militia? Customs? Navy?"

"Nope," the sergeant shook his head. "Nope."

"That weapon"—Jake pointed at the Gauss rifle— "that's Imperial property. Give us that. Any of the rest of you have Imperial property? Government-issued weapons?" The others shook their head. "Who gave you the armor?"

"We have to pay for it ourselves," the sergeant said.

"Then, it's yours. Leave the Gauss rifle, and you're free to go."

"What if I don't want to leave it?" the Gauss rifle man asked.

"Have you trained to shoot it?" Jake asked.

"I know the basics."

"I'll conscript you as its operator. You'll get Imperial wages, and you'll be a member of Legio XXI Magyar and subject to Imperial authority. The pay isn't great, but it's steady. But with or without you, that weapon belongs to the Emperor."

The man weighed it for a moment, then spotted the sheriff. "You're Tran. Sheriff from up north somewhere, right?"

"Yep," Tram said.

"What say I give it to you?"

"I'll give it to this Admiral Jake fellow. He's the real deal."

"Huh," the Gauss man said. He rotated the rifle and shoved it stock-first at Jake. "Here you go. Not my problem. We can go?"

"Sure. We're going to the city," Jake said. "Would you folks like to ride with us? We have plenty of provisions.

Courtesy of the Emperor Dashi."

The roadblock crew exchanged glances and muttered among themselves.

"Why not?" the sergeant said. "We haven't been paid in a while, and I want to go back anyways." He gave the cross-chest salute. "Long live Emperor Dashi!"

CHAPTER TWENTY-FOUR

It took another two hours to reach the coast road, and the group of riders was straggling by the end in the blazing sun.

"I see now why they made us wear these hats," Gabriella said, plodding behind Nadine. "Without them, that sun would kill me."

"Still might," Nadine said.

"And besides, it looks great. Sets off my highlights."

"I wear it better."

"You? No, it's too young for you. You need something more mature."

"Mature? You're saying that I'm too old to dress like this?"

"These hats are... frisky... that's it. Frisky. Frisky is a young thing."

"When we get to the water, I'll show you frisky, infant," Nadine said. "I'll frisky you so hard you'll bounce off the horse and onto those cactus things." Nadine sucked in her breath. "But first, a drink."

"A long drink."

"Very long drink. Drink as much water as I can hold."

"And maybe a rest."

"In the shade," Nadine said, holding her reins as her horse picked its way down. "A rest in the shade, where it's cool, with lots of water."

The group came down a hill above a dry riverbed. A grove of trees lined the wash, and the group collected under them.

"Ten-minute break," Vidor called. "Off the horses.

Walk them and check their hooves. See to your weapons. We will be at the road shortly."

Nadine and Brie slid off the horses and flopped to the ground. Nadine tried to bend and examine her horse's hoof, but fatigue made her stumble to the ground.

Gabriella dropped to her knees. "This horse is amazing. Tough, climbed up and down in the dark, hasn't complained about the lack of water."

"Vidor said he was giving us some of the best horses. 'A matter of prestige for the leaders,' he said."

"Or he thinks that we need the help."

"That's probably more likely," Nadine said. "Either way, I'm grateful."

Gabriella gestured at the canyon walls. "If I wasn't dying of thirst, this canyon would be pretty."

They were in a mile-wide steep valley. Sheer cliffs of sedimentary rock lined each side, light-green and dark red alternating bands on one side, black and ocher on the other. Stubby trees with needle leaves lined the dry riverbed, and barrel cactus spread out to the rock face. A dry wind blew down from behind them as the high dry plains whistled down to the cooler ocean littoral. The trees swayed, and a bug buzzed its displeasure at being disturbed from its nap.

They sat and listened to desert insects buzzing in the heat. Gabriella closed her eyes and started to snore after two minutes. Vidor came back and shook her.

Gabriella sat up. "Do we have to attack at the hottest part of the day?"

"There's nowhere to hide by the ocean. We're invisible to the road in this canyon until we're right on the road. Then they can't miss seeing us," Vidor said. "As soon as we hit the road, we ride."

"I drive spaceships," Nadine said. "Not chase people on horses."

"No spaceships here," Vidor said. He raised his voice. "Enough rest. Enough waiting. We ride to victory." He climbed onto his horse and marshaled the others."

"Pretty masterful when he wants to be," Brie said.

"Indeed," Nadine said. "Maybe he's not as stupid as he sounds."

"Does it matter if he is?"

"Not in the least. He just has to win this war, take over the planet, get us our charts, and we'll wish him well."

"Nothing else in the interim?"

"We'll find something to amuse ourselves. He's not Mr. Right, but he could be Mr. Right Now. Forward to victory!"

Gabriella furrowed her brow. "Really?"

Nadine clambered up on her horse. "Seemed like the thing to say. Let's go, spacewoman."

This part of the coast was a series of small bays, with rocky points between them, backed by high bluffs leading to hills and mountains. The road snaked on the flat land between pebbled beaches and the bluffs. The bluffs' height made the high mountains invisible except for the peaks. Seasonal rivers cut gullies out of the hills. They followed one such river downstream, hiding them from view, until they reached the road.

The group clambered out of the gully onto the crushed gravel road, stepping carefully past the cactus and prickly bushes. The whole sweep of the bay was visible from north to south. On the southern city end, a cartload of provisions was just rounding the far point. Away from the city, a two thousand-foot mountain blocked all view past the next point, where the snipers and the roadblock waited. The road was empty. Prickly bushes, dead and alive, filled the roadside ditches and hemmed the road in.

"Forward," Vidor said. "Canter till the point, then charge."

"I can't canter." Nadine said. " I never learned that."

"Just follow," Arpad said.

The group rolled forward. The four leaders pulled away from the others.

Nadine yelled and pointed back. "Don't we need those people?"

"Their horses are spent," Arpad yelled over the drumming hooves. "We have the best. It's up to us."

The group cantered to the point, then past it. The next bay opened up. Not more than a hundred yards ahead, two carts blocked the road. A figure was visible underneath, watching the north road. Four others lay in the shade of a tarp hidden twenty yards back behind the rocks. A cooking fire and tethered horses completed the scene.

Arpad and Vidor yelled a war cry, and their horses accelerated to a charge. Nadine didn't change her stance, but her horse responded to the yells and picked up speed.

"Whooooooa," Nadine yelled.

She nearly bounced off as her horse jumped a wide ditch and lost the reins before leaning in and grasping the horse's mane. The reins hung loose, but her horse didn't care, chasing the leaders.

The four drummed down the road. The figure under the carts rolled out from under and ran to the others. He yelled, his words lost in the drumming of hooves.

Vidor reached down, yanked his sword out, and waved it as he rode. Arpad did the same. Brie reached down and pulled a revolver. Smoke puffed as she fired the gun in the air.

Nadine didn't dare let go of her horse's mane, so she just watched as they raced down the road. Arpad and Victor booted the horses faster, then Gabriella followed suit.

The running sentry reversed course and scampered back to the carts as their charging angle threatened to cut him off. Vidor, Arpad, and Gabriella raced directly at the four stumbling sleepers, yelling, waving, cursing and firing a gun in the air. Three runners turned and dashed into the boulders.

The fourth stepped up, took a two-hand stance, and fired at the charging horsemen. A line of fire creased

Nadine's arm. The gunman lost his nerve, dropped his revolver, and ran.

Nadine's saw a glint of metal to her left, grabbed the reins and forced the horse to slow. Arpad, Vidor, and Gabriella pulled farther away from her. She slowed to a trot as they drove ahead.

A tall figure in lime-green with a long gun materialized from behind a boulder in front of Nadine. It was the Gauss rifle sniper who had been concealed in the rocks. He stepped behind the three leading horseman as they passed. The rifle came down, and he pulled the trigger, firing a burst with the cloth-ripping sound. He had fired high and shot only air. He stopped, corrected his aim, and centered on Vidor's back.

Nadine yelled, kicked her right foot free of her horse, and leaped on him as she passed. Her trailing foot caught in the stirrup, but she snagged the man as she went by. She banged her shoulder into his back and grabbed at his waist. He tipped over, and she grasped his belt. Her horse continued, and she held onto the shooter's belt as he was dragged along the road. He banged into the ground once and dropped the rifle. Her horse slowed to a stop, banging him into the ground over and over.

Once they stopped, she extracted her foot and rolled off. The shooter lay still.

Nadine stumbled to her feet. Clouds of dust obscured the road in both directions. The other riders yelled from behind her.

"Vidor? Arpad? Brie?"

"Here," Vidor said. "We have them."

Dust settled, and Nadine could make out four figures with raised hands standing under Vidor's sword and Gabriella's gun. Arpad dismounted and searched them for weapons.

"How many are there?" Nadine asked.

"Four here and one under the cart."

"Not how many we see, Horse Khan, how many total.

Ask them. We need to find the others."

The remaining group scrabbled in and milled around. Pista rode up to the two wagons blocking the road. He climbed off his horse, crouched, and pointed his revolver under the nearest one. After a short exchange, the sentry climbed out, hands high. Pista interrogated him, then came over.

"There're six total here, Khan," he said. "The sentry, four resting, and the sniper with the big rifle. Up in the rocks somewhere."

"Everyone," Vidor yelled, "we must find the rifle. Dismount and search the rocks. Quickly, before he escapes or gets to a place to fire. We are in great danger till he is found."

"What does this sniper look like?" Nadine asked.

"We don't need a description. We need the rifle," Vidor said.

"Lime-green colors, tall," Pista said.

"Oh, him." Nadine pointed. "That's the one I got over there." She grinned. "Was he important?"

***

"They'll stop us at the bridge," Jake said.

"No, they have to deal with the Ranchers," Tam said.

"What Ranchers?"

"They have an army, too."

Jake's group was proceeding down the coast road on the north side of the Central Sea, heading for the peninsula that the capital city occupied. A broad river passed through the plains and down into the sea at the county town ahead, the last and largest before they reached the capital city. At the town—called Bridgetown, of course—the road turned south and crossed a bridge. The capital city and its excellent harbor were a day's ride away at the southern tip of the peninsula. On the eastern side of the peninsula, the land was rockier and drier. Only a small fishing port occupied the road there. The two roads, eastern and western, connected just outside the capital city.

"The Ranchers have an army? Where did they get that?" Jake asked. "How big an army?"

Tam scratched her head. "Rumor is, thousands of Ranchers have come together under one of their leaders, Vidor, the old khan's son, and are heading into town to burn all the city people at the stake and raze it to the ground."

"You believe that?" Jake asked.

"That's what that sergeant person told me before he gave you that Gauss rifle."

"What else did he tell you?"

"That thousands of planters had collected under the ambassador's daughter and were massacring any city people they found before going to the palace and burning it. They had reports of dozens of massacres in every county town along the way."

"Thousands?" Jake said.

"Yep," Tran said.

Jake stood in his stirrups. His escorts yelled at him, and he sat but continued to count. "One hundred seventeen, including eight of the chancellor's people who are along for the free food."

"Maybe there are thousands around somewhere else."

"The former ambassador have any daughters other than Tam?"

"Not that I know of."

"Have we been doing any massacring that I missed?" Jake asked.

"Not today," Tran said. "Of course, it's still early. We have the whole day left to be massacring. Never done a massacre. Does it take long?"

"Not long at all, if you plan it right," Jake said.

"Done a lot of massacring, have you, Admiral Stewart?"

Jake thought back to Delta and their uncivil war and remembered spaceships crashing, stations exploding, and a city burning. "Quite a few. Planned, organized, scheduled. I'm quite good at it."

"Is this admiral here serious?" Tram asked Kivi.

"Yes," said Kivi. "Captain Jake, Admiral Jake, he does what has to be done."

"Perhaps I misjudged you spacepeople," Tram said.

"You did," Jake said. "Very much. What's the truth behind those rancher rumors?"

"I don't believe ninety percent of them."

"What's the other ten percent? A couple hundred riders?"

"Could be. Armed like we are. On their way into the city."

"Not very effective, then," Jake said.

"Could say the same of us," Tram said.

"No, because we know how to think. And plan," Jake said. "We'll arrive with plenty of people, appear well armed, be prepared to stay awhile with our own provisions, with off-planet support from a known Empire that's sent an actual ship, at the head of a group that has run their own affairs for years, ready to assume control and stop the anarchy. Who would choose a bunch of rural Ranchers stinking of horse dung or a group of incompetent leading families who let themselves get killed by accident over us?"

"When you put it that way—"

"I do put it that way. All we need is an inside man or two, somebody to support us. And I know where to find these." Jake turned to his escort people. "I need to talk to Tam. Can you bring me up there, please?"

Tam made him cross the bridge into the town before they stopped. After a few minutes' discussion with Jake, she gathered her best armed troops and stationed them around the plaza at the center of town. She and Ket arranged to have two dozen carts full of food and

213

provisions placed in the center of the square. Ket took ten people and dragged a desk into the square as a podium. Jake took ten others and gave them a list of things he wanted scrounged from the town.

"Wooden doors?" his escort asked.

"As many as you can stack onto the carts," Jake said. "And woodworking tools. Make sure you pay for them."

"Jake," Tam called. "We're ready out here."

She had collected the chancellor's people from the roadblock and any other city people they could find. They ended up with a group of eleven. The chancellor's people, passing traders, and a newly married couple on their honeymoon enjoying a rural retreat. Jake and Tam jumped up onto the desk and addressed the crowd.

"You folks are going to be our messengers," Tam said. "Pass on some info."

"I don't work for you," the sergeant from the roadblock said. "I work for—"

"Nobody," Jake said. "Your boss is dead. You work for yourselves now. The group of you are representative of all the city now."

"We're not representative," the sergeant said. "There isn't even anybody from the council families here."

"That's 'cause they're all dead, and their supporters, and subordinate families all died in that fire. It's just you now. And no government. You have options. Want to hear them?"

"Do we have a choice?"

"Indeed, you do," Jake said. "You can just run off and go home and tell everyone you meet some weird guy gave you dinner and sent you away, and that's all you know. That what you want?"

The crowd was quiet.

"Thought so," Jake said. "The government is dead. Baron, all of them. But nowhere in human space goes without a government for long. At the end of the week, there will be a new government on this planet. Here's your choices."

Jake held up a finger. "First, the former controlling families, what's left of them, will fight to take over the city. They've been planning it forever, but there's not enough of them anymore. None of them has a majority, none of them will win. There can't be a hundred of them total left, and they'll be killing each other forever. Meanwhile, no government, no salaries, no maintenance, and imagine one of them does something stupid, like blowing up the water supply. You want that sort of anarchy?"

The crowd murmured, "No."

"Second, the remaining non-first families could do the same thing. Fight each other, fight the remaining first families, and take over. And burn things down. And, frankly, do just as bad a job of it. Agree?"

"My family has been running the metal shop forever," one man objected. "We can run a shop, we can run a city."

"I've been to your shop," the sergeant said. "Your dad, as a planetary executive, he'd make a great metal worker. I don't want you in charge."

"Who, then?" the metal worker said.

"Those couple hundred Ranchers riding their horses into town? How about them?" Jake asked.

Everyone laughed.

"I'm an admiral in the Delta Militia," Jake said. "I represent an Empire. Yes, it's small, but bigger than yours. We have ships, we have technology, we have metal, we can trade, and most importantly, we have a legitimate claimant to the throne, and we're here. We want things to be stable, and we're too far away to interfere with your internal affairs. And we don't want to be local, so we'll give you legitimacy but leave you alone. The planters." He pointed at Tam. "The planters have run their own government for years. They're organized. Look around you. What do you see? Troops. Uniformed and disciplined troops. Sheriffs. Police. Food. Logistics. Smart people doing smart things. You know Tam, the late ambassador's daughter. I can make her a baron—a baroness. She'll be appointed governor. Sure, she'll change the rules about trading and how the planters can live in the city, but that would have happened eventually, and those rules just made your bosses rich. Your dead bosses. Prosperity, stability, rejoining the Empire. And, economically, things will end up better for all of you. We are going to ride into the city the day after tomorrow. You don't have to do anything. Just tell your friends not to fight. I'll proclaim her Baroness Magyar and Imperial governor. Problem solved."

"What if she dies?" one person asked.

"Unlike the old baron, this will be a dynasty. I'll make it a hereditary title in the name of Emperor Dashi. She'll have kids, and the kids will rule after her."

"Who will she marry?" the sergeant asked.

"How should I know?" Jake said. "Whoever she wants. One of you, probably. A city family."

Everybody started shaking their heads. "Nope, that won't work."

"Why not?" Jake asked.

"We had this problem before," the sergeant said. "Can't marry a city family and raise them up at the expense of the others. One winner, too many losers."

"But you had the baron's grandson, Marchello, before," Jake said.

The crowd laughed.

"The thing is, Mr. Spaceman," the sergeant said, "you may have noticed that Marchello wasn't the brightest moon in orbit, so to speak."

"He didn't seem very... quick," Jake said.

"That's the truth. His father and mother were... Well, let's say they were more closely related than immediately obvious. We couldn't do that sort of pairing again. It was a temporary solution, till we found a better one. We never did."

"Well, Tam's right here. She's a solution."

"But we're back in the same place. How to ensure

succession without starting another civil war. She needs to be able to marry somebody and have kids, but who?"

The crowd was silent, then one person pointed at Jake. "What about spaceman here? He's not related to any of us. He's from the Empire. He doesn't have any local ties. Why doesn't she marry him?"

CHAPTER TWENTY-FIVE

"We're just lucky that I was along," Nadine said. "Right, Brie?"

"You did catch the rifle person," Gabriella said. "But I covered the other four."

"Good point. Well done, spacewoman." Nadine high-fived her.

"Arpad and I were of some help," Vidor said. "And the others. You did not do this alone."

"Of course, of course," Nadine said. "All you other folks, once I showed you the way, you whipped them into shape. Good job, boys."

Men in the group grinned and cheered back at Nadine.

"How do you do that?" Vidor said. "They were ready to kill you earlier."

"They were confused and unsure what would happen then," Nadine said. "But I told them what needed to be done and made them do it. They were wrong, and I'm right. Plus, we won. Everybody loves a winner."

"This is true, Ms. Nadine," Arpad said. "We will all follow you to the ends of the Earth now. You and your friend Brie, of course."

Nadine grinned and waved at the troops, who raised a cheer, then drifted back to ride with Gabriella.

"Follow you to the ends of the Earth?" Gabriella said.

"He'll follow you to the nearest set of bushes, for sure," Nadine said. "Give me some of that water."

Brie handed her a water bag. "You keep drinking like that, and you'll pee your pants."

"If I had to choose between that or hiking that oven

desert we were in again, I'll pee my pants every day. I'll ride without pants if it comes to that. Speaking of taking off pants, how are you and Arpad doing?"

"We're taking it slow."

"Because you're a conscientious, traditional girl who likes romance?"

"Because his cousin knocked out a guy at the roadblock with the pommel of her sword. Hit him so hard he dropped on the spot."

"Too bad for him he wasn't wearing armor."

"He was. Left a two-inch dent in it. That girl packs a punch. What about you and your khan friend?"

"The war's keeping him busy. It's difficult for him. Lots of things to keep track of. There's math."

"He does look like the type who needs to be told what side of his horse to get on each morning."

"He's not that stupid."

Gabriella raised an eyebrow.

"Fine," Nadine said. "He's dumb as a bag of rocks most of the time. Arpad is smarter but not by much. But Arpad knows that. That's why he's always asking me questions. That, and he's always fishing for ways to impress you."

"I could grow to like this planet," Gabriella said, "if all the men are like that."

"They can be like that other places, too. Why, I remember once Jake... Never mind."

They rode in silence for a while. The full group of over a hundred riders spread behind them. After the fracas at the sniper point, the rest of the group had charged the original roadblock. The five people there hadn't even resisted, just kept turning back and waiting for the Gauss rifle to fire. Only one had offered any resistance to the thundering riders, the one Arpad's cousin had clocked. The two wagons blocking the road at the sniper nest were full of water. The whole group had watered up, collected the city people, and ridden down the coast.

Their convoy of water and provisions followed. A few hundred more riders had crossed the strait farther east with enough aloe sap to keep the horse fungus down and was proceeding apace, but they were still at least two days behind.

The main group moved down the east side of the peninsula. One small fishing village lined the road a few miles ahead, then an easy road down to the city walls. The plan was to overnight at the village and make an early start the next morning, arrive at the city, and demand entrance.

"At the city, what if we don't get in?" Gabriella said.

"We'll talk our way in. Why not let Vidor run things? He's here, he has troops, they know his family. And they won't have to knuckle under to some other city family."

"What if that doesn't work?"

"I have a backup plan. I need to talk to some people in the village. Regardless, once we're in the city, Vidor will be the boss. I've been quizzing the village people here. I don't think there's a hundred armed troops or police or customs left in that city, and they are from different groups that don't get along. We should be able to get inside."

"And if that doesn't work?"

"I have a backup, backup plan. Some families that have dealt with him in the past. I've talked to some of their junior members, put a few ideas in their heads. They'll support us once we're in."

"How do you think of all this?"

"I ask myself, what would Jake do? And 'cause I'm smarter than you, I come up with these cooler and cleverer plans."

"Really believe you're smarter than him?"

"Not really."

"He's a smart guy."

"Was a smart guy," Nadine said. "Village in twenty minutes. I want to get off this horse and drink a bucket of beer."

"Not water?"

"Beer is mostly water. Kills two planets with one asteroid."

Vidor, predictably, put his headquarters in a tavern. Ranchers thronged into the tavern for food and drink. Nadine toured the town and paid special attention to the waterfront, chatting with a group of fishermen and giving them some money. Arpad insisted on paying the tavern owner for everything they took and bringing in provisions from their wagons.

"Long live Khan Vidor," the tavern owner said, dropping off four mugs of beer.

"See?" Vidor said. "Even here, they support me."

"He's just saying that because he made more money today than he has in the last year," Nadine said. "By the time we've left he'll have sold every single item of food or booze he can lay his hands on. Which is, in itself, a lesson. You need to keep the economy running properly if you're going to be in charge."

"The economy, yes," Vidor said. He rubbed his chin. "The economy."

"You have heard about the economy," Nadine said. "Right?"

"Oh, yes. Very economical." Vidor stroked his chin again. "But that, I will delegate to Arpad. He studied it in school."

"Arpad studied economics in school?" Nadine pointed. "This Arpad?"

"You told me," Gabriella said, "you told me that you studied geology." She took a drink of beer.

"I did. For two years, from the computers, you know. But there were other modules. On many subjects."

"Arpad studies widely. He was most interested in many things," Vidor said.

"Economics? You studied economics courses on the computer?"

"No, it was part of a history of the Magyar people, from Old Earth. History of their economics."

"You studied the history of Old Earth economics?"

"No. Just Magyar. They called it Hungary then. I found out some historical information."

"When historical?" Nadine chugged her beer and signaled for another. "Imperial colonizes historical?"

"Pre-Empire. When they were part of a wide-ranging Earth Empire called communism."

"Didn't lots of people starve under this communism thing?" Gabriella asked.

Arpad blinked. "Yes."

Nadine glared at him until another beer arrived. She took a swig, put it down, and faced him. "Maybe not do anything that you learned in that course, then."

"Of course," Arpad said. "But you know economics. I can take your advice."

"I do not," Nadine said. "Who told you that?"

"Brie did," Arpad said. "She told me that you learned from Admiral Stewart, that he was a noted economist and economic planner on your world."

Nadine took another drink. "It's Brie now, is it? What do you call him? Arpy?"

"Whatever I want," Gabriella said. "And don't change the subject. Admiral Stewart is famous for his trades and economic planning."

"I'm not Admiral Stewart," Nadine said.

"But you trained under him."

"With him. Or near him. He didn't train me in anything. And not to make too fine a point of it, but I'm usually on top. Look. City people." Nadine pointed at a group of others coming into the bar. "These must be your friends."

A half dozen city people strode in and made for the table. Their two-toned bright-colored outfits contrasted the Ranchers' somber grays and browns. Everyone shook hands, clasped shoulders, and slapped backs. Vidor and Arpad introduced them, and Nadine promptly forgot their names.

"I declare myself khan," Vidor said. "Khan of all the Magyars. And since that is the entire planet, I will be the khan of you all. What say you?"

"I'm sorry about your late father," the oldest of the assembled group said. His house colors were a red jacket with green check pants, so Nadine dubbed him Red Jacket. "He was a good man, if a little hasty. But we worked well together. The ranches and our group have always done well together, yes?"

The crowd murmured an assent.

Red Jacket continued. "We will continue to work with you, and with the death of your father, it is just that you be the khan of the Ranchers, but the city people are not used to being ruled by outsiders."

"Outsiders?" Nadine said. "The population of this planet is tiny. None of you are outsiders—there's not enough of you to be outside. You're all insiders. You folks especially."

"Who are you again?" Red Jacket asked. One of his companions leaned in and muttered to him. "Right, you're the spacer that came from that so-called Empire. You escaped the boat."

"It's not a so-called Empire, it's a real Empire, with a real Emperor," Nadine said. "I've met him. Dashi the First. And our moon is bigger than your planet, with more ships, more industry, more technology, and we found you. You didn't find us. One way or another, welcome to the Empire, buddy."

"That's a pretty aggressive statement," Red Jacket said. "I don't like your attitude."

"You'll like it even less if we drop an asteroid in your Central Ocean and wash your little city away. You're part of the Empire now, whether you want it or not."

"If we don't?"

"What are you going to do about it?"

Red jacket looked at his friends, then grinned. "Your Empire will be far away. So nothing. Long live Emperor...

Dashi?"

"Emperor Dashi the First," Nadine said.

"A toast. Long live the Emperor!"

"The Emperor," everyone said, then drank. Nadine drained her mug and signaled for more.

"If he's really a descendant of the Emperor, then we're joining," Red Jacket said. "Why not? We like Empires. On to other matters. Matters more important to us. How do we fit within this Empire? Colony? Member planet? Duchy? Which is it? And how do we govern ourselves? As a democracy? Republic? Imperial officials?"

"Well..." Nadine grimaced, gulped more beer, then set her glass down and took a deep breath. "We'll make a list of who you want to be the governor. We'll take it back to Dashi. He'll pick somebody off that list and make them the planetary governor and make them a noble. They'll rule in the Emperor's name. You'll need a council to advise, of course. The governor, baron, whatever will handle anything to do with off planet. You'll be in charge of your own internal affairs, but you'll have to pay tax on imports and exports. That will pay for running things. The city people appoint or elect a council to run the city. Up to you. Ranchers rule under their hereditary leader. Those Planter people have their own system. The baron or duke—whatever—appoints all those leaders to the council and a few others. Now you're in the Empire. You can trade, and you have a planetary government. The rest of it can be a federation, a republic, whatever you want. Military junta for all we care. But a single planetary government. You got a complaint about the Empire, you take it to the governor, they deal with it. You handle police, fire, taxes, welfare, whatever you want."

Nadine took a big drink.

"Wow!" Gabriella whispered. "That was amazing. How did you think about all that stuff?"

"It's how we run things on Delta," Nadine whispered. "Dashi runs his council, but all the members are from competing factions. The Militia, different grower families, the Free Traders, his own company. He's got his own power base, but he lets the others do what they want. Some are hereditary, like the corporate families. The Free Traders are a democracy. They vote their captains in. Some families are democratic. They all do their own thing in their own space, but Dashi handles disputes between parties. And he's in control of all the trade. It's an economic Empire."

"You're so smart," Gabriella said. "Knowing all this stuff."

"I paid attention," Nadine said. "I read books." She frowned. "But, mostly, Jake explained it to me one day. This was his thing. I miss him. What?"

Red Jacket had started talking.

"If we join your Empire, we have to decide who goes on this list of yours."

"Only one name on the list," Nadine said. "Vidor here. He's going to be in charge, from the Empire's point of view. Remember, this only works if you all agree to support him."

"Why him?"

"Why not him? He's head of a large group. They have an army. They run businesses. They deal with you people in the city."

"They're not allowed in the city overnight."

"That's surely going to change, and, honestly, is this something you'll go to war for?"

"Nope," Red Jacket said. "We kept the last government because it was easy, and we were used to it. It had problems, but it was easier than changing things."

"And now the change is forced on you."

"Suppose we support Khan Vidor here as planetary executive. He can be the new baron. We'll want some trading concessions, of course, but if we let it be known that the local Empire supports him, it's probably a done deal. There might be some issues in the city, but a show of force and a few speeches and things will move on. People want somebody in charge. But what happens next?"

"Next?"

"What happens when he dies? The last baron was temporary."

"We'll make it whatchamacallit—his kids take over."

"Hereditary."

"Right. He's the baron and his son after him, too."

"Which means he needs children. Which means a wife."

"He's not bad looking. I wouldn't kick him out of bed for eating crackers," Nadine said. "I'm sure he'll find some willing woman."

"Kick him out of bed for eating crackers?"

"Sorry, Old Earth saying a friend of mine used. Just find him a wife. I hear his family was already doing that."

"And not doing so well," Red Jacket said.

"Try harder," Nadine said. She looked at Vidor. "Don't you want to weigh in on this?"

"You have said you support me as khan," Vidor said. "And want me to be the new baron, and you are convincing my city friends of this as well. I think I should let you talk."

"Don't you care who your wife will be?"

"I was told from an early age that she would be chosen for me, and for the good of the family, I must accept. I would like to pick my own, but that is impossible. Besides"—Vidor curved a glum smile—"I know a woman I would ask. She is incredible, but I am not sure she would have me."

"Pluck up your courage, then. Suggest her to these folks. Arpad, are you looking for a wife for him?"

Arpad nodded. "I am helping. But it is difficult. Vidor is impetuous. She must be strong-willed."

"And smart. If you're going to run a planet, horseleader, you need smart people with you."

"I know a smart woman. One who is extremely smart.

A leader in her own right."

"She sounds great. You should put her on your short list, then."

Gabriella kicked Nadine under the table.

"What? Stop that, Brie. Right. You need a smart woman, strong-willed. One who doesn't take guff from anybody. Know anybody like that, city man?" Nadine said.

Red Jacket agreed. "I have met a woman like that, yes. She would be a great consort to our new baron."

"And she is—I mean must be brave as well," Arpad said. "A woman who would ride into a fight without a weapon in hand and fight the strongest of her foes."

"Sounds like a great lady." Nadine jerked. "Brie, stop kicking me."

"And attractive, of course," Vidor said. "Physically beautiful. Outgoing. Outspoken. A sight to behold."

"Long list of requirements you all have here," Nadine said. "Your new baroness. She has to be attractive, athletic, smart, outgoing, brave, strong-willed. A fighter, a thinker, and a beauty all at once. Have you got somebody in mind?"

Red Jacket looked at his party. They all nodded. Arpad and Vidor were grinning.

Brie shook her head and put it in her hands. "I think they have somebody in mind already, Nadine."

"Well," Nadine said. "I'd like to meet her." The room laughed. "What?" Nadine said. "Why are you all looking at me like that?"

CHAPTER TWENTY-SIX

"Can we lock him out of the control room?" Yvette asked. She stifled a yawn.

"Willowby? Not without him noticing, no," Odette said, putting a hand to her mouth. "Stop that. You're making me yawn, too."

The two women were both seated in the front row of the control room at the pilot's seats. Yvette had the sensor program mirrored on her station.

"We'll just have to keep one of us here all the time," Yvette said, unbuckling her harness and drifting out of her chair. She floated up, back, and down, pushing off again with one foot. They were under thrust—barely, just enough to give gravity.

"We need sleep," Odette said. "At least I do. I'm not cut out for this type of work."

"Bad attitude if you want to someday be a shipmaster."

"I was happy staying in Delta on my family's run between the transfer stations, till you sucked me out, Shipmaster."

"Don't call me shipmaster, not where Willowby can hear. I needed pilots with lots of docking experience, and you were the best we had."

"Try docking a hundred-year-old family ship missing half its thrusters that has a stutter in the main fuel lines. It's amazing how good your reactions become and how practiced you are at manual dockings." Odette ran her hand along the control boards in front of her. "But Jake's ship is a joy to fly. Responsive, powerful, the best sensors. I'm in love. Anything you ask her to do, she does it with a smile."

"Ships don't smile."

"Jake's does."

"It's not Jake's ship. It belongs to the council," Yvette said.

"I notice they didn't make him give up the codes to it."

"You noticed that? So did I."

"Marianne is on the council. Why didn't she put it up for vote?"

"She said she didn't want anybody focusing on the special list of codes. Especially the ones for communications and encryptions."

The rear hatch of the control room flipped open and banged back against the stops. A gray-haired figure emerged.

"Good morning, young ladies," Willowby said, pulling the hatch shut behind him. "Sorry about the banging. I'm not used to micro gravity."

"That is fine, Professor," Odette said. "What brings you here?"

Willowby grinned. "Can't the chief engineer bring himself up to the control room, or is that forbidden now?"

"As long as you don't distract the control room crew, you are welcome."

"What if they distract me?" Willowby said. "In, you know, a personal way."

Odette laughed as she adjusted her board. "Don't worry, Professor, I respect you. You're safe from my attentions. And my distractions."

"At my age," Willowby said, "I'm safe from any and all women's attentions. But I'm up here to make you an offer."

"An offer we can't refuse?"

"You two are working shift and shift. No rest in between. No need for all of that. We're coasting to that gas giant. I'm qualified to watch a board. Why not put me in your rotation? I can log the sensors, and I'll be in the chair if something beeps. I'll wake you up if I catch any big problems, but I can certainly acknowledge the status reports and file the scans."

"Thank you for your consideration, but there is no need," Yvette said. "We're fine. It's not bothering us at all." She tried to stifle a yawn but failed.

Odette clamped her mouth shut but was also unable to stop a yawn.

"Doesn't look like you're doing fine," Willowby said. He touched the overhead bar with two fingers to stop him from drifting backward. "Looks like you are tired. Very tired."

"Odette and I were up late last shift, talking about old friends, and correlating our survey notes. We kept talking too late. It's just a temporary thing." She reached the hatch and spun the locking wheel open.

"I can help you out up here."

"You're better off staying with the engineering crew. I'm sure they are excited to be learning new things from such an eminent teacher." Yvette swung the hatch open. "I am going back for a meal. Will you join me?"

"The engineering crew is cursing the eminent teacher's guts because of the assignments he's assigned them, all the different surveys they have to do, and the lack of computer power to get them done."

Yvette held the hatch open. "We have a jump ship and a jump computer. This computer is more powerful than any on Delta except the one at the university and the main Militia computer. How do they lack computing power?"

"That program that Jake left running is sucking up all of our simulation time. We can hardly run chess games back there."

"Jake left a program running?"

"A big one. Haven't you noticed?"

Odette shook her head. "Control room, thrusters, main drives, and sensors have their own local controls. We only use the main jump system if we're doing navigations, or if we need to archive things."

"Jake has this giant program running. It's sucking up all the computing power. He's pulling in all the sensor logs and doing something with them—cataloging them, perhaps—and I can't shut it down or modify its priority. You didn't know this?"

"Nothing. All the sensor logs?"

"Yep, and communications logs, too?"

"Why would Jake be pulling the communications logs?"

"You can ask him when we find him."

"If we find him," Yvette said. "The planetary comm is still silent. There hasn't been a word since that big fire."

"We'll find him. Jake always comes through."

"Until he doesn't," Odette said. "It's a shame. I liked him."

"Me too." Yvette yawned. "Perhaps I am more tired than I admitted. Professor, if you will excuse me, I need to sleep. And I would prefer it if you would not bother Odette this shift. She has her own work to do." She pulled the hatch open and beckoned him by her.

"Work to do while we're nearly drifting through empty space?" Willowby said.

"I do not tell you how to run engineering, you do not tell me how to run operations."

"True enough," Willowby said, climbing through the hatch. "At least there's only one more shift of this silly micro thrust, and we can begin fueling operations at Magyar IV."

Yvette coughed. "I am afraid that we will be under micro thrust for three more days."

"Three more days? To get to Magyar IV?"

"We are not going to Magyar IV. We are on course for Magyar V."

Willowby flicked his glance between the two women. "And why did you change course? We agreed that we would go to the nearest gas giant to refuel. Magyar IV was nearest."

"We didn't like the... conditions for fueling at four, we felt they were better at five."

"And you decided this without consulting engineering, who is doing the fueling. What conditions, please?"

"Just—conditions," Yvette said.

Willowby kept one hand on the hatch and used the other to twiddle his mustache. He looked at Yvette, turned to see Odette, then back again.

"How long till we arrive?"

"We can commence fueling at five in just under three days."

"Fueling will take at least two days." Willowby scratched his head. "Or longer. I don't remember the gas concentrations. Regardless, then we will be fully fueled up, and we can head back to orbit, pick up Jake and company, and jump back to Delta, assuming he approves."

"Assuming he's alive."

"Well, whatever happens, we need fuel," Willowby said. "Enjoy your nap. But this discussion isn't finished. We'll talk more when we're full of hydrogen."

"I'm looking forward to it," Yvette said.

"I'll bet you are. I'll bet you are," Willowby said, pulling the hatch closed behind him.

Odette waited till the hatch locking ring spun shut before speaking. "He knows."

"He suspects," Yvette said. "Not the same thing. What's this about Jake running some program?"

Odette tapped her screen. "Now that I know where to look, I can see it on the daemon list. He's right. It's taking over everything, except critical functions."

"Why would Jake need that much computing power? What type of program pulls that much computing time?"

"Decryption program."

"He's cracking our codes. Are you sure you can't read those other messages?"

"The council only gave me three decoding keys. Low-level ones for course and arrival data. One works. One for in-system course charting. That one works. The other doesn't do anything on any of the other messages. All we get is gibberish."

"Could Jake have gotten the codes?"

Odette patted her Free Trader overall pocket. "I keep it physically separate, unless I'm working on trying to decode something. I never stored it on ship systems."

"And the messages you stripped from those beacons?"

"I don't store those locally, either, but they come in through ship sensors..."

"And Jake has access to those. He could record everything and be trying to break them, decoder key or not." Yvette rubbed her forehead. "I'm talking like he's still alive."

"You don't really believe he's dead?"

"All the evidence says he is."

"Never stopped Jake. There's another problem."

"Wonderful. Going to share?"

"Another ship passed here. Recently. It tried to strip the beacon, but the request was ignored when it didn't use the right codes."

"Another merchant ship?"

"Didn't send a merchant code. Just some random attempt. The beacon recorded the attempt but didn't respond."

"Pirates?"

"Not a merchant."

"But somebody who knew the beacon was there and knew enough to try to strip it. We don't need this."

"No, but we do need fuel. What happens when we get to Magyar Five?"

"We refuel. Crack some hydrogen. You and I get some sleep while engineering does their thing."

"And after? When we're done fueling."

"According to that message, we'll be contacted before fueling is complete."

"What happens then?"

"Something good." Yvette spun the hatch wheel and yawned again. "I hope."

CHAPTER TWENTY-SEVEN

"It's the logical thing to do, Jake," Tam said. "If I'm going to be a planetary executive, then I need a strong partner, somebody who can help me organize things. I can deal with the politics. You'll handle economics, currency, construction, labor, defense, external relations, technology trade, and commerce. Health and welfare, too—and employment."

Jake and Tam were riding with her "strike force," as Jake had taken to calling it. Just over a hundred armed planters, their new city friends, and lots of wagons. They had marched out early and expected to be at the city gates by nightfall.

"You give me all that work to do, and you'll do what?"

"Agriculture. I know farms and farming and any industries related to that."

"I'll spend all my time killing myself, trying to gain an expertise in areas I know nothing about, and you'll spend time talking to your friends and doing things you've trained for all your life."

"Yep," Tam said.

"Anything else you'll do?"

"Parties," Ket said. "We'll need to have parties. I'll assist her baroness in organizing those."

"Parties?" Jake said. "You want parties?"

"Parties are fun, and, besides, Tam is too serious most of the time. We'll need something to loosen her up. Neither of you can argue against 'bread and circuses,' right?"

"What type of parties?"

"Great parties," Ket said. "With great food. Lots of good wine. Entertainment. Music. Dance."

"What type of entertainment?" Kivi asked.

"Gladiators," Ket said. Everyone scowled at her. "Okay, no gladiators."

"That sounds great," Kivi said.

Jake glared at him. "So, I'll spend all my time working like a dog to run the planet, and the rest of you will be drinking wine, eating great food, and dancing all the time. And you think I'll be okay with that?"

"Absolutely," Tam said.

"Completely," Ket said.

"You wouldn't have it any other way," Tam said. "You're so detail-oriented and information-obsessed you'd go mad if we didn't put you in charge of everything. You'll get up every morning and work all day and still have a list of a hundred things to do when you fall into bed."

"You make me sound like a detail-obsessed killjoy with time for nothing but work," Jake said.

Ket grinned, then turned to Kivi. "Want to say something to your boss, Kivi?"

Kivi coughed. "Sir, it's been a great honor to work with you—"

"Please don't," Jake said.

"And I've learned so much."

"No," Jake said.

"But honesty requires me to give a fair assessment."

"Kivi, shut up," Jake said. Everybody rode in silence for a moment. Jake pulled a coin from his pocket that somebody had given him earlier. "You know, I never did find out how your currency system is set up. Do you have a mint? And what do you use for a central bank?"

Kivi smiled. Ket grinned. Tam outright laughed.

Jake bit his lip. "Damn you all."

***

"No, I will not be the baroness of the planet," Nadine said. "I have too many things to do to stay here."

"It wouldn't be so bad, Ms. Nadine," Arpad said. "Under your plan, the baroness would be mostly ceremonial. The real work of governing the planet would fall to the councils and the planters and the large rancher families. We would take care of all the details, the day-to-day work. You'd only have limited duties."

"I'd have limited duties, would I?" Nadine said. "Like, what type of duties?"

"Mostly just sit and look pretty," Arpad said.

"She specializes in that," Gabriella said. "Lots of experience to draw from there."

"Thank you, Ms. Do You Like My New Hat," Nadine said. "Look pretty?"

"Well," Arpad said, "if Vidor is to be khan and Imperial governor, we will have to receive the leaders of the councils regularly. There will be levies to attend. You will have to preside there."

"What's a levy?" Nadine asked.

"It is a meeting where the people get to meet and greet their sovereign and his consort. It's like a giant party. You dress up in your finest clothes, go to the palace, eat fine food, drink good wine, and talk. Music, dancing, everyone will want to speak with you."

"Finest clothes?" Nadine asked. "What type?"

"Well." Arpad looked over Nadine's shoulder. Gabriella waved. "Different types. Traditional clothes."

Gabriella shook her head.

"Or perhaps those space clothes you wear."

Gabriella shook her head again.

"Or perhaps gowns. Ball gowns?"

Gabriella nodded.

"Yes," Arpad said. "Ball gowns. Like the princesses in the vids you talk of. Many ball gowns."

"And her assistant would have her own ball gowns,"

Gabriella said. "Right, Arpad?" Gabriella nodded again.

"Of course. One for each levy. And you would be able to travel and participate in the activities of the khan's family. Like horse riding."

Nadine looked down at the dusty, sweaty animal she was riding. "Horses?"

"Or... knife fights. Knife training. Ranchers do much with knives."

"I like knives," Nadine said.

"And swords. Of course you would learn the sword," Arpad said.

"Swords could be fun," Nadine said.

Vidor spoke for the first time. "And you would be paid, of course. This is a job."

"You'd pay me to wear pretty clothes, dance and drink all the time, and fight people with knives?"

"Of course," Vidor said. "The princess consort baroness needs a salary. And her assistants, of course."

"Hmmm," Nadine said.

"How much of a salary?" Gabriella asked. "Imperial credits?"

"Yeah, what would the pay be?" Nadine said. "And how would you pay me. Not in horses or hides or anything weird like that."

"Well, we don't have much money, my family," Vidor said. He looked closely at Nadine's wrist. "Of course, we do have access to the mines out east. We could pay you in opals."

"Opals? You can pay in opals?"

"A princess baroness consort should have many opals," Arpad said.

Nadine rubbed her bracelet. "How many is many, exactly?"

***

"I can't do it," Jake said. "I have responsibilities at home. We have to get back."

"Can you get back?" Tam asked. "You were asking some very particular questions about charts and jump ship software earlier?"

"I was?" Jake said. "I don't remember that."

"You're a horrible liar, Jake Stewart. And you're not the only one who has spies nor the only one who pays attention to the questions others ask. And your radio communications aren't as secure as you believe."

"You know about our software issues?"

"I know you have issues. I know that you're concerned about getting back to your Empire. I know that you left crew on your ship to deal with something."

"We can go back anytime without any problems," Jake said.

"That might be true," Tam said. "But why not stay, at least for a while? Or longer. Your ship can go back without you. You have a crew. Or if it can't, eventually, your Empire will figure out you're overdue and come looking for you."

"Well—"

"And you'd be building relationships with neighboring friendly worlds. Haven't I been friendly to you, Jake?"

"Well—"

"You don't find me attractive, is that it?" Tam said. "I'm not pretty enough for you?"

Jake stuttered. The weather was hot, and Tam had switched back to her crop tops, showing a tanned midriff. She had replaced her dress with tight leather riding pants and heeled cowgirl boots dyed red. Jake had problems figuring out where to look. It didn't help that riding the saddle made... interesting changes in her form. "You look... nice," he said.

"Nice?" Tam leaned forward. "That's all you have to say? I look nice."

Her breasts look bigger when she does that, Jake

thought. I wonder if she knows. He shook himself. If she doesn't know, all she has to do is follow where I'm looking.

"You're one of the most attractive women I've ever met," Jake said. "Smart and funny and sexy, and you know who Vespasian was."

"Did I mention he was my favorite Emperor?" Tam said.

"I thought it was Antonius Pius?"

"I like them both. You know," she said, "I have a toga. Maybe we could play dress-up. Roman woman and gladiator sometime."

"I, uh, which gladiator? Early Empire?"

"More like the time of Commodus," Tam said.

"I can't," Jake said. "I made promises. I have responsibilities. I have a crew. I have a job to do. I have— Kivi, help me out here."

"A complete inability to see a great deal when it's in front of you?" Kivi said. "Sounds like a great offer."

"Excuse me for a moment," Jake said. He pushed his horse over to Kivi. "Stop taking her side. You're not helping."

"She wants you to be the coruler of her planet," Kivi said. "You'll be able to run things the way you want. You'll have complete control over different departments that you're just dying to reorganize. You'll be in charge of building factories and setting up trade routes. She's rich. She likes you. And the only way she can be wearing less clothes right now is if she wore just cowboy boots. Imagine what she'd look like then. How is suggesting you go with her 'not helping'?"

Jake gulped like a fish. "I just can't."

"She knows who Commodus is."

"You have no idea who that is."

"No, sir. But you do, and it matters to you. Sir, we might be in trouble here if that software doesn't work out. Consider her offer."

"Well—"

"Or just keep quiet, see how things work out. We'll be at the city gates in a while. How can it hurt to think about?"

"Right," Jake said. "Think."

"Just stall them for a day or two, till she gets control of the city. See how the software works. String her along. Haven't you ever done that to a woman before?"

"Not successfully, no." Jake looked at Kivi's face. "I'll try. Tell them I'll think about it."

Kivi turned his horse and walked it back to the women. "Admiral Stewart is considering your offer. He'd like a little more detail. Assuming you do make an offer, what sort of position will he have, what will be his responsibilities..."

"Kivi," Ket said. "You know as well as I do that he'll get whatever he wants. And even if he doesn't, he's smart. He'll figure out a way to get more."

"True, he's bright," Kivi said. "A brilliant planner and strategist."

"Wouldn't know it if you see him now," Tam said. "He's just kind of gibbering."

"He's not good with women he likes," Kivi said. "I've seen that. He and Ms. Nadine always fought."

"The other spacer? The one who drown—was on the boat with him? With us?"

"Yes, they've been on-again, off-again forever. They were together for a while, then they broke up."

"Why was that?"

"He had an affair with two Francais girls and a female Militia major during a voyage."

"Consecutively?" Tam asked.

"Concurrently, as I understand it," Kivi said.

"You're saying he was cheating with all three of them at the same time?"

"For a month. They seemed happy. Satisfied. Word is, they kissed him on the dock, all three of them, when the ship arrived."

"That's disgusting," Tam said. "But also somewhat impressive. All three at once?"

"That's the rumor."

"Have to investigate the strength of that rumor, princess," Ket said. "In the interests of understanding your negotiating position."

"Stop calling me princess." Tam shaded her eyes and peered back at Jake. "He doesn't look the type. Is it something to do with space?"

"Radiation has strange effects," Kivi said.

"What type of effects?" Tam asked.

"Perhaps you should investigate that as well," Ket said. "Also, to check your negotiating position."

Tam and Kivi laughed. "What happened to that spacer girl when she found out he was cheating?" Tam asked.

"There was no actual proof, and Admiral Jake denied it. But Ms. Nadine reacted."

"She yelled at him?"

"Shot him."

"You mean verbally?"

"No, revolver. She has a temper. And she's a good shot."

***

"Let me repeat," Nadine said. "Should that suggested event ever occur, first, I will shoot the floozy I find you with. Twice. I will shoot her horse. I will shoot your horse. Then I will shoot you." She and the others were still talking at the bar.

"That's unreasonable."

Nadine blew out her cheeks. "You're right. It's not the horses' fault. I'll just let them run free. Then I'll chase you down and do that thing. That cattle thing. Brie, what's that called? Gardening?"

"Gelding," Gabriella said.

"That's the one," Nadine said. "I'll geld you with a rusty spoon."

"You don't use spoons," Arpad said.

"I will," Nadine said.

"It won't work."

"Maybe not the first time, but I'm persistent."

"Good thing I'm one of the foremost horsemen on the planet," Vidor said. "You'll never catch me."

"If you run away, and I can't catch you immediately," Nadine said, "I will go back to the city. I will collect as much money as I can and hire the best horse trainers. I will learn from them. I will study all hours of the day and some of the night. I will become a better rider. I will study and practice till I am the best rider. Then you know what I will do?"

"Chase me?" Vidor said.

"No. Then I will recruit a personally loyal group of the best riders on this planet. And I will train them and have them trained with me until we are, all of us, the best horse posse in the history of your dung-covered people. Then we will ride out and hunt you down. But we won't just catch you. We'll chase you. For days—weeks on end. Summer, winter, and fall. We'll harass you, hunt you like a diseased dog, and ride you down until you collapse in agony in the middle of the desert, and I'll leave you there without water or food for days until your soul cries out in the agony of living. And then, only then, after you beg for it, will I grant you the release of the death you richly deserve."

Vidor and Arpad blinked. Gabriella smiled. "So," Arpad said, "we're hearing no other girlfriends and no concubines."

"Right."

"Got it," Arpad said. "And as to your other demand..."

"Five thousand carats to a kilogram," Nadine said. "Ten kilograms worth. That's fifty thousand carats. That's what I want."

"That's an extremely large number of opals."

"But you get an entire planet for it. And they're mine to keep, no matter what happens."

"So, you are willing to..."

"Discuss it. I need to speak with Brie," Nadine said. "We'll talk more later."

Nadine steered Brie ahead on the road. The column was heading into the town. Lights were visible in the distance, perhaps an hour's ride away. The first sun would have almost set by then.

"Nadine, that's an enormous amount of jewelry."

"They'll never get it. I just want them to think about doing this. Keep them interested while we get this own-the-planet thing sorted out."

"What happens next?"

"We help them get into the town. Vidor becomes the baron or governor, whatever. Arpad seems smart enough to run things. I get some new jewelry."

"You're going to marry him?"

"Let's see how many jewels he gets first..."

CHAPTER TWENTY-EIGHT

"That's the city?" Jake pointed ahead.

Their "strike force" was approaching the city from the northwest. The main sun was down, the far sun projecting a reddish glow bright enough to discern faces but hard to distinguish colors. The downtown palace and harbor area was visible in the distance. Single lights blinked from the roofs of buildings with batteries and local electricity. Some flickered—fires or torches. Not every household had modern Imperial equipment.

"And that's the wall," Ket said. She and Jake were riding at the front of the column. Jake tended to shy away and try to hide when Tam came to talk, so they had moved up front to be the scouts. "And the gates."

"Gates? Plural? You didn't mention that," Jake said. "We only saw one gate during our tour."

"There are three—east, west, and main."

"Named with the originality I've come to expect from this planet."

"They're just gates," Ket said. "The main gate is what you saw—that's where the market is. It's manned at all hours to keep us pesky farmers from sneaking in at night."

"What about the other gates?"

"Locked most of the time. They open them up for wagonloads of heavy freight coming or going."

"Good, so there won't be anybody around at night. We can get close."

"Close enough to use that cartload of wooden doors you had us bring along?"

"It's just an idea, a backup plan," Jake said.

"Given any thought to Tam's proposal? Her proposal of a proposal."

"It scares me to death."

"She likes you. You like her. What's to be scared of?"

"I thought you Planter people didn't like to marry outside your first families or whatever you call them."

"We don't normally. We don't like the city people or the Ranchers. Of course they don't like us, either, so it all works out."

"And you like us Imperials?" Jake said.

Ket looked over her shoulder. Kivi was riding next to Tam and Tran, gesticulating as he made a point. "Some of you aren't so bad."

Jake saw where she was looking. "He likes you a lot."

"I was wondering... if you leave, can he stay behind?"

"We never thought that through," Jake said. "This was supposed to be a trading mission. Meet local governments, offer to set up cultural exchanges, that sort of thing. I never expected this to happen."

"You never expected people to meet and fall in love, like humans have been doing for all of recorded history?"

"I don't read those histories," Jake said. "I read historical fiction."

"So does Tam. The two of you are well matched. You'll make a great husband for her."

"I never said yes!" Jake said.

"But you never said no, either, which a lot of people noticed."

Jake flicked his reins to move his horse closer to the middle of the road. The horse ignored him. Ket yanked the reins to move him over.

"Does she want to do this?"

"She didn't say no to the suggestion, either," Ket said. "You intrigue her, coming from another planet. You're a thinker, a planner, like she is. Not much of a romantic."

"You will never, ever, hear anybody call me a romantic," Jake said.

"Nor her either, but this could work."

"Is that all she wants—'this could work'?"

"She's always known that there will be some sort of political aspect to her marriage. You're acceptable."

"Yay," Jake said. "Women find me acceptable."

"So, say no. Publicly."

"Not yet," Jake said. "Besides, she hasn't actually asked me."

"Creative ambiguity," Ket said. "You both figured it out. Let everyone think that you are engaged. Get her appointed baron—great idea there, you pretending to be an Imperial admiral."

"I am one. I've got papers to prove it."

"Which means nothing, but it's a good story. And you're so serious about the whole thing. That makes people believe that you're not lying."

"I never lie. Too much work."

"Which is why you haven't said yes or no yet," Ket said. "But you'll have to commit sometime."

"When will that be?"

"Not soon, thankfully for you. What's that?" She pointed ahead.

Jake squinted into the dim light. "Looks like horses. People on horses."

"Lots of people on horses," Ket said. She turned her horse. "I need to tell Tam."

***

"An initial gift is traditional," Nadine said to Vidor. "It's not an actual proposal until you give me a ring. A big ring. With a diamond."

"We have no diamonds here on Magyar," Vidor said. "Perhaps someone in the city has one that I could buy from them."

"Better get shopping, then," Nadine said. "No ring, no

proposal, no off-world help or Imperial legitimacy."

"You make it sound like you are for sale."

"Yep. And am I making it sound like I'm very, very expensive? 'Cause that's the way it is."

"I don't believe in purchasing my bride," Vidor said.

"Then, you don't believe in getting naked with her, either," Nadine said. "'Cause that's how it works in the real world."

"But all those opals you demanded. What are those?"

"That's in the nature of a gift. A bride price. A dowry."

"Nadine," Gabriella whispered, "that's not how a dowry works. With a dowry, you're supposed to give it to him."

"That's not going to happen. We'll tell him we do it differently in the Empire."

"We do?"

"How should I know?"

Vidor and Arpad had waited while they whispered. "I will look for a diamond once we are in the city," Vidor said.

"I can wait," Nadine said.

"I am having difficulty with that," Vidor said.

"That's what makes it more fun," Nadine said.

"You are infuriating sometimes."

"Princess Infuriation, that's me." Nadine pointed to the city wall barely visible in the dark. "Why aren't we using that gate here? That one near the water."

"We go to the main gate. It is only proper that the city's new leader enter the city from its main entrance."

"Works for me," Nadine said. "We'll march in, make you the big cheese, then hit the software library and work on our ship."

"As you wish," Vidor said. Two riders rode up out of the gloom and spoke to him. "I have some details to attend to. Please excuse me. Arpad?" The two men rode ahead. Arpad smiled at Gabriella as he passed. She grinned back.

"Arpad invited me to stay at his house in the city," Gabriella said.

"Don't do anything I wouldn't do. Which is, well, nothing."

"I told him I would speak to you first. Ask your permission."

"You don't need my permission."

"Yeah, but he doesn't know that. I figured you would demand some sort of unreasonable thing from him."

"Silk sheets. Bags of money. I'll tell him you only get sexually excited if you are rolling in piles of cash."

"He's pretty yummy. I don't need the money."

"Everybody needs the money."

"His cousin keeps glaring at me and sharpening her sword."

"That makes it better for you. You like Arpad better because you're taking him away from her."

"I don't. Okay, I do." Brie rode in silence. "Does that make me a bad person?"

"Yes," Nadine said. "Horrible, awful, hateful person."

"Maybe I shouldn't think that way?"

"Never said that. Competition makes everybody sharper, makes us stronger people."

"Pretty philosophical."

"Princess Infuriation, the philosopher," Nadine said. "Who's that?" She put her hand on her revolver.

Vidor and Arpad and the others rode out of the gloom.

"Horsemen ahead, many horsemen," Vidor said. "We deploy for battle."

***

Jake, Tam, Ket, Kivi, and Sheriff Tran waited at the head of their group. Tam and the sheriff flanked Jake in case he did something stupid with his horse. Ket and Kivi waited behind. The five had all ridden up in front of the main gates where they could be clearly seen but left the bulk of their forces a looming mass in the background. Floodlights blazed from the walls, and Jake counted a half dozen city guards in a variety of colors above the closed gates.

"They're Ranchers," Tam said. "Perhaps the Ranchers group we heard about coming down the coast."

"Are they likely to be a problem?" Jake said.

"My information is that they are supposed to have the same numbers as we do. They could fight us, I suppose, but why would they? They don't like the city people any more than we do."

"Will they support you in your bid to become baron?"

"Probably not, but they can be bought off," Tam said. "They can always use money. I can put them in the government, and they'll be impressed by our Imperial connections." Tam smiled at Jake. "And my Imperial husband."

"Maybe we shouldn't talk about that," Jake said.

Tam just grinned. Jake tried to count the horsemen, but it was too dark. At least fifty. Four leaders rode out in front.

"Tam," Jake said, "it looks like—that's Nadine. And Gabriella." Jake stood up in his stirrups and tried to ride forward. He kicked his horse, who looked back at him, leaped forward, then stopped when Jake fell backwards, tugging the reins.

Jake hit the ground like a sack of superpotatoes dropped from a great height. Tam and Sheriff Tran dropped off their horses. Tran took the reins and gave them back to Ket. Tam leaned over Jake. "Are you okay? What happened?"

"Nadine. It's Nadine. And Gabriella. They're alive." He sat up.

Vidor, Arpad, and the two spacewomen arrived. Vidor and Arpad leaped down from their horses. Nadine and Gabriella followed suit more deliberately.

"Princess Tam? Is that you?" Vidor said. "You survived the fire." He looked down. "Is this the spaceman?"

"It's me. You survived the fire as well," Tam said. "Your father?"

Vidor bit his lip. "Killed in the flames. Unless you have knowledge of him?"

"He's not in the survivors we heard of," Tam said. "I am sorry."

"Your father as well. Did he live? No, we would have heard. I grieve with you."

"It was a great tragedy for everybody," Tam said. "I see you have a spaceman of your own."

Nadine led Gabriella into the light. "Spacewoman, thank you very much. Emperor's balls. Jake Stewart, you're alive. How did you get away from the fire?"

"Cut a float loose and floated ashore. You?"

"The four of us jumped off and swam for it. We made it to the shore. We were lucky. We were out on deck when it happened."

"Us too," Jake said. "I'm glad you're alive."

"Me too," Nadine said. She pulled Jake up and gave him a big hug. He hugged back.

Gabriella and Kivi exchanged milder hugs to the side.

Nadine stepped back. "I knew you'd have some sort of crazy plan. Have you called the ship?"

"Lost the communicator in the rush," Jake said. "You?"

"Salt water got it. Haven't talked to them, either."

"Well, we'll use the planetary net if we need to. Once we get to it."

"Who are your friends, Jake?" Nadine said. She looked around. "Your many, many friends."

In the excitement of his fall and the rush to help him, the mounted planters had pushed into the light, the Ranchers following. The two groups faced each other, with the closed gates to the side.

"This is Tam and her people. Her planters."

Tam crossed her arms. "Princess Tam," she said.

Jake stepped back. "You said you weren't a princess."

"I am now," Tam said. "What are you doing here, Vidor? And why do you have that armed rabble with you?"

"These are my supporters," Vidor said. "I am khan now, after my father."

"Supporters in what? Poor hygiene? We can smell you from here."

"The baron is dead. The council is dead. I come to propose a new council."

"Oh, really? Whose council?"

"My council. My people have settled this planet for generations. In the absences of legitimate authority, we will rule in the Emperor's name."

Tam unfolded her arms and pointed at Vidor's riders. "You rule? You and this mob? In the Emperor's name? You couldn't rule the needles on a cactus."

"The city. The planet. All of us. As is our right as first settlers."

"The first settlers? We have been here nearly as long as you."

"You admit we are the original settlers?" Vidor said.

"I admit nothing," Tam said.

"I'm not surprised. You always were a pigheaded troublemaker with the personality of a she-sow."

"A she-sow? That's rich coming from somebody whose horse bathes more often than he does."

Jake coughed. "Harrump. What's this about first settlers?"

"It doesn't matter," Tam said. "And even if it did, we have an Imperial charter. And Admiral Stewart, appointed as such by the Emperor Dashi the First, has named me as baroness and governor of this planet."

"Admiral Stewart has, has he?" Vidor said. "Interesting because Ms. Nadine has suggested that we exercise Imperial authority here in the Emperor's name. And she has agreed to become my wife and join me in being

Baroness of Magyar."

Jake blinked. "Nadine? You're getting married? To Vidor?"

"Well, mutual congratulations are in order, then," Tam said. "Because Jake has agreed to marry me and rule by my side as the coruler of Magyar. I'll send you an invite to the wedding. We're going to have it in the palace. We're going there now to take control in the Emperor's name."

Nadine crossed her arms. "Jakey, what's this about?"

"I thought you were dead," Jake said, "and we weren't getting along so well anyway, and, well, as the admiral and all that."

"Jake Stewart," Nadine said. "I leave you alone for a few days while I escape from a killing fire, and you hook up with the first farmer's daughter that rolls along."

"I was sort of shipwrecked, Nadine."

"You didn't even try to contact me!"

"We just said that the comms weren't working," Jake said.

"Don't interrupt me, you little twerp," Nadine said. "I leave you alone for a day or two, and you're engaged to this skinny little tramp. But I can see why—look at the way she's dressed. She's like an actress playing a harem girl from some fantasy vid."

"Thanks," Tam said. "I always liked those movies. But you could be in one, too." She gave Nadine an up-and-down look. "You could be the angry, fat older sister who complains a lot and never gets a man."

Nadine hissed. "Don't cross me, you Imperial weasel."

"That's baroness Imperial weasel," Tam said.

"Vidor will be the baron. I'm here to make sure he and his men have the support they need to become Imperial governors."

"Admiral Stewart has already arranged the support for me." Tam grabbed Jake's arm. "He's been very kind, very helpful. Very... accommodating. I will be the baroness governor. Khan Vidor can have a place in my cabinet."

She smirked at Vidor. "A small place, until he proves his worth."

Nadine put her hands on her hips. "We'll see about that. Vidor, come with me. We have planning to do." Nadine stalked away.

"Nadine," Jake yelled, "things have changed. We need to talk."

"Shut up, Jake. Vidor. Now would be good."

"Perhaps," Arpad said, "we can take some time apart and talk about this later—"

"Now, Vidor," Nadine yelled. "Arpad, if you keep talking, I'll have Brie chew your tongue off the next time you kiss." Nadine hopped up on her horse and rode off.

"Go with your bride, Khan," Tam said. "I'll be sure to invite you two in for discussions in a few days, after we've set up our new government."

"It is us who will be inviting you," Vidor said. "We will talk later when I hold my first audience in the main chamber. Arpad?" The two men rode away.

"This is a surprise," Jake said. "But with a little discussion, we can—"

"Shut up, Stewart," Tam said. She waved at Ket, and the two of them stormed off.

Jake sat back down on the ground. "My head hurts."

"Not surprised," Gabriella said. She had waited after Nadine left. "But I'm glad to see you're okay, Jake. You, too, Kivi."

"You should call him captain or admiral," Kivi said.

"I'm working for a baroness now, looks like," Gabriella said. "She outranks him now."

"She's not a baroness yet."

"One thing I have learned about Nadine is that I shouldn't bet against her."

"Same thing with Admiral Stewart."

"We'll see. And Kivi?"

"Yes?"

"What's that other girl's name again? The one who was

slobbering over you?"

CHAPTER TWENTY-NINE

"We will gather the troops and charge the gates," Vidor said. "Overrun the defenders."

"We will, will we?" Nadine said. "Charge in and attack everyone guarding the gates? Run them down and dash into the city, seize control in a blaze of glory? That's your plan?"

Vidor, Arpad, Nadine, and Gabriella had retreated from the meeting at the gates and gathered out of view of the main gate. They dismounted in a stand of scrub trees and tied the horses.

"Well, yes, Ms. Nadine," Vidor said. "We must take the city, of course. Capture the gate."

"The gate," Nadine said. She walked over and stood in front of Vidor, hands on her hips. "Take the gate."

"Yes," Vidor said.

Nadine put her hands on Vidor's shoulders. "Horseleader, does the baron of all the Magyars live in the gate? Does the Emperor's anointed rule from a gate?"

Vidor stared down at her. "No."

Nadine reached down with her right hand, grasped his sword, and pushed him back with her left. He stumbled back a step, and his sword slid out of the scabbard. Nadine gripped the sword and held it up.

"Correct. The Emperor's personal representative doesn't live in a gate." She flourished the sword. "Where does he live?"

"Ms. Nadine, may I have my sword back?"

"No," Nadine said. "You're talking about getting married. If we get married, what's yours is mine. Better get used to it."

"What's mine is yours, yes," Vidor said. "Of course. And what's yours is mine?"

"What?" Nadine rolled the sword in her hand. "Mine is what?"

"What's mine is yours, what's yours is mine."

"That's stupid." Nadine spun the sword. "Of course not. What's mine is mine. What's yours is mine, too."

"That doesn't seem fair," Vidor said.

"It's not. Get used to it. Arpad, how do these things work? With knives, you stab." Nadine swung the sword back and forth. "It's heavy."

"You can stab with it," Arpad said, "or slash."

Nadine stepped over and swung the sword at a tree. "Like this?"

"That's more of a hack," Arpad said.

Nadine hacked a small branch from the tree. "Works, though. So, our brilliant plan is to capture a gate and celebrate owning a hole in a ten-foot wall? Brilliant, Khan, just amazing." Nadine hacked another branch off.

"The baron lives in the palace. He rules from the palace," Arpad said.

Nadine hacked another branch free. "Go on."

"That is the seat of government," Arpad said. "Khan, we do not need a gate. We need the palace. The computers are there, the fusion plant controls. The library, all the main medical equipment, the council meeting rooms. That is all there. That is the only thing we must have."

"Right," Nadine said.

"And the planetary comm is there?" Gabriella asked.

"No, Ms. Gabriella, that is in the hills, some distance away. Something to do with line of sight to the transmitters," Vidor said.

"Everything but that is in the palace," Arpad said. "Everything we need is in that one place. That is the only place we must control."

"Right." Nadine cut the last branch off the sapling and

hacked at the bottom. "We take the palace, and that's all we need."

"But we need to go through the gate to get to the palace," Vidor said.

Nadine narrowed her eyes at him, then let loose a flurry of hacks till the tree finally fell. She hauled it up and held it out to Vidor. "Hold this."

"There's more than one gate," Arpad said. "More than one way in. We can check the others."

"Probably closed. And guarded. But worth checking just in case. Hold that higher, Vidor," Nadine said.

Vidor lifted the trunk. Nadine chopped the top of the staff off and trimmed the trunk to size.

"Ms. Nadine, please be careful of my fingers," Vidor said, shrinking back as she swung his sword at the end of the stick.

Arpad snapped his fingers. "There's more than just land gates. That's why you spoke to those fishermen in that other village."

"Always have a backup plan." Nadine held up the former tree trunk, an eight foot long pole pointed at one end. "Vidor, Arpad, I need another dozen of these. Get cutting."

Vidor scrunched up his brow. "We are cutting poles rather than fighting?"

"Because I spoke to those fishermen. There are small boats back at that fishing village," Nadine said. "We're going back there. Get eight, ten people. We can pole along the shore in the shallow water to the seaside of the city, push the boats in. Then we walk—not run, just walk—to the nearest gate, open it up, and let the rest of the boys and girls in. Then go surround the palace and walk in and take it."

"That's a brilliant plan," Vidor said.

"It's my plan. Of course it is. Vidor, if you think what's mine is yours, you have another think coming."

"Of course, Ms. Nadine."

"And if you think I'm going to charge a fortified gate for any reason, I'm going to take your sword off you again, and, this time, I will cut your fingers off."

"Yes, Ms. Nadine," Vidor said.

"And if you think that you can tell me what to do at any time, charge a gate or not, I'm going to cut off more than your fingers. Arpad, get cracking on those poles. Soon as we have them, off to see the fishermen. Chop-chop."

Arpad turned to Gabriella. "Is she always this... combative?"

"For her, she's being reasonable," Gabriella said. "If it was Jake Stewart she was talking to, she'd stab first and explain later. This is her being accommodating." Gabriella grinned at Vidor. "Still looking forward to the wedding, Khan?"

***

"I can do this," Jake said, putting his foot in the stirrup and lifting. "It can't be that hard."

"Jake, we need to retreat and discuss our next move," Tam said. "And you're using the wrong foot."

"I am not. This is my right foot. Oh, I see what you mean." Jake levered himself up. He had successfully climbed onto the saddle, facing backward. "This is harder than it looks."

After Nadine's departure, he had spoken briefly to Kivi and Ket, then sent both off on an errand. Tam had detailed a group to follow the Ranchers when they rode away. Jake stumbled over and tried to remount his horse. The gate guards stood and watched his antics. Some were laughing. Others were making bets.

"Jake, all these Ranchers here adds a whole new dimension to this. We need to think about it."

"I'll just pull myself around," Jake said. He pulled his

259

leg out of one stirrup and tried to swing it over the other side of the horse. "We need to strike now. Whoever controls the Imperial administration building controls the planet."

"You're going to lose your balance and fall out," Tam said. "It's just a building."

"I am not," Jake said. "You don't have a formal system of government here—all you agree on is that you're part of the Empire and that the Imperial representative appoints a council and the council is in charge. Control who's on the council, control who runs the planet." He twisted more and threw his left leg over the horse before standing with his right leg balanced in a stirrup, his left swinging free. "Nice horse, good horse. Nice horsey."

"You can't get turned around that way," Tam said. "You'll just end up losing your balance and falling."

"Of course I won't," Jake said. "I just have to be more careful. Hey, up there?" He yelled at the guards on the gate.

"What do you want, farmer?"

"We want to talk to whoever is in charge in there."

"They don't want to talk to you."

"How do you know that? I'll bet you don't even have somebody in charge since the sinking."

"The city families are discussing it now. They want somebody... Imperial."

"I'm an Imperial admiral. You heard us talking."

"Talking nonsense," the guard yelled.

"It's not nonsense. Open up the door and let me in."

"Not by the hair of my chinny-chin-chin. Also not by the rule of the baron. None of you farmers or Ranchers are allowed in at night."

"You don't have a baron," Jake said. "Princess Tam is the new baron. Baroness."

"We did. We will. She isn't. Go away."

"You want to fight us for that?" Jake said. "Get hurt? Possibly get killed?"

"We've got guns, spaceman."

"So do we. And there are only six of you. Shouldn't you call for reinforcements?"

"We don't need reinforcements, but we're up here behind a wall, and you're down there where we can see you. If we start firing, it won't go well for you, will it? And you don't know anything about getting on a horse."

"He's got a point, Jake," Tam said.

"I know he does. I just need to stretch this leg some and twist." Jake leaned and tried to turn the stirrup.

It slipped backward, Jake's other leg pivoted out, and he slid from the horse with a crash. He let out a huge grunt as his shoulder hit the ground. He hung upside down, staring up at the gate people, with his right foot still in the stirrup. The horse turned his head around to see what the noise was, looked at the squirming spaceman, then bent down and cropped a bite of grass.

"Good job, spaceman," the gate guard yelled. "Thanks for the fall. I just made ten credits off you. Hey, I'll bet ten credits with your lady friend, and I say you'll fall off the left side next time."

"We serve the Emperor," Jake yelled. "Who do you serve?"

"The Emperor," the guards chorused.

Jake climbed to his feet. "Remember that." He stretched his shoulder. "That hurt a lot. Is there a book on this?"

"A book?" Tam said. "A book on what?"

"Climbing up on horses. A how-to book."

"The Complete Moron's Guide On How To Not Fall On Your Butt While Getting Tangled Up On A Horse For Idiots?"

"The title's redundant and not complementary, but it would be easy to find in an index," Jake said. "I should read that book."

"The book you should read, Jake," Tam said. "Is Don't Do Stupid Things Where People Can See You."

"I'm a spaceman. Everybody knows I'm useless on horses."

"You do look particularly useless on horses. And you're sounding kind of useless. We didn't plan for the gates being closed. We thought we'd just walk in."

"Some of your people thought we'd waltz in," Jake said. "I had other ideas."

"We should go back and discuss our options," Tam said.

"No, we should charge forward and get into the city and grab that administration building. Before the Ranchers. Whoever controls that building controls the council. Whoever controls the council controls the government. And whoever controls the government appoints the baron, and that's going to be me and you."

"Together?"

"Could be. We'll discuss that later. After we've taken the city."

"We can't take the city with the gates closed. And we certainly can't do it with you acting the fool in front of those guards."

"Those guards who are all watching me be an idiot?" Jake positioned himself next to the stirrup. "All six of them? Who have just admitted that they don't have any reinforcements available, while everybody argues over who is the new baron?"

"And betting on your idiocy? I should have taken that guy's wager. You will fall off the left side."

"This is harder than it looks. I need more practice."

"Let's go back and talk to Ket and the sheriff. And where's your friend?"

Jake pointed out into the gloom. "Here he comes now. And, technically, I'm his boss. He works for me. But he's a good kid."

"He's smarter than you—or at least not so much of a fool."

"Not as foolish as me?" Jake stepped into the stirrup

and swung his foot over. This time, he faced the proper direction but was overbalanced and fell off the far side.

"Told you, pretty lady," the gate guard yelled. "Left side this time. You owe me ten credits."

"I don't owe you anything," Tam yelled. "Jake, stop being an idiot."

Ket and Kivi trotted up. Kivi hopped off his horse and bent to help Jake. "Are you okay, Captain Stewart?"

"Everything is going according to plan," Jake said, letting Kivi pull him up.

"That's good," Kivi said. He turned back to his horse and climbed up in a smooth, easy motion.

"Kivi, I hate you a whole lot right now," Jake said. "Just so you know."

"Yes, Captain Stewart," Kivi said.

"Things are going to plan," Tam said. "Does the plan include Captain Stewart falling off his horse over and over again?"

"That's what he told me," Kivi said. "He was staying here and keeping them occupied while we moved the siege materials."

"Moved the what?" Tam said.

"What did our Gauss guy say, Kivi?" Jake asked. He patted his horse. "Good horse."

Whiskers snorted and continued eating.

"What Gauss guy?" Tam asked.

"That city guy who had the Gauss rifle," Ket said. "Admiral Jake here had Kivi put him in the woods over there and use the sighting scope to survey the wall. Those Old Empire scopes are like high-quality cameras. It has infrared sensing and some sort of lowlight thing. We could see everything. Six guards. Four at the gate and two walking post along the wall, but they have all come back here to watch your antics and bet on you."

"No heavy weapons," Kivi said. "Nothing like his rifle. They have swords, two shotguns, and everybody has a revolver. That's it. He says he could kill half of them with one burst."

"We'd rather not do that," Jake said. "Don't want to start your rule with a massacre, princess. What about the doors?" His horse farted loudly. "The Emperor's sweaty knuckles, that stinks."

"They support a horse's weight," Ket said. "I walked over one myself. We practiced with the angles. We'll need eight of them in a row to make the ramp for the horses."

"Do we have enough doors?" Jake said.

"Yep, and we took advantage of the noise and fun to drag those carts close to the walls. They're hidden in trees close to the wall." Jake's horse farted again. "Wow, that does stink."

"Jake," Tam said, "I don't want to ruin your brilliant plan, whatever it is, but unless you step two feet to the right, that horse will—"

Whiskers blew a huge pile of liquid dung out of her butt. It splattered all over Jake's chest, and he jumped back with a curse. The farmers snorted, and the six guards on the gate went wild with glee, catcalling and gesticulating.

Jake shook dung from his hands and dabbed his poop-covered chest. "The things I do for the Emperor. How long till the ramps are in place?"

"We're still building them, and that will take some time. A couple hours at least. They have to be braced up to hold the horse's weight. But once they're together, we can drag them up to the gate with the carts. They'll reach up there no problem. And the ladders will be done by then as well."

"Reach up where? What the heck is going on?" Tam asked.

"In two hours," Ket said, "our people will have ramps that we can tow up to the wall. They will be strong enough to support a horse and rider, and wide and stable enough that we can walk the horses right up to the top of the wall."

"They don't have any Gauss rifles up there," Jake said. "We put two groups of riders up—two a side. The top of that wall is nice and wide—six people abreast, plenty of room for a horse. At the same time, we'll charge the gate, put two other groups on each side with ladders, and start to climb. Those people up there will have five different groups coming at them—right at the gate, ladders to either side, and horses racing down the wall, with troops behind them. Plus a Gauss rifle in the woods that can chew up any wooden wall they hide behind. And they're not out here to die. They're not fanatics, just folks doing their jobs. Once we're charging at them, I bet they'll just stand aside and let us do our thing."

"And being an idiot in front of them was part of the plan?"

"We've moved half our troops into an assault position on their flanks," Jake said. "We've constructed—well, almost constructed—siege equipment close to their walls. They haven't noticed a thing. In two hours, we'll storm that wall in five places, capture it with light or probably with no casualties on either side, open that gate, ride in, and seize the palace before anybody knows what's happening. All because I was distracting the guards with being an idiot."

Jake tried to wipe the horse poop off his chest again, then just gave up. He held his smeared hand up to his nose and sniffed, then extended it to Tam. "Smell that. Know what that smells like?"

"A man too uncoordinated to avoid falling in horse manure?"

"Victory," Jake said. "Smells like victory."

CHAPTER THIRTY

"Gas giants are boring," Odette said, watching her display. Magyar IV shone in alternating bands of red and white on her screen. "They look like somebody mixed milk and orange juice and shook it."

"They're beautiful," Yvette said, buckling in next to her. "Cloudy mixtures of the stuff that made us."

Odette raised her eyebrows. "Listen to the poet."

"You have no romance in your soul," Yvette said. "Peasant."

"I'm just a simple ship driver, not some high-class shipmaster. You should be happy that this peasant is here. Otherwise, you would have gotten no sleep at all in the past week."

"Doesn't matter now," Yvette said. "But thank you for covering for me for a full shift."

"I napped in the chair," Odette said. "Nothing to do during fueling."

She and Yvette had agreed that, since Willowby was busy with the fueling maneuvers, he would be unlikely to sneak onto the bridge. The on-watch person could take a catnap in the control room chair. They had both managed a full shift of sleep while he fussed with his hoses and mixes.

Red lights flared on the screen, and the ship shook for a moment.

"That gets worse every shift," Yvette said.

"Can't fight atmospheric density," Odette said. The ship shook again. "But Willowby says we're streamlined enough to handle this. And I will say, he does seem to know orbits."

"Speaking of," Yvette said. She tapped her intercom. "Engineering?"

"Willowby here."

"Could we have a status report, Professor?"

"I'm hungry and grumpy," Willowby said. "I want some dinner and a nap."

"We meant the ship, Professor."

"Should have specified, then. Nothing has changed from last shift," Willowby said. "Atmosphere hydrogen density is same as before. Much worse than it would have been at Magyar Four, I might add. But we made do. Nitrogen and oxygen are both better than expected, though. Those tanks are full now. We just need one more shift to top up the H tanks, and we'll be full up. Exactly as I predicted when we got here."

"You are a beacon of certainty in an uncertain world, Professor," Yvette said.

"I'm going off shift now. I'll talk to you two later," Willowby said.

"Of course. Enjoy your rest shift," Yvette shut the intercom off. She tapped a few screens. "How much longer?"

"Earliest is now," Odette said. "But you know that."

"I'm just nervous. Good timing with Willowby off shift."

"Just luck, just worked out that way."

The two women ran through their checklists to prepare the ship for maneuvering, asking and answering questions. Both looked up when the hatch banged open.

Willowby climbed through. "Stupid microgravity. I'll never get that worked out."

"Professor, you said you were going to go to sleep," Yvette said.

"Never said that. Said I wanted a nap, not the same thing. I've been saving my water ration. Had a nice shower and a big cup of tea. I'm bright-eyed and bushy-tailed, ready for the festivities."

"What festivities?" Odette asked. "What are you talking about?"

"I will say, you two ladies look presentable today," Willowby said. "Both of you have washed your hair, and unless I miss my guess, you've rebraided it. I may be old, but I appreciate it when handsome women like yourselves make some effort. Why, you'd almost think there's something special about today."

"We wash every week, Professor. And we always braid our hair after that."

"Last wash was less than a week ago. Could be you were just bored, of course. Decided to pretty yourselves up for a change. Of course, it's interesting that you also decided to clean and iron your uniforms. And Ms. Odette has an expensive-looking neck ruff on, which is unusual. And you, Ms. Yvette, you've pinned on some collar tabs. I believe those are Free Trader rank tabs, aren't they? I've seen those before on Free Traders, at council meetings, but I've never seen you wear them before. Are you a shipmaster, by chance?"

"Sometimes, we just like to dress up," Yvette said.

"With Odette's scanners all focused on the jump limit of this planet?" He pointed.

Odette instantly blanked her screen.

"We like to contemplate the infinite," Yvette said.

"Me too," Willowby said. He slid into a console in the second rank and tapped it until a screen came up. "I'm feeling contemplative today. I'll just mirror your sensors and contemplate them right here." He sat back.

Odette reached for a pocket, stopped, visibly thought about it, then returned her hand to her board.

A bong sounded. Odette looked at Yvette. Yvette nodded once. Odette tapped through her board. Willowby watched the mirrored settings on his display. Odette stopped at a warning message.

Willowby crossed his arms. "Well, look at that. The

proximity radar just went off." He uncrossed his arms and cracked his knuckles. "One of you want to get that, or should I?"

CHAPTER THIRTY-ONE

"Next time," Gabriella said, "We have them scrub out these skiffs before we borrow them."

Nadine gagged. "I thought the horses smelled bad. This smells worse."

The four of them had bought a skiff from the fishing village and headed back to the walls.

"Horses do not smell bad," Vidor said. "Horses smell like the endless green fields that they ride upon. Fresh, clean, and exciting."

"Perhaps I'm being unfair to the horses." Nadine set her pole and sniffed his back. "Mumm. Yep, I am being unfair. The horses smell fine. It's you who stinks, Vidor."

"It's not my fault I slipped on those fish guts," Vidor said. "How was I to know they were there in the dark?"

"Maybe the smell would have been your first clue?" Nadine said. "Or perhaps you were just excited because the fish guts smelled like the endless stretches of ocean that the fish swim through."

"And defecate in," Gabriella said. "Don't forget that. Don't drink the water."

"It's salt water," Arpad said.

"Exactly," Nadine said. "And fish crap in it. It smells like endless seas of roiling fish guts, fetid, stinking, and exciting. And break is over, keep poling."

The four created a rhythm. The two in front set their poles in and pushed, and as they reached the end of their thrust, the two in the back did the same, and they alternated. A second skiff followed them, with Pista and three other warriors barely visible in the dark.

"Brie, how far to the castle thing?"

"It's right there." Gabriella pointed.

Lights of the city ahead cut off abruptly where the surrounding wall ran to the water. The end of the wall had a stone tower with a single electric light on it. It illuminated lapping waters fifty meters in all directions. Two hundred meters farther along the shore, according to Gabriella's memory, was a dark dock.

"Right, everybody keep it down for the next twenty minutes," Nadine said.

Everyone quieted, and they pushed the skiffs farther out away from shore.

"I can barely touch," Gabriella whispered five minutes later. "I'm not getting any leverage. The water is too deep."

"Me neither," Nadine whispered back.

Arpad, with his longer arms, was able to reach the bottom for a few dozen meters more, and he, too, couldn't push.

"What do we do now?" Gabriella said.

"Give me your pole," Arpad said. "I can fix it."

Gabriella handed him her pole, and he balanced the two across the boat and lashed them together.

"You're good with those knots, Arpy," Nadine whispered.

"Boy scouts," Arpad whispered back. "We had to learn to build a lean-to in the woods, with just some twine and what wood we could find."

"And you always carry twine with you?"

"Of course," Arpad said before cutting the twine off with his teeth. "A scout is always prepared. Ms. Nadine, your pole?"

Nadine handed him her pole, and he bound it to Vidor's. The two men spoke briefly with the boat behind, and the second boat tied their poles together and followed.

"See that, Brie?" Nadine whispered. "They're boy scouts."

"And always prepared," Brie whispered back. "I'll bet

271

they and Captain Jake would get along. Being into preparation and all."

"Jake is probably preparing something different with that floozy Planter girl."

"She's pretty," Brie said.

"Of course she is," Nadine said. "He has good taste."

"And she's smart. Very smart. Knows all those Roman things."

"Jake likes that type of stuff."

"And dresses well. I liked her boots."

"I'm sure Jake does, too, if that's all she's wearing."

"You're upset that Jake is attracted to smart, good-looking women with great fashion sense."

"Shut up. You're supposed to be on my side."

"I am. Besides, right here, you have this big handsome, brave, mustached..."

"Ox? Thoughtless bag of rocks?"

"I was going to say impetuous, but you're the boss. What you say."

Nadine sighed. "I miss that boy, Jake. If he was in charge, we'd be inside already."

"Ms. Nadine." Arpad bent down. "We are nearly ready to turn to land."

"And nobody said stop pushing. Get a move on. We haven't got all night."

The two men continued poling. Their speed was halved from before, but they were able to stay well out of the circle of light thrown from the wall. The bottom shoaled rapidly, and, soon, they were pushing in just a few feet of water.

"We have forgotten about the tide," Arpad said. "The water shallows here near the wharf. The wharf will be too high above us."

"How far above?"

The boat slurped to a stop as it got stuck in the mud. The wharf loomed above them, sitting on top of greasy, wet, wooden piles. "About nine feet above," Arpad said.

***

"Gaston, can you see them?" Jake asked.

"Clear as day," Gaston, the Gauss sniper said. He held the rifle to his face, using the imaging scope and its sensors to scan the top of the gate.

"What are they doing?"

"They're talking about this crazy space guy who can't ride a horse, falls off into the mud, and is too stupid to get out of the way when his horse shat on him."

"That's to be expected, I guess," Jake said.

"They also are wrinkling their noses at the way he smells. Says he still reeks of horse turds."

Jake sniffed himself. "I washed in that stream. I'm a little ripe but not as bad as I could be. Wait. We're hundreds of meters away. They can't smell me. What are they really doing?"

"All six of them are standing there laughing," Gaston said. "And if they're laughing, they must be laughing at you."

"You have no way to know that."

"Stands to reason. Hello, princess."

Tam, Ket, and Kivi crept up behind Jake.

Tam flopped down beside him. "The ramps are ready. Give us the okay, and we'll get going."

"I wish you weren't the one doing this," Jake said. "Somebody else can ride up the ramps."

"You just gave me that lecture on seizing the brass ring, and he who dares wins and leads from the front."

"I did say all that. But, well..."

"Well, what?"

"I'm not used to people listening to me," Jake said. "About physical things. When I talk about actions and doing things, people mostly ignore me. They only pay attention when I talk about metal purity or insurance rates or what a crop derivative contract is."

"Jake, I know what a crop derivative contract is. I don't need you to tell me. How to storm a fortified gate—that, I don't know. I need you to tell me how that works."

"Be careful," Jake said.

"I always am. Ket, you take the right side with Kivi. I'm going left with Sheriff Tran," she slid back and called into the woods. "If you ladder people are ready, then move out."

Four groups of two carrying ladders muttered assent and jogged off in the trees.

"The rest of you, split up, like we planned. I want twenty up each ramp as soon as we hit the top, twenty up each ladder, and twenty with Jake in the front. Let's go." Tam slipped through the trees to her horse, and the other groups moved to mount up and follow their leaders. Ket followed.

Kivi stayed behind. "Don't worry, Captain Jake. We won't let you down. I'll be up that wall in no time. I'm sure we'll just overwhelm them."

"Overawe, not overwhelm. Steady progress," Jake said. "No running, just inevitable, unstoppable progress." Jake compressed his lips. "I wish Nadine was here. She's better at this sort of thing than I am."

"You're doing great, sir," Kivi said. "I have to go."

"Up the Empire," Jake said.

"Up something," Kivi said, then rode off.

Jake walked to the front of the woods to his group. His two escorts didn't even let him try to mount up. They leaned down and hauled him up to thrust him on top of his horse, then held him steady while he settled himself.

"Good horsey. Nice horsey," Jake said.

Whiskers ignored him and kept cropping the grass at the edge of the forest.

Magyar had so many moons that there were always a couple up in the sky. It wasn't daylight, but the night was never dark. Jake could see figures moving in the gloom but couldn't make out clothing colors or faces. On his left, Tam, the sheriff, and their group exited the woods at a fast pace. Two carts pulled by eight horses rolled alongside them. Wooden framework joined the carts, a bunch of old doors hammered together. Cart pullers yanked the whole contraption to the wall. To his right, Kivi and Ket pulled a similar group of carts. They didn't yell or fire guns, but the horse's hooves drummed, and the cart's wheels squeaked and screeched. The figures on the gate turned left, then right, to see what was happening. Two detached themselves from the group of six guards and jogged right.

Two other groups departed the woods in tandem. On each side of Jake, four lead riders balanced long ladders between them, and more planters rode on horses behind them. They cantered forward, reaching the wall just after the cart pullers. The two guards running on the wall to the right stopped and yelled out at the approaching farmers.

Jake let them yell for thirty seconds. Planters on horseback, carts, and ladders crowded the walls in the cleared area in front of the wall. Only a hundred planters total, but the darkness and the noise made it seem like five times that number.

"Forward," Jake said.

His escorts grabbed his bridle and led his horse on a fast walk. They had flat-out refused to let him gallop. His group of twenty collected around him in a circle and moved into the view of the guards.

"Back. Everybody back, or we're going to shoot," a guard yelled. He brandished a shotgun over his head.

"You can't hit anybody with that," Jake yelled back. "And there's too many of us. Just put it down. There are hundreds of us. We'll be inside in a few minutes. Nobody needs to get hurt."

Ramp carts on the left thudded into place on the wall. Figures in the gloom jumped at the rear cart. Hammers thudded, and, one by one the wheels were knocked off the cart. It dropped two feet, and the rear of the ramp tilted down and bumped the ground. The front rocked up and reached the top of the wall. Two small figures on horseback deliberately mounted the ramp and clopped up.

To Jake's right, the ladder people reached the wall first and thrust their two ladders up. Escorting horseman swarmed off their horses, grasped the ladders, and climbed. None had weapons in their hand, but they kept climbing. A guard yelled, ran to the nearest ladder, and tried to push it off. Hands at the bottom held it steady, and the riders continued climbing.

Both ramp carts came into contact. Tam, Ket, Kivi, and the sheriff reached the ramparts on opposite sides. Tam carefully maneuvered her horse over the top. A hop and a jump sideways and she was on the walkway of the wall, facing the gate. She cleared out. The sheriff landed behind her, and other planters on foot followed. Kivi was stepping up on Jake's right, and people swarmed both ladders. The guards pulled out their swords and threatened the groups advancing on them but backed away from the horses. Other planters hopped off the wall on the inside, and Jake heard their yells as they ran to open the main gate.

His group had arrived at the main gate and pounded on it. A guard up top was yelling and pointing a revolver at them, but they just yelled back. The inside group reached it, and the gate swung open. The guards drew back together with drawn swords and faced the interlopers.

"Quiet," one of the guards screamed. "Everyone, shut up. You're in. Fine. We didn't let you in. Not my fault there's a hundred of you." She took her sword and snapped it into her scabbard. "I'm not fighting a hundred people for no reason. I'm done here. I'm going home. The rest of you want to fight? Fight, but let me through."

"Let her go," Jake yelled. "Let them all go if they want. They keep their weapons if they don't use them."

Five other guards surveyed the crowd, muttered among themselves, holstered revolvers or lowered shotgun barrels, and stepped to the ramps. The planters parted to let them down.

"Admiral," one of the guards said.

"What?" Jake asked.

She saluted. "The Empire."

"The Empire," Jake said, fumbling to return the salute and, of course, losing his balance and falling backward off his horse.

He thudded into the dirt behind his horse and saw stars. Several planters pulled him up.

"Jake," Tam said, reaching him. "Are you okay?"

"Just bruised," Jake said. He rubbed his skull. "I normally let Nadine do these type of things. She's much better at it than me. I wonder where she and the Ranchers went?"

CHAPTER THIRTY-TWO

"No. No. No. If you grab my butt, it will be the last thing you touch with that hand," Nadine said. "Ever."

"It's the only way, Ms. Nadine," Vidor said. "I must. At least one hand."

"No. No. And no. Figure out another way."

Nadine, Vidor, Gabriella, and Arpad were crouched in the skiff. They were bumping against the pillars of the wharf. Four times, they had tried to climb up to the dock above and, each time, slid down after the first few feet.

"We will do it like so." Vidor gestured. "I crouch down and put my hand out. You step up, and I hold your foot on the left, Arpad on the right. Then we stand quickly and heave your feet up. We should push you high enough to grab the dock and climb up. But we must guide you in the back because if you lose your balance on the way to—"

"My balance is fine," Nadine said. "I sing, I dance, I cavort. All without losing my balance. Sometimes, I do all three at once. Put your hand out and get ready to boost me up."

"Very well."

The four shuffled sideways. Brie sat on the bow and leaned out to balance the boat. Vidor put his left hand out, and Nadine put her left hand on his shoulder and stepped up, swinging her right leg into Arpad's extended hand. As she stepped into the two men's extended hands, they rocketed upright, firing her up six feet into the air, lifting her grasping hands above the level of the wharf and four feet backward from the dock as she overbalanced. She plummeted, hitting Gabriella in the head on the way, and the two women splashed into the harbor. The water was only inches deep, covering soft, stinking mud. Nadine fell in headfirst, with Gabriella rolling underneath. The two women thrashed, surfaced, and spit up water.

Both were covered with stinking black mud. Gabriella cursed quietly, then spat again. Nadine wiped her mouth and nearly barfed as the mud spread over her lips.

The two women stood there a moment, huffing. A seagull screamed above them, then another.

"You okay, Brie?" Nadine asked.

"Yes. Just muddy."

"Sorry about that."

"Bad toss." Gabriella pried a clump of mud from her shoulder and threw it in the water. "This mud is sticky."

Nadine scraped her hands. "Very."

"Ms. Nadine," Vidor said.

"Yes, khan of all the horse people?"

"Are you okay?"

"Do I look okay?"

"Not exactly."

"Glad to see your powers of observation are in better shape than your throwing ability."

"We said..."

"Said what?"

"Nothing, we said nothing. Are you sure you're okay?"

"I'm not hurt."

"That's good. You fell because—"

"I know why I fell. Don't talk about it."

"Yes, of course. Should we try again?"

"Ms. Nadine?" Arpad asked.

"What is it, Arpad?"

"You have seaweed in your hair."

Nadine ran her hands over her mud-bedecked head and extracted two pieces of straggly seaweed. "You're right, Arpad, I do. Is it gone now?"

"Most of it."

Nadine exhaled with a ruff. "We'll try again. Brie, back

in the boat."

Nadine and Brie climbed into the skiff and arranged themselves.

"Vidor?"

"Yes, Ms. Nadine?"

"Balance me with your right hand."

"Yes, Ms. Nadine. But I will have to—"

"I'm telling you to grab my ass."

"Of course."

"Just balance and push. No grasping, no rubbing, no comments."

"Of course."

"No fondling."

"I promise."

"And, Vidor?"

"Yes, Ms. Nadine."

"Under no circumstances enjoy any of this."

"I would not dream of enjoying this, not for a second."

"Everybody ready?" Nadine said.

They all murmured assent.

Nadine positioned herself for the throw. "Ready? Go."

The butt-balancing did the trick. This time, she was catapulted right up over the edge of the wharf. She easily rolled onto it and lay there, listening.

"Ms. Nadine?"

"Quiet. I'm okay, just wait." Nadine rolled onto her side, then her knees.

Gabriella's memory was correct. The dock was dark and empty, with fishing gear heaped up along it. It ran fifty feet to the shore to intersect the promenade. A narrow alley extended back into the city. Dilapidated signs hung over doors. One pictured a frothing beer, and light shone through the windows. Nadine had been in that tavern before, when she first met Vidor and Arpad.

"This will work. Let me find something to get you up."

"We need rope. For us and the other boat," Arpad said.

"I know that, horseman. Just wait." Nadine dug

through piles of fishing gear containing nets, traps, and metal hooks.

"The night grows late, Ms. Nadine," Arpad said.

"Take the time to practice your throwing, then," Nadine said. "Because that obviously needs some improvement." She opened a box with buckets of metal hooks inside.

The next one was just buckets.

There has to be rope. How else do they haul the nets up? Wait, nets... Nadine snuck back to a pile of fishing nets. The mesh openings were small but big enough for a toe, so they could be climbed.

"Got something," Nadine said. "I'm dropping a net. Wait till I get it attached."

Nadine dragged the net down the dock to where the skiff waited. She needed both hands to tug it into place. Once there, she pulled a corner out and threaded it through the metal fitting the boats tied their mooring ropes to. Then she dragged the far corner and wound it on another fitting. The net was attached on the far side from the skiff.

"I've got the net tied off. Let me drop it down to you," she said.

Dragging the net didn't work—it stuck. She fumbled with it in the gloom, pushing and pulling. It resisted moving until she figured out that it was rolled up. It was so long she had to unroll it five times till she was nearly at the edge above the skiff.

"Ms. Nadine," Arpad said.

"Shut up, Arpy. Almost there." Nadine unrolled the side, then the middle. She climbed along the net to the end and unrolled it one more time to bring it to the edge of the dock. "Just one more, almost there." She rolled the net out and let it hang over the edge. She stuck her hands in and felt a line of square objects attached to the net. Wood. These were the floats that held the net up. The fisherman must roll the nets up from the surface and then load them on the boat.

She continued down the line of the net, unrolling, and stopped at the end. Most of the net hung loose. She unrolled the final bit and let it hang, whispering, "Here it comes, catch!"

She kicked the end to free it, and it spun and unwound down to the boat, pulled by the wooden floats. Nadine heard a curse, then two thumps and two splashes.

Then nothing.

Nadine waited. "Brie? What's going on."

"They're both in the water. The floats smacked them. They're both knocked out."

***

"Jake, do you mind riding over there?" Tam asked.

"Where? There?"

"Or anywhere farther away and downwind," she said. "You stink."

"Don't all horse people love the smell of horse manure?"

"We're planters, remember? And I don't want you getting my house dirty."

After storming the gate, Jake's group had gathered and marched into the city. They were on their way to Tam's father's—now Tam's—house. Carts rolled along behind them in the twilight.

"You do stink, sir," Kivi said. "But we can get you cleaned up at the house."

"No time," Jake said. "We need to get to the palace."

"After we drop the carts there," Tam said. "We'll take a break, meet up with some people we know in town, gauge our support, and discuss our next move."

"No," Jake said. "No discussing. We move fast. Drop the wagons at the house for sure, but we took too long getting into the town."

Arriving at Tam's house, Jake and Kivi arranged to have everybody fed—it had been a long day.

"I need a nap," Ket said.

"No napping. We need to gather supporters at the palace and proclaim Tam Imperial baroness."

"Do you have the authority to do that?" Ket said.

"Governments derive their just powers from the consent of the governed, so if Magyar wants to be ruled by the Empire, if they consent to her appointment, then I have that power."

"Circular reasoning."

"Most political reasoning is, she'll become the government if everybody agrees. We just need to get everybody together who agrees with that."

"Shouldn't there be a vote or something?"

"Did you vote for the Empire? For the Emperor?"

"No."

"That's your answer. We need to get to the palace, with friends. How many people, city people, can you scare up at this time of night who are in favor of Tam, will support her?"

"Dozens—or more, I suppose."

Tam had stepped up behind the two of them. "Anybody who supported my father and opposed the old council should support me. I've already sent out some riders, and I'll get the rest out shortly."

"What time is it?" Jake asked.

"A few hours till dawn."

"Good," Jake said. "Tell everybody we'll be in the main square at the palace at dawn. Get all your supporters to show up there and bring friends. We'll ride down there with our strike force. Get them fed, cleaned up, dump the carts and equipment, and march down there. Then we'll proclaim you baroness."

Tam and Ket spoke to all their riders and sent thirty racing off in all directions. A hunt through the parked carts produced one specific cart loaded with black-and-yellow singlets that everybody donned over whatever else they were wearing. A second wave of a dozen riders rode out with packs full of black-and-yellow armbands to be distributed. Tam's father's old housekeeper awoke and brewed hot tea for everybody. Kivi raided a cart loaded with cheese and dried fruits and distributed them. City people warned by her riders arrived and spoke with her. Jake talked to anybody who would listen about the "new" Empire, how they would be left to their own devices. He answered questions on trade and ate a lot of an unidentified fruit in a bowl.

Some people left looking thoughtful. Some frowning. Two others left with big grins.

"What made those two so happy?" Jake accepted his third glass of tea from the housekeeper.

"New minister of finance and minister of transportation in my cabinet. Thanks, Weldin. You're a dear." Tam accepted her own glass of tea.

"Friends of your father?"

"He hated them. They hated him back. But one is the only banker in town who would do business with us, at ruinous prices, of course. The other is a lawyer who owns several coastal ships and has been suggesting we do railroads for ages. I'll let them pass the laws they need to build and finance it. Even loan them some of our money. A new transportation grid will benefit everybody. More and cheaper goods available in the city, better markets for my people. Even those Empire-dammed Ranchers will benefit if we get a line out onto the plains."

"Empire-damned Ranchers?" Jake said. "Are all of them damned, or just one in particular?"

Tam grimaced. "One in particular I don't like very much."

"Why is that?" Jake sipped his tea. "Sweet. We need to talk about sugar at some point."

"He kept trying to tell me what to do."

"I've been doing that for two days now."

"But you're smart. You have smart ideas." She slurped her tea. "Like trading sugar."

"And they're ideas you want to do, regardless."

"You think that I wanted to become leader of this planet?"

"Not this way, not by your father dying. But, yes, I think you've chafed under the city rule for too long. You want the opportunity to grow things here."

"I do."

"And do those Ranchers oppose it?"

"Not exactly. They just..."

"Didn't do everything you wanted immediately? And probably kept pushing you to be more daring and less timid?" Jake stuck a finger in the bottom of his cup and scooped up some of the sugar sludge. "This sugar is great."

"I'm not timid," Tam said.

"Not anymore," Jake agreed. "But without me, do you think you would have got this far?"

"No. Not nearly. And that's gross. Stop licking your fingers."

"I'm not letting this sugar go to waste. And as for me, I'm normally the timid one, but I've discovered that, sometimes, it's better just to forge ahead. I understand now why some people get exasperated with me."

"Ms. Nadine."

"Yes."

"You're in love with her."

"What makes you say that? How did you know?"

"You only get that angry with people you care about."

"You never get angry with me," Jake said. "You're always willing to discuss things. Can I have more sugar?"

Tam handed him a bowl full of it. "Help yourself. Of course, you're smart. You're well read, you're... not unhandsome."

"Not unhandsome?"

"Yes."

"You find me acceptable?" Jake spooned the sugar into his mouth. "Sugar is amazing."

"Shut up, Jake. We have a planet to capture."

Jake licked his lips, then reached for the bowl of fruit. "These fruits are great. What are they called?"

"Apricots, but be careful and don't eat too many."

"Why? They taste so good."

"Trust me, your stomach will thank me later—and your butt," Tam said. "Me, they give me a lot of gas."

"That's bad?" Jake said.

"You'll stink."

Jake sniffed his mud- and dung-stained clothes. "Can't get much worse."

***

The door of the Cuttlefish Tavern swung open and crashed back against the wall. Vidor and Arpad strode in, leaning on each other. The crowd clapped, and the tavern owner held out his arms to embrace them.

"Vidor, you survived the fire. We thought you were dead, we—whoa!" The tavern owner retreated. "Horse's hair—what is that smell?"

"Fish, we had to take a fishing boat back," Vidor said. "We are not dead."

"You smell like you are. Your head? You're bleeding?"

"A scratch." Vidor staggered. "But perhaps Arpad and I could sit for a moment." They stumbled to an empty table near the door and collapsed into the chairs."

"I'm sorry to hear about your father."

"He was a great man. I grieve for him."

"You are khan now, I suppose."

"Yes. In his place."

"I offer you a drink to celebrate his life," the tavern owner said.

"I don't feel I am well enough for a drink, perhaps

some water—"

The door rocked open again, and Nadine and Brie came through. "Did someone offer a free drink?" She shouldered her way to the bar. Pista and his crew crowded in behind her.

"Milady," the tavern owner said, "And good Ranchers. Welcome back! You-gahhhah." He recoiled.

"I smell as bad as horse khan here, yes. Have you got whiskey?"

"Rum."

"Good enough. Line up four shots of that on the bar for Brie and I."

"Of course, of course. But, we have just cleaned, and you seem somewhat, ah, seem to be..."

"Seem to stink like the corpse of a dead stallion after it's turned rancid on the steppe?"

"I could not have said it better. Perhaps you could wait till after you clean up—"

"Pour Brie and I four shots, line them up on the bar, and step back. Otherwise, I will give you the biggest slinkiest hug you've ever had and rub my exquisite body all over you. And after you've felt that, you'll never want to be with another woman again."

"The way you smell," the tavern owner muttered, "no woman will want to have me."

"What?"

"Please stand here. I'll put the drinks on the bar." He hurried back and poured four shots. Not from a bottle, from a jug.

"This is a change for me," Nadine said. "The first time ever, I've had a man want to pay me not to touch him."

"Nadine," Gabriella said, wiping her stinking, muddy hands, "I'd like to wash up before getting this on my lips..."

"No time," Nadine said. "Need to keep the momentum going. Follow my lead." She stepped up to the bar, kept her hands at her side, leaned forward, grasped the shot glass in her teeth, flipped her head up, and downed it in a single gulp.

The crowd clapped and cheered. She spat the glass out, smashing it on the floor. She waved at Gabriella, who stepped up next to her. Gabriella wasn't as smooth as Nadine—half the rum ran out of her mouth—but she got some of it down before she spat her glass out.

Nadine stepped up and did it again, sucking the shot down in one go. This time, she kept the glass clenched in her teeth, shook her head from side to side, and flung it across the bar to shatter the mirror. The crowd cheered louder. Gabriella did the same, even managing to fling it farther down the bar before it smashed.

"Outstanding. God save the Empire!"

"The Empire!" the crowd chorused and cheered.

"Pista?" Nadine yelled.

"Ms. Nadine?" Pista said from the door. "Your wish?"

"Leave one man here to see to Vidor and Arpad. Take the others to the gate and let our troops in. Bring a small escort here. The others are to gather in formation in the square, to witness the ascension of the new baron, Vidor, Khan of the Magyars."

Some in the crowd cheered. Some clapped. Some just looked stunned and muttered to their neighbors.

Pista marched to the door.

"Pista?"

"Ms. Nadine?"

"Walk slowly, with dignity, as befits a representative of the baron, appointed by the Emperor Dashi the First. God save the Emperor."

"The Emperor," some in the crowd chorused.

Others looked confused.

"I shall," Pista said. "Khan, I leave to return with your escort." He and the others walked out the door.

Nadine gestured to the remaining warrior standing near Vidor. He came over. "Get them some water, clean them up, and get some coffee or something with caffeine into them. Bandage up their heads, get them ready so they can ride. As soon as that escort gets here, we're going into the square and into the palace and proclaiming the new government." The man ran off.

"Ms. Nadine?" The tavern owner had come up. "This Emperor Dashi, he is from your Empire?"

"Yes, Emperor Dashi the First. Not our Empire. The Empire."

"You may have heard, we have had several Empires recently—"

"Listen, bartender," Nadine said. "Those Empires aren't here right now. Ours is. Somebody has to run this town. This planet. All the old rulers are dead. Your choices are a bunch of city people who probably hate you, a bunch of dung-smelling farmers who don't care about you, or some nice rancher people who know you, who buy your booze, and have been doing business with you for a while. A bunch of nice rancher people and their one hundred armed warriors who, as we speak, Pista is letting in the gate to take over. In a few hours, there will be a new government here, one way or another. Are you going to be their friends or their enemies?"

"Friends!" a patron yelled.

"Well?" she said, "whose side are you on? All of you?"

"The khan doesn't look good," somebody yelled. "What happened to him?"

"He got in a fight with some rogue fishing equipment," Nadine said.

"Will it affect his mental capacity?" the voice asked.

"You're asking about his mental capacity?" Nadine said. "You've all met him. A knock on the head might make him smarter." The crowd laughed. "Besides, you've never cared till now."

"Who are you again?" the voice asked.

"I'm the one who's going to be standing next to Vidor in an hour in the palace. And I'm going to be writing down the names of who came out to support your new baron. So if any of you want to have any dealings with the new government, I expect to see you out there yelling 'God save Emperor Dashi and his new baron, Khan Vidor, that's who I am.'"

A man in the back stood. "I'm going to go wake up some friends. How much time do I have?"

"Less than two hours," Nadine said. "Dawn. We'll be in the square then."

"God save the Emperor," the man said, then left.

The crowd cheered more. Nadine gestured to the bartender, who poured them another round of rum.

"Nadine," Gabriella said. "That's amazing. Where did you learn all this?"

"Jake Stewart," Nadine said. "I've spent all day thinking WWJD?"

"Who wants jelly donuts?"

"What would Jake do. He always has a plan. I'm trying to think like him."

"What's he planning to do?" Gabriella said.

Nadine downed her drink, using her hands this time. "I'm not so much worried about what he's doing." She stared at the bottom of the glass. "I am worried who he's doing it with."

CHAPTER THIRTY-THREE

"I told you not to eat all that," Tam said.

"My guts feel like I'm going to explode," Jake said.

"Serve you right, little stinking bits of Jake intestines bouncing into the square."

"Stop making fun. It might happen." Jake buzzed a huge fart. "I hope it happens."

Kivi and Ket rode behind Jake. They both twitched away. "I didn't think he could smell worse," Ket said. "I was wrong."

They crowded down the streets leading to the square. The main sun was rising, and Jake could see colors, not just shadows.

Groups of yellow-and-black bedecked people waved at them from side streets or lined the main road. Their horsed group of a hundred had black-and-yellow surcoats over their uniforms and led groups of similarly colored pedestrians.

They arrived at the main square, entering from the side. The palace was to their left. A group of two dozen blue-and-red-uniformed guards stood in front of the main doors, facing in all directions.

"Didn't expect guards," Jake said. "Somebody got up early."

"Can't be running around the city smashing carts into the wall and running horses everywhere in the dark without some people noticing things," Tam said.

"Who are those folks over there?" Jake asked.

"They're not wearing colors," Tam said.

"The opposition. We need to get this finished before

they arrive."

A cheer ran through the crowd as Tam came into view. The riders trotted to the left and the right to line up and face the center of the square.

"What happens now?" Kivi asked.

"What we need to do, what you need to do, Tam, is get inside, occupy all the offices of the civil administration with your own people. Have them tell each department that they've been appointed by the council, and they are in charge now. Ask for reports for the council meeting this afternoon. Then we disarm those guards and send them home, then get up on that balcony up there." Jake pointed. "The one above the main entrance. Give a short speech about how much you love your planet and its people and how you're looking forward to a new era of stability and prosperity in partnership with the new Empire."

"What's your job, then, Jake?" Tam said.

"I stay next to you, and anytime the topic comes up, I remind everyone that the Emperor, the real Emperor, Dashi the First, is pleased to welcome your 'return to proper Imperial jurisdiction' and how much we're looking forward to resuming trade and economic ties with Magyar."

"Proper Imperial jurisdiction?" Tam asked.

"Return to proper jurisdiction. The return part is important." Jake leaned sideways and let out a huge fart. "That feels so much better."

"Trade?"

"Nobody likes wars. Everybody likes trade. New things. Cheap things. Technology. Metal. All good stuff."

"What about us?" Kivi gestured to Ket and himself.

"Kivi," Tam said, "stay close to Jake. Keep him from farting himself off his horse. Make sure he doesn't fall down or trip over his sword."

"I won't trip over my sword." Jake glared at Tam.

"Not what I saw happen when you tried to mount earlier."

"I fell once."

"Fell putting the sword belt on. You tripped before you buckled it."

"Kivi can watch him," Ket said. "What do I do?"

Jake shuffled and ripped another burst of gas. "Stay close to Tam, and every so often, lean in and whisper in her ear."

"What should I whisper?"

"Remember, Caesar, thou art but a mortal man."

"I have no idea what that means."

"That's fine." Jake grinned. "But Tam does."

***

"Twenty guards in front of the palace," Pista said. "Old baron's colors. My cousin says they don't want to fight, but they're not cowards, either. They'll stop you from coming in, if their officer tells them."

"Who's the officer?" Nadine asked.

The Ranchers had met up two streets away from the square, along with their supporters. They wore lots of black leather, which made them stand out from the city people. Gabriella had suggested a colored armband or scarf they could share with their city supporters.

"I don't know him. My cousin said he supports nobody now, but would be difficult to convince of our cause."

"Because he dislikes the Ranchers?" Nadine asked.

"No, because he's dumb like a plow-beast," Pista said. "He's too stupid to care. Brave and cheerful, but not bright. His job is to guard the door, and he'll do it. The only way we'll get in will be to fight him."

"And his men?"

"They don't particularly want to fight, but they won't let us just murder him, either."

"It's hard dealing with brave, stupid people," Nadine said.

"Does that happen often, Ms. Nadine?" Vidor said.

"More often than you can imagine."

"Well, we have no time for this," Vidor said. "My riders and I will attack them and kill them all. They cannot resist us. We will drench the square in blood."

Nadine closed her eyes. "Case in point." She looked at Gabriella. "I get it now."

"Get what?"

"Why Jake used to get so exasperated with me. Horse lord?"

"Yes, Ms. Nadine?"

"There will be no drenching. There will be no attacking. Understand?"

"Ms. Nadine—"

"No. No. The properly constituted, Imperial-appointed Baron Magyar will arrive at his administrative center to take up his duties, in a normal and civilized fashion. No drama. No fighting. No massacres."

"Massacres could be fun," Arpad said.

"Depends on which side of them you're on," Nadine said. "As I well know. What's that?"

Voices chanted a name from the square.

"I will find out," Pista said. He rode off.

Vidor and Arpad continued to greet late arriving supporters. He was genial, cheerful, and affable. Everybody left smiling.

"He's good at that glad-handing thing," Gabriella said.

"Yes. He'll be popular as a ruler if he doesn't ruin the economy, trade, employment, and technology."

Gabriella raised her eyebrows.

Nadine blew out her breath. "This isn't fun anymore. We have to help these people. Vidor's fine, but he needs somebody with brains behind him."

"Arpad?"

"Smarter but not enough."

"You, then, Baroness Nadine?"

"I'm not smart enough, either. Oh"—Nadine held up

her hand—"I know what you're saying. But I'm just parroting things I heard Jake say. I know they're important, but I don't understand them, not completely, and I don't know how to fix problems. Or avoid them, like Jake would."

"As soon as we find the planetary comm system—"

"We call our shuttle down, get that software we need, and vamoose back to civilization."

"What about Jake? And his friend?"

"What about them?"

"You said this planet needed somebody smart to run it. That Tam girl sounds pretty smart. Vidor has said a few things about her, but none say she's dumb."

"She's probably smart enough to run things, but she needs more support. The Ranchers all like Vidor. They think he's a great guy. They want him to run things 'cause they like him. They all know he's stupid. They just don't care. He's stupid, but he's their stupid."

"But he'll screw things up, won't he?"

"Badly. That lady Planter would be much better."

"Why not dump our support of Vidor and support Jake's friend?"

"And give Jake the satisfaction of dumping me for some random tart? Never."

"You're going to destroy the political and economic system of a harmless little planet because you're mad at your ex-boyfriend?"

"He is not. I am not. I'm just..."

"Worried that he might stay here with her?"

"Shut up. Remember, you're supposed to be on my side."

"I am on your side. That's why you're so angry."

Pista returned. "Tam and the farmers are in the square. They have perhaps seventy armed riders and several hundred supporters. The crowd is cheering them."

"Guards on the palace?" Nadine asked.

"They are still there. I spoke with their leader. He says

he will fight anybody who tries entrance to the palace, whoever they are, until he gets orders from the new baron."

"Did he say who he thinks that is going to be?"

"He was confused on that point. He was not confused on protecting the palace."

"Fine." Nadine looked back at Vidor. "He's got a lot of friends here in the city, doesn't he?"

"Many, Ms. Nadine. He's very popular."

"Right, we need colors, like they do. Those armbands, Brie, what do we need?"

"Something festive. Something different. Something easy to get."

"Festive?"

"The old baron's colors were blue and red. Lots of people will have blue things around. Black is easy to find. We're all mostly in black already."

"Blue and black it is," Nadine said. "Pista, you and Arpad get as many of our supporters to wear blue-and-black armbands or something blue. Tell them that Vidor chose it to match my eyes and tell them to get in that square and start counter-cheering."

"You think his supporters will believe that he choose blue to match your eyes?"

"Unfortunately, yes. Give them thirty minutes to get in there. Once we hear them cheering, we're going into the palace."

"But if we go in the front, the guards will fight."

"Who said we're going in the front?" Nadine said.

CHAPTER THIRTY-FOUR

The inbound ship was huge. Odette snapped the display up on the screen. "According to the computer, it's twice as long as us and almost ten times our mass."

Odette zoomed the telescope in till the new ship filled the screen. The center of the ship was cylindrical, with rows of colored containers attached to trusses, circling a common center hull. The containers stacked three or four to a row, and they rose in a staircase pattern to the center of the cargo area, then retreated to the stern. Drive nozzles stuck out the back, and tiny hab modules were stuck on the front.

"Are you sure?" Yvette said. "Those hab modules seem tiny. Are they for short people?"

"Computer says they're standard hab modules, and that's a standard control room on front. In fact," Odette typed and the screen overlaid the Accounting Error in wireframe, and the control room fitted almost exactly. "According to the computer, it's the exact same modular control room we're sitting in."

"That makes the rest of the ship fat," Yvette said. "What are those things next to them? Is that a giant air lock?"

"It's spinning for gravity," Odette said. "You can see the rotation. Those piles of containers are spinning, too. Why spin your containers?"

Willowby laughed. "Clever, clever people."

"Mind telling us why they're clever, Professor?" Yvette said.

"Mind telling me how you know that this ship was

going to be here now?"

"We knew no such thing," Yvette said. "This is just a coincidence."

"And it's just a coincidence that you changed our refueling site to the closest planetary body in the system to their emergence," Willowby said. "Is it?"

Yvette pressed her lips together. Willowby waited. "I see I have to go first. Well, the control room and the container area—let's call it the cargo section—and the engineering sections are not spinning. It just looks that way from our perspective. It's the hab modules that are spinning. The others are in zero G, I'm sure. But the hab modules are spinning, so they always have gravity. We get gravity by spinning the whole ship, but we've got a big ratio of human-occupied compartments to cargo compartments. That ship is ninety, ninety-five percent cargo mass. It's wasteful to spin it, so they just spin where the people live. Saves fuel."

"Clever," Yvette said.

"That's my word. You can't have it."

"Why the shape? It looks familiar, but I can't quite name it."

"Think of a spinning sphere with the top and bottom cut off and replaced by a spike. Or just take a big netball, cut the top and bottom off, stick hab modules on the top and nozzles on the bottom where you cut it off."

"Jump field," Yvette said. "It's because of the jump field."

"Right," Willowby said. "Jump fields are spherical, so that's why the containers are stacked that way. They push right out to the boundary to maximize cargo space. I'll bet the middle of that cargo section is a big jump drive and even bigger fuel tankage to support it. Then the containers are just stacked one on top of the other from the surface till they hit the radius of the jump field. The back is cut flat to attach the nozzles, and that front area is all the hab modules and anything that needs gravity. I can see air locks on the front, what looks like some sort of shuttle tucked into one of them, and some big empty metal boxes—probably internal holds with atmo and heat for smaller or special packages."

"Nice theory, Professor," Odette said. "But if that's so, then why aren't we built like that? We're a jump ship, too."

"Good question," Willowby said. He regarded the screen. "We're more of a cylinder, but we have scoops. Are they heading for us?"

"Why would they be heading for us?"

"Probably because you told them where we were, but we'll leave that for now. What I mean is, are they heading for this gas giant or the other one? Like they want to refuel."

Yvette crossed her arms. "You seem pretty relaxed about this ship showing up, Professor."

"Perhaps I'm copying you."

"I doubt it."

"That's true. There's no way I could ever braid my hair as well as you do." He ran his hand over his head. "Or have any hair to braid at all. I listened to you back a few jumps. Captain Jake gave you a choice of red dwarfs to jump to—two of them. You chose this one. And there were two—well, at least two—gas giants in this system to refuel in, and you changed our destination to here. You must have expected them to come out here. It's either some Free Trader thing or you're psychic. Are you psychic?"

"I'm not psychic."

Willowby put his hand to his brow and closed his eyes. "I'm thinking of a phrase, a group of words. Tell me what it is. Read my mind."

"Bite me."

Willowby opened his eyes. "That's the exact phrase I was thinking of. You are psychic! I knew it."

Odette popped a course plot up on the main screen. "They're going to the planet. Magyar. Distant orbit.

Unusually distant orbit."

"They're not trying to refuel?"

"Nope, least cost course for the planet."

"They can't refuel at a gas giant," Willowby said. "They're not streamlined."

"We're not streamlined," Yvette said. "We can refuel. We are refueling."

"Untrue," Willowby said. "We can't land on a planet with atmosphere, but we can circle these gas giants high up and suck in hydrogen and make fuel out of it, as long as we watch the density. If they tried that, they'd break into pieces, even with a few percent of a planetary atmosphere."

"None of the ships in Delta are streamlined," Yvette said.

"Except for shuttles and that lifting body that Jake took out of a junk yard. But that doesn't matter because we have orbital fuel factories, and we have specialized, streamlined shuttles and a mass driver to move things up to orbit and tugs to drop them down if need be. We've got a whole infrastructure to deliver fuel and goods. That jump ship—call it a jump freighter—goes from system with infrastructure to others, and offloads and onloads in orbit. It can't just drop things on any random planet like we can."

"Then what's it doing here?" Yvette asked. "There's no infrastructure for loading or unloading here."

"Good question, and I'm assuming you know the answer."

"I don't."

Yvette's comm board lit up. "Looks like they want to talk. Why don't we ask them, then?"

It turned out they couldn't. The jump freighter kept trying for a secure connection, but they didn't have the codes to handshake with. Yvette ran through a whole series of Delta codes, Delta Free Trader codes, and Delta Militia codes. None of them were accepted. They even tried some old Imperial codes included in the database. Nothing worked.

"Well, isn't that interesting," Willowby said as Yvette methodically went through her list of codes again to double-check. "They only want to talk to certain people. I wonder why. And I wonder if you don't have some sort of secret Free Trader code chip to talk to them."

Yvette slammed her fist down onto her board. Odette looked back. Yvette nodded. "Do it. Try them."

Odette, watched minutely by Willowby, pulled her code chip out of her pocket and inserted it into her board. She typed in a long password sequence and then selected from a menu. The comm lights flashed as they handshaked, then failed again. Odette tried a second time, then a third. The third time, the light flashed green. A moment's tapping, and two figures appeared on the screen.

"Who are you?" the man said. "What do you want?"

"I am Shipmaster Yvette," Yvette said. "And you are?"

"Why are you here?"

"I asked who you were."

"And we asked why you are here."

Willowby leaned into the video pickup. "Hello, Free Traders! I'm Professor Willowby. This is the good ship Accounting Error, and welcome to the Magyar system."

"We never said we were Free Traders."

"You're talking to a couple of Free Traders right now and don't seem surprised enough about it. You've got an earring that looks to me like a shipmaster's rank badge, but more importantly, that pretty young lady behind you has her hair in an elaborate braid pattern, which just happens to match young Odette's hairdo here. Put Odette up so they can see her, Yvette."

Yvette scowled at Willowby but tapped her screen. From the view in the control room, it showed Odette and the mystery woman side by side. Not only could they have been sisters, but their hair was braided in exactly the same pattern.

"Gotta be some sort of cultural cross-connection there," Willowby said. "Why don't you tell us who you are?"

"You first. Who are you."

"We're the people who are going to trade with you because your regular people aren't coming."

The couple on the screen looked at each other, then tapped at hidden boards. "Stand by," the man said, and the screen blanked.

Yvette and Odette looked at each other. Willowby waited in silence.

Finally, Yvette said, "You have any questions?"

"Who, what, where, why, how, the whole shot," Willowby said. "Can I guess?"

"Guess away."

"You have some pre-abandonment Free Trader records, ones that were closely held within families. You got codes and a method to leave secret information in a system when you pass through. Those messages that you thought we didn't catch you downloading told you something would be here and when."

"You knew about the messages?"

"Not me. Captain Jake figured it out and told me."

"I don't believe you. Jake didn't know."

"If he didn't know, why did he give me the engineering lock codes to keep you from scooting off to meet your friends?"

"What did he tell you?"

"He didn't tell me everything. He just suggested the codes for engineering might be useful. And they were, to avoid abandoning him."

The other ship appeared on the screen. The man spoke. "We expected somebody else here."

"Who did you expect?"

"Someone else. Why are you here?"

"We're here to trade. Which someone else? What do you have to trade?"

The man on screen shook his head. "We're asking the questions."

Yvette shook her head at the screen. "We're willing to trade, trade cargo, and trade answers. Are you from the Empire?"

The man pursed his lips. "We're from a nearby system. That's all you need to know. Yourself?"

Yvette snorted. "We're from a nearby system. That's all you need to know. Just like you. How about this. We will send you a list of things we have to trade, and you tell us what you have to trade for them."

"It would be better if you also gave us a list of what you wanted in return."

"Better for you, maybe, not us. We'll let you guess." Yvette made a cutting motion to Odette, who chopped the connection.

"Pretty private people," Willowby said. "What's going on?"

"You were right. They were expecting to meet somebody else. Another trade ship. They didn't expect to meet us here. They want to know what we have. The person who speaks first loses, usually. They give up more information than they get."

"So, you're not going to tell them anything?" Willowby said.

"Perhaps. Tell me, Professor, was this refueling difficult?"

"On a scale of one to ten, perhaps a seven or an eight. You have to find the right density of atmosphere, and the scoops have to suck in the atmosphere, and, of course, the fueling systems have to be set up properly..." Willowby stopped, then tapped his screen.

Sensor pictures of the inbound freighter appeared on their screen. He zoomed in and studied the engines closely, then flipped to a forward view. He superimposed a grid over the telescope picture, then methodically quartered the front of the freighter, examining each square. He zoomed in on different extrusions, analyzing each before moving on to the next. Several long minutes were spent on the two shuttles and their air locks.

Odette started to speak, but Yvette waved her off and put a finger to her lips. They sat in silence for five minutes, till the professor finished his search. Midway, the comm light blinked a connection request, but Yvette shook her head, and Odette ignored it.

"You, Shipmaster, are one smart lady," Willowby said, looking up after reaching the last grid on his search.

"We get nervous when you're complimentary," Odette said. "What's happening?"

"They can't refuel." Willowby leaned back and put his arms behind his head. "I don't see scoops, they're not nearly streamlined enough to play nice in atmosphere. They'd lose sensors, thrusters, probably one of those air locks, too, and even strip containers off the main cargo section."

"You spent a lot of time looking at the shuttles."

"One of them might have scoops, but I think it's too small to have much of a fuel processing plant. Even if it did, it's not effective."

"They can't refuel?"

"They could send the shuttles out, but that would take ages. They could send the shuttles down to the planet for water, and if they have an onboard processing plant, they could crack it. Even if they don't have a plant, they could jimmy up something. The process is straightforward."

"This model freighter doesn't have a built-in processing plant," Odette said. "I checked the database."

"I don't have that type of freighter in my database," Willowby said. "The database the Delta Militia gave me."

"Odette has a... different database," Yvette said.

"Of course she does," Willowby said. "Well, it will take them weeks—no, it will take them months to refuel fully if they have to use those jury-rigged methods we're talking about. Or we could sell them fuel."

"We could. Maybe we will, maybe we won't."

"We can always get more, quickly," Willowby said. "No problem for us."

"But it is for them, and if we are solving their problems, they should be solving ours. Besides, they haven't been very friendly. Odette, cheri." Yvette switched to Francais and spoke at length.

Willowby waited till they were finished. "I speak a little Francais, and I got the gist of that. Plus, I have access to bridge recordings that I can translate. Do you want me to put in the effort?"

Yvette shook her head. "I told her to give them a list of the top three things on our trading list—metals and food trays—and add three things that Jake had said were available on Magyar. Sugar, leather, and some fabrics. We can easily get those. Fuel will not be on the list. Then ask them what they propose to exchange. Then we wait."

"Wait for what?"

"For them to realize that they must buy fuel from us, even at inflated prices."

"They might wait."

"We can wait, too."

"Now you're willing to stay."

"What are you complaining about? You wanted us to wait for Jake. We're waiting."

"But not for Jake."

"We're waiting. It will have to be good enough."

Odette's board bonged again. "Now those freighter people want to be chatty."

"What do they want now?"

Odette raised her eyebrows. "It's not the freighter. It's the planet. Magyar. Their comm is back online. They want us to have a meeting in a few hours to discuss issues of mutual interest."

"That sounds promising," Willowby said.

"And"—Odette looked at Willowby—"you will be happy, Professor. They say Jake and the others are alive."

"That's great news!"

"Alive and fighting some sort of revolution. Jake and Nadine are leading it."

CHAPTER THIRTY-FIVE

"There's more of them now." Ket pointed at a group waving black-and-blue flags streaming into the square. "We're outnumbered."

"They look like Ranchers," Tam said.

"That's the beef buyer guy. Vidor's trade contact. And those guys are from his favorite tavern," Ket said.

"How do you know they are from his favorite tavern?" Jake asked.

Tam reddened.

"She used to spend a lot of time in taverns," Ket said. "We both did. With Vidor and his friends."

"Right, you and Vidor were an item. What broke it up?" Jake asked.

"He was a selfish, overbearing nincompoop who could barely read," Tam said. "He had no appreciation for literature, history, or the arts."

"Spent a lot of time discussing books with him, then, did you?" Jake said.

"He has no culture. He'd rather go to a horse race than a concert."

"What were you doing all that time in the taverns together, then?" Jake asked.

Ket giggled. Tam glared at her. "You don't know him at all."

"I don't know him well, but he seems a... a very attractive man."

"Oh, he is. Yummy," Ket said. "Those rancher types always are. Those tight pants, leg muscles from all that time on the horses. And those tight leather shirts."

"I didn't need the details," Jake said. "But I was curious why things didn't work out. You dumped him because he didn't like music?"

Ket giggled again. "Khan Vidor and some of the other Ranchers had difficulty with women who spoke their minds."

"Like fiscal policy, trade relations, commodity futures, things like that?"

"Well, those things didn't bother him," Ket said. "Not when Tam talked of them."

"He agreed with Tam on them?"

"He didn't know what the words meant. But the general concept of a smart woman was new to him. And he thought she wasn't... proactive enough for him?"

"He used the word proactive?" Jake asked.

"Arpad picked it for him and helped explain it to him. He said she was too timid sometimes."

Tam seethed beside them. "We don't have time to discuss my ex-boyfriends. We have things to do. Governments to overthrow."

"Technically, it's more of a terra nullius-type of thing," Jake said. "There being no extant government—"

"Shut up, Jake," Tam said. "Ket, collect twenty people. Make sure they're in our colors. Send them out in front of the main entrance. Where the guards can see them. Get them to start yelling and causing a ruckus. Yell at Vidor's people. No violence, just yelling."

"Tam," Jake said, "a riot won't serve us—"

Tam clenched her teeth. "I. Said. Shut. Up. Jake. Stewart."

"Shutting up," Jake said.

"Get back here when you're done," Tam said. "The rest of you, everyone on a horse back to the edge, keep out of the middle of the square but stay visible. Sheriff, I need ten people. Armed but steady. No nervous types. Get them off their horses, put the horses on the edge of the square, and come with me." She slid off her horse.

The others followed suit. The other mounted riders did the same.

Five minutes later, the center of the square was full of a frothing mass of yellow and black, chanting Tam's name. The riders were back against a side lane, and horse handlers held the spare horses. Ket returned, spoke briefly to Tam, and rushed back into the crowd. Tam marshaled her group, marched them down a side street parallel to the square, down an alley, and came out facing the side windows of the palace complex.

"Tam," Jake said. "What's happening? There're no doors here."

Tam waved over her head. Second-floor curtains twitched, then the window opened and a hand waved back.

"You're not the only one who can plan ahead," Tam said. "Everybody, with me."

***

Nadine, Gabriella, Vidor, and his escort rode through the backstreets. Nadine had explained her needs, and Pista led them away from the square, through a park, and down an alley. They turned left out of the alley and rode down a secondary street to the back door of the palace.

Two guards in the blue and red of the old baron waited at the door. Both wore swords, the taller one carrying a shotgun. One had a black armband.

"Halt," a tall guard said as twenty riders pulled up in front of him.

"Out of the way," Nadine said. "We're going in."

"I can't let you in," the guard said. "Those are my orders. No unauthorized personnel."

"Baron's dead," Nadine said. "Vidor is the new baron."

"Fine with me, but I need orders," the guard said.

Nadine glanced over her shoulder.

Vidor and the others collected behind her, Gabriella at the front. Nadine caught Gabriella's eyes. Gabriella nodded.

"There's twenty of us and two of you," Nadine said. "We're going in, whether you like it or not."

"I'm not afraid of some itty-bitty girl," the guard said.

Nadine flipped her arm, and a knife appeared. "How about now? You afraid now?"

The guard gulped. "You can't come in."

"If you don't let us in, I'm going to skewer you like those meat-on-a-stick things I keep eating."

"Shish kebabs?" he asked.

"Whatever."

"Just meat or with vegetables?" the guard asked. "'Cause you need to mix the potatoes and the onions in as well. Otherwise, it's not a kebab."

"I don't care about your culinary issues," Nadine said. "In fact, I don't care about any of you on this stupid, stinking planet. We're from the Empire. We're coming in. Either politely or over your dead body."

"Listen, you off-world twit." The guard stepped in front of the door. "Do what you need to. But nobody's going to say that I gave in to some tin-pot Empire bimbo who thinks she can drop down here and do what she wants."

"Ms. Nadine," Vidor said, "if you will give me a moment—"

"Shut up, horse master. The Empire doesn't need your input."

"I think—"

Nadine pointed at Vidor and snapped her fingers. "Be still. Okay, Brie, which first, knife in his chest or his head?"

"Well," Gabriella said, "like a lot of people on this planet, his looks could stand improving, but there's no need to be cruel, so why not both?"

"Ms. Nadine, Ms. Brie, please be—"

Nadine snapped her fingers again. "I said quiet,

horseman. Well, doormat man? Do you want—"

"ENOUGH," Vidor yelled. All eyes turned to him. "We are loyal servants of the Empire, but we need no help managing our own affairs." He slid off his horse and handed his reins to one of the Ranchers, then strode to the door.

"I know you," Vidor said. He rubbed his chin. "Your aunt works at the metal repair shop, does she not?"

"Salians is her name. She works in billing."

Vidor waved his finger. "You were there when we paid for a repair to our gate locks. How is your aunt? She was always most pleasant to us."

"She's off work—pregnant."

"Her second child, as I recall. You already have a niece."

"Yes, on both counts. You have a good memory."

"She was always kind and friendly." Vidor said. "The Ranchers have decided I will be khan after my father. The ambassador. You knew him."

"Yes, of course. He came here often. I'm sorry he's dead. That fire was a great tragedy, so many lost."

Vidor pointed at the guard's back armband. "Your own family. You lost some as well?"

"A great uncle. He was on the council."

"You miss him?"

The guard laughed. "I'm sorry he's dead, but he was an overbearing Imperial anus when he was alive. Pompous."

"Many on the council were."

"Not your father. He was, well..."

"He was a loud, obnoxious drunk. We all know this."

"Yes, but entertaining. He always made us laugh." The two guards grinned at each other.

"I'm the ambassador now. The position is hereditary."

"So I hear. I hear that you're going to marry this Imperial lady and become baron."

"That distresses you? Perhaps you want the job?"

Both guards laughed. "Not in a million years."

"But somebody has to do it. Why not me?"

"Why not you? Or that Planter girl. Either or. But I can't let you in."

"Of course you can't," Vidor said. He smiled. "You have your instructions. But soon, you will be working for me, and I am upset with people who work for me who don't do their job. Guarding the door is your job. We will not force you to fight."

"That's good. I don't want to."

"What were your exact instructions?"

"Guard the door. Don't let unauthorized persons enter the palace."

"Who is in charge of authorization?"

"Well, the baron." The guard held up his hand. "I know he's dead. The chancellor. He's dead. The ministers, they're all dead. I'm not sure who can authorize people now."

"What about the ambassador to the Ranchers? Was he allowed to authorize people?"

"Of course, his staff and attendants. He just told us who they were."

Vidor spread his hands and pointed at himself.

The guard nodded. "And you're the ambassador now." He swung the door open. "How many of these others do you want to authorize?"

***

One of the younger planters in Tam's group had a rope. It took a few tosses, but they were able to get it to the person in the window. Some tying and yanking, and, soon, they were climbing the walls. One of Jake's escorts preceded him, and one followed. They braced him up and pulled him through the window.

"I'm not helpless," Jake said. "Just because I can't ride a horse doesn't mean that I'm an invalid or something."

"We haven't seen any evidence of that," Tam said, helping drag him in.

"When we get on a ship, I'm putting it in zero G for the whole trip," Jake said. "See how you like it for a week."

"But we're not on a ship. We're on Magyar, and we're climbing, so you need help," Tam said.

"Speaking of help," a black-haired woman said from behind Tam.

Jake recognized her as the woman who let down the rope.

"And thank you for yours," Tam said, turning to her. "Ket, can you..."

Ket produced a pouch and handed it to the woman. She examined it and smiled. "Praise to the Emperor... ?"

"Dashi," Tam said. "Dashi the First."

"Praise to the Emperor Dashi the First, and Baroness Tam, his representative," she said.

"Thanks. Let's go, everyone," Tam said.

Jake walked next to her. "Great plan, bribing the palace staff to let you in. Good planning."

"I always was a planner," Tam said.

"When did you contact her? How long were you planning this?"

"We contacted her last night, told her to get in here and wait for us in case we needed it."

"How did you know she would help?"

"She can't afford not to. I've been paying her monthly for nearly five years," Tam said. "My father and I both."

"You've been planning for a takeover for five years?" Jake said.

"Longer. We've been setting things into place since I was born. I'd ask my father, but..."

"Sorry," Jake said. "Well, let's take a minute and figure out—"

"Nope. Not anymore."

"Well, I just wanted to talk—"

Tam put her fingers over Jake's lips. "No more talking.

No more planning. You're right. We need to do this." She raised her voice. "Councilors, go to your departments and inform your staff that you're their new bosses. Then bring everybody to the council room, or to the overlook. Admiral Stewart will invest me with the Barony of Magyar, and I will promise to take over Imperial stewardship of the planet. Let's move."

Jake scratched his head. "Don't you think we should—"

"No. Let's go." Tam strode off. Ket grinned and followed her, leaving Jake and Kivi talking.

"A little hasty," Kivi said.

"It is," Jake said. "Good word, though, stewardship. Implies that she's holding it in trust for the Empire but that the Empire isn't going to be here all the time."

"Interesting. You think she's decided that she doesn't need us?"

"Maybe she doesn't."

"Not right away but sometime."

"But, if not now, when?"

Kivi grimaced. "Good point. But I'm surprised that she's been planning this for so long. What made her come over all aggressive right now?" He turned to Jake. "It's almost like somebody has been pushing her."

Jake winked.

CHAPTER THIRTY-SIX

Jake and company pounded down the palace's second-floor corridor from the western annex building, kicking doors open as they passed. Office suites and meeting rooms lined either side. Tam had collected twenty people in her retinue, including Jake, Kivi, Ket, the sheriff, and various potential cabinet members. The cabinet officers and assistants peeled off into their offices as they went by.

"You already picked the cabinet people?" Jake asked. "Isn't there some sort of appointment process or something?"

"It's whoever the baron and council wants," Tam said. "Besides, they've all either worked in those departments or run them in the past till they got fired."

"How do you get fired as a cabinet minister?" Jake asked.

"Don't take enough bribes. Or take the wrong ones."

"You picked them for their honesty?"

"No, I picked them because they would take my bribes," Tam said.

"You paid them bribes?"

"Big ones."

"But how are you sure they will, I mean, be supported by their own people?"

"I bribed them enough money that they can pass it down to their subordinates. Trust me, every senior administrator is this instant getting a pile of cash dropped into their hands."

"LONG LIVE BARONESS TAM" came a shout from one of the offices they passed.

"Told you she was rich," Ket said. "A princess."

"I'm not a princess."

"Baroness soon," Ket said. "Uh, we need to let the special group up front, Tam."

Tam stopped. "Right. Hang on here. Specials, up front." Six of her men pushed through from the back. Five wore swords and carried shotguns. The sixth had a bulkier gun.

"That's the Gauss rifle," Jake said. "We don't need that here."

"We might need to convince some people of our legitimacy," Ket said.

"By blowing holes through reinforced concrete? Because that rifle will legitimately do that."

"Sometimes, it's not what you do," Tam said, "but what people think you can do."

Jake stumbled along behind them. "I hate it when people listen to me."

"Sir, are you all right?" Kivi asked.

"Things are just moving in a different direction than I expected. She seemed so... reluctant... before."

"I guess all your nagging about seizing the day is taking effect," Kivi said.

"I do not nag," Jake said.

"You nag all the time," Tam called back. "All. The. Time."

The group came onto the balcony surrounding the throne room and turned left.

"I guess I should keep my stupid suggestions to myself," Jake said.

A figure dashed up the stairs below him and intercepted the group. She spoke with Tam, who nodded and waved everybody on. A hum of talking seeped up from below. People crowded in from the rear entrance to the throne room. People wearing black and yellow. Jake jogged to catch up as she turned right to descend the stairs to the main floor. "What's happening?"

"The Ranchers are in the building. Vidor is here."

"Well, we can talk to them."

Tam pointed at the shotguns of her escorts. They clacked as they cocked them. "I've done enough talking till now. Time to finish things off."

***

Nadine surveyed the council room as she came in the back entrance. It was rectangular, three stories, with an extensive mezzanine surrounding the second story, and open windows piercing the third. Half of the roof was skylights. Split stairs ran from the second floor to the ground at either end, and railings allowed observers on the second floor a clear view of the proceedings. Imperial light strips and heating and AC units were hidden under the second-floor extrusions.

The room was adapted for multiple purposes—not just a throne room or a council room, more like a ballroom. The floor was a polished granite, with green-and-brown swirls on a yellow background. Walls were similarly polished up to the first floor, beyond that painted concrete. The Imperial Polaris star adorned one wall, a stylized collection of suns and planets on the far wall.

Nadine took that to be the Magyar system's planets and moons. The biggest piece of polished wood Nadine had ever seen served as a table.

"Holy Imperial wood carvings," Gabriella said. "That table has no joints. It was cut from a single tree. A six-foot-wide tree. I didn't know trees got that big."

"A piece of wood that big back on Delta you could trade for a spaceship," Gabriella said.

"Two spaceships," Nadine said. "If you could get it in one. It wouldn't fit a standard container."

Vidor slapped the shoulder of the back door gate guard who had accompanied them. The guard scuttled to the front of the room and slipped out.

"He will bring the front guards in, to see me, acclaimed? Is that the word? Acclaimed by my authorized guests."

"Vidor," Nadine said. "That table—where do you get the wood?"

"They cut it in the northern mountains and bring it down by river. Why, I—"

Four shotguns cocked to their left. They turned to see Jake, Tam, Ket, Kivi, and a group of others coming down the stairs.

A crowd of black-and-yellow garbed workers filled the mezzanine and balconies, peering over the rails. Jake stopped at the bottom of the stairs next to Tam, facing the Ranchers, flanked by Ket and Kivi. The shotgun guards split to either side, holding their weapons vertically. Gaston, the Gauss rifleman, waited on the stairs, his weapon pointed at the ceiling. Nadine, Vidor, Arpad, Gabriella, and Pista faced them from ten feet away. Ranchers crowded behind them and fanned out across the room. Blue and red former chancellor guards joined them from the front.

"Vidor," Tam said.

"Tam," Vidor said.

"I see you brought your friends. And your brothers and cousins. And your Imperial floozy."

"Ms. Nadine will acclaim me baron. On behalf of the Emperor."

Tam wrinkled her nose. "Will that be before or after she has a shower?" She sniffed some more. "Perhaps she's not used to those. We could arrange a firehose, hose you down like you do your cattle."

Vidor narrowed his eyes. "She used a firehose before— we both did before we leaped off the ship. She tried to save the ship. She was very brave."

Tam gave Nadine a once-over, head to toe. "Of course, Vidor. You are well known for choosing your female companions for their... bravery."

"As you are known to choose your male companions for their susceptibility to your money."

"Admiral Stewart led me into the flames on the ship to find my father. He led me through a burning door twice and only retreated when the ship began to collapse around us. He is very brave as well."

Vidor turned to Jake. "You don't look the brave type."

"I've heard that you're not bright enough to tell the difference," Jake said.

Vidor laughed. "That, that is brave." He regarded the colored groups around the room, looked up into the galleries, and finished by addressing Tam. "You have brought friends as well, I see."

"I have already established my administration. The workers, the councils, the ministry are with me. We will ensure continuity of government, our stewardship for the Empire."

"Of course you have," Vidor said. "Always the planner. How long ago did you start bribing the palace staff?"

Tam gave a rueful grin. "Dad said I always did plan too far ahead."

"But how are you here?" Vidor said. "You always planned, planned, talked, planned. It was nothing but boring. Boring talk. Never any action."

Tam jerked her head at the guards. The shotguns dropped several inches. Gaston pushed a button, and his rifle hummed. "How's this for action? Stand aside or we start shooting."

"Are you threatening me?" Vidor asked.

"No, Vidor, I'm suggesting you let me dust off the chairs so they will be nice and clean when you dump your stupid rumps on them. Stand aside. Admiral Jake will acclaim me the baroness."

"This isn't the Tam I know. The Tam I know would want to discuss things."

"People change, Vidor. I've been taking advice. Advice

from some smart people." Tam slapped Jake's shoulder. "And these smart people say I should shoot first and talk later."

"I never said—"

"Shut up, Jake," Tam said.

"An amazing change," Vidor said. "Surprising. I would not have believed it."

"Well, believe it." Tam looked beyond Vidor. "Arpad. I will confess, I'm surprised to see you here. And these others. I hear you have hundreds of Ranchers with you."

"Many hundreds. Brought in from the plains," Arpad said.

"How did you feed them?" Ket asked. "Let's face it, Vidor. Everybody knows that you're not good at thinking. Friendly but not the sharpest tool in the shed."

"Short a sock or two," Tam said.

Arpad chimed in. "Couldn't organize a party in a brewery."

Vidor glared at Arpad.

Arpad pursed his lips. "I'm sorry, Khan, but you know the truth."

"I take advice," Vidor said, turning back to Tam. "Advice from smart people. Like you do."

"What type of advice?"

"Advice on many things. Logistics. Supply. Administration. Economics. Commerce."

Tam and Ket looked at each other and laughed.

"I don't think you know what those words mean," Tam said.

"I did not before, but I have paid close attention to my friends. I can learn."

"Learn from who?"

"Ms. Nadine has taught me things. Only the other day, she lectured me on the need for a sound monetary policy."

Jake laughed. "Nadine? Monetary policy? That's a hoot."

Nadine narrowed her eyes, then marched the ten feet

separating her from Jake.

"Something funny, Stewart?" She jabbed her finger at his chest. "Something amusing you, Jake?" She leaned closer and glared at Jake, swept her eyes right to Tam, turned her head slightly left in Vidor's direction, and nodded. "Somebody being funny, Jake?"

Jake glanced over her shoulder at Vidor, then back. His face opened wide in a grin. "You, Nadine. It's funny. I don't believe you have any idea what you're talking about, and I certainly don't think you'll be qualified to advise Mr. Vidor back there."

"Ms. Nadine knows a great deal," Vidor said.

"She knows as much about economics as you know about jump drives, Mr. Vidor," Jake said. "In fact, I'm surprised you made it this far, if you've been following Nadine's advice."

"I give excellent advice, Jake, you know it. And right now, I advise you to keep your mouth shut," Nadine said.

"Make me, Nadine," Jake said.

Nadine reached, grabbed Jake's neck, and squeezed. Jake rose on his tiptoes and gasped. Nadine kept squeezing. "How do you like my advice now, Jake?"

"Ms. Nadine," Vidor shouted. "That is enough. Stop."

"Shut up, horseman," Nadine yelled.

Jake kept gargling. Kivi stepped forward, Gabriella signaling him, shaking her head and mouthing no. He stepped back.

"Let him go." Tam stepped up.

"Nope."

Jake gargled.

"Let him go, Imperial wench," Tam said.

"Like Jake said, make me."

Tam stepped back, set her feet, made a fist, and swung a massive right roundhouse at Nadine. It connected with her face, and Nadine's head snapped back, then she slumped to the ground. Jake collapsed forward and dropped to his stomach, clutching his neck and rolling to face Nadine.

Vidor sped forward but brought up short. Tam had stepped in front of him and raised her fist. "You want one of these."

Vidor held out his hands. "No, no."

Gabriella slipped by and bent over Nadine. She ignored the croaking Jake, leaned down, and cradled Nadine's head. Nadine's eyes remained closed. "Are you okay?"

Nadine mouthed some words, and Gabriella bent closer. "What, what?"

"Stay down. Keep your head down."

"I, what?"

"Whatever happens, keep still and down low," Nadine hissed. "Don't draw attention. How's Jake?"

Gabriella glanced to the side. "He's lying there, holding his neck. Kivi's with him. What's going on?"

"Just keep low and don't act surprised. Move me so I can see the two Imperial wannabes."

Gabriella repositioned Nadine to see the confrontation next to them.

"... and if you think all I do is talk,"—Tam shoved her fist in Vidor's face—"then talk to this. Talk to my people, who are here and ready to KICK YOUR ASS if you don't back off, you ignorant, idiotic, brainless dupe." Tam's clenched fist forced Vidor back a step. "First, I'm going to beat you about that stupid mustache, then my people are going to beat your people, then we're going to beat your friends, and then—then we'll kick your horses."

Vidor looked at the fist two inches from his nose. "I don't think the horses deserve that."

"No, they don't. I'll spare the horses. I'll just hit you more. Now get out of my way, you stupid lummox."

"If I'm such a stupid lummox, how did I get here with all these people? Bring all my troops and friends here. Feed them, arm them, sneak them into the palace."

"You had good advice."

"And I listened to it. Of course"—Vidor bent around

322

to see Nadine on the floor—"Ms. Nadine is not the only good source of advice on this planet. There are others who know as much as her. Perhaps I will start listening to them, too."

"Who are you going to take advice from now?"

"How about you?"

Tam dropped her fist. "You never listened to me before. Why start now?"

"I understand now. There are many things I don't know. If I can learn to take advice from an off-worlder— and a woman, at that—anything is possible, yes?" Vidor said.

Tam dropped her hands to her hips and glared at him. "If you learned to take advice from her, the universe has truly rocked on its foundations."

Vidor smiled at her. "I have missed you, princess. Did you know you are sexy when you are angry?"

Vidor caught her slap and pushed it away. She drew her hand back again, cocked it, then growled and leaped up at him. He caught her as she jumped up and straddled his waist, then kissed him.

"Stupid ox. I missed you, too."

Gabriella, leaning over Nadine, covered her mouth.

Nadine looked up from the floor, watching Vidor and Tam kissing. "Whatever you do, Brie, for Empire's sake, don't laugh. Not now."

CHAPTER THIRTY-SEVEN

Jake, Nadine, Kivi, and Gabriella found themselves pushed to the back of the room as the two groups conferred. The newly somewhat-reconciled Planter/Rancher power couple had seated themselves at the council chamber and were hashing things out, along with their advisers. The off-worlders were neither invited nor pushed themselves in. After exchanging hugs and hearty handshakes, they faced each other.

Jake rubbed his neck. "You didn't have to be so realistic in the choking, Nadine."

Nadine stepped back and put her hands on her hips. "You were pretty friendly with Ms. Skinny But Big Boobs back there, Jake."

"Who wouldn't be?" Jake said. "She's attractive, rich, smart, and she doesn't abuse me all the time, like some women I know. Besides, she knows who Vespasian is."

"Vespasian was a Roman General," Nadine said, "back on Old Earth. But Princess Tam is right. Antonius Pius is more your style. Less fighting, more planning. Did you know that Antonius Pius never commanded an army?"

The three others dropped their jaws.

"She doesn't look sick," Kivi said. "But she sounds weird. Like somebody else."

"Did that hit from Tam knock her wits out?" Gabriella said. "Scramble her brains."

"What?" Nadine said. "A girl can't know history? I could have learned all this years ago."

The others shook their heads.

Nadine rolled her eyes. "Fine, Arpad had a reader,

there were some history books on it. I wanted to see why Ms. Princess was so into those people. She was kind of right. Planning is hard."

"Planning is hard? You're saying that? Maybe your brains are scrambled after all," Jake said. "Maybe Tam's punch did turn them to mush."

"A little punch like that wouldn't do anything. But let's have a test." Nadine held up a fist. "I'll punch you, Stewart, and we'll see if I scramble your brains."

"It was all fake," Gabriella said. "All of that. The argument. Your falling down."

"Justice must not only be served, it must appear to be served," Nadine said.

"Who said that?" Jake asked.

"You did," Nadine said. "You were quoting somebody else, don't remember who. We can't just fix things. They have to appear to be fixed. We need a stable planet here, and it wouldn't be stable if it was run by off-worlders. They'll put up with their own people abusing them but not outsiders. Besides, Vidor was getting boring."

"Didn't look like you were bored," Jake said.

"I was getting tired of always having to explain things to him."

"Yes, that can be exhausting."

Nadine clenched a fist. "Have somebody in particular you want to mention, Stewart?"

"Nope." Jake smiled. "I'm glad you're okay, Nadine, and I'm glad those two are back together."

"I would have been bored being a princess," Nadine said. "Or a baroness—whatever. And I'm glad to see you, too, Stewart."

"How did you manage it? Getting all those Ranchers here, keeping them fed, supplied, and move them into the city. It's quite a logistical accomplishment. All the information I have is Vidor wasn't up to it."

"I just kept thinking what sort of thing would Jake be talking about right now that would be annoying to listen to? What sort of irritating thing would bore me so much that I'd stomp off and stab things." Nadine grimaced. "I'd make a list in my head of things that would bore me the most, and I'd go look into them right away because it turned out that those were always the most important things to look into—at least, in retrospect. And yes, I know what that word means."

"That's amazing," Jake said. "I wouldn't have believed it of you."

"Everybody told me that Tam was a planner, a plotter," Nadine said. "Even Arpad said so. That's one of the things that turned him off about her. But somehow, she managed to swim ashore, find an army, march on the palace, and storm the council chamber, all in a few days. It sounded like your work. How'd you get that done?"

"I used muscle memory," Jake said.

"Muscle memory?"

"I'd just hit myself in the chest like I was being shot, which hurt my muscles, and that would make me think of you, and I'd think of what sort of crazy idea you'd suggest, and I'd make Tam do some variant of it. I just kept asking myself, 'What would Nadine do in this situation?'"

"I'd have probably dragged Ms. Princess off into the bushes every night and her friend there, too."

Jake crossed his arms. "How do you know I didn't?"

Nadine narrowed her eyes and made a fist again. Then she laughed.

Jake laughed as well, then he and Nadine hugged. After a moment, they separated.

"Come on, Stewart," Nadine said. "Let's go see the happy couple. You talk sense and planning, and I'll hit somebody."

The group marched to the central table.

Vidor and Tam were standing side by side at the council table, peering down at a map. Jake and Nadine and the others approached from the back.

"Ms. Nadine," Vidor said, "I must tell you—"

Nadine smacked him hard, and he rocked back into the chair and tripped over it. Nadine waited till he rolled over, grabbed his free arm, and hauled him up. He stood there, rubbing his chin.

"I heard already," Nadine said. She stuck out her hand to Tam. "I understand congratulations are in order. When will the wedding be?"

"You just smacked Vidor," Tam said.

"We all know he deserved it," Nadine said.

Tam nodded and shook her hand. Vidor rubbed his chin again, then smiled and put his hand on Tam's shoulder.

"We have agreed on a joint rule," Vidor said. "Both factions can agree to this. We will be co-baron and baroness, and our children will rule after us, In the Emperor's name, of course. I hope our first child will be a boy. I will teach him to ride."

"Or a girl," Tam said. "Then I will teach her how to run a planet while the boys ride horses in circles out on the plains."

"Perhaps we each instruct the children in different things. We go before the people shortly. Some of the councilors"—Vidor gestured at Tam's two appointees—"have an idea for building a rail system. We have some details to be worked out, but we will benefit from easier access to food and resources from the Planter groups, and they will have better trade access to us, the Ranchers as well. Also, we have a plan for some coal-powered ships to bring goods across the strait. We will be able to trade directly with each other and with all in the city. Since we will be providing the money, the city people have agreed to this change." He pointed at two blue-and-yellow garbed councilors, both wearing the black armbands of mourning.

"Big loss for them, horseleader," Nadine said. "What do they get?"

"They will get better access to our new off-world ally's trading goods, which will be landed here and traded with our new friends. In the name of the Emperor Dashi the First, of course."

The crowd cheered.

Tam turned to Jake. "Jake, we didn't have time to talk about our suggested trading arrangements, but I hope, I hope..."

"Don't worry," Jake said. "I find them acceptable."

"Acceptable is good."

"Well, in the name of the Emperor Dashi the First, welcome, and blessings on the newest Imperial appointees—Baron Vidor and Baroness Tam."

The crowd cheered more, their voices drowning out all further discussion. Jake grabbed Nadine and hauled her off to a corner. Gabriella and Kivi followed.

"Right," Jake said. "Crisis averted, planet organized, trade assured. Let's find out what's been going on with our people up top."

There had been a direct link to the planetary long range comm system in the palace, but it had failed forty years ago for unknown reasons. The only way to have a real-time orbital conversation was to climb the tallest hill in the area, where radio and microwave towers rested with their controllers. It had taken almost a full day to arrange a guide and horses, get access, and raise Accounting Error.

"I'm glad to be alive as well," Jake said, answering questions over radio. "Thanks for asking, but my butt hurts a lot. What's your status up there?"

"We've got visitors," Willowby said. "I'll let Yvette tell that story, since they are friends of hers."

"They're not friends," Yvette said, then explained all she knew.

"But you were expecting them—or someone like them—according to those coded merchant messages you've been receiving," Jake said.

"What coded merchant messages? They're getting coded messages."

"Not now, Nadine," Jake said. "I'll explain later."

"We should ask her—"

"Shhh. Let her sweat," Jake said. "Just wait."

Yvette came back online. "How much do you know?"

"Most of it. Dashi knows more."

Jake waited for almost thirty seconds before speaking. "By the way, how's my decryption program going? Should have chewed through your codes by now. I can download my messages..."

Yvette came back on. "Fine. We were expecting a Free Trader ship. Not this one. There have been Free Traders coming to this planet every few years for the last thirty or so. They have traded technology for some hard-to-get things. Gems. Some of those fabrics. They would trade a few containers of Imperial technology for a few dozen containers of fabrics and some boxes of gems."

"But they missed the last two or three trips, haven't they? And then one started up again recently."

"How do you know that?"

"Delta may have been part of their regular route at one point, but they stopped coming to Delta and here."

"Yes. A gap of years, yes. Then, two years ago, a different ship arrived on the circuit."

"And your friend up there is supposed to meet this different ship, swap some goods, trade with the planet below, and then the two of them go their separate ways. I'll bet they are supposed to go back Coreward—they came from the direction of the Empire, right?"

"Yes, they came from the Empire."

"And they want to go back. But they can't without fuel."

"Right."

"We've got them over a barrel. A big barrel. Let me think a moment."

Jake keyed off the comm and drummed his fingers. "Nadine, Can Odette fly us back to Delta?"

"I'm the only one who's flying you anywhere, Jakey."

"Humor me. What if you were sick or worse."

"Odette," Nadine said. "I don't like her much. But, yes, she could do it. But I'm not sick."

"You'll be busy. You won't be able to fly Accounting Error."

"And why not, Jakey? Where will I be?"

"Flying that freighter. Back to Delta. So they'll trade with us."

Nadine raised her eyebrows. "You do think big. You're going to hijack it."

"Nope, I've got them over a barrel. I've got a better idea."

"Does it involve boring lists of trade goods?"

"Trade goods from Magyar. I'm going to load them up with tons of stuff."

"Because you have the princess over a barrel, she needs the trade."

"Exactly. Let me sort a few things out with Yvette, and we'll go back to town to talk to them. Huh." Jake smiled a big smile, then turned to Nadine. "That's a nice visual."

"What's a nice visual?" Nadine asked.

"All this talk, you know, about barrels and so on."

"Yesss..."

"I was just picturing the princess, Tam. You know?"

"Know what?"

"What she'd look like, over a barrel."

Jake had expected the punch, so he ducked easily.

CHAPTER THIRTY-EIGHT

Turned out Tam and Vidor had a few barrels of their own.

"You need your software update to get home safely," Tam said. "You need it, so you can't just have it for free."

"It doesn't cost you anything to give it to us," Jake said.

"What's that have to do with it?"

"It's Imperial property. It's in the administration computers."

Tam tapped the council table. "You are right, it is. So, that means you can't have it."

"Pardon?"

"It's Imperial property. For official Imperial missions, military, Militia, customs ships and the likes. Therefore, you can't have it."

"I'm on an official Imperial mission."

"And yet, not on an Imperial ship. Somebody made a point of saying how they owned their ship privately, that it didn't belong to the government."

Jake squirmed. "It is my ship, yes. But I told you that to stress my close relationship with the current Imperial council, how they trusted a private entrepreneur like me with such an important mission."

"Really?" Ket asked. "We thought you were just trying to impress Tam so you could get in her pants."

"Both could be true," Gabriella said.

"Good point," Ket said. "But we've got the only software around here, so you need to deal with us."

"As an Imperial citizen, I'm going to appeal to the local Imperial governor, who I believe is the current baron/baroness combo, to support this Imperial mission, blessed by the Emperor Dashi the First. I'm sure the Imperial governor of Magyar will support the Empire."

"Oh, they will, they will," Tam said. "But it's a bit above our level to approve that, so we'll need to seek advice. As part of our first meeting with the Emperor Dashi the First, I'll send him a message asking him what we should do with those type of Imperial assets. Let me know his response when you bring it back, Jake."

Jake glared. "Fine. We'll pay. Suggest a price."

Ket tapped her screen. "We won't rip you off. Not too much. Next item, fuel."

"We don't need fuel," Jake said. "We can make our own. Or scoop it. Or even lift water to orbit and crack it there."

"But your trading buddy that's coming in, they need fuel."

"They do," Jake said.

"We need to set a price on that as well. A high price."

"And how are you going to get it to them?"

"Well, lift it..."

"On our shuttle, which is the only one here. What was it somebody just said, 'You need it, so you can't just have it for free.'"

The bickering continued. Nadine had pulled out a whetstone. She had bought a new knife from one of the local artisans and was sharpening it.

Gabriella watched her. "Are you bored?"

"Bored? Of course I'm bored. Aren't you?"

"This is kind of interesting. It's like a dance."

"The Emperor's greasy elbows," Nadine said. "Jake just infects everybody he comes in contact with."

It took a few days but both sides considered the trading went well. Jake got several dozen containers of exotic raw materials. At least exotic for Delta. Sugar, coal, leather, hemp, the local silk plant, the biggest pieces of wood they could handle, fruits, olives, and free rein of the Imperial archives for planetary and trade data. And a giant container of ice cream. In return, Magyar got copper, silver, gold, zinc, and lots of steel—enough for a start on their burgeoning rail network. And they wanted Jake to carry six Magyar locals to Delta to study at the Delta University.

"Passengers? We're not set up for that," Jake said.

"Think of it as a technology transfer mission," Tam said. "You said you have a university. We're sending doctors, engineers, a veterinarian, and two agricultural specialists. I'll bet they know something you don't and vice versa."

"I'm not sure."

"I'll give them guns. I've told them they can shoot Ms. Nadine if you ask them to."

They had space, so Jake agreed, especially after Tam sweetened the deal by offering him as much cracked hydrogen as his shuttle could carry every lift.

"Why are you being so generous with the hydrogen?" Jake asked.

"First, because it's surplus. The fusion plant makes it during off-peak times. We've got lots of water and an integral cracking plant for the fusion plant itself. So, for us, it's free. But of course there's a catch."

"Which is?" Jake asked.

"You agree to lift and drop our trades with that freighter, the Flandre. For free."

The lifting body's landing was much smoother on their second trip to the planet. Greetings were exchanged, Tam's people—or, to be correct, the 'consolidated group of Imperial charter holders of the Planet Magyar's' people pumped hydrogen into it, setting it up for the next lift.

Jake and Tam had agreed on a number of things, but the limited cargo capacity of the lifting body and the physical limitations of hatch and container sizes had limited what could practically be exchanged. That, plus all the metal Tam wanted was heavy.

In a complicated exchange process, Accounting Error

detached empty and full containers to float next to the ship. The ship's "boat," as Jake insisted on calling it, would load up as much metal as it could carry, drop to the harbor, and offload to a barge with a crane that floated next to it. Sealed bales of leather or sacks of sugar would replace the metal. Next they stuffed the boat with as much fuel as it could carry, lifted to orbit, , then docked the hatch to the free container and cross ship. It was cumbersome and needed a lot of muscle power.

Jake sent the six "passengers" up to help lift at the start. Nadine flew the ship's boat, and Jake and the rest of his party dealt with issues dirtside. Communications was still an issue.

The newly arrived Flandre had communicated sporadically with the Accounting Error. After the initial contact, Yvette and Odette had no luck getting into any sort of two-way conversations. They preferred to communicate via written messages, mostly lists of things they wanted to trade for, with rejections of Yvette's offers.

"They seem to be short of metals and basic industrial items," Willowby said, reviewing their latest suggestions.

"We need to get Jake involved," Yvette said. "He has a gift for this sort of thing."

"Or they need to get a radio link at the top of that hill," Odette said. "Why can't they just talk to us on the radio?"

"Planetary-wide communicators are in short supply," Willowby said. "Our comms are Old Empire technology, powerful and long ranged. They've got some sort of local setup down there and not much of it. Fine for line of site, or calling the guy on top of the next hill but not part of a network. We didn't realize how lucky we were on Delta," he said.

"And how are we lucky?" Yvette said.

"First, our planetary and system networks are intact. We've got satellites, constellations of satellites, plus a whole whack of stations that can talk across planetary distances. Every ship has one, even some of our suits. Rare and expensive technology. Because our environments were so harsh and so big, we had to equip for them. A comm that's built to sit in your pocket and talk to a local carrier mesh that's less than a kilometer away and uses that mesh to connect to others is way easier and cheaper to make than one that can punch through a planetary magnetic field and go a hundred thousand kilometers. Our stuff is all more powerful and better built because of the society we're in. We lucked out."

"Can't build jump drives though," Odette said.

"But we can build a lot of other things, and we have the materials to do most of it. We can repair starships, refine almost any kind of metal, have effectively unlimited fuel processing capabilities, and do some basic technological stuff. We're even self-sufficient in food, and we can make it into trays to preserve it."

"If we're so great, why are we out here trading for things?"

"We're short on things that grow, or have to be mined, on a planet instead of an asteroid. We don't have nearly the variety of food we should—we've all been eating potatoes and algae most of our life. We don't have cotton, sugar, rubber, or anything grown. We have some wood, but the quality is poor. And anything that isn't on asteroids—coal, oil, carbon-based items, we're short. And our technology palette is limited. If it's not for spaceships or steel mills, we don't have much expertise in it. We don't have any consumer electronics, like entertainment systems, for example. We could make them, but the printers are too busy making spare parts for ship systems."

"What's that have to do with the price of copper?"

"More like the price of sugar," Willowby said. "Those Flandre trading people—they turned down a bunch of things that are planetary based. Not interested in the sugar at all, but they jumped on our nickel. I think they'd take as much as we could give them. And look what they offered in return."

"Electronics for terrestrial telephone systems," Yvette read. "A thousand units, with base stations. Sounds great."

"We couldn't use it, though," Willowby said. "Look at the specs. We're too spread out. They might be able to use it here, but it's for densely populated planets. Not orbital setups, or even rural."

"So what?"

"So, they need to come to Delta with us. I'll bet they've got some even better stuff they're holding back because they really, really want a load of metals. I think they'd trade a lot for it."

"What's a pepper?" Odette asked.

"It's a spice, for food."

"They say it's worth a lot. I've never heard of it."

"Not something we can grow. We could take some."

"Well, in a few hours, Jake will be in orbit, and we can drop it on his lap."

Her board bonged. "I'll bet another useless trade offer from our friends." She looked more closely. "Whoops."

"What?" Yvette asked.

"Not our friends. Or not these friends. Another ship just arrived."

"Wonderful. I think. What type of ship?"

"Let me run it through the database." Odette held up her hand. "Yes, both databases. It will take a minute while it chews through the scan."

They waited until the console bonged again.

"There it is," Odette said. She stared at her screen for a long time.

"Well? Going to tell us?" Willowby said.

"Warship," Odette said, popping it up on the screen. "Computer says Imperial missile boat. And it's heading this way, fast."

CHAPTER THIRTY-NINE

Nadine docked the ship's boat with the Accounting Error, and Jake and the others swarmed aboard. This was the first time many of them had seen each other in person, and the crews exchanged hugs near the air lock. Some were more genuine than others.

"Great to see you back, Captain Jake," Willowby said, slapping his back. "A little thing like fire and water can't kill you."

"It's great to be back," Jake said.

"And now you can get us out of this mess."

"I have a plan."

"Of course you do, mon capitaine," Yvette said. She and Odette gave Jake big hugs. He hugged them back.

"I missed you both," Jake said.

Nadine stepped out of the air lock behind them. "You must miss people lying to you, then, Jake." Jake let go of Yvette and stepped out to let Nadine greet them. Or perhaps just to clear the line of fire.

"Yvette, Odette," Nadine said. She glared at the two Francais women.

Yvette glared back for a moment, then stuck her hand out. "Ms. Nadine. I'm glad you're not dead."

Nadine looked down at the hand, then up at Yvette, then reached out and shook it. "Thank you. I'm glad... you're still here."

They broke contact, and Nadine said, "Jake, you wanted us all in the lounge. Everyone, let's go."

The group trooped off to the lounge.

Kivi dropped back to walk next to Gabriella. "I'm

337

surprised she said that. Glad they're still alive."

"I'm not."

"Why? You don't think they want each other dead."

"I'm sure they do," Gabriella said. "But they want to be the one to do it to each other."

The crew assembled in the lounge. The two Francais girls, Willowby, Jake, Nadine, Kivi, and Gabriella, and six new faces from Magyar crowded the lounge. The engineering crew connected via video.

"How much fuel do we have?" Jake asked.

"Topped up," Willowby said. "To the brim. And before you ask, all systems go. We can jump out of this system anytime."

"Cargo loading?" Jake asked Yvette.

"Containers are latched up. Two left to secure. We've been moving shuttles nonstop since you came back online. We've loaded most everything that the surface folks wanted to trade with us, and we've dropped most of our metals to them."

"Great job. This other trading ship, the Flandre, have they taken anything from us?"

"There's been lots of back and forth, mostly text. And they haven't committed to anything. They haven't brought up the subject of fuel yet."

"Because they want to try to get it from the planet, but they can't because we have the only transport craft," Jake said. "Outstanding. We'll deal with that."

"Jakey," Nadine said, "shouldn't we be talking about this warship pirate thing that's zooming in-system and causing problems?"

"Not really. We do have weapons of our own. We can take on a pirate, or at least damage them. Pirates don't like to be damaged. We could even outrun it."

"Weapons that we've never fired. That you say you don't know how to use."

"We can learn."

"Better learn quickly, then. And what about that big

freighter out there? The freighter that has no weapons and can't outrun a pirate?"

"You mean the Flandre? The one that's not talking to us and only wants to trade for certain things? Unfairly trade, I might add. Doesn't sound like our problem."

"You don't think we should help—"

"Nope. We're going to help our new friends and allies, the Magyars," Jake pointed at the six groundsiders. "Their government and the people who sent us here. Others who want to take advantage of the situation, not so much. Professor?"

"Yes, Captain?" Willowby said.

"We've got good sensors on this ship. Better than most merchants, military-grade, I think. Is it possible that the freighter can't see this missile boat zooming in?"

Willowby nodded. "Possible. Probable. Unless they know where to look."

"Let's tell them," Jake said. "Yvette, send a message, give them coordinates of this unknown ship and repeat them until you get an acknowledgment. Professor, I've done some reading, but tell me about this missile boat."

"If it's the same as the ones in our old Imperial databases, it's an extremely small warship designed for commerce raiding. Jump drive, minimal facilities, and just eight missiles. No other weapons. They're small and stealthy, and they would hide in asteroids or behind moons or suchlike. And when a convoy came close, they would sneak out, launch their missiles, then get the heck out of things."

"Can't stand up to us in a fight, then?"

"Not at all. But the missiles are pretty dangerous."

"To freighters."

"Sure."

"I'll bet our lasers can shoot down missiles."

"But we don't know how to use them," Yvette said. "Not properly."

"They don't know that. And if their main weapon is

stealth, and we can see them... can we count how many missiles they have?"

"Three," Willowby said. "Already checked. They carry them in external pods, like containers. And there only three left."

"And I wonder how many of them work after not being near an Imperial shipyard for eighty years. Maybe none."

"We can't take that chance," Nadine said.

"Are you suggesting caution, Nadine?" Jake said. "Don't want to go charging at them in a blaze of glory."

"I'm... Well, I'm confused." Nadine said.

"Good." A gong bonged from a nearby comm board. "Unless I miss my guess," Jake said. "That's our friendly freighter realizing they're in big trouble. Put them up please, Odette."

Jake stepped up to the monitor. It flashed with a view of the two men and women who had appeared before.

"Who are you?" the man asked.

"Hello," Jake said, "I'm Jake Stewart, Admiral of the Delta Militia. Representative of the Emperor Dashi the First, commander of this ship and agent on behalf of the newly proclaimed rulers of the planet Magyar and their trading department, factor, along with Shipmaster Yvette here, of the Free Traders of Delta. And also owner of this ship and trading on my own behalf." Jake gave a big grin. "That covers all my conflicts of interest. Oh, and I'm also the commander of the only warship in this system that can protect you from that pirate ship you just noticed on your sensors. Any questions?"

The man and the woman exchanged glances. "Not yet."

"Now you," Jake said. "You two are here to meet either a Free Trader from Delta to trade for Delta products, which hasn't shown up here in over..."—Jake looked at Yvette—"probably thirty years. Ms. Yvette can give me a more accurate count."

Yvette grimaced. "My parents talked of trips here in the past. Distant past. Twenty years, at least, on a jump ship from the Empire."

"So," Jake continued, "no ships from Delta for twenty years. There have been other ships from your sector here, perhaps once a year for the last few years. You expected one here to trade goods and refuel from, and it's not here, either."

Jake blew out his breath. "And you also know that ship chasing you down are pirates, and you probably have some idea which pirates—they've been backtracking your trade routes and those of your rivals and have finally tracked you down here, and they're going to board and seize your ship—unless you stop them, which you can't. Am I good so far?"

The couple on the screen looked at each other, then back at Jake.

"I'll take silence as a yes," Jake said. "To sum up, you're stuck in a remote system. You have no fuel. Because you're based at a planet similar to this one, there is nothing of interest for you to trade for here. You need a planet with a space-based infrastructure, which this one doesn't have. This trip would be a bust if you could get back— which you can't, having no fuel, and couldn't, because even if you did, that pirate will catch you and destroy you. I think I've covered everything."

The man spoke finally. "We're in trouble. Will you help us?"

"No," Jake said and crossed his arms.

Everyone in the room stared at him. The man and woman on the video stared at him. Jake stood.

"You're not going to help us?"

"Why should I? You've had eighty years to go to Delta to try to establish some relationship. We could have been dying for lack of simple medicine or basic technology, but you couldn't be bothered. You've been ripping the people here on Magyar off with overpriced technology for decades, and you haven't even tried to help them out. If it hadn't been for that pirate, you'd have ignored us. And I'm not even sure they are the pirates. You might be the pirates, and that might be a legitimate Imperial ship trying to suppress you. But I do have an offer for you."

"An offer? What is it?" the man asked.

"On behalf of the consortium mentioned earlier, Delta, the Free Traders, the Magyars, me, the Emperor, my crew, and all that. I have an offer."

"What's your offer?"

"I'd like to buy your ship. Right now."

The man and the woman regarded each other, then Jake.

"We're about to be destroyed by rogue pirates, and you want to buy our ship?"

"Bet I get a good price," Jake said.

CHAPTER FORTY

"As Jake Stewart's plans go, this is one of the crazier ones," Nadine said, piloting the ship's boat into the docking ring of the Flandre.

"I would have to agree," Yvette said.

She, Nadine, four of the Magyar's crew, and two engineering crew crowded the ship's boat, along with clothes, extra food, and a few critical spare parts. All of them were armed.

"Odd, the only thing we agree on is Jake's craziness," Nadine said.

"Crazy like a fox, is that the expression?" Yvette asked.

Nadine pivoted the shuttle slightly, then fired the rockets to twist it. A display changed to green. She tapped her screen, and the docking magnets engaged with a clank. "I guess so. Ever seen a fox?"

"In pictures," Yvette said, stepping back into the main area. "Everybody armed? Weapons up."

The Magyars produced shotguns, the spacers all had revolvers. Nadine squirmed through the group, checked the displays, and spun the shuttle's hatch open. It opened to display a second hatch inside.

"Everybody ready?" she asked.

Shotguns snapped up, revolvers pointed, and a chorus of yesses rang out. She spun the inner wheel and pushed the hatch open. Hammers clicked, and everybody glared, then all the guns lowered at once.

Nadine couldn't see, so she secured the locking levers and shoved her way sideways. The two occupants from the screen were there. The man was a shade taller than

Nadine, with dark hair and eyes and three days of stubble. He could have been Yvette's cousin. The woman, also dark-haired and dark-eyed, was a shade shorter than her, with her hair braided exactly like Yvette's—could have been her sister.

The man held a briefcase. The woman, visibly pregnant, held a bawling two year old.

"Know just what you mean, kid," Nadine said. "And I agree completely."

***

After the weapons were holstered or safed, the man, Jacques, led the engineering crew and three armed Magyars to the engineering spaces to check on drives, fuel, and the general engineering state of the ship. The woman, Kianna, led the remainder to the bridge.

"Jake said you were most probably a family ship gone awry," Nadine said. "But he didn't say in the family way."

"Are you going to hurt us?" Kianna asked.

"Of course not. We're going to make you rich. That's why we all signed those contracts." Nadine grimaced. "Those very, very, many contracts that Jake produced. You and the whole fam-damily here. Why just the two of you adults, though? That's not enough for a ship."

"It was only supposed to be for one jump. We were to meet the rest of the family two systems away. They didn't show. This was a different rendezvous, and..."

"They didn't show, either. Maybe the pirates got them."

"I hope not."

"Me too. But that's for later, when we have time to talk things out. We have our own pirates to get away from. Let's get to the control room."

It was only a short walk through a connecting corridor to the universal air lock behind the control room, under gravity the whole way.

"This spinning the hab section all the time is a great idea," Nadine said. "I could get used to this constant gravity."

"You don't have constant spin?" Kianna asked.

"Ship's too small. You need to unlock the board. That was part of the purchase deal." Nadine sat in the pilot's chair.

"You ripped us off on the ship."

"Could be. Jake handles that sort of thing. But this lease-to-purchase thing sounds pretty good for you. You're guaranteed payments as long as he can ship cargo on it, and you own it till he pays it out, if I understand it properly."

"We wouldn't have agreed if the pirate wasn't there."

"But the pirate is there, and we could just have taken the ship, and you've got that rider thing about percentages. The way I read it, if we make money, you make money. If we make a lot, you make a lot."

"And one thing for sure," Yvette said, slipping into the other chair, "Jake makes money."

All three of them sat and stared at each other.

"The board?" Nadine asked.

Kianna tapped in a code, and the board unlocked.

"And step back," Nadine said. Kianna didn't move, and Nadine flicked her eye to the Magyar behind her.

The man stirred, and Kianna sighed. "Fine, it's your ship now. I'll wait in the lounge." She slipped back.

"I'll put in the master code," Nadine said.

"No, I will," Yvette said.

"I'm the pilot." Nadine glared at her.

"I'm the backup pilot and sensor operator," Yvette said, tapping a Hold button.

"I'm Jake's official representative," Nadine said.

"I'm a shipmaster and the Free Traders' representative."

"Want a knife in your gut?"

"Want a bullet in your chest?"

The screen pulsed yellow. Neither woman moved. Then the intercom squawked. "We're ready back here. Why aren't we moving?"

"Empress's vagina," Nadine said. "Dual codes?"

"For now," Yvette agreed. Both women typed in long strings of characters, and seconds later, the board moved to green.

"Get me a course," Nadine said. "Straight away from that pirate." She tapped screens, and slight vibrations hummed through the ship.

It twisted gently sideways and back as she tested thrusters.

"Course A—least fuel course," Yvette said, "gets us farthest away on available fuel, but takes hours and hours, with multiple burns and three gravity assists."

"What else you got?"

"B is similar, about ninety percent of the way, but only one gravity assist and does it in half the time."

"And..."

"Course C. Blast away. Full thrust for two hours, then drift. Gets us furtherest fastest. Just enough fuel left to run basic life support, and we're in grand trouble if Jake doesn't come get us."

Nadine keyed the intercom. "Stand by for high accelerations in thirty seconds. Strap in and hold on." She and Yvette adjusted their harnesses and tightened straps. Nadine pivoted the ship gently using just the thrusters, and they spun till they were facing away from the planet, away from the approaching pirate, and into deep space. "Ready?"

"Oui, mon ami."

"Mon ami. I like that. I'll use it myself. Here we go."

Nadine thumbed two screens simultaneously, and the Flandre leaped forward.

***

"They can see us now," Odette said. "As we come around the planet." After the departure of the ship's boat, the rest of the crew had scattered to their stations and gotten all the systems running. "They can see your other ship as well. It's pulling out of the planetary shadow."

"You mean our other ship," Jake said. "You and the Free Traders' guild own a fifth of it now."

"Kind of a purchase under duress."

"Yvette didn't think that, and she's a shipmaster. Shipmasters can commit the resources of the Free Traders' guild. Says so in your bylaws."

"You've read our bylaws?" Odette said.

The intercom crackled. "Of course he has," Willowby said. "Probably memorized them."

"Not all of them," Jake said. "The important ones."

"You know I know nothing about running a merchant ship," Willowby said. "I don't see why you made me a trustee for Dashi's part. Should have been you."

"I have great faith in you," Jake said. "And I can't act both on my own behalf and on the Empire's, not on the same contract. Which makes you the trustee for the Empire."

"A trustee who knows nothing, so I'll just go along with your advice."

"I give good advice."

"I think so, and so does the crew and their shares. Which means, between me and them, you have a majority control of this new trading venture, without having majority responsibility."

"Don't forget the Magyars. I'm sure they'll listen to me. And I've got their proxy. Besides, there is the small matter of this inbound pirate."

"The pirate that is chasing an unarmed ship through the system, an unarmed ship that will shortly run out of fuel and drift helplessly, while the only thing protecting it is a small ship, barely armed, charging directly at them."

"That's what you see," Jake agreed. "Ready for the course?"

"I guess. I'm not happy, though."

"Didn't ask that. Engage at point alpha."

Odette raised her eyebrows, shook her head and typed on her board, then tapped the ENGAGE screen. "All set in. Full accel in thirty seconds."

Everyone leaned back and waited. Once the clock ticked down, the Accounting Error fired its main engines and went to full acceleration.

Directly at the incoming missile boat.

"We just charge them and hope that those auto programs give us a hit as we pass?" Willowby said.

"That's part of the plan."

"Jake, I'm still not happy. We can still run."

"And leave the others here?"

"It's better if some of us survive, rather than—"

"Your codes don't work anymore," Jake said.

"What? I—"

"I deactivated them before we started. Odette, will they have had time to see us change vector yet and react?"

Odette tapped her screen, and two countdown's appeared. One said One-Way Delay, the other: Two-Way Delay.

"They've seen us," Odette said as one countdown hit zero. "But we won't see their reaction yet."

"They'll react badly," Willowby said.

Jake rubbed his eyes and ran his fingers through his hair. "What do they see coming at them?"

"They see a crazy trading guy who thinks he's a fleet admiral," Odette said.

"They see a warship coming out to meet them, to protect the merchant ship fleeing behind us," Willowby said.

"A merchant ship, which will run out of fuel shortly," Odette said.

"They don't know that," Jake said. "It could be full of

fuel. They can't tell how much fuel it has. Right now, for all they know, that freighter is good to the jump limit and can jump out. In the meantime, we're between them and the freighter. They don't know it's out of fuel."

"But we know that."

"They don't. What type of warship do we look like, Professor?"

"Well, a courier," Willowby's voice said. "Or some small ship—or I don't know, an Imperial corvette?"

"Tell me about Imperial corvettes," Jake said.

"Small ships. Convoy escorts mostly. Not much firepower. But designed for..." Willowby laughed. "I'm reading the database entry now. Designed to engage and destroy missile boats. Missile boats were anti-convoy ships. Corvettes were anti-missile boat ships. Purpose-built convoy escorts. If they're checking their databases right now. They think they're being charged by their worst enemy. A ship that's designed specifically to destroy them."

"That's the case," Jake agreed. "And those ships had special anti-missile programs, didn't they?"

"Yep, says so here. If we were a real corvette, we'd swat away their missiles no problem, then engage them directly."

"But how do they know that we're going to do that?" Odette said. "How do they know that we're armed that way? And even if we were, none of us know how to run these confusing Imperial gunnery programs at all."

"As I said before, they don't know that," Jake said. "All they see is a warship heading straight for them."

"A single missile hit will badly damage us," Odette said. "Possibly destroy the ship. We could all be killed if we engage."

"Are we acting like somebody who thinks they might be killed? No," Jake said. "We're acting like somebody who is confident we'll kill them, and the sooner we get closer, the better."

Odette checked the timer clocks. "But, Capitaine Jake, they've seen us rushing toward them by now, but they haven't changed their vector. They're not buying it."

"We just have to sell it better. Give them something more to think about."

"Like what? Wave our arms and yell? We don't know how to fire these weapons."

"Then let's show them something we do know. A prebattle test." Jake typed on his screen, and a weapons screen popped up on the main display. Jake selected an option, and the screen changed to Laser Weapons, Level-3 Diagnostic. Engage?

Jake tapped YES, and lights sparkled on the main screens as the computer ran a series of test firing sequences of low-powered shots to test targeting and control. Lights played down the screen until the list was complete, then the display changed to Tested OK. Main Battery Ready.

"Now, we just wait till they see that and realize we're not an unarmed escort." Jake sat back in his chair and leaned on his elbow.

It let him rest, and it hid the growing pool of sweat forming in his armpit.

The clocks reset, and they watched them count down. "One minute till they see us," Odette said.

The one-way delay clock ran to zero and held there. The two-way one kept counting down.

"That felt longer than a minute," Willowby said.

"You're just nervous," Jake said.

"I am not."

"No?"

"No, I'm terrified. I'm too old to get killed in a random missile attack in a strange system."

"You'd rather die of old age in your bed?" Jake asked.

"Well, no, I... Dammit, Jake. You've been hanging around that Nadine too long. You're going to get us all killed."

"Maybe," Jake said. "We'll know for sure in twenty seconds."

Odette flicked her hands. The counter filled one screen, and the missile boats vector appeared in the other. "We will know. A bold move. Mon Capitaine?"

"Yes?" Jake said.

Odette unbuckled and stood, then gave Jake a Free Traders salute. "An honor to serve." She buckled back in and turned. "Five, four, three..."

The timer ran down to zero, then started counting to negatives, and they all looked at the other screen. The course plot of the missile boat stayed a solid blue—no change.

After ten seconds of silence, Willowby spoke over the intercom. "Well, I guess I better put together some sort of ad-hoc damage control teams, and maybe we should look at everybody sealing their skin suits because—"

"Status change," Odette said. She tapped her screen. Yellow-and-red text flashed on the main display. "That pirate is now firing main engines. They're generating a vector at ninety degrees to their course. They'll miss us, the planet, and the freighter."

"Headed for the jump limit?" Jake asked.

"Eventually."

"Chase them, the whole way."

CHAPTER FORTY-ONE

It took two days for Jake to reverse course after chasing the pirate out-system. Once he dumped his outbound velocity, he then had to chase down the freighter.

Nadine and Yvette had reversed course for as long as their fuel lasted as soon as the pirate jumped out, but they didn't have nearly enough to return to orbit. It took most of Jake's fuel reserves, but, eventually, the two ships were back in Magyar orbit. Another two weeks were consumed, boosting fuel from the surface for the Flandre or running out to the nearest gas giant to refine it, but, soon, both ships were fueled up.

Jake engaged in a complicated five-way discussion between Magyar, the Empire, the Free Traders, the former owners, and the crew—who owned shares—about who was to pay for what.

Tam provided all the fuel and agricultural products for free—food and all the steaks they could freeze—in return for medical robots and computers, extra computer-controlled milling machines, enough pieces and parts to construct a decent railroad system, and a promise to come back with goods from Delta.

Jake got a freighter stuffed with sugar, wheat, and dozens of other commodities, as well as some interesting Imperial tech. The former owners got adopted by Yvette as Free Traders, and everybody promised to get together during the next trading visit. Jake gave the crew options of either receiving a share of the goods carried, purchased on credit from him as the emperors executor as a reward for good service, and offered to lease them storage space for the return journey home, or if they preferred to join him in a limited-liability co-operative that he was trustee of that would pool resources with his shipping company that owned the ship and provided transport services as his contribution to the co-operative.

Nobody had any idea what all that gobbledygook meant of course, and Nadine was particularly suspicious.

"So if we join this co-operative," Nadine said, "You, as the Trustee control it, and you decide the costs, and how much we get at back on Delta?"

"I'll issue a dividend," Jake said.

"How much?"

"I can't tell in advance. It will be fair, your share of the profits after cost."

"But you decide how much?"

"Yes," Jake said. "But I'm a shareholder as well, so I can't cut your dividend without cutting mine."

"It sounds like a great deal, sir," Kivi said. "I'm in." Gabriella nodded her assent as well.

"It does," Nadine said. "Which is why I'm super suspicious."

"You could always take your share now," Jake said, "And I'll just charge you for shipping and associated costs. The good will be yours, as of now."

"Gimmie," Nadine said. "This is another Jake Stewart scam. I'll take care of selling my own stuff."

"Of course," Jake said, producing a comm pad. "Whatever you want. You will have to sign some paperwork though."

They all went down to the surface for Vidor and Tam's wedding. After the service, Kivi and Gabriella decided to depart with Jake and company. Gabriella gave Arpad a sloppy kiss goodbye, whereupon Arpad's admirer poured a drink over her head. In the resulting brawl, both women got torn clothes and black eyes, then decided Arpad wasn't good enough for either of them. They got drunk together and ended up puking on Jake's shoes, which everybody considered an acceptable outcome, except Jake. Nadine was particularly proud of her protege.

The badly hungover spacers crewed the two ships the next day, locked down various containers, air locks, and shuttles, and moved the two ships sedately to the jump limit en route to Delta.

"We're rich, aren't we?" Nadine said, driving the Flandre.

"Depends on your definition and what all this stuff sells for," Yvette said.

"With Jake's record, we'll make bank," Nadine said. "He always makes out."

"He didn't get as much as he could have," Yvette said. "Seems like he left some on the table somehow."

"It's always like that," Nadine said. "You think you've got him on something and bang—he drops the hammer and ends up walking away with everything. He does it every time."

"I wonder how he did it this time?"

The radio bonged at them. "Well, there he is. Let's ask him."

Nadine hit the intercom. "Hi, Jakey."

"Nadine. Everything good over there?"

"Five-by-five, Jakey. Say, are we rich? Am I rich?"

"Rich? Well, you both own substantial shares in two ship loads of unusual cargo, electronics, technology, and agricultural goods that should sell for a fortune."

"So, we're rich."

"You can say that."

"And yourself?"

"I own some shares, the same as the crew group. Not as many as everybody combined, of course, but still substantial."

"And... you're not going to steal it from us, are you?"

"Steal it? Why would I do that?"

"Why indeed," Nadine muttered. "Jakey, it's just that, sometimes, things work out better for you than was originally evident."

"You can hardly blame me for working hard on my own behalf, can you?"

"I guess not. Well, I guess we'll be able to keep our ill-gotten gains. This time."

"This time. Speaking of time..."

"Yes, Jakey?"

"It's the first of the month."

"Thanks for keeping a calendar, Jakey. Why do I care?"

"Lease payment is due. For your goods. And shipping. And insurance."

"Lease payment. What lease payment?"

"The one you owe on the first of every month till the cargo is sold."

"I owe a lease payment?"

"Of course. Your individual crew group does. It was in Schedule C of your agreement. Didn't you read Schedule C? You pay lease payments till the cargo is sold."

"I did not read Schedule C. I was busy stealing a ship from pirates."

"Well, I understand that, but, later, during the mandatory cooling-off period—"

"Jake. Shut up. What's the bottom line?"

"Thirty-six thousand credits."

"What?"

"Thirty-six thousand three hundred seven credits, to be exact."

"I owe you thirty-six thousand credits?"

"That's what the contract says. First of the month. But it's not me. It's the corporation on behalf of the lease. It's too bad you didn't stay in the general group – they don't owe payments because they gave me more shares in lieu of charging shipping."

"Shut up." Nadine released the channel and banged her head on her console.

Yvette giggled, then chortled.

"You shut up, too," Nadine said. She picked up the channel again.

"I owe the corporation thirty-six thousand credits."

"The corporation, yes. Me, and the others. Gabriella, Kivi, the rest of the crew."

"I don't have it."

"That's unfortunate. Can you get it somewhere?"

"Jake, we're almost in jump space. The middle of nowhere. Where am I going to get thirty-six thousand credits?"

"You could sell something."

"Like what?"

"Well, I heard you have some opals. I'll buy them from you."

Nadine banged her head again.

"For a fair price. Well, pretty fair. Considering. I mean, " Jake said. "I have to strike a good price, on behalf of the other members of the co-operative. You don't want me to rip off young Gabriella and Kivi right? I have a responsibility to them.

Nadine dropped the channel and banged her head again while Yvette laughed and laughed

GET A FREE EBOOK

Thanks for reading. I hope you enjoyed it. Word-of-mouth reviews are critical to independent authors. Please consider leaving a review on Amazon or Goodreads or wherever you purchased this book.

If you'd like to be notified of future releases, please join my mailing list. I send a few updates a year, and if you subscribe you get a free ebook copy of Sigma Draconis IV, a short novella in the Jake Stewart universe. You can also follow me on Amazon, or follow me on BookBub.

Andrew Moriarty

ABOUT THE AUTHOR

Andrew Moriarty has been reading science fiction his whole life, and he always wondered about the stories he read. How did they ever pay the mortgage for that spaceship? Why doesn't it ever need to be refueled? What would happen if it broke, but the parts were backordered for weeks? And why doesn't anybody ever have to charge sales tax? Despairing on finding the answers to these questions, he decided to write a book about how spaceships would function in the real world. Ships need fuel, fuel costs money, and the accountants run everything.

He was born in Canada, and has lived in Toronto, Vancouver, Los Angeles, Germany, Park City, and Maastricht. Previously he worked as a telephone newspaper subscriptions salesman, a pizza delivery driver, a wedding disc jockey, and a technology trainer. Unfortunately, he also spent a great deal of time in the IT industry, designing networks and configuring routers and switches. Along the way, he picked up an ex-spy with a predilection for French Champagne, and a whippet with a murderous possessiveness for tennis balls. They live together in Brooklyn.

Please buy his books. Tennis balls are expensive.

BOOKS BY ANDREW MORIARTY

Adventures of a Jump Space Accountant

Decline and Fall of the Galactic Empire

Made in the USA
Las Vegas, NV
09 May 2023

71812905R00215